Professor Nim's Possibility Collapser

And Other Stories

by Steven Muir

Table of Contents

Dawngames

You went to bed with the strong determination to get an early start. Enough are the days of laze, of seeing a chipper sun and a powder blue sky out the east facing window from your bed and yet turning over again for yet another round of indulgent sleep. Tomorrow will be different, you say: I will reap the many splendored glories, oft-praised virtues and logistical advantages to waking up early: to get in a morning walk before work, to have ample time, slow and easy like molasses, to sip a cup of oolong while reading, or to sip while doing nothing at all, replete with time like someone with a freezer full of provisions in the fall; to align with the sun and that oh so important circadian rhythm you've heard about, to shower and shave unrushed (though perhaps while listening to Rush), stretch, practice breathing exercises, prepare, enjoy, and then thoughtfully clean up a satisfying breakfast like a sourdough toad-in-the-hole topped with micro greens and sauerkraut. Maybe you'll even have the time to research a place you'd like to visit this summer, some hitherto unknown supremely enticing ecosystem at a different latitude. It's all there, your perfectly satisfying feel-good productive yet relaxed morning. Can you pull it off? Can you turn one morning into a continuous habit?

Your alarm, a not-so-abrasive three bars of a standard samba, echoes from your phone at the far end of the bedroom. Though most sounds or devices to wake you up come off as really quite rude - ripping you from the world and story of your dreams with the cold and heartless indifference of waking punctuality, this one, this tone is a least offender. Now comes the hardest part: to part from the loving warmth of your nightly cocoon, to feel the discomforting temperature differential of the air beyond the blanket, to face gravity again - weight, balance, resistance, solidity. To face the ongoing trials and tribulations of daily life, a rush of reasons to both get up and to stay in bed...no. You don't have to do this, and you know it. You don't have to think of everything you have to do today and for days more all at once, and right this moment face the sheer cliff face of reality, its expectations across time all felt right now together, no. This sense of overwhelm needn't be. Instead you, the wiser, know to face it a bit at a time, one step at a time. First foot forward, and only that: what is to be done now, in the quiet, tender hours before you head off to work. That's it, bit by bit. The linear day stacks realistically as places and happenings are encountered, not hours before, when breakfast hasn't even been had. It would be unhelpful, actually, to try and consider everything there is to do at once. How many balls, after all, can you sustainably juggle? Not even three.

There - the hardest part is over. You're up and moving. The alarm is off, the bed is made even (you don't always make your bed in the morning, but you always feel good when you do) and you've stretched a few nearly involuntary morning stretches, butt out, arms up, deep body yawns. Your body temperature is increasing again, your blood pressure is rising from the lull of life supine, your cerebrospinal fluid is...doing something. It's there, and you heard in some podcast semi-recently that it's important.

Fresh out the shower, toweled off and fresh of face (your shaving cream pleasantly tingling), you make yourself a cup of tea. Best not to dive right into the coffee - something you also heard on a podcast recently. Water boiled and poured, you place the kettle back on the stove top, and hear a knock at the door.

Stopping in your tracks, you pause, ears perked and head slightly turned to hear again, yes again, three quick solid knocks. You continue to wait, another ten seconds perhaps, before slowly and cautiously approaching the door. You wait, listening attentively for a few seconds more before opening it and stepping outside to be blasted by cold and dark, a pronounced absence of the light and of heat you had inside. Even the sun is still sleeping. You enjoy the cold air for a moment, on your face, in your nostrils, as you realize that there is no sign, no sign at all of whoever knocked on the door; no fleeing person in sight, no sputtering car ignition, no bodies, no steps, no sound except for the gentle swish of the occasional car passing by on the road, people well-established in their early morning routines heading off to a job that demands their pre-solar presence, or coming back from one, brave nocturnal folk.

This very moment you've stepped outside proves to be the very end of night's third trimester, for you see the first ray of the new rising sun peak out over the distant horizon. Like a laser it beams right to you and as if through you, as you see it faintly illuminate your porch, trailing indoors behind you and into your apartment, a buttery yellow arc slowly widening. The light warms and wakes in a way that the artifices of centralized gas heating and LED bulbs simply cannot compete with. Like the spearpoint of heaven's army descending upon the earth, the single light beam beaming forth from the horizon expands gloriously by the moment. It is like a bridge to the motherland, to the origin of all things. It calls you forth - the warmth, the light, yellow now orange now pink. On the other side of the sky, to the west, you notice the ghostly fading moon waving goodbye. Closing the door to your apartment behind you with one hand, you start walking forward towards the increasing light. You cannot rationalize why; it just feels right. Like a magnet you are drawn towards the widening arc of the dawn, without resistance, without complaint, utterly compelled like a babe to the breast, like a moth to the flame.

Ignoring roads, shoulders to roads, road barriers, white and yellow lines, your bee-line towards the sun takes you across state route 34 in front of your apartment complex and into a patch of woods. The morning light caresses the sides of thin trees, rolls casually across fallen ones being swallowed by grass and decomposing forces. Here it widens with some open space, there it is eclipsed by leaves gently shaking in the cool a.m.

breeze, trees receiving their wake up call. The frosted mud of the sometimes marshy forest ground crunches satisfyingly underfoot. Teaming orange now with the light of day, it will soon begin its daily thaw. Having come too near, a few chickadees and bush wrens flit about in a cute panic, sounding their chirping alarm. Their homes of rose bush and blackberry have just recently begun leafing out for the year. The small, vital green of their baby leaves - they too long for and soak up the sunlight like a free all-you-can-eat buffet.

Reaching the edge of the woods, you realize that following the sunrise has brought you to your favorite local park, where you like to play frisbee with friends, walk around easily on dates, sit in the grass and read. But you've never been here at this hour, never seen it in this light. You think you're the only one here until, advancing further into the park, you see a group of people under the shelter in the middle of the main field. You squint your eyes: they've formed a circle and expand out from the shelter, keeping the shape while widening. Do they see you? Have you disturbed some mysterious morning meeting, secret and solemn? The part of the circle facing you is coming closer, just as you somnambulantly take a few slow steps forward yourself. Is this some sort of occult pact or ritual, one you, an outsider, aren't supposed to see? Who are these people, and why are they gathered here at dawn, within the first few minutes people are legally allowed to be here?

Suddenly they stop and stand in place, the circle now perhaps sixty feet in diameter. Surely you can be seen by some of them. You've stopped moving too, frozen in curiosity and a light but pressing apprehension. They all turn inwards, backs to you, and begin, it seems, to play a game.

They're taking turns calling out, after which various members of the circle race across, high-five someone else moving and take a new spot at the circle's edge. You know this game. They're playing Common Ground, a fun way to get to know a group of people. They continue, going round the circle, taking turns calling out things they've done, things they can do, places they've been, pets they have or grew up with, favorite colors, foods, other preferences. As they run about, you can hear their laughter, see their smiling faces. You look at your watch. Still some time before work. Now the question grips you - do you join in? Are you feeling bold enough?

Calmly and silently you walk up to the group playing the dawn game. Finding a place gracefully between two people who yield space easily - an invitation implicit - you join the circle. They both look at you briefly, smiling and nodding their heads kindly, a gesture of welcome. The unquestioning ease with which you join the game informs: it is not 'as though' or 'like' you belong; you do, truly, belong. You *are* welcome.

Now it is your turn to call something out to the group. You look to the sun as you think, closing your eyes, engulfed in the now omnipresent light of the new day. Oh joy, you think, oh joy, you feel, look where the sun has led me this morning: to connection and to joy.

Professor Nim's Possibility Collapser,
or Choose

Golden gears spin in succession like the smooth passage of the baton at a track and field event. Steam hisses at the turning of the central gyre, and the room warms slightly. The professor curls his lips in, pressing them against each other, and skews his eyes slightly - habits of concentration established long ago, now automatic. The student, his intern, stands by, preserved in equal amounts nervousness and awe at what she is seeing, and that she is allowed, finally, to see it. For her entire time at the university she has heard tell of this machine, whispered rumors trickling down from upperclassmen of this one mad professor's mind-blowing invention, something with the potential to change lives.

Over cheap beer off campus or endless quantities of lukewarm, mediocre chow at the dining hall, the legend was told of a certain professor of philosophy and history, Professor Nim was his name, and of how he had figured out a way to make life much, much easier. He'd created a machine, it was rumored, that somehow could empower you to quickly achieve your goals. How quickly? Well, if ordinarily, people walked towards their goals, this machine somehow activated your hidden, inner potential or transformed hindering outer circumstances to the effect of taking a jet plane to the destination of your ambition.

The boldest and blandest of rumors ended there, and that is all that most students 'knew' about the professor and his machine. Sometimes, students uninterested in philosophy or anything the man actually had to say would take a class of his purely to figure out more, as if undercover and trying to learn more of this purportedly wondrous machine incognito. With that as their sole motivation, they soon flunked out or switched out, lost interest or didn't have the patience to see it through (for he gave no encouraging hints along the way, not to most students at least), and went back to the comfort of their chosen major, baffled and warning other students of the professor's eccentricities and how difficult it was to pass his class. This tended to scare off more students than it encouraged. But not Vishwanath Singh. An engineering major out of the gate, the more he heard about the State University of New York's infamous "mad" philosophy professor, the more determined he became to learn more, and some day see and use the machine himself.

He had his motivations. He felt passionately about solving the modern quandary that plagued so many of his generation: with the world at our fingertips, with all the possibilities placed knowable and accessible through the internet - internships in this city or that one, time abroad in some sister university or a semester at sea, summer jobs or exploring this or that mountain range with friends or by oneself, to go home and save up money, or to chance it and move to this up-and-coming town and attempt to strike it rich with an innovative tech start-up by jumping on board a gravy-train at just the right time - came a phenomenon of overwhelm and underperformance, a situational paralysis and high potential for stagnancy. Like a large tree broadcasting thousands of seeds, only a fraction would find purchase in the soil and, by tenacity or luck or a blessed mix of both, germinate, survive initial hardships like frost and drought and live on, perchance to thrive, so does what's possible seem to us. Vishwanath was unique in that he didn't just face and feel the paralysis of the too-much information age like everyone else; he saw it for what it was: a huge issue in and of itself. While millions of others hurdled past it, through it, effected by it, wobbly with uncertainty and influenced by it to their suffering detriment, to the disquietude of their minds but blustering on anyway, Vishwanath wanted to tackle this issue before anything else: living in/with the reality and/or illusion of nearly infinite choice that is the hallmark of our time. He wanted to figure out how best to steer his ship of self through this huge and wild sea, and help others become better navigators too. Most people affected by this dilemma kept on with their lives, like animals with thorns in their hooves that don't take the time to stop and take it out or don't even know how, doing whatever it is they wind up doing without the full, undistracted rays of their mind at their command, without unleashing or even being aware of their full potential. Not Vishwanath. He wanted to fully gather the rays of his mind and unknot the hose of his volition before continuing on to pursue a career. Maybe solving this dilemma for himself and others would be his career, his life's work.

Quickly into his first semester at the prestigious east coast university he deigned to pursue philosophy as a minor, out of both genuine interest in the subject - the 'love of wisdom' - and a desire to meet Professor Nim and see what might happen. Like many freshmen, word spread quickly to him of this professor, someone to avoid or to pursue depending on which category of rumor happened to reach you first and whether you found it intriguing or discouraging. Vishwanath heard both schools of thought on Nim, and decided to weigh the fish himself. By his second semester, having taken his first class with Nim, he was determined to make philosophy his second major. He would sacrifice social time and turn down as many party invitations as he had to. He was up with a red-light headlamp on his head at night, examining and re-examining the readings assigned by Nim as well as the supplemental ones (which Vishwanath thought might be the real track to follow to uncover the professor's secret) while his roommates played Minecraft, or failed at having sex quietly. Vishwanath made sure Professor Nim noticed him, not by being a loud presence in his class (PHIL 201, Epistemology) but a consistent and competent one. He submitted everything on time, and was one of the only students to complete all the supplemental readings as well, turning them in with unasked-for short essays to boot. By the end of the semester in May, Professor Nim had certainly taken notice of student Singh, though in his classic style, didn't make much of it. Spring in upstate New York was undeniably in motion, soon to give way to the peerless joy and frivolity of summer: freedom, travel, summer jobs...once finals were over, that is. Vishwanath aced his, all of his, and was already thinking about what he might take with Nim next semester. He would have to get written permission from Nim to take it, as it was an upper-level class and this was to be his sophomore year coming up, but his new specialty lecture (meaning, no other professor taught it) Implications of Artifice, sounded very interesting indeed.

Determined to take the class and continue his mission to gain the professor's utmost confidence, Vishwanath approached Nim after handing in his Epistemology final, after first returning to his seat and waiting for the class to end and everyone else to leave. Nim was looking down at his desk, pen in hand, immersed in grading the stack of finals.

"Excuse me professor but I'd..."

"What? Hmm. You handed in your paper. I thought you'd left."

"No, not yet. I was waiting to be able to speak with you...

"Speak? Converse? Chat? Something important or something casual? I'm at the Morpheus Cafe every wednesday morning, my informal office hours, if there's something you'd like to go over or talk about."

"It's about next semester. I'd like your permission to take Implications of Artifice. I know it's an upper-level lecture but..."

"But you're interested. Yes I can see that, Vishwanath. You've done well this semester. Epistemology can be a tricky subject to get through and to express thoughts cogently on. But this you have done. And done well," Nim said smiling, tapping his finger on the exam in front of him: it was Vishwanath's, and from what the student could see peripherally, the page was largely unmarked - a good thing, generally, when it came to grading.

"Yes, I think you'd do well in that class. I think you should take it. You're a philosophy major?

"Yes, and engineering too."

"Perfect! Well, Implications of Artifice will be of great interest to you then. I'll put that in writing and get it through the system. Check your online web portal at the end of the week and you should be able to get in. Let me know if you find you can't.

"Thanks very much, professor...I'm excited...it's been a great semester, I..."

"Yes yes, academia can be dry and dusty but classes with the 'mad professor' are more fun, aren't they?" He broke into a Cheshire cat smile. "They have their challenges too. But you seem up for the task. Have a good summer, see you next semester." Nim stuck out his hand, which Vishwanath gripped immediately. His arm was hairy, his palm was sweaty,

but Vishwanath didn't mind. If this interaction was any indication, he was well on his way to Nim's good graces.

"When the calculating power of the computer met with the breath-taking and unprecedented interconnectedness of the world-wide web, humanity began making quantum leaps on an exponential curve. Quantum leaps in what? Technological advancement to be sure, but how about also in the rate and scope of resource extraction and consumption commensurate with increasingly energy-intensive lifestyles? For the wealthier third of the world to be living, materially speaking, like the kings of old, or at least have the ability to, ease and access with Amazon or Alibaba at their beck and call, for the average person to have access to technological capabilities hitherto only dreamed of by marginal, top-class innovators like Da Vinci or Tesla, smart-phones and the rapidly approaching ubiquity of internet access, for all this, we approach omniscience and omnipresence."

Professor Archibald Nim's class was aflutter with the scribbling of pens, animated with ponderous stares on the part of students lost, amazed, incredulous, and in sartori states variously, gawking at the instructor or their eyes peering off into space trying to work out or think more about something he'd said. For most people this meant looking to the upper-left or upper-right as their thoughts sought completion and mental dots connected. Some students' mouths went agape from time to time as they listened, or alternatively, furtively looked over at their peers as if to corroborate the wildness or profundity of what they were hearing, to double-check they'd heard correctly. Their facial expressions implied a range of reactions spanning from either 'this guy is off his rocker,' to something more like 'this man is a god, a modern Faust'. Some students' mouths were tightly closed, bottom lips swallowed and beards being chewed on as they strained to keep up. Pencil tips that broke were hastily re-sharpened. As this was an upper-level elective taken for the most part by genuinely interested philosophy majors, every human in the room was alert and engaged. There was an almost constant low level background noise of papers shuffling and pens or pencils scribbling, very much the cosmic microwave background radiation of Nim's classroom.

Professor Nim insisted that everyone take notes on paper in his class and then type them up later on their own time. This not only nixed the issue of students abusing the internet and going off to la la land; he made a point to clarify that his motive here was more a matter of refinement. A rough draft first in ink or graphite meant at least one re-read as it goes into a word document. The brain is more engaged, stimulated by both different external writing tools as well as internalizations of space, expression, text, engaging muscle memory...or so he would preach on the first day of each of his classes.

The room was a classic descending half-bowl of a lecture hall, with Nim at the bottom, the sun of his solar system that convened for fifty or ninety minutes at a time, the conductor of this intellectual orchestra gesticulating wildly when in front of his cluttered desk or more mild-mannered and measuredly when sitting behind it. He mostly taught while seated on his treasured rolling office chair, a modern one with pronounced lumbar support, which he moved and manipulated with surprising dexterity and grace. Engaging students actively throughout his lectures, he always knew his audience, could feel the collective mood at the start of class and transform it into one of enthusiasm and studiousness if he needed to, or if that was already there, add more wind to the sails of their interested learning. He took it for granted that the most interested students sat in the first two rows. Sitting here told him that you were open to his engagement, would meet his eye-contact and wouldn't mind, would actually like his calling on you or including you in an example. This was the 'Nim splash-zone' as some students called it. If you sat further back in the lecture hall, he assumed you were just trying to get through the class, had to take it as a requirement but weren't particularly interested. Though certainly, he called on all hands raised, in any row, without prejudice.

"There have been other shifts as well, changes as a result of internet-powered computation I wouldn't call 'quantum leaps' but rather would label 'effects unaccounted for, unseen or uncared about.' Many of these effects are of a sociological nature, such as the growing trend to look at screens more than other people's eyes, to touch plastic more often than skin. Correct me if I'm wrong here, but is it not almost too bold now to engage a stranger or ask someone on a date without the nouveau vetting-process of at least a little conversation online first?" He paused, waiting for a counterpoint from his students, waiting for an objection...but it didn't come. Instead he saw heads nodding in agreement, faces poised in exasperated acknowledgment belying a forlorn acceptance of the way things were now. The silence, the absence of a response, spoke for itself. Then, when he felt that had sunken in, he continued. "Our social norms are changing faster than we can keep track of, too fast it seems to even reflect much on or have conversations about them...at least meaningful ones in which we might decide if we actually like and want to keep on with these changes, or whether they are not, upon honest examination, actually for the best. This is not unlike when a child first learns that they can lie, and later, after doing so, either reflects on their own or more likely has a conversation with an adult about how even though you can do that, even though you can speak something that isn't true, you ought not to. Please, anyone, correct me if I'm wrong about this, if I'm being too much of a Luddite, but it seems fairly obvious and dire to me that humankind has not had this conversation with itself." Again he paused, waiting. Nothing, only the speedy taking of notes, and the somewhat sad recognition of the veracity of the professor's claim hung in the air. "Well," he continued, "now is that time. Here in this class, on this campus, in the cafeteria, in your dorm rooms. Now is the time to have that conversation. Have it now while we still have the luxury of intelligible discourse and the freedom of speech to do so. These effects unaccounted for, unseen or uncared about I call I-ffects, a term commensurate with the 'I-this' and 'my-that' jargon of the day, feeble attempts to make the inherently impersonal virtual world uniquely yours."

Professor Nim stopped speaking, scanned the lecture hall to assess the range of student responses, and wiped a bead of sweat from his forehead with the back of his sleeve. He counted three students chewing on their writing implements, four, now five students cupping their chins in thought, eighteen students still writing and at least two that had fallen asleep. Less than optimal, he thought, but he bore no grudges; it was hard to balance earning a degree with maintaining an active social life and getting enough sleep.

"Please complete the reading and response questions for today's lecture, and the supplemental reading, if you wish. Refer to the syllabus if you need a reminder of where we're at and the reading connected with today's class. That's all for today. See you all next week, when we begin to dive more deeply into the 'online economy'." The noise of students packing up, rising from their chairs. "Have a good weekend, everyone. Stay hydrated." he said, with a smile and a shine in his eye.

For many students it was 'thirsty thursday', where weekend partying began a day early. Some students organized their schedule so they didn't have any classes on friday, or maybe one in the afternoon. Vishwanath did have class, three classes, and would not go out and get drunk tonight. He rarely did. He completed his class assignments straight away. He was of a rare breed of student that possessed one-pointedness of mind, and a burning drive to achieve his goals: his dual bachelor degrees, and an answer to what he saw as the quandary of his time: paralysis by possibility and mediocrity by volume.

This semester, Vishwanath had pushed for and to his great determination and luck landed a single room in Argyle Hall. It was unheard of for an underclassman to get a single room, much coveted for their privacy. Very little got in the way when Vishwanath settled on something. Last semester (the second half of his freshman year) he rounded up recommendations not only from his residence hall advisors but several of his professors as well, expressing his high academic drive and the deserved boon having a single room would be to Vishwanath. Including a short supplicatory essay of his own and the blessing of a graduating senior who's single room would be available, the hunter caught his quarry. Now he was able to work and rest according to his own schedule and without the distractions of other, not-as-studious students. He did not look down on his peers who partied. He did not cast judgment. He knew the world was full of people of all sorts of different intentions and means to achieve them, whether that was figuring out the cure to an intractable disease or getting laid every weekend. He simply wanted to be able to pursue his academics under the guiding star of his own ambition to make life clearer and less stressful, to somehow, someway eradicate the obscuring fog of modern information-overload. And this, he thought to himself at times in a semi-conscious effort to justify to himself and others his tendency towards perfectionism and workaholism, this would make life easier for everyone!

Nim's class that afternoon, ending at 5:45PM, was his last for the day. By 6:30, after having dinner at the dining hall, he was back in his room, his 'study' as he thought of it, and hard at work. He had completed his assignment for MATH 202 Problems in Logic, a set of complex truth-tables, during his lunch break between his morning and afternoon lectures. This evening he had ENGR 254 and 301 assignments to work on. Sipping on a tall cup of matcha, he made short work of them. He saved Nim's reading and response questions for last, which he often did, as he found the work for that class set his brain up, as it were, for an interesting wistful sort of speculatory mode with which to end the day, often times leading, he found, to curious, ponderous dreams.

The alternating gold and platinum bars of the machine whirled so quickly as to appear still, like a top spinning at high speed. In the perfect, lubricated execution of their duties they purred audibly, like a large, hollow, mechanical cat perfectly at peace. The machine's three centrifuges - one chrome ruby, one chrome sapphire, and the last chrome emerald - grew in their glowing intensity. She, the student at her professor's side, heard an inner voice not her own say, "Choose". For some ten seconds that felt more like an hour, she waited, unsure and indecisive. "Choose one," she heard again, this time the machine lighting up in tandem, as if...as if it were speaking to her in her head. The voice was that of a female older than herself, resolute and metallic sounding. Of course, thought the student-assistant, the professor's machine communicates telepathically. Which then means...she quickly realized self-consciously..."Yes," the machine set up in front of her replied in her head, "your verbal commands are superfluous. You can communicate with me via thought. I do not understand the sounds your larynx makes when aspirated through the

----

"There has been a trend as the online economy proliferates into all of the aspects of our lives that it can, to see more, but less deeply. To come into contact with more information in a given day, heck, in a single hour or minute of the day than ever before, but for most of it to not mean much at all. For everything you see when scrolling, ask yourself, how much of this is practical or actionable information? How much of what I see can I do something with or about *right now*, other than dubiously donate to or repost for more to see? This is the new forest we are out hunting in: the meaningless dross of webpages, like the myriad bushes and trees of a woodland environment, literal clones of each other, as we move with purpose, on the hunt for something of value. As the career content creators - be they online stores and brands, photographers or musicians, news media or fitness influencers peddling the same powders in different packages - pump out and upload content, sweet ephemeral, dopamine-engaging, virtual content, the sheer flood of data, of things to at least look if not also respond to or bookmark, does several things to us. For one, we are adapting towards volume and superficiality pretty much across the board. Two, it has become exceedingly easy for someone's unoriginal, nay, fully repetitive take on something to engage us disproportionately and stir, sometimes command our emotional, hormonal response. How do mediocre brands, singular influencers, or news agencies with nothing unique or original to say achieve this? You've all heard the term 'clickbait' by now. Well it is just that - studied, formulaic online maneuvers that have been shown to grab attention: strong words in capital letters, thumbnail images for videos exhibiting the host or guests' incredulous reaction. We can clearly see that these sorts of attention-grabbing techniques work by simple analytics like views and time spent on page. Now, fully steeped in this clickbait culture, what was once taught as keys for online success are second-nature. Worse, they are expected. One almost cannot compete without engaging in these flashy, attention-grabbing tactics. By the continually successive desensitizing of our senses to language acuity, taste, and proportion, what were once considered extreme tastes are now normal to our palette, baseline. This happened throughout the 80's and 90's first with fast and packaged foods. Just try sharing a standard American sweet with someone not from North America, and see how they react. Now this is happening with our sense of language and facial expression. My question for you all is this: will we not, with these successive forays deeper and deeper into our senses of taste and speech for the express purpose of grabbing and holding attention to earn ad or product revenue, lead ourselves to a 'boy who cried wolf' type scenario? After seeing online for the thousandth time that this person CRUSHES or DESTROYS that person or group, what language is left to truly invoke the proportionally correct emotional response when seeing or hearing about someone or something *actually* crushed or destroyed?"

"The quality of the content to which we are exposed is being diluted to a dull and boring mean not worth anyone's attention. In this day and age, how many Mozarts are being swallowed up in The Great Flood of content? What will come of that five year old that can play along perfectly to Rush's 'Tom Sawyer'? It doesn't matter, because you're already on to the next video, and it's something that's sure to grab your attention, because we inform Google, Facebook, Apple, and Amazon everyday of what we like and are willing to spend time oogling at through our devices, our hand-held ponds of Narcissus! How many Hemingways are slipping through the cracks between the million blogs you could subscribe to? And being advertised to through, always being advertised to. It is as if now everyone can dump their mind-stuff into the public square and make money off you merely looking. How many sleek new products, brands and lifestyle blogs vie for your attention and your dollar with keto-this and plant-based-that, the top five new superfoods you can't live without? The ten under-explored places you *must* visit this summer? The five best cruelty-free skin-care products of 2022? This easy weight-loss hack you can do while you're asleep? When are we satisfied? When does it end? How many goji berry-reishi-lucuma-raw cacao bars and liposomal glutathione gel pills does one have to buy to get rid of x vague, nagging health concern? How much carbon must I pay extra to offset in order to save the whales? How many faceless charities must I round up my purchase for to see God?!"

Professor Nim, all but spinning around in his chair animatedly, took a moment to collect himself. Closing his eyes, running a hand through his hair and solemnly regaining his cool, he carried on, lowering his voice back down to the soft, impartial calm of academic discourse. "In the new virtual economy, an infinite, holographic bazaar projected out to you through your device by the amazing capabilities of real, physical metals like cobalt, tin, and tungsten (in essence, sigils for information-projection), the major commodity sought after, fought over, obsessed and hoarded, is our attention. The main battle being fought today, fought every waking second and likely even while you're asleep is the battle for your attention. We are the product we are being sold. Regurgitation of our interests back to us as part of a dopamine-driven perpetual feedback loop keeps us engaged, and thus the impersonal - something thousands of miles away, people we haven't and won't ever meet, news stories from communities far removed from our own - becomes intimately personal. How personal? As close and meaningful to us as our felt experience. Once realized at the advent of the internet only by technological far-seers and business-minded chess players, the command of our stress hormones and neurochemically-induced state has become a given, an industry standard. This has become a whole job class unto itself: consumer engagement and retention - how to get and keep people interested. This is precisely how the impersonal can affect us so strongly: because we have a real neurochemical reaction to the stories, the media, the content we access through our devices, the crucial and bankable middleman."

Vishwanath did not raise his hand very often. He did not come to class, to university even, to debate. He wanted to glean what knowledge he could from his professors and the work they assigned, and move on. He trusted that his own creative process would occur more or less automatically and subconsciously, and was a believer that the best insights and innovations popped up on their own at unexpected moments, often while doing something else, usually something menial and related to personal or household upkeep: while shopping, showering, cleaning one's room, these sorts of times. If during a lecture there was something he didn't immediately understand, he would wait to see if his question was answered incidentally within the next two or three minutes. If not, he would then raise his hand and ask. He was not shy or self-conscious; he was just focused, stream-lined and terse in his vocalizations as well as his movements. He sought to conserve energy as a rule. There was another student on the other hand that he was noticing was participating in Nim's class with animated interest and increasingly acute and provocative questions. She also sat in the second row of the lecture hall, on the side opposite Vishwanath. Her name was Vivienne Donnelly, and she, a dedicated philosophy major, attacked her coursework and engaged in her classes with an intellectual rigor and sense of discipline and drive similar to Vishwanath's.

"It's true," Vivienne said, responding to Nim's last pontification with an anecdote that grounded Nim's tendency to go (or appear to go) off the rails in his excitement. "My brother got a job last month doing just that, as a social media manager for a company - I won't name it - that just repackages herbal powders in bulk and upsells them, claiming various health benefits. So if you've looked up anything to do with 'superfoods' or diets or even talked about them near your computer or phone, it's now my brother's job to keep you interested. That's how he's paying his rent and supporting himself: tracking people's expressed interests and marketing to them."

"Precisely!" Nim continued enthusiastically, clearly appreciative of Vivienne's corroboration. "And as the online economy expands, per-sordid-chance to one day eclipse that of the physical world, what are the implications of thousands, millions of people no longer contributing anything tangible to society, but earning their bread organizing spending and interest trends expressed online? That is the key: the keystroke. What you say or search for, whether you actually care about it or not. For instance, if you cleared your browser history, which is something I recommend we all do from time to time," he said with a wink, "and just searched for products for your pet, just looked up animal videos and made sure to mostly be talking about pets when in earshot of your phone, that is all you would see online - advertisements for doggy day-care, pet grooming, the best food for your pet, pet CBD for your aging furry friend. Show this to an alien or a caveman, someone who's never seen the internet before and has absolutely no pre-standing concept, and they'd think that's all it is. You can reproduce this experiment with just about any interest. And since we are all combinations of interests, our online experience has evolved to reflect that. And so that is one major way in which the online 'world', not a world so much as an experience, the online 'experience' is different from the outside, objective world. The hard, organic, fleshy physical world we are born into is not, by default, a subjective experience. We all walk down the same hallway to get here, drive the same roads to get home, see the same mountain range looming in the distance. Downtown does not change for us into an assortment of only the things we like or would spend money on. It is what it is, whether those stores pique your interest or not, whether you go hiking in those mountains or not. However, we all know that though we experience the same objective reality, our subjective experience is the lens through which we view this hard, tangible reality. The virtual experience flickering a few feet or inches in front of us, ruining our eyesight by the way, is like a handheld pond of Narcissus for us all. So enamored are we by the things we like, we'd gaze into our handheld reflectors all day if we didn't have other responsibilities to tend to. And when awareness of this, when mindfulness of self, habits, and lifestyle - introspection, in a word - isn't part of the overall picture, either not encouraged or cultivated or even considered as a possibility, what happens to that individual? What does this unchecked I-ffect *do* to the non-introspecting individual being marketed to? It keeps them static. That would be the ideal state for businesses in the online economy, wouldn't it? For people to be interested in what you're selling, forever. For them not to change, not to grow without you, for them not to move on and become interested in other things. Or worst of all, for the clientele-consumer base to lose interest, look at their phones less, engage online less, take a break from their social media or, heaven forbid, delete their account and go 'off-grid'!"

"As things now stand, the unwisely unregulated, algorithmically inclined internet experience is anti-personal growth. It is, in its very make-up, designed for and dependent on your static and unappeasable desires. But what, you may ask, about the other things we use the internet for? For communication or for finding information? Well, originally, this was clear enough. At first the internet was a more objective virtual repository of information, facts and opinions, and it was incumbent upon we brave 'surfers of the world-wide-web' to parse this growing database of rants and raves, as well as calmly stated facts. That, however, has changed too. In our next several classes we will talk at length about what has become, ominously, another implication of our obsessive artifice: modern tribalism and the formation of distinct and increasingly disparate opinion camps; the disappearing middle-ground of opinion by the, once again, algorithmically-driven nature of content suggestion and control of what you see. I'll leave you with this: if you haven't seen the Wizard of Oz, watch it this weekend. Oz is alive and well in our world today, sitting at a million desks simultaneously as he, a multitude, shouts and storms for your passionate ire! See you next week!"

Vivienne Donnelly came from a working-class Irish-American family from Boston. Both sides of her family were Irish Catholic. She was, genetically-speaking, a thoroughbred. She did not grow up with wealth or much of anything in the way of material excess. Growing up, she did not get new winter coats as often as other kids did, and it showed. She did not get the newest accessories - dolls, bikes, computers, video game systems - when they came out; she got them used the following year. Her family's one hairdryer was from the 90's, stubbornly clung onto by her mother with the almost daily refrain, "it still works!". Their longstanding tv was bulky and very clearly did not have the resolution quality other peoples' tv's had, or what she saw at school. The youngest of five, her clothes were hand-me-downs. Taking all of this in, she resolved from an early age to do better, to become wealthier and more successful than her family had ever been. At first this resolution was unconscious, born of the differences she saw between herself and her peers. Sometime in high school it became an explicit goal. She journaled about and vision-boarded for greatness. She worked hard during her teens years to achieve the sort of academic success that would land her scholarships to be able to go to the sort of university her grades would get her into. She attended and grew to run clubs at school, did tennis and swimming, and volunteered in the memory-ward unit of a senior assisted-living facility.

Vishwanath on the other hand was the product of a chemist and a dentist. He and his sister grew up comfortably. His parents had the good sense not to spoil their children, and so while they could've, they did not live exorbitantly. Rather, his parents saved up judiciously and were able to put both of their children through college completely, and would be able to pay for their masters degrees too, if they chose to pursue them. Though he grew up not in want of anything, he was raised with a strong sense of morality, thanks to his family's steadfast participation in the local Hindu community and daily morning pujas and evening arati ceremonies at home. They were simple, quick, and obligatory times that the Singh family would come together to remember the divine, a sort of cultural north star for them. These daily rituals, along with secular ones like self-imposed exercise, gymnastics, and violin lessons, formed the backbone of Vishwanath's strong sense of discipline he was able to carry on so seamlessly into his time at SUNY, a stone's throw away from his home town in Connecticut. Now with twenty trips around the sun under his belt, Vishwanath could spot others like him, those with a similar drive and intellectual prowess, a certain ferocity or hunger for study and personal growth, leading to self-mastery, the ultimate end.

"So," Vivienne started with Vishwanath, making eye contact and keeping pace with him and his quick, purposeful strides after Nim's class that day, "How many classes have you taken with Professor Nim? Are you a philosophy major?"

"This is my second. And yes, I am. Engineering also."

"Ah a double major...how's managing that? Betcha don't have much free time on your hands."

"I don't, you're right," said Vishwanath, a tad put off by this student's forwardness. She hadn't even introduced herself yet and she was already making assumptions. As if reading his mind, she continued, "I'm Vivienne," and extended her hand.

"My name is Vishwanath," he said. Sometimes he would next give his nickname 'Vish', as an appropriate shortening of his somewhat exotic full name, but with this one he did not. There was something too fast, too brash about her, Vishwanath decided to himself. Vivienne seemed

object-driven, and he had the feeling she was only engaging him for some
end, not out of genuine, unpremeditated social curiosity. Whatever her
intentions were, she did not do a good job of hiding the fact, or the
likelihood rather, that she had intentions. He caught this perception of her
quickly, and as a result his replies to her were short, terse, and
informational, giving no more than she
asked for. Something about her put him on guard, and he was rarely wrong
in his perceptions.
"Where you from?"
"Connecticut,"
   "Where in Connecticut?"
"Danbury. Are you familiar with Connecticut?"
   "Somewhat. I grew up in the Boston area and would drive through
Connecticut to get to New York. Or take the train sometimes."

"Nice," said Vishwanath emptily, just to say something.
   "You seem pretty smart. You get any scholarships?"
"I did," replied Vishwanath, saying no more, inviting no more from her. She
must have picked up on this because she stopped inquiring. Okay at least
she's not socially daft, thought Vishwanath. She can pick up on cues. They
walked side by side for about eight seconds in complete silence as they
crossed the campus' main quad, as it was called, a large often wet green
lawn, gently sloping downwards towards town. The tan diagonal concrete
paths crossed the quad to form an asterisk: two diagonal paths forming an
x, overlaid onto a vertical and a horizontal path that formed a t. The chill of
mid Autumn was in the air and soon the college grounds-crew would be
salting these paths after running snow-blowers through them.
Eight awkward seconds and Vivienne got the message. "Well," she said,
stopping walking, getting Vishwanath to stop too. "I think I know what
you're after." Vishwanath turned to look at her fully now, narrowing his
eyes ever so slightly, defensive. "I can see it in how you look at him,
Professor Nim. The admiration. The trust you have in him. Trust that there

is something more there, something beyond his words. It's like, he's beckoning us toward some secret, right?" Vishwanath raised his head slightly, turning his chin in question. Vivienne smiled, not kindly but...what was it? What was in that look, wondered Vishwanath...competition. Something flashed in her eyes and she gave him a look of competitive encouragement. "I'll see you at the finish line," she uttered, with conviction and gravity. She then turned and took another path from the center of the quad. She had terminated their conversation exactly at the center of the quad, the center of the asterisk of paths. Well-timed, thought Vishwanath, staring at her for a few moments longer as she walked confidently on into the distance, her long red coat flowing behind her like a cape.

Vishwanath found himself at the top of the quad, looking down at all the students passing through, of various grades and ages, from all sorts of backgrounds, circumstances and walks of life. Some tall and some short, some moving quickly, some zipping by on bikes or segways, some moving more slowly and perhaps pensively, not in a rush. Here and there across the vast lawn, clusters of students stopped to talk in two's, three's, groups of four or more. All coming from different places, going towards different places, different desired careers, different life goals and motivations and of different hindrances and obstacles, whether outer barriers like finance or inner pathological hurdles born from trauma and life's compounding complexities. Some obstacles, as well as strengths and assets, were visible while many were invisible to the casual onlooker. A wind blew across campus, and the leaves, mostly red, orange or brown at this point in the year, rattled on the branches of the many maples and oaks planted long ago. With every gust, with every autumnal stirring, some leaves, dry, brown and crunchy, would fall down to their nearby base, sometimes brushing against students or university staff as they fell. Vishwanath stood for a solid minute or two, unfocusing his gaze, taking in the whole of the scene, his eyes and his mind no longer jumping from one eye-catching person or group of people to the next but instead perceiving the entire scene, a portrait alive. Are we really all so different? he wondered. Is life truly full of such endless permutations and possibilities? Or does the common denominator of our desire for happiness simplify the unfinished equation that is life? He mused only until he felt his stomach grumble. It was time for dinner.

"One of the more obvious consequences of our devices increasingly becoming the medium through which we interact and attain the things we want or need is simply spending more time on them. We then enter a problem of finitude, of bandwidth. We have only twenty-four hours in one full day, subtract six or eight for sleep and we're left with sixteen or eighteen hours, on average, in which we're awake and doing things. It stands to reason that that which we devote the most time to consistently will also be our greatest influence, as it is simultaneously that which we exert the greatest influence on. On a physical level this is clear: construction workers, professional sports players and fighters are prone to injury given the hours they put into doing what they do and the nature of their physically taxing work. But they'll also build and maintain muscle better. Scholars or clergymen spending most of their waking hours pouring over books tend to lose their eyesight sooner, and suffer stiffness in the body as a result of their sedentary occupation. Believe me I can attest to this. The same is true of office-workers in general. When the percentage of our time spent looking at our screens - whichever screen it is, the totality I suppose - increases, our bodies, our eyes, our necks, our hips and lower backs feel the repercussions of this. So does the body, the traps and deltoids of a farmer. But then there is also the mind, our ongoing conversation with ourself, our mental diet so to speak, that is influenced by the social atmosphere we spend the most time in. This was fairly cut and dry before the advent of the internet, in that people only found themselves in social situations possible where they lived. To a Norse Viking of the 1400's, life in Japan's concurrent Shogunate or the life of a merchant within the Mayan civilization would've been inconceivable. No one before the printing press, save adventurers bent on exploring the world at large, would've or could've had even the potential to emote or sympathize with, let alone know about, the goings-on of human life outside their own town or tribe or kingdom. The not-so ancient art of history, of records-keeping, collapsed this inconceivable impossibility somewhat, but there still was a time delay. For instance, when George Vancouver sent his travelogues back to his acquaintances in Europe, he was relaying his experiences in a different place, amongst very different cultures and climate, yes, but with the time-delay of however long they took to get back. So his targeted audience could not possibly imbibe or be affected by Vancouver's foreign escapades in a timely manner; their experience of his experiences would not be in sync. As well, the stream of information from him and other explorers was not constant enough to escape novelty status with their audience. The majority of everyone's waking hours were still steeped in where they were. Now almost a quarter of the way into the 21st century, a simple village life - the standard for most people for most of human history - no doubt seems quaint, small, and old-fashioned. Pandora's box of information-exchange has been blasted open. There isn't even a box anymore; we live in a mostly boxless and globalizing human experience, an exciting and also confusing time, as I'm sure most of you would agree. Now, we here in New York can spend as much time in New York each day as we do reading and learning about the goings-on of the world outside of New York, outside of our country, outside of our planet even. And we can do more; we can spend more time *outside* New York than we do experiencing it, even as we live and breathe here."

Nim paused, allowing students to catch up with him as he moved along to his next set of powerpoint slides. The second's hand of the old clock in the lecture hall ticked away, its light click deafened by the scribbling of pens, the shuffling of papers, the shifting of postures, the occasional squeaky chair.

"But, as we have seen in the last couple of years, something curious has happened. One might expect the broadening universality of internet access to result in a veritable plethora of information deposited and found online, a teeming, writhing multitude out of which sense cannot be made, like a billion people and evergrowing shouting their desires all at once. In the resulting cacophony, you would hear quite a bit and yet nothing intelligible. It would seem, given the initial conditions and premise of the world wide web, that the ensuing Information Age would be akin to an infinitely expanding virtual universe in which the weight and gravity of any one thing thins out as the totality unceasingly expands."

Nim cleared his throat. "Beyond merely sub-par navigators of this blooming virtual dimension of our lives, we are overwhelmed by it. We are getting consumed by it, lost in it. To just go on the internet and scroll mindlessly, as we now say, is to freely give in to being lost. It is to desire to lose yourself in content, content you are implicitly agreeing is worth your time and worth your eyeballs' preoccupation merely because it is online. What has happened in the last decade or two however has been the creation and continual fine-tuning of the internet's algorithms dictating what you see along your guided tour through the digital swamplands, as we spoke about last week. This, as we all know all too well, extends beyond advertisements. It extends to opinions. We cannot actually converse online, try as we might or substitute it for a social life as we are now increasingly prone to doing. For the most part, online conversation fast-tracks sharp emotional responses at the expense of the truth of nuance. The tempting, deadly anonymity and convincing finality of publishing and/or reading someone's opinion online - whether that's the New York Times' or the CDC or your second cousin's assertively conclusive statement on Twitter - simply does not stimulate debate in a manner and context in which we 'smart primates' are used to. Online we cannot read facial expressions, try as we might to simulate them with emoji's. We cannot feel the sting of what we say to offend someone viciously, and when we aren't in their physical presence we are all the more likely to give in to the impulse to say something that ethically would not check out if only we had the social context of their face, their presence, the presence of a group *irl*, in short the checks and balances of live, real-time human response to inform and mediate our statements. Humanity, folks. We need real, living, breathing, sweating, smelling, warmth-giving humanity in order to have realistic, proper conversations. The online social experience has been and dangerously remains more sociopathic-leaning than humanistic because of its inherent limitations."

"What has happened as well as a result of our algorithmic online shepherds, our coded sorting-hat pointing us to this or that faction, all complete with associated stances and things you might buy like a BLM lawn sign or a backup generator and a year's worth of dehydrated food depending on which trend of news is reaching you, is a less nuanced and more divisive social experience, harkening back to the automatic suspicion, aggression, and incredulity of our hunter-gatherer, tribal band past, where even a tribe of similar-looking, similar-sounding people would be regarded with extreme caution before trade or inter-marriage was allowed, lest one tribe steal from, slaughter and subjugate the other. And then if your people, your culture came face to face somehow with a different-looking, different-sounding people? How much more difficult would that social reconciliation be? How much more understanding, caring, open, trusting, and enlightened would both groups have to be in order to get along? It has been a sore several thousand years of history, setting the vast wake of prehistory by the wayside, to get to the point of the recent past where the enlightened ideas of universal rights, rights by birth, universal suffrage, the rights of children, and the inalienable rights by virtue of citizenship and of humanity were first seriously contemplated and legally established *somewhere* in the world. They still are far from being a given everywhere. But I digress; this is not a law or civil rights class. We are here to talk about the implications of artifice, are we not? The effects, accidental and intentional, of our modern tech-assisted lives."

Someone in the second row raised their hand to speak, Vishwanath, face aimed down at his desk, realized as he heard Professor Nim say encouragingly, "Yes, go ahead." And she went ahead. Still scribbling away, Vishwanath heard the voice of Vivienne Donnelly. "Technology, and specifically I mean being able to converse and plan within a virtual space, has greatly benefited the people of countries whose governments seek to keep control despite their cruelty and unpopularity. If someone is kept in a cave, bound there in chains and *doesn't* know of the outside world, illuminated and free, then that is one thing. They may be content to stay in the cave, because that is all they know. But when someone else races back into the cave in excitement as they tell the others of the amazing brighter, freer world that exists out there, then the cave-dwellers, be they a small band of three or fifty-three or a nation of millions, will be curious to see what's out there. And as they find themselves in an objectively better, freer situation, they will inevitably demand that for themselves and refuse to go back to the way things once were. I remember when I got my first job in high school and started making money consistently, certain things that were once rare treats that I felt semi-guilty about, like a big iced latte in the morning or getting tickets to see a concert, became more normal for me. In short order they even became expectations. A small, silly example perhaps, but I'm sure the people of Egypt or the former U.S.S.R. can relate in terms of learning about and first experiencing democracy and international trade and investment."

"Precisely!" replied Nim in enthusiastic approval. "An excellent use of Plato's 'allegory of the cave', Vivienne. Very good. Yes I believe one of the only peoples truly still trapped in 'the cave' at large are a sizable demographic of the citizens of North Korea, whose government seems hell-bent on keeping them all bound in chains toiling away while supplying them with ludicrous shadowplay on the cave-wall for entertainment and warped views on the nature of things: their lives, their government, the state of the world. A true dystopia of physical and informational control, it seems. We are all very lucky to not have been born there; we should count our blessings." Nim paused again, thoughtful, perhaps literally counting his blessings that very moment.

"However, we living here in America are not out of the woods. We are actually, to extend the allegory, no longer in an informational cave but a dense forest. A forest of information so thick with content that we are having trouble seeing through to the light of truth, it seems. What we are seeing and experiencing now as a society is this: algorithmically driven shepherding and partitioning of us all, to the extent that we use and express ourselves on the internet. This wouldn't be a problem with such long, proliferating tendrils if only the internet weren't such an essential aspect of our lives, as it has become in such a dizzyingly short amount of time. And so, once again, as we spend more time online because in today's world on some level beyond mindless scrolling we have to in order to get by, and thus are inevitably exposed to virtual influence as we get our opinions, interests, and biases reinforced in something of a dopamine-driven feedback loop - expressing our opinions and seeing more of the same online, searching for political hot-takes on search engines and seeing continual confirmations of what we are looking for, even if what we are looking for isn't represented in reality, hasn't actually transpired in the physical world."

"You find or are given your 'tribe' when it comes to this issue or that, whether it's the environment and sustainability or gender rights or international relations or domestic politics. That then, your side of the issue, becomes entrenched as your curated online experience. And because we give such automatic authority to the written word when things like capitalization and grammar are observed, as well as still naively believe that by virtue of being 'online' it - the opinion, the perspective, the hot take - has some clout to it, some oomph, some power, some reality, because of this, we tend to believe it without much scrutiny. To the extent that we personally identify with a side of an issue, a political party, a sports team, a brand, we do not question them as much. Scrutiny of our tribe slows or even stops to the extent that we are comfortably identified with it. That is part of what it means to be part of a tribe or a family even: when it's healthy and functional, we no longer question its perspectives; we simply save energy by shutting that part of our brain function down in regards to *our team*, as well as curry favor. To express concern or doubt is to imply disbelief in the stances of the tribe, lack of confidence in the tribe itself. Taking such a position, even if it is ultimately not in the name of dissolving or overturning the group but instead to shore up its ideological integrity and make it stronger, is, inherently, taking a risk. And most people, it seems, would rather quietly conform to their group despite whatever small or not-so-small hangups they may have, preferring the comfort and steadiness of unwavering loyalty and unquestioning solidarity to risking social banishment or even worse, their livelihoods in some cases, in the pursuit of truth, integrity and accountability. To cut through the jungle-like morass of opinions with the machete of discernment in order to see one's way clearly takes courage. We are most of us more socially inclined than philosophically or morally steadfast, and so engaging in a degree of cognitive dissonance is for most people a small price to pay or no price at all for the non-disruption of our lives, socially or economically."

"I will leave you all with this thought today, which is what our week's readings pertain to, this interesting idea that some are calling for: turning the internet into an impartial utility, like heating, electricity, and water. What would our online experience be like then, and how would the effects of that sort of online experience ripple out into the physical world? Read, reflect, respond to the comprehension questions, and we'll talk more about this all next week. Our next two classes will be different; they will be an open forum for debate on all we have discussed, in which I will prompt and moderate instead of delivering a lecture. So come next week well read and well rested with your take on the implications of our beloved device-middleman-artifices, the one you're about to check as this class ends, and have likely checked thirty or so times over the course of the last forty-five minutes!" Students looked sheepishly at each other in recognition of this calling-out. "Which, by the by, I do not begrudge you for. Narcissus simply could not tear himself away from his pond! Ha!"

And with that, Nim turned to his last slide for the lecture, prompting an embedded recording of Modest Mussorgsky's Night on Bald Mountain to start playing. Smiling and excited, students packed up their belongings and began to exit the lecture hall to its striking, ominous melodies.

The semester was coming to an end. Debate week in the Implications of Artifice class was two weeks before the final exam. Nim recommended students begin drafting the essay component of the exam as they prepared for the debate by responding to the questions, "How have you noticed technology and the way we use it change? How has this impacted your life? How do you believe these changes have impacted society at large?" By the end of the debates, students would have the opportunity to revise and expand on their essays before turning them in, adding or editing in whatever they may have gleaned over the course of the debate classes. Despite Nim's clear tech-hesitant leaning, the student body of the class was split. Some students, like Vishwanath, were right there with him, believing that our understanding of the breadth and pervasiveness of our new social technologies was of a somewhat negative forecast, and that the changes to the way we socialize they've brought about have been deleterious thus far. Others, like Vivienne, saw the power and the potential in our rapidly advancing and far reaching communication technologies and believed it to be a good thing, or at least an exciting and empowering thing. Most of the class lay somewhere in between, frankly indifferent. They would go along with whatever technological advancements the industry cooked up and fall in line with whatever social implications came along with changing, quickening tech. To them, available and popular technology and its role in human society called the shots by authority of its popularity, an implicit vote of confidence. Vishwanath sat poised and thoughtful in his study, eyes closed, two fingers on his temple, habits of concentration established long ago, now automatic. Rachmaninov's Isle of the Dead was playing at a low volume from his computer. He was done preparing for the debates to come; now he was thinking about Nim and his machine, what it could be, what clues he may have hidden in his lectures. Somewhere hidden, tucked away in a powerpoint slide that only the most fastidious of pupils would even think to click around and look for? Or was the clue, the invitation somewhere in what he said aloud? Of his sayings, Vish took thorough notes. Was there perhaps an acrostic to be found somewhere? What could the famed machine be when Nim so clearly was weary of today's computational-relational technology? Just what was it? Where was it, and why?

Vivienne sat at a small round table by herself in the campus' main cafeteria. It was on the second story of the student services building, and with its vast glass window-wall on its west side, was a favored vantage point for catching the sunset over dinner. Many students had dates in the cafeteria for this reason. Vivienne liked to spend time here because it also afforded a view of most of the college campus. She liked being above ground level, able to see the many comings and goings of all who lived and worked on the SUNY campus, noticing trends like rushes of students when classes let out, students flocking towards the cafeteria at meal times and back to their dorms for the night or to prepare for a night out on the town.

On this night however, Vivienne was not people-watching. She was thinking of Archibald Nim, thinking back on her classes with him, analyzing her notes and his memorable quotes, marked with an asterisk as possible leads. Leads that might give an inroads into making conversation or asking directly about his alleged machine. The 'mad' professor sure talked a lot about the ills of modern communication through social media and screen-devices, but it wasn't clear to her that he was against these technologies in principle. It was more their immature application, one we are in the process of learning from and working through as a society that he was painfully aware of, and sought to make others. Perhaps, in secret, he had perfected some machine, some search-potential-engine that cut through the 'jungle-like morass' of content online and somehow got to the heart of the matter, the heart of what matters to the individual using it, cut to the core. Walking back to her dorm room, Viv was already feeling sleepy. Quickly and dutifully she completed her nightly ablutions, lay softly onto her bed, and soon fell into a deep, nourishing sleep.

Behind the three centrifuges was a large motherboard, green with various other colors in the form of microchips and embedded wires: silver and gold, here a blue wire, there a red one, a short yellow cable linking this circuit to another further down the board. "My machine is programmed to factor all possible outcomes of all possible timelines, beginning as its standard setting at the formation of the Earth."

"But how, professor?" she asked him, her awe compounding. "Simple enough," he replied, running his hand through his grey hair and gazing at his machine as if looking at a lover in quiet admiration, "While I may not have been there to know the spin of the Earth, so to say, at its very

beginning, the metals present in the supercomputer were." Her mouth dropped a bit more. Genius, she thought. At which the machine's motherboard lit up briefly as its centrifuges alighted, glowing for a moment or two. Nim and Vivienne smiled at each other in silent marvel and secret knowing: the machine had heard Vivienne think that complimentary thought, and in its own way, had blushed. "It is only at rare points in time that the Earth ever gets something new sent down fast, flaming, and angry into its planetary sandbox. Well, statistically it's seventeen times a day, but they are usually quite small and land somewhere where no one is, and therefore negligible. What I mean to say is much of the Earth's resources, from liquid to gas to metals, have always been here, moving through a cycle of cohesion, degradation, dispersal, or sublimation often on a time scale that we humans simply cannot appreciate. And so the metals that compose Selenia as well as the energy that powers her has always been here, and so keeps a record of all that was at the beginning as well as accounts for all that has transpired since. Harnessing this record and applying some modern computational algorithms, the metals respond to the person thinking at it the strongest - an ability-lever, so to speak, we are just beginning to be able to measure. Think observational collapse of particles, a principle discovered in the field of physics in the last century. As such, you may wonder why she is responding just to you and not me. Knowing just how she operates, I have been suppressing my thinking since I turned her on to show you."

Yet again, Vivienne marveled at the master standing to her side, the mad professor who was equal parts philosopher, historian, inventor and genius. Vivienne turned to him and asked, "You named it...her, Selenia?"

"Yes," he said. "Her full name is Selenia 5-D. 5-D for 'fifth dimension', which is to say..." Nim closed his eyes. "The order of movement outside

time, or, possibility." Now he opened his eyes again, looking right at Vivienne head on, peering at her with the intensity of gaze that only he had, "Yes, if the fourth dimension is time, the previous three dimensions defining shape and form subjected to duration, then the next dimension of existence, the fifth, is time in multiple. Multiple lines of time, the knowledge thereof, and the ability first to see this and then to master it, to master them, to be able to skillfully navigate the forking river system of one's own possible timelines: this is what it means to be a being of the fifth dimension - to be able to walk or even waltz through it with all the ease and aplomb of a garden stroll." Vivienne continued standing there in growing awe mixed with growing respect, and now, the onset of a new emotion: elation and a sense of boundlessness, something akin to feeling like she could fly. "Selenia is a short-cut to this," Nim pronounced proudly. Once again, Vivienne realized, with appreciation approaching reverence, technology was reducing work by magnitudes: now she would not have to work all her life to maybe achieve what she wanted; instead, it would be given to her in an instant. All confusion, all doubt hindering the reaching of what she wanted, gone. "Selenia is waiting for you," said Nim. "Please, choose from the scope of what you believe to be possible for yourself, and my possibility collapser will make the necessary adjustments to extant earth-matter to make it so." Just as Vivienne's mind began to turn with the possibilities of what she might want to come to pass, Nim added, "so long as what you choose is actually possible for you."

The Implications of Artifice class met on Tuesdays and Thursdays that semester. The first day of debate, on Tuesday, had proceeded as one might expect: broad lines in the sand were drawn, and students interested enough to express themselves aloud were roughly divided into the two predictable camps: that technology these days was leading to our demise as a species and needed to be either done away with entirely or radically re-envisioned, or that it was fast-tracking our inevitable and optimal way of communicating with each other and that the kerfuffles and awkwardness we're experiencing today are only necessary growing pains as we advance in our capabilities. Nim, in his academic mercy, did not make everyone speak, but required students make their opinions known on paper at least. The end of semester debates were, after all, a portion of each student's final grade. The most vocal of the class thus spoke:

"The industrialization of agriculture has led to the lifting of millions out of fear of starvation, while international free trade and its corresponding technologies have alleviated just as many from the ravages of privation in general."

"Yes but these advancements have allowed the human race to rise dangerously above our carrying capacity as a species on the planet. As long as the aim of industry is to extract resources more and more efficiently, responding to the demand of tech companies to power their products, to be made into products that people then feel the need to get year after year out of dissatisfaction with their lives, out of work or social necessity or both, we are effectively assaulting the Earth with our unchecked and insatiable desire."

"Every year, sometimes twice a year, it's a new thing. A new model. Endless software updates that aren't even always improvements, all keeping you beholden to the parent company. Planned obsolescence. First hit's free, they say."

"The idea that today's communication technologies are a bad thing is an absolutely ludicrous take only possible from the cozy vantage point of the sort of heady, out-of-touch and hyper-privileged individuals living squarely in the first world. It's only when you can take Amazon's same day or next day delivery for granted, tired of its normalcy and critical of its fossil-fuel usage that you can make such inane statements. Thanks to the technology that powers the companies you decry, their customer interface and product delivery, more people now have the ability to live like royalty than ever before. If that isn't a quantum leap towards egalitarian abundance, I don't know what is!"

"If you've ever seen one of those massive cargo ships packed with shipping crates like a horizontal Jenga tower looming massively into the port of a coastal city, you have seen the cost of our desires. The implications of those ships' noise pollution and round-the-clock fuel usage on ocean ecosystems goes unbidden and ignored...and it will all come back to haunt us someday. Mark my words."

By the time the bell rang that day, the intrepid students Vishwanath and Vivienne hadn't even gotten in a single word; such was the passion, to their surprise and Professor Nim's delight, of their fellow students. And so they each, separately, resolved to ready themselves all the more for the next class, the last day of the debate, Thursday.

But there was one day before that to contend with, to see through from sunrise to sunset, and a unique opportunity to check in with Professor Nim.

When Vishwanath stopped in at the Morpheus Cafe wednesday, fat, fluffy snowflakes were falling from the sky. It was the first snowfall of that year's winter, not too cold, but cold enough so that it wasn't raining, and likely wouldn't again for the next few months. For the first time this season, winter boots and jackets were being taken out of closets and worn. It was the perfect day to hole up in a cozy cafe with fingers wrapped around a warm beverage.

"Ah Vishwanath, good to see you off campus," Nim began jollyly. Vish smiled, trying not to let his nervousness influence his ability to converse. In speaking with the professor today, he did not want his ulterior motive to be so obvious. He genuinely did not want Nim to think that that was all he was after, that he was just another curious student questing for his supposedly powerful secret. Mystery aside, he earnestly liked and respected him. "Have you been here before? Nim continued. "The special lattes they have on rotation each month are truly wonderful. Clearly some creative folk at work here."

"No, I haven't, what are you having today professor?"

"I'm having a chaga peppermint mocha." Nim took a frothy sip, smacking his lips. "Mmm dee-licious," he said, baring his teeth in an obvious display of delight.

"That sounds great," Vishwanath replied, smiling back at him, "I think I'll get one for myself. May I join you?"

"Of course, please do. I was just grading assignments from one of my other classes this semester, Empirical Reasoning. But I am in no rush; I come here to be social. Please, join me."

"Let me just put in my order and I'll be right back."

Walking up to the barista's counter, he saw a full menu containing all the usual coffee and tea options, iced and hot, decaf and not, as well as sandwiches, muffins and cookies on display. Written in chalk were this month's specialty lattes. He saw Nim's choice and two others: Cardamom Apple Rose and Feisty Chocolate Sea Salt. Seeking to embolden his resolve, he ordered the latter and walked back over to Nim. Taking a seat across from him in Nim's customary corner booth, the professor continued on without missing a beat. "So, you seem well prepared for the debate this week. You've come to make the impression that I ought not to expect anything less. Tell me Vishwanath, if you don't mind, what are your aspirations after you graduate? This is your sophomore year, correct?"

"It is."

"Certainly I do not wish to impart any existential dread, or any kind of dread for that matter in asking this, but have you any idea of a potential line of work after all of this? A dream job, a problem plaguing humanity you wish to apply yourself to solve?" It appeared as if Nim was lobbing him a soft, easy underhand pitch. Vishwanath swung.

"I would like to help people be at ease."

"A noble premise,"

"And of course in helping people I would be making my own experience of life easier, more straightforward."

"An honest premise,"

"It's just that, life can seem so full nowadays, no matter the subject in question, and yet also so very chaotic and uncertain. I imagine, I've been told at least, that things weren't always this way. Life used to be more straightforward, didn't it?"

"Certainly was. Less imaginative, too. Just a few decades ago, and practically for all time before that, people were expected to stay in their lane when it came to profession, gender, social caste, socio-economic bracket..."

"Right, and now it's as though the lane lines have faded, are almost gone. In the western world at least."

"Yes, I see your line of thinking. The dilemma of form and fundamentals and their place in the creative process. In terms of outright artistry as well as general life creativity - what one does with one's life, how one shapes it."

"I don't want to stifle creativity or curb anyone's potential," Vishwanath said, growing impassioned, "but I do wish it were more straightforward for people to act on what they're passionate about and make a solid impact.

It's like we would benefit from having some kind of blinder on, like a horse that races better without distraction. It's as if..."
Nim, listening intently, was beaming. In that moment he embodied the same sort of stored energy a cat does just before it pounces on a mouse or a bird. In a word, focus. Vishwanath, noticing this, continued.

"It's as if we would all benefit from some sort of technology that narrows and focuses what's possible into what is most likely or best for the individual based on their skillset and interests, a streamlining of sorts, as opposed to the naked infinity we experience online, barraging our eyes, storming our inbox."

"Inboxes, Vishwanath. Everyone who's anyone has multiple email accounts," Nim said with a smile. "If there's one thing you learn from me this semester, let it be that."

"Everyone who's anyone has multiple emails, got it," said Vishwanath. "Thank you professor, that's vital information." At this, they laughed together. A barista brought over Vishwanath's drink.

"Cheers," said Nim, raising his mug, "to a splendid semester, and more to come."

"I'll cheers to that professor, thank you." They sipped their brews, and talked on for a while about lighter subjects. The cafe was full of people, positively bustling with activity and conversation. Students and faculty from the college as well as town residents filled the room. The Morpheus Cafe was a lively place, a town staple, with regulars that kept its seats filled and its shelves stocked at all times of the year. The tourism season was beginning to pick up in upstate New York, a fact to which the lines, sometimes out the door, testified. But for true devotees, the ones who kept the cafe busy throughout the year, rain or shine, snow or sun, the staff of the coffee house always made sure to go the extra mile, holding onto their favorite mugs for when they stopped by, making sure service was snappy no matter what, remembering preferences. And the music selection was perfect. There was no music playing over a sound system to fill space, playing just to make noise and obscure the sometimes challenging clarity of silence. There was almost always enough hustle and bustle to create an organic ambience of its own anyway, relaxing in its own right and true to life at that. The cafe had live music several days a week. Wednesday and Sunday nights were open mic nights. Fridays and Saturdays professional musicians or bands were booked to play, with a preference for local talent. All in all, the Morpheus was a beloved and longstanding business in the college town.

As they each drained the last drops from their cups, Archibald Nim steered their engagement to a close. "It's been very nice chatting with you, Mr. Singh."

"Agreed, professor. It certainly has," Vish replied, starting to stand up, sensing where the conversation was going.

"I can see from the work you've turned in this semester, and our talk today has confirmed: you are at least as concerned about humanity's relationship with technology as I am."

"Yes, I would say so. I am very concerned. I feel inspired to give myself to the task of reconciling our, as of now, immature use and integration of the profoundly powerful technology that has come to be over my lifetime." Nim narrowed his eyes, studying Vishwanath Singh as if he were a portrait in a gallery. "And you will, Vishwanath. I believe you will meet with success," he paused, looking, thinking, contemplating. Behind the remarkable hazel eyes and expressive face he'd come to respect and somewhat adore, Vish saw some sort of human machine, a whirling cerebellum of acutely keen intellect and connective faculties working away quickly, processing, weighing, deciding. "Continued success, in fact, will be your lot. At least, that is my hope. More than mere hope, I would bet on it." From Nim's kindly, smiling face, his countenance, his very being he felt a wave of goodwill surge forth. "Now if you'll excuse me, I do have to make a dent in grading these papers. I'll see you tomorrow. I'm looking forward to the next day of debate!"

"As am I, professor, thank you. Take good care." Vishwanath put on his coat, returned his mug to the bussing bin, and took his leave from the Morpheus Cafe.

When Vivienne Donnelly walked into the Morpheus Cafe that wednesday, Professor Nim was on his third chaga peppermint mocha, hard at work grading papers. As she strode confidently up to the service counter, putting in her order, he saw her in his periphery and put down his pen. As she walked towards him - direct, focused, of one mind - he put all his papers back into one stack, laying the ungraded ones horizontal on the vertical stack of graded papers. "Miss Donnelly," he said, looking up from his table,

"A fine day to you." It was as if he'd been expecting to see her today, as if he'd known she'd come. If he had a hat on, he would have tipped it towards her, was how his cordial, gentlemanly greeting felt.

"How's it going professor? Getting some work done while getting your latte on?" Vivienne asked with a smile.

"I do not know a better way to get done what needs doing," Nim replied. "A warm brew can ease along even the most difficult of tasks. Not that what I'm doing is all that difficult. No..." Nim took a long sip. "Grading essays was not a labor of Hercules, if I recall correctly. But I shall put that by the wayside for now. Come for a chat? Have a seat Vivienne, please."

"Thanks professor, it's nice to be able to talk one on one."

"Very different social experience than one on thirty-four. You and I can have conversation. I find that hard to do with thirty-four people. I don't know if you've ever tried to talk with thirty-four people at once, but it's quite a challenge. In fact, I don't think it's truly possible, talking *with* that is. The best I find I can manage is talking *to* or *at* thirty-four other people. Not a conversation. At best, a lecture." Nim and Vivienne both smiled. "And you know, seeing as that is what you all signed up for - to attend a lecture - I suppose that it's well and good that that's the way it is. But conversation - back and forth, inquiry, conjecture, the sounding out of concepts and the revision of ideas - well, it's vital for us, social creatures we are."

Vivienne could tell the professor was amply caffeinated. Perfect, she thought to herself, he's in the mood to gab. "We are social creatures," Viv picked up, "and try as we might, no single one of us has all the answers."

"No, that's right. No one will have success 'going it alone' as they say. Monastics typically belong to an order replete with seniority-based hierarchies or at least some sort of loose but important fellowship in the sparer cases. Even the noble hermit living in solitude cannot remove herself from the web of life, from the interconnectivity of existence. She must still procure food and water, make her home from wood or stone or earth. And veritably, would she not look forward to morning birdsong, to the beauteous and mystifying call of the loon by the lakeside? Only a true scrooge, a true grinch would bemoan the friendly little steps of the curious squirrel around her hut. I would venture to bet that she looks forward to it, looks forward to another mammal shacking up with her, sharing in the warmth of her home and that she might provide, if incidentally, a safe and cozy place to spend the night for another living being."

"I agree. Even stoically and purposefully living alone, one would have to have a real heart of coal to shun all other animals from one's life."

"It wouldn't just be incomprehensibly mean, it simply wouldn't be possible. From the moment we are born into this world until the moment we make our exit, however gracefully or fearfully, we take and we give. We cannot stop this process, or we die. Breathing is the greatest example of this: we take in a draught of space, inhaling oxygen and also dust, skin cells, bacteria, viral particles, and many other minute things I'm sure, and exhale a warm blast of our self, out to commingle with our immediate environment and in a small but not insignificant way, the entire world. Every time, each breath. If we do not do this, if we fail to engage in this exchange, we suffocate and die. This giving and taking is necessary for terrestrial life to function. It is both miraculous and the most ordinary, common occurrence we experience."

"It is important to help others, to give back." Vivienne tried to redirect the trend of the conversation from the philosophical to the practical.

"Nowadays, to get ahead in life, for instance socio-economically speaking, it does not appear to be as simple as it once was. Merely working hard and 'pulling yourself up by your bootstraps' doesn't seem to cut it anymore. Most of us find ourselves treading water despite our skill or talent. Skill specialization is encouraged early on, and so we must pay someone for everything we need done but don't know how to do. To 'become an adult' in our culture merely means, from what I've gathered so far, that you're the one who pays all the monthly fees required to keep playing the game. That you're the one that handles all of the upkeep. And as they all require regular monetary diligence, the race and competition for well-paying employment is paramount. Interests, passion-projects, and activities that satisfy non-monetarily fall to the wayside in the wake of the reality of modern adulthood, despite their value to the health and sanity of that individual and the world."

"Yes, as we have discussed in class, I do find it to be the case that now in the hyper-information age it is not necessarily the cream that rises to the top. We do not, unfortunately, exist in an honest meritocracy. More often now it is simply the loudest ones in the crowd that are heard, not the best or the brightest. And there are clear guidelines to amplifying oneself to attract more attention online, garner more views, more clicks. It is a road well-traveled at this point, with proven methods evolving into task-outsourcing and pyramid-scheme-esque hacks that some continue to fall for while others continue to swear by. The promise of the comforts of worry-free wealth, the sense of security buoyed by seeing bigger and bigger numbers in one's bank account, it's all very tempting. Work hard yourself to stay afloat, keep your family afloat, or take advantage of others and tap into your virtual network, sifting through your 'online friends' and 'followers' for what suckers you might get to sign up for this or buy that through your affiliate link. Bah! I'm glad to be holed up in the ivory tower, to be secure enough to not have to commit these semi-mortifying social faux-pas's that more and more people are willing to bend, to tap into for the alluring promise of 'passive income'. Morality, decency, dignity are all going to hell in a hand-basket by way of obfuscating anonymity, what we might be able to get away with when others can't see who's doing it. It's childish."

"How do we, as you said, "cut through the jungle-like morass of opinions" most effectively? The "machete of discernment" might not be enough. If someone really, really wants to, um, 'make it', let's say, make a splash in their chosen field or even on the world stage, and I mean meaningfully…how does one stand out these days?"

"Well, if your skills and intellect are sufficiently worthy of notice and merit - as I believe yours are, Vivienne - and you still find it difficult to move up in the world, to make the splash you want to make, there are other ways to do so, to get ahead. In their own way, this is what esoteric alchemical traditions around the world have sought to do: transmute the ordinary into the extraordinary, recognizing the intrinsic worth and potential of all objects and particles under the sun. If that is your aim, then it is the path of alteration, the alchemists' way that you must make your own."

"Now that sounds exciting. Any pointers for starting down this path?" "For starters, I would recommend looking into the works of Hermes Trismegistus. And to balance out that perspective, I would also recommend looking into Adi Shankaracharya and Meister Eckhart."

Vivienne jotted these names down into a pocket notebook she had with her. "Thanks, professor," she said.

"Oh and I would cautiously recommend looking into colloidal metal supplementation. Expands certain mental and psychic faculties. A bit obscure, a lost art for sure, but they do affect the brain in interesting and helpful ways. Be sure to be thorough in your research before you actually start taking anything, as I'm sure you will. I would recommend looking into colloidal gold, platinum, palladium, iridium, cobalt, nickel, and selenium. Start small, see how they affect you, increase infrequently and cautiously, perhaps after working with one low dose for a month or so."

"I've heard of colloidal silver, but nothing else 'colloidal'. Very interesting. Thank you professor. Do you take them?"

"I experimented more with them in the past. I've had many experiences of both under and over-doing it. It takes time to figure out the optimal dose for oneself. Nowadays I just...well I don't want to influence your idea of what is best or what to aim for, so I won't say. I'll let it be your journey. Go slow, small, and cautiously is all I'll say. I'm confident you'll handle them the right way and derive benefit."

"Fascinating, I'm excited to give them a try."
"Very good," said Nim, savoring his last sip. He stuck out his arm and looked at the watch on his hairy wrist. "Look at that, it's time for lunch. Both my watch and stomach are in agreement." Nim and Vivienne stood up from their chairs and began to pick up their belongings from the booth. "Take good care, Vivienne. Passionate and galvanized as you are, do take care to rest and nourish yourself properly. The engine of your ambition needs proper fueling to run. Never forget that."
"Thank you professor. Have a good lunch. See ya tomorrow."

————————————————

Students were filing into one of the last classes of the semester that thursday. Everyone felt a mix of emotions hard to put into words: excitement and/or dread for finals, elation for the semester's end and the summer to come, and a bittersweet sense of tenderness at the finishing of Implications Artifice with Professor Nim. The man himself, Archie as his friends and colleagues called him, was seated in his ergonomic rolling chair as usual, wearing his large spectacles, a checkered button-up shirt with tan slacks and a gold pocketwatch attached to one of his belt loops by chain. As he usually did, he watched the students pour in the doors to the lecture hall, one to the upper right, one to the upper left. He felt a growing sense of pride as he saw student after student come in, remembering ah-ha moments, great insights, and other evidence of growth for just about each student he saw. This was the first time this class, an idea Nim had been nurturing for years, had ever been taught. Now nearing the conclusion of this class's debut, he mused to himself about the journey they had all taken together, at once thrilled that the class had done so well and would certainly run again the next academic year, and somewhat sad that it was coming to a close. Nim wasn't a particularly sentimental person, but this class was his baby, and seeing it succeed and inspire as well as it did made everyone who was a part of it special to him. Especially the students who were really into it, who really attacked the coursework with vigor and participated passionately in class, asked questions with an earnest desire to know, the ones Nim saw with their noses in their notebooks, scribbling furiously. They made this class what it was, for which Nim felt gratitude as well as a paternal sort of affection.

"Welcome everyone, welcome. As you know this is the last class of our two-part, in-class debate, so if you have something you wish to say, today is the day to do so. Please, don't be shy. I understand we all exist at various levels of comfort with public speaking, and it is no flaw on your part for being averse to speaking aloud amongst a group. It's not for everyone and by no means needs to be. There's a place in the functioning of society for politicians, orators, or 'influencers' as they are called now, and there's a place for producers, accountants, book-keepers and editors, silent and efficient at what they do. I encourage you to speak today, especially if you didn't on tuesday, though as I hope you know, am not requiring it. What I am requiring of everyone is a selective written transcript of the debates this week along with your actual opinion on the matter we're discussing. As you can see from the papers I handed out on tuesday, you have large boxes in which to capture several quotes you hear that resonate with you, quotes uttered by your fellow students that I would like you to respond to in writing. In this way, even if not everyone speaks aloud - which, seeing as there are thirty-four of you, I do not expect - everyone will still experience something of a debate as you jot down and agree, disagree, or partially agree with what you hear today. And to remind you once more, this debate and its worksheet are part of your final grade. Use this week's debate and the notes you take to help inform and craft your final essay, due a week from today, next thursday. The following week, the last week of class, will conclude with our final exam, which will be a simple though lengthy multiple choice test with a few short answer questions showing me that you've been awake this semester. Now, does everyone know where to find the essay questions in our syllabus? Does everyone know where to find the study guide for the final exam? Please, raise your hand if you don't. I would like to embarrass you in front of everyone." Laughter from among the studentry. Everyone was ready.. This was a class of philosopher majors, after all.

"Okay, very well then. Let us pick up today with the following prompt to start things off. As before, I will call on the first hand I see shoot into the air. How has today's social and communications technology leveled the playing field as regards artistry, craft and commerce, and journalistic expression? Or has the way we communicate put up barriers to entry? Made things harder for anyone?"

At the cessation of Nim's voice, Vivienne's hand shot up into the air like a Tesla accelerating from zero to sixty. The professor motioned his hand at her, palm upturned, entreating her to go ahead. And so she went.

"These days we hear a lot about 'living your best life.' It is a phrase said in passing, vapidly on Instagram stories or encouragingly at friends when they decide to do something for themselves like splurge on a shopping trip or take a tropical vacation somewhere. Like so much of our lingo, it has become watered down through the banality and frequency of its use. But I see a real reason emerging why people say this now, as opposed to during the Klondike Gold Rush or the fall of Rome: it is because the scope of our ability, the average person's ability these days to summon the resources they want, let alone what they need, is currently the easiest and most stream-lined it's ever been. I would say this is due to the current state of technological advancement, the ease of 'getting yourself out there' whether you are a small-business owner who now has the ability to sell across the world through Amazon or Etsy, or whether you are an exercise instructor, teacher or tutor who can now reach practically anyone anywhere through platforms like Zoom. Our interconnectivity as a world-wide species is powered by today's communication technology. I firmly believe it not only has leveled the playing field but has allowed us, is allowing us, each of us separately and together, to reach our highest potential."

Vishwanath sat, still, thinking, waiting.

A hand from the fourth row went up into the air, and Nim signaled in approval. "I agree with Vivienne. Nearly anyone now can upload a video to Youtube or express themselves on Twitter, share a snippet of their life on Instagram, or talk and share more at length on sites like Patreon, Substack, and Ghost. The barriers to entry into the global conversation have been lowered way, way down. Like never before can anyone reach everyone."

Another hand, another student in agreement, "To go along with that, young people and people without the financial ability or without the time to spend on upgrading their credentials - earn degrees as we privileged folk here have the ability to - have new and easy-to-set-up ways to earn their keep, provide for their families, fund their dreams or create a side-hustle."

Vishwanath now had a hand to his face, his left palm meeting his jawline. Still, thinking, waiting, poised. Like a cat storing potential energy, waiting to pounce.

One student picked up with their comment from the last class, repeating their train of thought, obviously proud of what they had to say and feeling it deserved repeating, feeling it was poignant and insightful: "I said it on tuesday and I'll say it again, because I think we really need to hear it and think it often: if you are using your phone to complain about the state of technology today, you're being childish and naive. If you are posting pro-minimalist, anti-tech, anti-capitalist witticisms on Facebook, Instagram, or Twitter, espousing the old 'return to Nature' narrative, you've already contradicted yourself and invalidated your own opinion by virtue of the very technology you've used and had to use to do so and reach as many people as you wanted to see how 'enlightened' you are. It is all too easy and appealing to romanticize 'Nature' as a state of perfection and innocence that we've fallen from, and prescribe a return to this 'natural state' as the solution to all or most of the world's problems. But think about how life would change if, say next week, all our devices - everything requiring mobile service or wifi - shut down. Practically all of life as we know it would go to hell in a hand-basket remarkably fast. It would leave us spinning, cranky and pining like a baby without its pacifier. Even a less extreme reduction in the use of our devices, a forced rationing say, of only being able to use our phones or computers for...let's say four hours a day, would result in a noticeably dramatic slowing down of commerce and information exchange. And this would trickle down to just about every aspect of our lives, from food to utilities, transportation and entertainment. Societies that employ top-down rationing schemes are never happy ones. People who are just trying to live their lives, meet their needs, provide for themselves and their families if they have one, are only inconvenienced by this. Life would just be shittier without our technology or with less of it. Why go back? It doesn't make rational sense."

At this, there was a pause. The student's pronouncements seemed wise and irrefutable. Nim sought to keep the momentum of the debate going and asked, "Does anyone care to follow that up or shall I begin us on another debate prompt?" After he spoke, no hand was raised. Instead, a voice was heard, steady, calm and confident.

It was Vishwanath's voice.

"Does it make rational sense to curse people you've never met out in the strongest possible terms? Does it make rational sense to walk around this beautiful world with your head down, ignoring the magnificent source of light and life above and all our fellow organisms around in favor of a small blue blinking rectangle of plastic, glass, and indium held in the palm of our hands? Does it make sense to converse more, know more and think more about individuals we'll never meet than to walk across the yard and greet your neighbor good day? Does it make rational sense to be more affected by and interested in people on the other side of the country or the other side of the world than in the people you share a street with, walk past everyday? Does it make rational sense to cringe in anxiety at the prospect of having to say hello to your neighbor while you walk your dogs around the block, only to come home and excitedly and obsessively check your phone to see if someone thousands of miles away has messaged you back? When you see a group of people standing around each other, all within a three foot radius of each other as if they were conversing socially, only to see that they are all craning their necks staring down and thumbing away at their little screens while saying absolutely nothing to one another, does that look rational? When you see toddlers being wheeled around in strollers, not looking out and marveling at the wondrous world around them but glued to their touch-screen pads, does that look rational? And when they scream and storm when their parent takes it away, does that seem healthy? Is it rational to be angry at your cousin who hasn't responded to your request to be listed as 'cousins' on Facebook, when in actual life this is self-apparent, requires no listing or affirmation and is incontrovertible biological fact? Is it rational to spend hours every day building your home in an online fantasy world, gathering resources, improving skills and making connections with lines of code given anthropomorphic recognizability to the detriment of your ability to do any of that in the life and level of reality that forms the substratum of the world in which you have the ability to check out and get lost in such fantasy games in the first place? Please, someone tell me: does it make sense to say something online that you wouldn't ever say to someone's face? No? Clearly, something is amiss here. Clearly, I would say, we have some learning, some growing up and self-moderating to do in this new, vast and undeniably engulfing arena of our lives. And I am of the belief that we'd better self-examine and self-correct quickly, before we become afraid to look off-screen or go 'afk' for more than a minute or two. Because that is hell, anxiety-ridden and dysfunctional, bordering on solipsistic species self-destruction."

The next voice picked up after a moment or two of stunned silence, again no hand, straight to voice. It was Vivienne's. "Some personal anxiety for each of us or perhaps only some of us to work through is a small price to pay for the ubiquity of information and opportunity we gain. We can learn. We can adapt. We can work through awkward latencies in the integration of our empowering, connective technologies because they are worth it. Just think of the repercussions, the unfathomable butterfly effect of not having the access to information that we've had growing up...how many of us would be here in this lecture hall right now? Without the boundless, ever-expanding Library of Alexandria that is the internet to level the playing field, giving everyone access to nearly everything, I would be cleaning up in a sheet-metal shop in Boston. Where would you be today without twenty-first century technology, Vishwanath? Where would any of us not born into wealth, class or power be? You, like me, likely wouldn't be out of the stuck impasse of intergenerational farming or artisanry. Stuck where we are, doing what our families have always done for as long as anyone can or cares to remember. Face it: you probably wouldn't even be in this country right now!"

At this, a gasp from the class. No one had anticipated that, a personal affront and a calling-out in the debate. Vishwanath scowled silently. Vivienne, surprised at herself, felt her heart racing, her mouth hot with the excitement of conflict, yet that the remark had been worth it: it was like a slam dunk that the anti-tech side, of which Vishwanath had taken up the beat as chief, would have a hard time recovering from. The morale, the energy in the room had changed, for the debate had gone from abstract to personal. Professor Nim sought to restore order. "Please let us keep this civil. This debate has been productive, but let us make an effort not to veer off into personal attacks, which have no place in this friendly debate. That is a reminder to you all, and a warning for you, Miss Donnelly. I would appreciate if you would please apologize to Vishwanath, as I'm sure he would as well."

Vivienne relented. "My apologies, Vish, for going there. I'm just getting passionate. I didn't mean anything by it."

"That's Vishwanath to you, Miss Donnelly," the young man uttered pejoratively in response, emphasizing her name farcically. Some laughter came about at this. Nim stepped in once more. "Alright, alright. Tit for tat. There we are. Let's everyone cool their jets, take a deep breath, hold, one, two, three, exhale, one, two, three...there we go. Everyone back in a calm, respectful mode? Everyone's vagus nerve chilled out? Good. We still have about twenty minutes left today, so let us continue."

"I would like to, if I may, professor," said Vishwanath, raising his hand. "Please," said Nim.

"The benefits of our rapidly advancing technology are clear enough, and it is not my desire nor my focus to look past that and dash it all away, throw the baby out with the bathwater so to speak. I am confident that we will not 'go back' willingly in terms of a technological drop; I don't think any civilization does that willingly. What may happen one day though, and has likely happened in the past - there is archeological as well as circumstantial evidence for this - is that some planetary catastrophe may set us back. But that's just speculation for now, and not quite the point I'm trying to make. What I am trying to say, trying to remind us all of, is the importance of weighing the cons with the pros, and then taking proactive action to mitigate the cons. For instance, data is starting to come out on the socially deleterious effects of intensive screen-time at young, developmental ages, screen-time over real face-to-face time, that is. Face-to-forest time - the inexpressible advantages that come from spending time in an ionically-charged, mycelium-rich, bio-diverse landscape. Young people, whose brains and attitudes have not yet fully developed, are not allowed to smoke or drink alcohol until a certain age, see R rated movies, rent cars, or join the military, among many other things. I think we need something like this, some in-built, age-based social wisdom for our up and coming generations. As I look around everyday and bear witness to the normalcy of anxiety that is the experience of so many of my peers, I wish our generation had something like this. We've been guinea pigs, and everyone younger than ourselves even more so. To be clear, I am not advocating for a slew of new laws to be passed instituting age-based restrictions if we can manage without them. I am advocating for, ideally, the popularization and societal embracing of non-codified, colloquial wisdom regarding social media and screen-time, something voluntary, arising as the next stage in the evolution of our common sense."

Vivienne, who had been raising her hand for the last minute or so as Vishwanath spoke, was now called on to respond.

"If there is something to know, I don't think it actually benefits anyone to withhold it, to prevent someone from knowing that which is out there to be known. We, all of us here and those younger than us, those yet to be born, do not need to be shielded from what is possible in life. We would only be doing ourselves a disservice since we will never agree globally on imposing such restrictions. However we elect to restrict ourselves is exactly how much we will be behind, because you can bet that many countries oceans away won't be imposing such restrictions, and therefore they will lap us, technologically, economically, and educationally. We cannot afford to handicap ourselves."

As Vishwanath began to respond - again, foregoing the hand-raising - much of the class had settled in to watch the V. vs V. debate with interest. He responded, "But we have already handicapped ourselves! We have bought wholesale into the dishonest sentiment of our devices 'making life more convenient'. That may appear to be so, but at what cost? Think about it: your phone is now the middleman, the medium through which you interface with the world. It may be fast, it may be a quick way to connect with any resource you need or want, but it is a pinch-point for you the consumer as well as those supplying the goods or services, a socially sanctioned and utterly controllable channel for doing business, like the virtual version of a port of commerce, imposing taxes and tariffs and dictating what can or can't come in. Our phones have become the rolodex's of our life contacts and connections. Instead of having meaningful, genuine and direct connections with tradespeople, craftsmen, grocers and shopkeepers, we reach out to the nearest and often the cheapest service provider through our device, discover that person or business through our device. What happens when the device is gone, or when it slows down? What happens when who we see is available through our devices for this service or that is controlled? Exposure online to professionals and to information is not merit-based, it is under an agendized control that we, most of us, are consumer pawns helpless in effecting."

"What's happening to us as these dopamine-driving devices become more and more necessary, more and more expected? What happens when physical currency disappears? What happens when you need work done on your home or your apartment, and without the skills yourself or personal connections to people with them, all you have is your phone or computer to reach out and attempt to schedule someone to come - someone you don't know and only sees you and your problem as just another invoice to kick down the pipeline for a few months? What happens, as more and more of life goes online, when your social credit score prevents you from getting the work you need done? The medical care you need? Or the vacation, the wedding trip you desire to attend? That is a chief concern of mine: the pinch-point and middleman to experiencing life that our devices and the virtual world are becoming. It's other humans, after all, that control these gates. Like a few sociopathic sheep that have figured out how to open and close the gates for their own flock, and so have an enormous degree of control over the rest."

"Your doom-saying hypotheticals may engage us viscerally, but have no basis in reality as of yet," Vivienne countered. "There is no social credit score, there is no prepper-apocalypse waiting fiendishly in the wings. These scare-tactics are bandied about as reasons to pump the brakes on the engine of our advancement, but the call of the luddite is as old as the wheel itself, probably even as old as fire. For as long as humans have been working to improve life, there have been other humans putting their intellects to ill-use to detract from them. And why? It's never for a good reason. Jealousy, perhaps? You all can judge for yourselves."

"There is another side to this conversation," said Vishwanath. "So far I have been arguing in favor of voluntary restriction, voluntary simplicity because of how we are, in practice, actually limited by the technology we're obsessed with. But what about the sea of possibilities that this interconnective technology supposedly brings us to the shore of? Is it really there, tantalizing and true? Or is it only a mirage, like the shimmering illusion of water in a desert, like the effect a kaleidoscope has on the set, physical world? Are there really so very many possibilities out there, so vast as the number of search results Google purports each search to have? For however many possibilities there appear to be, we decide on one, we choose one thing to buy for someone's birthday, one place to have lunch at, one person to be our therapist. Of all the businesses and organizations we may send our resumes to and of the ones that respond with a job offer, we decide on one. Possibility has become tantamount to paralysis, the myriad opportunities supposedly at our fingertips little more than smoke and mirrors."

"Thank you Vishwanath, we'll have to end it there. We are officially out of time today. Thank you Vivienne, and everyone else who contributed to our discussion today, and those who contributed on tuesday. I think I'm correct in speaking for the whole of the class when I say that the conversation today has been riveting and productive. I was on the edge of my seat! Please remember to turn in your debate responses along with your final essay next week, and to continue studying for the final exam the week following. You know where to find the study-guide and all of our lecture slides...as long as there's wifi, that is, you can access them at your discretion." Nim smiled knowingly. "So long everyone. It's been a pleasure. Have a great weekend. See you next week."

As the semester at the State University of New York drew to a close, each day passed like molasses, or more regionally appropriate, like maple syrup in freezing weather, slow and sweet. It was clear from people's moods, from the way they looked shuffling about the buildings of the college campus, from the attitude of students in the dining hall or out in town, that everyone was savoring this last bit of the semester: students, campus services employees and teaching faculty, the people working the businesses in town all but tried to slow down these last few days of what was for most, a very enjoyable last few months. Each student of Nim's, students all over campus for just about every class, strove to perfect their academic voice, their 'mic-drop' on the ending semester. While a certain demographic of students gave up on caring or had given up weeks or months ago and partied hard, many students paired this time of celebration with an intensifying of their academic work. Work and play, study and frivolity, resolution and hedonism, all as the world turns. Though the subjects about which they thought and wrote, about which we think and write, change, the song remains the same, as old as time, as old as there's been a curious, large-brained hominid species to muse about time, to remember memory and the recurrent themes of this ineffable co-creative adventure we call life.

Obviously, Vishwanath and Vivienne belonged to the former category, waking up early and staying up late to draft and redraft their best work. Vivenne however, extrovert she was, did do some partying. She worked hard, obsessively hard, and still made time to celebrate with her friends, often to the detriment of her sleep cycle. Vishwanath just worked obsessively hard. He found almost all the satisfaction he wanted in the complete, and as far as he was concerned, perfected and crystalline final drafts of his essays for his classes, his personal statements on the important matters put to him by his esteemed professors, academic statements which he saw also as statements about himself, reflections of the fitness and acuity of his mind. And he would cut no corner, give nothing less than his all in the crafting of these final assignments. His name was Vishwanath, after all, a name he did his very best to live up to.

On the day of the final exam, Professor Archibald Nim's class was aflutter with the scribbling of pens, animated with searching stares and narrowing eyes on the part of students who strained to remember this or that, looking both at the instructor (as if for some telepathic leniency) and off into space. For most people this meant looking to the upper-left or upper-right as their thoughts sought completion and mental dots connected, the human equivalent of a loading screen. Some students' eyes widened as they suddenly remembered what they felt confidently was the answer, or alternatively, furtively looked over at their peers, as if looking at someone who was acing the test would somehow rub-off on them. Some students' mouths were tightly closed, bottom lips swallowed and beards being chewed on as they strained to beat the clock and finish the massive test. Pencil tips that broke were hastily re-sharpened. Every human in the room was alert and engaged. Philosophy majors through and through. There was an almost constant low level background noise of papers shuffling and pens or pencils scribbling, the cosmic microwave background radiation of Nim's classroom they had all come to know and he, the conductor of it all, loved and lived for.

As the clock ticked on, the superlative students Vivienne and Vishwanath turned in their tests. They were neither the first nor the last to do so. In fact (not that this meant much), they happened to turn in their tests around the same time, within three minutes of each other. After Vishwanath turned in his, he did not say goodbye to the professor and leave like everyone else. Instead, he waited. He sat at his desk with his eyes trained on Nim, who looked exceedingly happy as he graded the tests that were being turned in, looking up every once in a while to take in the room, check for any hands raised in question, make sure there was no one was cheating. No one was, and he did not expect that anyway from this class. Every so often Vishwanath would look back down to his notebook in front of him to jot down some insight. Vivienne also stayed posted at her seat, waiting. She too wanted a word with Professor Nim. But as the minutes passed and student after student left, turning in their tests and bidding their professor farewell, her lack of sleep caught up with her. Falling prey to the nearly irresistible siren song of her tiredness, she made a pillow of her jacket on her portion of the long lecture table in front of her, folded her arms, laid her head down, and swiftly drifted off to sleep.

Vivienne found herself blinking in front of Professor Nim and his contraption, as if waking up, as if coming to. They appeared to be waiting. They appeared, in fact, to have been waiting patiently for some time for her to make her choice, for her to choose her fate…and evidently she had been standing there blankly and indecisively, for their patience suddenly felt to her like it was wearing thin. She was still overwhelmed by the barely fathomable power now available to her. To influence life from a higher dimension and to see the effects of her decision, of her will, trickle down into the mundane solidity of life, to see obstacles removed and goals and desires accelerated towards…her mind was still racing with all that she could possibly do. How she could dramatically alter her life, and in doing so, life on earth in sum. Dizzy, she felt what it must feel like to be a slot machine, only, she wasn't slowing down. Her mind, her choices, her possibilities, all of them continued to rush unbound in her mindspace, to dance in front of her just out of reach. She attempted to sort through them rapidly, sensing that she might be running out of time to decide on just what it was she most desired and was also within her realm of possibility. How could she possibly know that? How could she, in mere human form, know what was and wasn't possible for her? There were some opportunities that clearly were not within her wheelhouse, but that didn't mean they weren't fun to think about. She would not, for instance, become a world-class musician or international sports phenom, that was for sure, for tempting as that sort of skilled fame was, she had no proclivity towards either of those skillsets. Yet still, even as she attempted to narrow things down for herself, her frustration growing, whims of irrelevant but nonetheless tantalizing fantasies danced on seductively in her head.

She took a deep breath, closed her eyes, and tried to calm down her racing thoughts, her runaway mind. Okay, she thought to herself, what do I like? What am I good at? What do I ultimately want in life? As she made a mental list, Professor Nim and his machine, Selenia 5-D, continued to wait, and as they waited, began to slowly disappear. Unseen by her as she focused on her own procession of thoughts, they began to fade away, slowly going from opaque to transparent to nothing, like a screen going dim and then blank from non-use.

Okay, Vivienne thought: I want financial security for myself and those closest to me, I want to never again feel the dread sense of lack, of not having enough. I want to never miss out, to always be on the cutting edge of what's going on socially and technologically, and to always know what's happening in the world politically, what's actually happening beyond the dumbed down theater we commonfolk are shown. I want to always be one step ahead of catastrophe, to know how the stock markets of the world will go, how the trends of international trade may dive or grow so as to be able to profit off whatever happens, or at least be sheltered from the economic storms that befall us. But wait, would that just be for me? That would be lonely, and likely appear to others as suspicious. I want my family and friends to be safe too, to be able to weather whatever comes our way…what would that look like? A community of us? Actually living together or just linked tightly through virtual space? Hmmmm. Maybe we should all live somewhere safe together, yes, safe from both volatile economies and environmental disaster. We should all be on an island somewhere together! Yes that's it! But islands are especially subject to rising sea levels. So it should be an island with elevation, with mountains…an existing island like the big island of Hawaii or the highlands of Sri Lanka? Or, should I create one for us? If this machine can rearrange matter as the professor said then it should be possible. Okay that's a good idea. Hmmm. But what about putting myself into a position of power where I can prevent these problems in the first place? Govern and legislate in such a way and on such a global scale as to prevent both economic and environmental turmoil? Yes, I believe I can do that. I have the power to do that, the strength, the will, the intellect. Not everyone, not many others at all, but me, me, yes me! I can! I know I can! I want it so! She stopped thinking and spoke aloud, forgetting the very principle by which the machine operated."That's it Professor, that's what I want! Did you hear me? Did Selenia hear me? Make this all happen please! It is possible! I know it is!"

Vivienne awoke with a neck strained from having been laid sideways on the table in front of her. Groggy as she woke up from what had been an irresistible nap, she used her hands to stretch and crack her neck as she looked around. The lights were still on in the lecture hall, on this, the last day of class, but no one else was there. All the students had left. Vishwanath had left. Even Professor Nim was gone. Vivienne Donnelly had been left alone, seemingly forgotten.

————————————————

Approximately eighteen minutes before her waking, Vishwanath, diligent and ever-wakeful, had found the opportunity he had been waiting for. What he had been waiting for was for everyone else to leave the room before he approached the professor, and now everyone had. Vivienne's body was still in the room, but her consciousness was adrift; for his intents and purposes, she was gone. Professor Nim, surely aware of the only two students left in the room, his star pupils, continued grading the stack of tests like he had been. Vishwanath took a deep breath, filled his diaphragm and held the air in his chest for a few seconds, feeling a surge of oxygenated blood, of warmth, of courage. With everything of his packed up, he left his seat and walked over to Nim.

"Professor," he began, "I was wondering…"

"Hmm?," he pronounced, looking up from what he was doing and at the young man in front of him. "Oh yes, it's time isn't it?"
"Umm, I…" Vishwanath was flabbergasted, taken aback. His heart began to race. Could the professor have intuited his reason for lingering around? The question and the quest that had been guiding his heart and intellect for the last year? The better question - and for not thinking this first he quickly reproached himself mentally - was, how could he have not? Or, his confidence taking a sudden dip, was he merely projecting onto the man the conversation he'd been anticipating having for months on end?

"From time to time I choose to impart onto worthy students an extra lesson. It's not part of any of my course material, though certainly and in a uniquely experiential way it is relevant to the philosophy I am prone to prattle on about. You are, beyond a shadow of a doubt, a most worthy student, Vishwanath. You are unsurpassed, *aparajit*. Come with me, if you please." Smiling, he nodded his head and turned swiftly to his right, walking towards the large whiteboard behind and to the right of his desk. It appeared like he was going to walk right into the wall, but at the last second Vishwanath noticed he snapped his fingers in succession, first his right and then his left hand. A second later the whiteboard swung inward, creating a large rectangular window that Nim stepped on through and without even turning around, beckoning Vishwanath to do the same with a wave of his hand.

The room was dark and airy. By Nim's command, they had taken a few more steps forward before he snapped his fingers again, this time left then right. Lights turned on overhead and the whiteboard door behind them swung slowly shut, barely making a sound.

The room they had entered was not large, perhaps eighteen feet in length and ten feet wide. The ceiling was much lower than that of the large lecture hall they had logged so much time in this past semester. If the lecture hall was the wide-mouthed, high-roofed entrance to Nim's cavern of philosophy, this room they had just entered, which apparently had been hidden back here this whole time, was the cozy end of the cave, where the cave-dweller might make a fire and take rest. "We live in a sensitive age, Vishwanath. Thank you for showing trust in me enough to follow me here," he spun slowly around the room, arms out and palms upturned, "to my meditation room." Vishwanath could have been full of questions at this point, but he had the wherewithal, the presence of mind to pause his investigative thought processes and simply take it all in. "I'm sure you have many questions," Nim continued, "that is not what sets you apart. Many of us have questions. At various points in the development of a free and fair society, routine questioning, healthy skepticism and holding ideas, laws and policies up to scrutiny is encouraged and indeed quite important. It has appeared to me that in recent years 'healthy skepticism' has gone out of style and is no longer encouraged on a societal or even an academic level. But no matter; the pendulum will swing back in time. There are other applications of the mind, anyway. Intelligence denotes an understanding of the way things work, while wisdom is shown in an understanding of the way things are. As you may know or have an inkling of, the mind can do more than formulate questions and answers. It can do more than objective problem solving. Do you practice meditation?"

"I have, somewhat. I was encouraged to growing up, but it always felt ritualistic and more like a cultural obligation to fulfill. I did for short amounts of time as a child, muttering various mantras my father encouraged me to spend time repeating. But I had no stamina. Like I said, it was for short amounts of time, what a kid would commit to something on his own, and beyond that was given very little guidance or encouragement to say, cultivate a practice. More recently I have tried some breath meditations, but haven't been very consistent, I must confess."

"That's okay. Sometimes the practice of meditation can seem like a chore. Other times it may feel like a daily hygienic ablution, like flossing or brushing one's teeth. Mental floss, haha". At this, Vishwanath chuckled too. "And still other times, through dedication, meditation can be like taking a deeply relaxing ten or twenty minute vacation. In fact, I am of the opinion that meditation is the only *true* vacation one can take. When we go on a physical vacation, changing our place and daily activities for a time, we still take the same mind with us. That much is inescapable. The actor is given a different role for a time, acting on a different set, but it is the same actor nonetheless. Meditation rests the actor himself." Vishwanath nodded, having nothing to say at the moment but following along with the professor's metaphoric explanation. "And then beyond a mere vacation or break from our woes, when we are *dedicated* to this practice, meditation can be like visiting the most refreshing spring or well imaginable. Categorically beyond imagination, the refreshment we receive from this well is without peer. Not everyone likes to sit and practice at concentration or intrapersonal inquiry, I get that. But my fear is that in the growing calls for our attention to respond outwardly, in their increasing frequency and rapid normalization, we forget the path to the well within. You will go on to do great things Vishwanath, of this I am sure. It is my greatest hope, however, that you and humanity at large do not forget how to walk back to this well, do not forget to take a drink now and again of the stillness and the peace that is found at our ever-contented, often obfuscated core. When humanity forgets that there even is such a well in our being, forgets our birthright to peace and our innate ability to know it," the professor's face grew serious, now grimacing slightly, "the nadir of the iron age will have been reached."

"Why am I telling you this? Why have I taken you into a small, hidden room to pontificate on the virtues of what most people either see no value in or do see some vague value in but are too intimidated by or feel too busy to try? Because you see…" he paused for a moment, closed his eyes, quieted and slowed down his speech, "this is the only 'machine' that I have, and the best one I know of to make life simpler and easier. It allows us to experience life more joyfully and more richly. To consciously turn the mind from an outward objective-seeking mode to an inward clarification and relaxing mode is something too small a fraction of humanity realizes they can do. And though not as prevalent, this is more quintessential to us than complexity, violence or greed. The mind is the only machine I know that empowers us to do practically everything better when turned back on itself, not because when applied in this way it alters what is being done, but because it refines and gradually perfects the doer, bringing us peace and clarity no matter how loudly the storm rages out there," he pointed a finger off into space, away from himself, "or in here," he said as he pointed to his head, "or even in here," he said finally, pointing to the center of his chest, his heart.

And with that, no more words were spoken. In a small, bare room behind and beyond where hours of inspired lecture and heady discussion about the complexities of modern life had taken place, Professor Nim and Vishwanath sat for meditation.

Letter and Rebuttal

Dear Loyal Subject,

In a place far off and unknown sits your King on his throne. The throne room itself is massive, representative of the overall mammoth size of the entire palace. The only entrance to the castle - the drawbridge - is made from the wood of a single oak tree, similarly humongous and uniquely ancient. It is reputed to be the patriarch of all such trees in existence today. Past the drawbridge is the courtyard, filled with gardens and then hedge plant mazes. The gardens are vibrantly colorful to the point of utter distraction, filled with plants of every known species and even species unknown to mankind. These plants are arranged, grouped, and grown to compliment each other, forming rainbow arcs and swirls, spirals of varying hues. Fruits are grown in the garden that have tastes untasted - flavors and special sweetnesses savored by none other than the King.

Eventually the gardens end and the vast hedge plant labyrinths begin. Through these mazes is the only way into the palace's interior. Self-proclaimed maze-masters and curious court visitors alike test their aptitude and patience in attempts to make their way through these labyrinths. Some want to explore and master all of them, while most people just want to reach the palace itself. No one knows how many there are or exactly which of the labyrinths one must pass through to reach the exit, and even though the design of the numerous mazes seems predictable enough - some swear there is a pattern to them - a curious and subtle sort of amnesia seems to waft over the would-be conquerors of the maze system while exploring, making finding the exit near impossible.

The system of labyrinths empty into a small square of violet grass, directly in front of which are three small steps to a golden door leading into the palace. On the steps are the words, written in a rusty crimson, "You Know Not", with one word on each step. Beyond the door is the entry room, a giant square space thickly carpeted red. Here, whatever clothing the visitor wore into the palace they must change out of and into an entirely new outfit, supplied by the palace and of the King's choosing. There does not seem to be any rhyme or reason to the choices he makes for people; he has been known to demand visitors wear a dozen layers of clothing, or nothing at all. The decision rests on his whim alone.

The entry room leads into the general room, a long rectangular room painted sand-tan, from which many other rooms can be reached. These include the gallery - a circular room entirely black save for spaces on the wall and ceiling where the King's favorite artwork hangs, the game room - a space devoted to life-size chess, the floor itself being the chessboard, the blue room - painted entirely pink, the zoo - where the King's favorite exotic animals are kept, the burning room - a room perpetually on fire, the kitchen - where the King's culinary attendants live and work, and the pool - which is empty. Each of these rooms have several others adjoining, that splinter off into more and more rooms of decreasing size, as well as a hidden door that leads to the throne room.

Its gigantic triangular shape - with the King and his throne at the scalene tip - is supported and nearly cloaked completely by a forest of green stone columns, so many and packed together so densely that the King cannot be seen. After walking perhaps a mile through the stone forest, the King is just barely perceptible. In fact it is not he, but the hardly visible gleam of his crown that verifies his presence at this point in the room. Walking further still, presumably toward the King, the gleam of his crown is known to disappear and reappear at random, the unfaithful lighthouse it is. Visitors and even the King's very own kitchen staff are fooled and misled by this phantom light. Those wishing to see the King or those summoned by him wonder if he is even there, if that gleam is indeed coming from his crown - evidence of his presence in the room - or if it is coming from something else, some royal jewel, or trick of the King's concoction. But, advancing further into the room, presumably toward the King, those seeking him are rewarded for their patience at this point with more possible evidence of his existence: sporadic and shrill laughter that begins piercing the air and ends flattening it with a harsh, baritone boom. Because the ability to laugh is taken from visitors in the entry room and from kitchen staff when they first come to the palace, those on their way to see the King typically reason that the laughter belongs to him, denoting his presence somewhere in the room. Once the manic laughter starts, visitors are punished for having come this far by the ghostly golden gleam disappearing for good, leaving them with the laughter as the only help they have to find their way through the now darkening green column forest of the throne room. Finding the King becomes particularly difficult when one begins hearing the laughter come from different directions, instead of just straight ahead. Those seeking the King typically cease moving in one direction at this point, and begin to change directions as sporadically as the laughter is heard.

It is not long before all hope is lost, even hope of finding the way back. By all accounts, the throne room is an endless forest of dementia and stone. It is certain that all who enter will become lost and never find the King, who in all likelihood is probably lost himself, wandering the throne room mad, cackling to himself in his insanity.

I am writing to you now because I have become lost and am beginning to fear for my own sanity. I am, or was, a member of the kitchen staff. As a staff member, it is my duty - my pleasure as I was told - to prepare for the King a meal of his choosing and deliver it to him. Now that I think of it, I'm not sure how the King even makes his sartorial and culinary tastes known, if he is indeed lost like the rest of us, as I believe he is. A kitchen staff member in reality - though we are by no means told this at first - delivers but one meal to the King. We enter the throne room and follow the process I have just described, eventually coming to walk around aimlessly, carrying the King's meal all the while. Once we realize the truth of our task, one of three things can happen: a staff member will either eat the entire meal overtime, realizing that starvation is a very real possibility, eat part of the meal and leave part of it for the King, somewhere on the floor hoping that the wandering King will find it, or leave all of the meal for the King, faithful in duty and willing to starve in order to keep the King alive. Whatever the staff member decides, the King - if he even exists, something I doubt sometimes - is most likely kept alive by the meals left behind. If, in actuality, no meals are left behind, the King could, in theory, keep himself alive by eating the bodies of dead kitchen staff members and visitors, perchance he finds them.

I have become unnerved at the recent notion of mine that the mad and sporadic laughter that fills the room may not even come from the King. It may not even be real. If this is the case then the laughter is a product of my own mind, a tell-tale sign that I have begun to lose it. I certainly hope this is not the case. I write this letter in hopes that you find it soon after entering the throne room, so that you know to TURN AROUND IMMEDIATELY. I could be close to the entrance; I could be infinitely far away. I don't know anymore, but if there is any chance of saving someone from this awful fate, it is a chance I will gladly take. The strangest part of this madness is that I have seen no evidence of any other staff members or visitors. I have seen no clothing, no bodies, no plates nor food - I ate mine long ago by the way. The green columns, the green brick floor and ceiling have become terribly commonplace; they have lost their once intriguing, exotic, jade luster and have for some time now appeared to me as sulking, overgrown jungle plants, taunting me to just try and outlast them. They are all I've seen for so long. The King doesn't even matter at this point. I just hope I can make you aware before it is too late. I have given up on myself.

Sincerely,

An Unfortunate Kitchen Staff Member

P.S. I hope with all my heart that someone finds this. I hope with all my heart I'm not the only one.

Re: Slanderous Libel

Dear Loyal Subject,

It has come to our attention that letters attempting to slander the reputation of the palace, the King, and the very sanity of the royal family have been sent out to upstanding citizens of our kingdom so fine and pure, such as yourself. You've possibly heard any of the following mad and misbegotten tales regarding our dear royal family on the subject of where and how they live, from gardens of hypnotic sense-intoxication to undulating amnesiac mazes of Escher-esque design, to foreboding steps to a misgivingly small and ominous palace door. These rumors, shameful, incredulous, and yes, treasonous, continue: that the interior of the palace is an unorganized mess of random rooms and wild demands, and that the throne room is only found by one out of every thousand visitors, the one who, upon reaching the dark room, tortures a starving spriggan matriarch until she coughs up an angel's feather; she, chained to a wall smeared with streaks of unnervingly iridescent, metallic hues that blind the eyes of all visitors who didn't pick up and take with them the goggles found near the drain at the bottom of the Pool, which is empty.

We aim to satisfactorily put to rest and move on from these rumors, slanderous libel they are, and indeed, this entire period of unclarity and discomfort surrounding your rulers. The King, the Queen, the Prince, and the Crone are happy, well, and sane, and invite you to visit any time, day or night. Especially night.

With a deft wave of his hand and sonorous sounding of his saccharine voice, the Prince (our justly Prince of Jade), has slashed in half the ferry fee from the city to the palace isle. And now, citizens of all ages are allowed to visit the royal grounds. In fact, families bringing children ages three and younger receive a further discount, so much does the Royal

Family wish to see its new subjects, bright, cheery-eyed, and full of delicious life. The Prince, able to walk through walls and positively overflowing with virescent vim and vigor, rewards visitors who find him with enthusiastic arm-wrestling matches. He has never been bested, even in his times of deep, kingdom-quaking melancholy.

The Queen has taken over and revamped the interior design as well as the outfits of the palace staff. Color-coded by department and bedazzled by years and excellence in service (maroon crescent moons for the former and cerulean-tinged silver stars for the latter), the range of outfits cover not only the spectrum of visible light and all their perceivable hues, but also, so vast is the number of departments necessary to the full functioning of the palace isle, light outside the spectrum visible to most humans. We revel in the confirmation of one rumor in this letter: that the Royal Family indeed does see more than a mere three primary colors, allowing them to perceive magnitudes more combinations and permutations of reds, oranges, yellows, greens, blues, indigos, violets, ultraviolets, and ***********s.

The King, mighty in his forbearance and augustly discerning in his judgment, sits steadfast on his throne. Curious court visitors privileged to make his acquaintance are routinely dumbfounded, and rightly so, by his size, stature, and regal air. Last he was measured, our King stood eight feet two inches tall and weighed a svelte five hundred and forty two pounds. He wears a robe that changes color in accordance with the feeling of the perceiver (and is quite rapidly responsive, so the King always knows your inner state, often before you do), and wields a scepter made of obsidian wrapped in basilisk hide, at the tip of which is a jewel in a shape no known language has words for. He is perfectly fine with the publication of this information; in fact, he encourages parents to recite these facts about him to their newborns as nursery rhymes. Families of children who can recite said details of His Regalness to staff at the ferry terminal may ride to the palace isle for free.

The Crone, a slender eunuch reputed to be several thousand years old, sits in a windowless room at the heart of the palace, past all throne rooms real and imagined, and deeper than the splendid sewer to which the pool drains. He is brought no food, only a small dish of water once a month by a very, very lucky kitchen staff member, and does not ever stand in the light. He wears a long sable cowl and robe that hang loosely around his hairless body and drape down to cover the entire floor of his room, and sits on a wicker chair made of a yew tree from another era, one that was reported to have been struck by lightning ten times in two years. With one pointer finger with an exceedingly long and sharp nail he scratches at the pitch black air entreatingly, sighing a barely audible though not unhappy sigh approximately once a week. He speaks aloud to no one at all, not even the other members of the royal family. It is said that he communicates with them telepathically, and is fond of time travel. That is one rumor, however, that this letter will not confirm nor emphatically deny.

With this, we hope to have put to rest any and all unpleasant uncertainties regarding the palace and the royal family. The King is sane, the Queen is orderly, the Prince is joyful, and the Crone is wise. Our dear royal family is not only fit to rule, but among the best this manifest universe has been privileged to be led by. Fear not, for we have found the source of the awful slander, and eviscerated it at once. There isn't much worth saying on the subject, save for this: an unfortunate kitchen staff member seemed to lose his head, and then once discovered, actually did!
Please visit soon!

Yours truly,
A Most Fortunate Palace Scribe

Mickela's Kaleidoscope

Take a boat to a certain island in the Pacific Northwest, temperate and emeraldine. The waves, unless in slack, will lap up entreatingly on its rocky shore. Walk, pedal or drive to the island's northern end, its wettest part, replete with fir forests, salal and salmonberry understories, red cedar and alder groves. You will see lichen-lined trees and moss species, fluffy and green several shades between, covering many things.

You must shake hands with these beings, so to speak. Wave back to the wispy usnea clan as they waft in welcome by the wind. Otherwise you won't see *it*. Otherwise you won't find *it*. You could easily *pass it by*. Yes that's right: if you do not honor the plant people here, *it* very well could remain invisible to your eye. That is how she intended it.

Go down a few long, straight gravel roads; right angles, evidence of a certain ape species with an apparent affinity for quadrangles. Past the second eye catching moss-covered boulder you encounter, turn left. The street names are all gone; the plant kingdom, in its entropic intelligence, has vined long and, grown profuse and ambling over, taken down these signs.

Now you should find yourself on a narrower gravel road, not as flat, and with dripping forest canopy overhead. Shadows multiply tremendous, and you are in a darker place, crowded out by all the photosynthesizers. The road here twists and turns a bit as you find yourself going slightly uphill. At the Y in the road, bear right. Soon you'll reach a clearing, the edge of a couple acres of overgrown field. The forest is taking it back slowly, like a once shaven face left alone, like a wound slowly healing.

Following the gravel to its end, you'll see a dense stand of young trees to the left, surrounding a small pond, and to the right a two-story house, falling apart. Here is where *it* is. Here is where you'll find *it*.

Carefully push open the door; it won't be locked. The house could be in any sort of shambles. Who knows what the insects, rodentry, and birdage have done here in the absence of humanity, turning this found spoils cache into their Xanadu for a time. Ignore them respectfully as you walk past what was once the kitchen and what was once the living room and head up the first flight of stairs you see. They will creak and groan, but continue onwards sure of foot. You have my word the steps that aren't already broken won't break. It is likely at this point that the bed in the room you've journeyed to has been warrened beyond recognition by untold rat generations. So it is.

On the night table by the bed *it* remains, in its box and undisturbed, despite a thousand verminous attempts. Realizing they couldn't get into the mysterious box no matter how hard they tried, screeched, hissed and clawed at it, eventually the rats and other creatures of the derelict house learned to leave it alone. They taught their subsequent generations to leave it alone, and have for some time regarded the impenetrable box with awe and reverence.

Walk across the room.

Open the box, small and ornate with frenzied claw marks and inscrutable carvings in its smokey dark wood. In this unopened box, in this dilapidated house in the middle of the woods on an island in the corner of a worried empire sits Mickela's kaleidoscope. Contrasting stained glass shards emeshing and enfolding into one another reveal more than trippy interlocking splotches of color. Each shard, each individual fragment in the constantly revolving prismatic tube shows a scene from one of the lives she's lived.

This kaleidoscope is proof of reincarnation.

Moments both profound and mundane are included, such as the moment when she, in her lifetime as the widow Judith beheaded the Assyrian general Holofernes, and also when she, as an unremarkable French boy living in the countryside in the 17th century, farted quietly and satisfactorily to himself in an unoccupied stall in his father's horse stable. From the year 784, when she, as a young girl, first felt confident in basketry weaving, and fifteen moments the prior year she did not. The first time in all her lifetimes when she was taught that the world was round. The fifty sixth millionth four hundred thousandth and seventy second time she took a breath. When, in 1873, she learned her multiplication tables to the satisfaction of her teacher in a one room schoolhouse on the Dakota prairie. When, in 1152 BC, chasing a deer in the Laurentian Mountains of what was later called Quebec, she twisted her ankle and began to cry, fearing for her life. The first time she ever wore something pink. The 18th time she smelled something pink. The time she ordered the atom bomb to be dropped. The time when, as part of a coven in the Carpathian Forest, she and her sisters prayed for the fertility of the Earth in a time of drought. The eleventh time she choked on a grape. One hundred moments of joy and all-consuming excitation looking into the eyes of her lover; one hundred moments of sorrow, longing, and unrequited feelings. Sixty-seven frustrations, and eight hundred and eight 'a ha' moments. Seven hundred and seventy-six awe-inspiring sunrises, and two hundred and twelve full moons shining profusely silver.

You could find yourself standing there a long time as moment after moment she folds in or out, each scene captured, frozen still in time and rimmed by purple frames, ruby red or emerald green, cerulean or kingly gold. With a thousand lifetimes marveled at, you'll only have scratched the surface. Eventually you may begin to wonder: suppose there is a kaleidoscope of moments from your lifetimes somewhere out there, would this moment, this very moment of inexplicable wonder be included?

The Properties of Moonlight

Mystified by its argent glow, I once sought to learn more about the distinct properties of moonlight. I wondered to myself, to others, to no one at all, does this light impart something essential to biological life? Is it necessary like sunlight, offering a different kind of vitamin d? Or unexpectedly, vitamin c? Or something rare and not yet understood, a vitamin m? (I don't know if vitamins are entirely "understood", or if they're not just placeholders for more complex processes it would be a nuisance to fully describe each time they came up in conversation.)

Like Earth, the Moon has an outer crust, a mantle, and a core. Its outer crust is mostly made of oxygen, silicon, magnesium, and iron. The two types of rock that form the moon's surface from these elements are called mafic plutonic and maria basalt, which sound like a relationship style and the name of the girl with whom the relationship was had.

Again and again in my research (which I'll admit was mostly non-specific internet searches, casting a lure haplessly out into the information ocean) I came across the condemning notion that the light of the moon was *merely, only, just* the light of the sun shining down upon us much diminished, 400,000 times weaker, said someone on the web. The mass of the Moon in kilograms is .07346 x 10^24. Its equatorial radius is 1738.1 kilometers. The escape velocity of its sparse atmosphere is 2.38 kilometers per second, where Earth's is 11.2. NASA's fact sheet goes on, but that much should suffice to illustrate how, on paper, the Moon is puny compared to the Earth. Diminutive, dwarfed, stunted. And yet, the profundity of its influence is vast and undeniable. Its presence is responsible for water tides, and how much more the motion of the ocean, I do not know. With that one empirically observable axiom, what more can be inferred about how the Moon pulls on us and all beings, made mostly of water? Certain flowers somehow, some way, only bloom in the moonlight. It draws me out barefoot onto grassy fields in explosive martial arts sessions or calming qi gong, my fighting form eclipsing moonlit shadow, inspiring me to ebb, slack or flood my own movements according to a greater lunar intelligence, a mystery to daylight thinking. I have heard stories of magical evenings in caves on remote islands where the moonlight shone down therein and induced people to a dancing, celebratory rapture, with whale calls bouncing off the cave walls in agreement.

I have also heard that statistically there are more hospitalizations on the full moon, especially those of a psychiatric nature, and that boxers are more likely to bite each others' ears off on that night. In me, the full moon induces a powerful calm; in others, mania, a surge of energy they cannot control, according to a whim that could only barely be considered their own any other day of the month. Sleeping in the moonlight does not bother me; it doesn't keep me awake like other lights do, but rather, lulls me gently on into the dream kingdom at the other end of consciousness.

There are some nights when the sky is clear and the moon is big enough, swollen full as if pregnant with the potential for a hundred secret happenings, that the profusion of moonlight on the Earth makes it seem not like night, but rather, a silver day. On those night-days I wonder, what if I were to stay up, remain awake for hours more, perhaps till dawn, chasing the radiant, celestial downpour illuminating the once waking world in sepia? What secrets might I find? What differences might I notice, looking through this mercury lens, that remain unseen during the solar day? If I were to stay up chasing moonlight, dipping, ducking, walking and waltzing through woods I knew by day, in hidden joy and out of my right mind, might the dappled moonlight's shine illuminate a deer path I hadn't seen before? One that would lead me to an egg-shaped pond of perfect tranquility with two wood ducks gliding silently down the middle, bisecting the water with symmetrically gorgeous fractalizing ripples. Perhaps the moon would lead me to a cabin I hadn't ever chanced across - despite walking these woods most days - the moss-covered cabin of an old woodland wizard, complete with a gnarled staff and beard down to his belly button, colored the self-same silvery white of the moon that led me there. He would invite me in and together we would pass the night drinking tea from roots, leaves, and bark he'd harvested, sometimes talking casually, sometimes intensely, and other times not at all, perfectly content in the undesiring, undying unity of quietude. At some point in my visit, probably towards the end, it would be revealed to us both that we were the same person - he an older version of me, and me, a younger him. There might be no words exchanged in that understanding, just sure gazes and meaningful glances in the recognition of both the passage of time and the immortality of the soul, the weariness of endless days spent toiling in the sun and the motherly reprieve of night.

At dawn the spell would break, and the woken world would return.

Solar illumination presents to us a reliable continuum of known things, processes, projects, lives. There is a predictability and a sense of building, of knowingly working towards as the sun shines time away. That which is seen is known, and vice-versa. This fact of life can be grounding, it can be boring, and at worst it can be hindering, a preclusion of possibility. But in the land of diminished light, less is seen, and so more is possible. Less is knowable, and so more is magical. No, I haven't come up with a list of scientific facts, tidy and satisfactory, about the moon's photonic discharge that I am now able to present to friends semi-pridefully in conversation. No, I do not *know* much more about it than when I first aspired to. The conclusion I have come to is this: my quest to better understand the properties of moonlight ends itself, not in complete resolution, but in excited mystery. This is not a rejection of knowledge; I am not burying my head in the sand to facts extant I do not wish to hear. It is, in this instance rather, a recognition that there are places where the light of knowledge simply does not shine. It is there you'll find, as I have, the moonlight of the mind begins.

The Giant Clam

At the very bottom of the largest and deepest ocean rests a gigantic clam, situated comfortably within an endless forest of seagrass tall and thick enough to cloak it. The clam does not move, does not float, but sits, and has sat solitary in the same spot for longer than anyone can guess. The eating habits of the clam and the details of its survival are unknown; the only known movement on its part, the only indication of its even being alive, is the fact that once every thousand years it will open its shell, grazing the ocean's surface in the process, and reveal its contents to all things deep enough underwater and deep enough in the impenetrably thick seagrass forest to see them. The clam will keep its shell open for a thousand days, during which time there are numerous efforts to reach its center led by several of the world's best divers and ocean scientists. Though with every opening of the clam's mouth the exploratory missions come closer and closer to reaching its center - in search of its pearl (if it has one), and more information about the creature in general - they are still, after the passing of countless thousand day and thousand year periods, unfathomably far away from where it lies in wait. Even with the technological advancements of numerous compounding millenia specifically directed at reaching the clam's open maws, civilizations fall short, rise and collapse, forget about the clam and rediscover it, try again and ultimately fail each time. And even if the explorations were to get remotely close to the bottom of the clam, it is rumored that at that depth sea monsters of biblically large proportions swim, acting as eternal guardians of the clam's contents. After the thousand days have passed, a thousand days of failed quests to reach its precious inner core, the creature closes its trap in one swift movement, like an adult pedagogically snatching away some item that does not belong to its child. As if saying in that up-and-down tone of parental refrain, "un uh, that's not for you..." the clam emits a few bubbles of ancient air just as it closes its shell completely for the next millennium. They rise through the ocean depths, bounding up towards the surface at impossible speeds so that the dive teams now leaving the area in dejected sorrow may be granted some small, entreatingly bitter evidence that the clam is still alive, and is still, as it always has been, waiting for some 'intelligent life' to come down, plunder its treasures and understand its mysteries. Even now, it lies in immobile tranquility at the bottom of the ocean, sleeping a thousand year's sleep.

The Shadow Walks Backwards

On a weekend smack-dab in the middle of the semester, my favorite professor at school, a great help and mentor to me over the years, invited me out to his family's woodland cabin for a night. It was the end of October, or Samhain by Celtic reckoning. The leaves of our seemingly endless deciduous trees had been turning this past month from ubiquitous green, telling of summer's plentiful and effulgent sunlight, to yellow, orange, red and brown in strides, in cohorts depending on the tree species and microclimate it was rooted in, dictating just how long the photosynthesis game was worth playing. Time it was on the cycle of the solar year for the life-force of all things to slow-down, hunker-down, conserve energy and survive the slight tilt away from the sun for the next few months.

Having had dinner and a drink at one of the professor's favorite tavern haunts, we were now completing the drive, about forty-five minutes out from town, to where his family's parcel of land was, had been for quite some time apparently. The cabin was, uniquely, on park land. Much of the park was public land, meaning his family had had a spot there before the town sought to incorporate the park as public, also meaning that his family had held out and refused to sell their lot to the town or the county for a very long time, too.

Our small town doesn't create much light pollution, but even so it was noticeable as we left the lights of civilization behind, burning on into the night since time immemorial to provide a haven of safety for the human residents therein, to keep at bay the wolves and other beasts of the night. I was a little sleepy from my hearty pub fare, a shepherd's pie and a drink, a pint and a half of cider, and fairly gassy, to be honest, as well. Still, Professor Lemkehin sought to engage me, pleasant host and ever-thoughtful philosopher he is, as I fought nodding off in the car as well as contended with the alternating waves of embarrassment and acceptance one faces when having to pass gas in a vehicle with others.

"Have you ever been out walking at night, and really paid attention to your shadow?" His voice grew decidedly and ominously serious, and I noticed his grip on the steering wheel tighten. His velveteen gloves gave a faint squeak, audible only for the new refocusing of my attention, as I could sense the conversation now demanded. I looked down into the darkness surrounding my feet in the passenger's seat, giving the question some thought. Of course I've noticed my shadow, and like every child has, played in it, with it, moving arms and legs wildly and watching the show it put on, trying to outrun it, step on it, punch it. Punch it? Punch him? The more I thought about it, the more my shadow became a veritable character, deserving gender.

Just when my mind started to veer off into feeling bad for trying to fight my shadow as a kid, the professor, as if sensing this, asked again hoarsely, "Have you?"

"No, I would have to say I haven't *really* ever paid attention to my shadow. Beyond being entertained by it as a child, I never gave it much thought or attention."

"By *it*," I heard him mumble reflexively. He didn't seem to mean to project this into the conversation, so I let it slide without comment or question. "For shame, Alex. A young person such as yourself, intelligent and inquiring as you are, should be curious and scrutinizing of everything. Presume nothing. Investigate and explore for yourself the questions and the answers, especially when the answer is given to you abruptly and without explanation. This you already know, and this I know you know. I restate this point only because, having come to this topic, you seem to have laxed in your scrutiny."

"Will you reproach me every time I 'seem to have laxed in my scrutiny'?"
I asked the question mostly straight and earnest sounding, but hints of
irritation are almost unavoidable when we rephrase things sometimes, if
only imagined in perception. He picked up on this and, sharp and mindful,
answered me straight, "Yes, unless I grow lax myself," he said with a little
chuckle at the end, "then, I'll need someone to reproach me. And then it's
turtles all the way down I suppose..."

His old olive green sedan winding down the long, dark forest road,
Professor Vladimir Lemkehin was a man I truly admired. I must have not
only admired but trusted him too, to go along with him on this trip. And he
must have liked me well enough to have invited me to get away from the
university for a night and enjoy the serenity and quiet of the woods while
staying in a family heirloom of a cabin, one that had been in his family's
possession for generations starting with the first batch of his ancestors that
came over and, upon settling in Vermont, built it. They came over early for
eastern Europeans, sometime before the major boom for the demographic
in the early 1900's. How much earlier or exactly when, I never heard him
say. And to a strangely remote hinterland of a place for them, what with
most Jews coming from Europe settling in the burgeoning metropolis of
New York a bit further south. A stroke of luck, for the eastern European
and Russian language department at our school wouldn't be what it was
without Professor Lemkehin. He wasn't liked by everyone, not by all
faculty, unabashedly eccentric, opinionated, and invincibly tenured as he
was, and certainly not by all his students. Touch of a curmudgeon he was
at his age, he was nonetheless a thorough and effective teacher. He got us
interested in the subject matter whether it was Dostoevsky's
pre-imprisonment novels or Russian conjugation, encouraged discussion,
and had a way of bringing the best out in people, so long as they put in the
effort themselves. His family was very proud of their heritage, proud and
amazed that they could openly be who they were (Russian Jews), and
persisted in passing on their native tongue and naming all their kin in

America with full-on ethnic-sounding names. So no, the professor did not have a thick Russian accent intriguing and exoticising his every utterance. But he sure as hell could turn one on, and often did in both his language and literature classes, to the delight of his students, or at least to those not lost trance-like in the din of their electronic device.

The wheels squeak as the car comes to a tight stop, audible enough to wake me from a light, blank doze I didn't even realize I fell into. I look up from the darkness of the car to see what I can only assume is the professor's cabin, caught in a torrent of illumination from the headlights of the car - a streaming path of light, of visibility in the otherwise pitch darkness of the night. I turn to look at the professor and catch him smiling a wide, Cheshire cat smile, looking towards where the headlights hit the cabin. There doesn't seem to me to be a reason for him to be smiling; he was driving in dark woods, basically alone, as his co-pilot was asleep. Why the smile? What for?

In my still-sorta-sleepy state of mind, I was irrationally peeved by this. And then in the moments that immediately followed I got a little angry at myself for allowing this to annoy me. Do smiles need reasons? Does happiness need a cause? I felt raw irritation, short-lived frustration congealed into the sort of anger that can only follow sleep, the sort with a very specific half-life that comes from either being woken up unexpectedly or finding oneself, upon waking, in an unfamiliar setting or an unpleasant situation. Waking up in such a state, it takes some time for wakefulness to fully return. In that interim, in that dusk state between two realms, not fully in either while not wholly in one, there is no memory, no regular discursive, ruminating mind, the kind we are plagued by throughout the day. And so there, one is really present to face and feel the moment at hand, either clashing or at peace with raw experience. If one isn't prepared for that clash - the irritation of blissful self-annihilation's nightly end - then habitual, sleepy responses and actions ensue. Unmindful of your actions as reactions, and just what you are reacting to, you might as well still be asleep. On some deep level, you probably still are. A paradox, isn't it, that to finally be fully awake to raw experience, immersed in feeling only feeling, one has his legs in two realms, in shadow and in light. But then again, that is only a conclusion come to in full wakefulness, in one of two said realms, intoxicated on rationality and thoughts-as-words - a conceptual overlay onto the raw. The duality of light and shadow, of sleeping and wakeful states is assumed to be the way things are, unthinkingly taken from concept to 'given' more rapidly and more often than we are generally vigilant enough to notice. So if it's only in the in-between state that one is fully awake to raw, noumenological experience, what could be the value of the previous statements, if come to in full wakefulness where one isn't necessarily fully awake to the present reality, to truth? The designation, 'in-between state', can be understood as conventionally applicable, but ultimately erroneous; it's 'in-between' from the perspective of dream, where 'dream' is understood as thought or mental activity obfuscating a clear, baseline state. From the perspective of that baseline state however, to be fully asleep or fully 'awake' renders one especially susceptible to dreaming, where dreaming is firmly believing in or taking for granted the concepts we think up, the shadows on the wall.

It's enough to make you sit in a chair for an hour scratching your head. Enough to make you rest your head on your clenched fist, statue-like. However, this all comes to an end when thought stops, for there is no continuum for concepts; they are only the stuff of dreams, or flitting shadows.

The jangling of keys wakes me up from my still-sleepy musings. Is there such a thing as a not-sleepy musing, in light of my establishing or realizing true wakefulness as being the raw state behind thought, onto which thought projects? A life of mind is a life of sleep, or like sitting at a drive-in movie long enough to forget that you're just watching a movie. And if the movie is always playing anyway, what vigilance is needed, what grace, to keep from nodding off from time to time, or like most of us, indefinite hibernation.

The door swings open, a large, strong brown door, made of old, loyal logs, closer to gray upon further inspection. The cabin smells good, indicating proudly a history of cherished use. Musty and welcoming, empty yet well-maintained. Respected. "If you respect a cabin," the professor said, "it will serve you well beyond your time, outlast you and your children." He turned towards me and lifted his arms up and out widely, smiling and wordlessly welcoming me into his family's treasured cabin. At that moment, I had the sense that I had been allowed into his inner sanctum, and should appreciate what this meant about our relationship. It was his way of telling me, again, in gestures and actions, not words, how much he liked me.

An ossified chandelier hung from the ceiling, composed of a combination of deer antlers and bones, and contained several candles at various mathematically sensible points along its construction. Handing me the lantern he had been carrying - I just noticed it now, I suppose he had had it since leaving the car - he reached up to the chandelier and, pulling a small box of matches out of his coat pocket, deftly lit all the candles to thoroughly, surprisingly, light up the room very well. The cabin was not very tall or very big, so the chandelier, while not low enough to make it accident-prone, was easy to reach up to, light and maintain. He dropped a bag onto the floor that had been slung across his back. Rather automatically I did too, letting a backpack I must have put on as I left the car sink down to the wooden floor. Even the floor felt welcoming, its comforting wooden tone wise and well-worn. The cabin was clean, but not neurotically so, not lifelessly sterile. It was tidy.

Late in the evening as it was, the professor showed me my bed. There were several along the walls, the perimeter of the cabin. Two beds were against the back wall on either side of a large, black, ancient-looking stove, riddled with engravings. The letters were of a language I could not make out, though I could tell, strangely, that it wasn't Cyrillic, the character-script of the Russian language. Doubling as an oven, the stove piped up to the ceiling in a sturdy, impressive-looking metal pipe. Tin perhaps? I don't know what these things are made out of. "Neither do I, Alex, neither do I," said the professor. It was easy to tell that these beds, their frames saddled almost right up against the stove, were the best in the house. That is where we would spend the night, and rest well, I thought.

I sat down on one of the beds, my initial intention being simply to take off my shoes. The professor had gotten right to work getting a fire going in the stove. For what seemed like ten minutes or more, far too long a time, I struggled with my shoe's laces, struggled to get them undone like a child still baffled by knots. I felt slow, heavy, and dumb, fumbling with the little threads of waxed linen or hemp or whatever material they were. Behind me, the fire came to life with a sunburst flourish, its orange corona a comforting visage that began to assuage my frustration with myself. "Take your time, Alex, take your time. The fire I just made is to get the cabin warm. I'm starting one outside too and there we can talk for a few before turning in. I'll be just outside, when you're ready."

"Thank you professor," I grumbled sedately. "I'll be out soon."

He closed the door behind him, and the cabin darkened, and I could not resist the allure, oh how nice it would be, to lay down for a few moments, to give in to implacable inertia.

When I woke up, I found myself covered in blankets up to my chin, and my body quite warm under the thick felt sheets. The crackling of the wood-fire in the stove had died down to a soothing low. Climbing out from under the blankets, I found myself still in my day clothes, as well as ascertained quickly the warmth of the room. I could tell the cabin was well-insulated.

Behind the tempered glass port of the stove, a thick trove of glowing orange embers radiated pulsingly with heat. It was a feel-good, confidence-inspiring sight. Taking a step off the bed and onto the floor, I was surprised to hear and feel that I still had my shoes on. I looked about me. Professor Lemkehin was nowhere to be seen. The candles on the chandelier were out; the large room of the cabin was only lit by the strong heat bank of the fire. I inspected the stove once more, closer than before, coming right up to it and looking intently at the mystery script I noticed earlier. In the faint light diffusing outward, the engravings seemed to dance mischievously, waving in the thick heat close to the stove. I stepped closer still. The letters, it appeared to me, began to rearrange themselves, like several simultaneous games of three card monty. I watched for a pattern in their movement. I watched patiently, intently for one, two, what felt like three whole long minutes. Suddenly, as the letters danced on, still fuzzy and indefinite in the darkness and glowering heat, I recalled a very specific feeling I felt once as a child.

The etchings of a memory trickled in, piece by piece; it was as if I had to strain and engage some internal pneumatic muscle, some focusing of the will, subtle yet primary, to keep it coming, pull the faint memory-shards together and summon the impression, the deja reve: I was walking around my neighborhood at night with my parents. They were walking at what I felt was too quick a pace, and I had to push myself to keep up and remain in the radius of safety they exuded in the dark of night, outside of which potential dangers lurked, stalking me - a child, their preferred prey. Though I was at an age where I could speak, for some frustrating reason I could not express myself to them at the time, ask them to slow down or carry me. They talked quickly and with words I couldn't understand. They laughed loudly, ignorant of my anxiety. It felt like they were forgetting about me. And eventually, like how someone treading water can only tread for so long before tiring themselves out and slipping under, I lost pace with them, fell outside the zone of their illuminating parental protection and into the dark, where anything was possible and some terrifying fate felt probable. With all my available strength I tried to call to them, but my voice didn't work. At most, I could faintly, squeakingly engage my epiglottis, strained, pained and dry. As they turned a corner now perhaps fifty yards ahead, a weak wheeze came from me, the frustrating and pathetic sum of my power. Not enough, it was not enough to be heard, to save me from the darkness that was swallowing me, swallowing me, slipping under, losing control - pain, death, dark, gone.

All of a sudden I heard the sound of footsteps coming from outside the cabin. I roused myself, now feeling too hot near the stove as I was. I realized my hand was on the stove, and retracted it immediately, suddenly becoming conscious of intense, white-hot pain. How long had I been sitting there? How long had my hand been on the burning hot stove? And how in the world would any answer other than a split second make sense? Before backing away from the stove to respond to the noise from outside and finally join Professor Lemkehin, I looked down at the mystery letters on the cast-iron one more time. While I still could not make them out, I now noticed the small script-like shadows they cast on the floor nearby, projected out, I suppose, by the light of the hearth. I squinted to see, and saw in black they read, "*thgin ta shgual ohw eH*".

Outside, Professor Lemkehin was sitting by the fire he had made, a small, tidy fire encircled by several stones each about the size of an adult's head. He frowned as soon as he saw me and, not saying a word, gestured, seemingly annoyed, for me to come over and take a seat by the fire. I did, hearing first my footsteps on the creaking wooden porch resound into the night followed by the crunch of leaves underfoot as I approached the circle. There was the crackling of the fire and three rhythmic hoots from a nearby owl composing the night's soundscape. The air was crisp and cold. Again, three rhythmic hoots. The professor then said in a whisper, "You missed the start of the show." Something was strange in his demeanor. Why whisper? There was no one else around for miles. His strangeness continued: "Sleepy student, sleepy student," he said several times childishly, at a louder volume each time. Now back to whispering, he said, "I noticed every time you fell asleep in my class."

 "I never," I reflexively tried to break in to say.

"Every time," he said, overtaking me in a louder, now harsh whisper, twisting his face and lowering his jaw to look like a monster, "Every time I saw you fall asleep in class, I went home that night and broke a pen into my mouth, swallowed all the ink. Now I've saved up enough dark inside to put on this show!" he said with a flourish, gesturing grandly to the cabin wall, upon which shadows cast from the fire flickered wildly. Though I wanted to move, wanted to run away, I felt locked to my seat, the leaf-covered floor outside the circle of stones that surrounded the fire. Even as I summoned all of my strength to only teeter from side to side slightly, straighten my back and lift my head slightest bit, my shadow, I noticed, did not move. He sat stock-still and stuck to our seat as if in disagreement with me, as if he wanted to stay and see what professor had to show us.

They owe their existence to light, the light from the fire that burns at our feet, I thought suddenly, the whole thought appearing at once and as if it wasn't me who thought it there. The sentence had a peculiar quality of feeling inserted, incepted into my mental experience; thought insertion, a quality of schizophrenia, I suddenly and desperately had the wherewithal to remember. It was all there was time for, all there was time to think and then realize about that thought before the professor put on his shadow-play.

A single line on the broad wall of the cabin, denoting 'one'. Two makes 'two'. Three lines, a trio, then back to two. The two lines go up and down, gradually connecting by a bend at their bottoms, to look like the ears on a bouncing rabbit. A fox appears from the corner, waiting patiently as the bunny hops along in the fresh morning meadow. A gentle morning fog - moisture, dew, and the blooming of life that is Spring. The rabbit is young, the grass is older, longer, a teenager - tall enough to hide the rabbit and other animals, as well as the insects of course, enveloping them all in a cozy woodland world. This small, gentle meadow, a glen within an infinite and eternal forest, nestles and nurtures life womblike. As the young rabbit plays on, hopping and nibbling innocently at grass and perennial herbs, the fox slowly approaches. Sensitive to sound and ground pressure as the rabbit may be, the fox is simply more experienced, and proceeds undetected. With the rabbit's fuzzy little back turned, the fox closes the distance, the last few steps between them. Right up against the rabbit's back, they both freeze. Then there is only the panting of breath, the subtle, almost silent heaving of their bodies the only movement left. Unexpectedly, the rabbit turns around to face the fox. The fox remains still and focused, pretending it's not there, pretending it hasn't been spotted. The rabbit opens its mouth wide, cartoonishly wide, unhinging its jaw like a cobra.

Before the stunned fox can do anything, the rabbit chomps down on its stalker, and slowly but consistently works the body of the fox into its mouth and down its throat, to be digested. Sounds of sucking, whirling, and frenzied, hopeless resistance fill the meadow. The fox is panicking. Frantically it moves its two hind legs not yet in the rabbit's mouth; they paw desperately at the soft, dry dirt underneath them, finding no traction, no grip from which it can attempt to work its way out. There is no defense it can mount. It never would have expected this, just how outmatched it was,

how unprepared. The fox never could have anticipated that the rabbit
could've done such a thing, let alone actually dare to. Swallowed whole in
seconds, the rabbit closes its mouth and returns to what it was doing,
looking just as it did moments before, frolicking innocently in the pastoral
forest field.

"Never before has such an exchange played out in just that way,"
Professor Lemhekin whispered into my ear, "never before has prey turned
the tables on its predator like that. Wouldn't you say, Alex?"
  "Yes, professor," I said reflexively, robotically. He could tell my response
was disingenuous, the quick, unfocused affirmative belying sleepy
students caught in the act the world over. He frowned and grumbled. "Oh
Alex," he said like he was giving up, like he had given me my chance and
I'd failed the test. "Nck nck nck nck nck," he sucked and clicked his teeth in
disapproval.

The shadows that had been putting on the show on the cabin wall merged
into one as they slid down, down off the wooden wall and onto the forest
floor. They made a beeline for me and quickly closed the perhaps eighteen
foot gap between me and the cabin. I suddenly felt even heavier, even
more immobile. My breathing became shallow, and all I could do, all I
could cognize with my eyes fluttering slowly shut, open, shut, was the
professor staring into the fire, the fire that burns at our feet…

Rays of light from the rising sun cast into the car as it sped out of the
woods and onto an open road flanked by idyllic, honest Vermontian fields,
a road that just beckoned you to accelerate. Our overnight behind us, I
think it would be reasonable to conclude the professor was a little
frustrated with me. He had a paper of mine - I had written about 'the
doppelganger' in Dostoevsky's The Double - waiting to be read and
graded. "Actually, I have read your paper already, Alex. It is quite good.
You have a way with words my boy, a way with words and a knack for

gleaning insight...for gleaning insight, and expressing it." he pronounced finally, definitively. His voice grew decidedly and ominously serious, and I noticed his grip on the steering wheel tighten. His velveteen gloves gave a faint squeak, audible only for the new refocusing of my attention, as I could sense the conversation now demanded. "Yes, such a shame. Such a shame you fall asleep so often in class, in car rides, in cabins." For the last word of his sentence his voice dropped down low, deep and bassy, sounding like he was talking in slow-motion.

I had no time to speak, no time to react or explain myself, as I so strongly wanted to do. I felt an immense pressure working against me, preventing me from opening my mouth, from moving my body. At a chillingly slow, steady pace, the professor turned his head to look at me, his eyes wide and bulging. He removed his hands from the wheel, and in one lightning-quick motion, opened my passenger door with one hand, and with the other pushed me out of the car. My body tumbled, scraped and skidded against the hard black-top road bifurcated by the rays of the mid-morning sun. After my momentum stopped and my body lay still, I heard small birds chirping innocently, and a farmer starting up some machinery in a nearby field. I hurt terribly in several places as I looked up and saw the car speeding away, the passenger door slamming shut. Looking about me, I noticed my shadow cast long and dangly in the road. Resigned and irritated, he apparently had had enough of me. While I remained still, on my knees clutching myself in searing pain, my shadow, growing longer and longer, walked backwards, back towards the forest where he belongs.

...sdrawkcaB sklaW wodahS ehT

The birds sitting up in the trees, darting around the woodchip floor by the jungle gym but not near the tire pyramid, chirp just the same. For years now I've heard them, yet I don't know their names. This past year we've studied geography and learned the names of the world's supposedly most important countries and places, several in each continent, and fifty states near and far, yet I don't know the names of my bird neighbors, my tree and plant neighbors, only a few of my bug and animal neighbors. Those closest to home get neglected, taken for granted, it seems, while the abstract - the world out there - is revered. For what? For naught.

On this particular day, as I swang on my usual swing, galloping woosh! with my legs and heaving myself into the air, lifting my tuckis off the seat as I reached the high-point of my swing, I enjoyed the elevated, almost bird's eye view for that onemagicalsecond before heading back down. Day after day, recess after recess, I swang on my swing. Five, ten, fifteen minutes if I was lucky. If all the swings were full and another kid wanted on, I was usually the first one asked to get off; the teacher knew I was at it everyday for as long as I could. Swing up, peer around, take it all in, that majestic greater-than-human view, and woosh! quickly back down. Sometimes so quickly as to evoke a warning or meaningless scold from a teacher or recess aide. Doesn't phase me, their empty threats.

On this particular day, in one particular magicsecond, amid a flurry of nearby bird chirps, I saw a kid I hadn't seen before. She had black hair, a pink shirt and, woosh! back down; hard kick, the exhilaration of momentum and woosh! back up, she was crouching, no sitting, woosh! back down. Strong kick, woosh! back up, she was looking down towards the ground. I couldn't make out her face at all, but saw that her hands were, woosh! back down; one more kick, woosh! back up, the bell rings, signaling the end of recess - and I saw that her hands were neatly on her lap, palms face up in what appeared, within the magic of the second, a most serene gesture. As I let the momentum of my swinging die down, down to a halt, feet dangling to kick the woodchips below, I was mystified at this new kid I noticed. Mystified because, noticing her for the first time, the school year was already three-fourths over and done with.

Another day passed by, Spring was in full-swing, and so was I, woosh! up and woosh! down. Our sorry twenty minutes of recess was almost up, when allovasudden Mystery Girl pops into view during a magicsecond again. She's there for the next. And the next. And the next. And then I am called off the swing. It's Jarad's turn. Approach her, I think. Approach Mystery Girl and see what the deal is. What her deal is. From where had she appeared so suddenly? Had her and her family just moved to the area? Thrust into a new school at this point in the year? I start to walk towards the spot where I saw her from my swinging-high, almost-bird's-eye-view. She was standing near the door that leads back into school, open-palmed yet again, a sense of stillness surrounding her subtly, like a muted silver effulgence. Soft crunching as I walk across the woodchips of the playground to the door. Grey overcast sky adds to the sense of mystery I'm sensing that day, and propounds my interest. I would call her name if I knew it. I would engage her at eye level if she were looking in my direction. But both of those connections would have to wait; she slipped back into school ahead of the rest of us restless kids still stubbornly clinging to our playtime. It was already clear to me that she was beyond us; within view, someone, something to aspire towards, but ever, it seemed, ever out of reach.

After recess another two hours of listless school-time awaits us. I scan the immediate stretch of hallway near the two big, heavy, metal doors we're let out everyday, compulsory exercise for us young cattle. Turning to the left, nothing, no one; turning to the right, a gaggle of kids meander to their respective classrooms. Shepherded by aides and teachers, I notice a few friends among them. Kevin turns to me and makes a face, goading me into some play-time he and I both know it isn't time for anymore. I pretend I don't notice him while I continue in this direction, a few more steps on the school's imposing granite floors, until I see her again, a trace, a shred, a morsel of her, of her pink skirt, her immaculate attire overall as far as I can tell. She disappears into the classroom, my classroom. I repeat, it is the third semester of the school year, and only the second day I've noticed this girl, this girl who is apparently in my class. Something is up.

Mrs. Tumms calls me to attention. Caught me with my head down on my desk again, somewhere in between sleep and dream and class. I suffer a stiff neck as I jerk my head up. I had been resting to one side on the pillow of my hands for what looks like, oh the last eighteen minutes or so. The history clip we've been watching on the thin white projector-screen at the front of the room about pilgrims and natives, 'indians' as they were called then, is almost over. I didn't catch much of it - movie time in school always means nap time for me - but what I did see seems suspiciously congenial. Did they really get along so well and agree to come together for a harvest-time celebration like that, the natives and their strange, demanding invaders? And why is Canadian Thanksgiving celebrated in October? Strikes me as a better, more temperate time for autumnal festivities.

Reflexively stretching my neck, I turn to the right, opposite the side my head was resting on my hands - and see Mystery Girl napping on her desk in just the same fashion. My heart skips a beat, and then thrums thickly in my chest. There she is: so close, so still, so real; right there sitting next to me as if she had been the whole year. And yet I swear this is only the third time in my life I've seen her. See her I do: dark hair, straight and shoulder-length, some kind of East-Asian in her heritage from the looks of her complexion, blue shirt on with a faded pink skirt and rouge-red leggings. Bold, unique. Somehow the look comes together, and for her age, for our age, spells confidence and personality. Oh and just what a personality! The mind races to fill in the blanks, to build the myth of one's crush as some sort of uniquely awesome and utterly one-of-a-kind person. The chemistry of attraction takes over, and I feel that ineffable, irresistible essence of intrigue. My words stop here. If you have lived, you know what I mean, what I now feel as oh crap my name is called again in even more annoyed a tone. And for the moment it takes me to turn and face forward, for onemagicsecond Mystery Girl and I lock eyes, she now awake from the swelling decibels of the teacher's scold, or from the universe's sense of timing and conspiring, or both. Yes both; these descriptions are not mutually exclusive but complementary and different, descriptive of different vantage points, different perspectives from which life - our experience - may be viewed and put into words. We may have many different ways of describing things, but ultimately, I believe we are bound by an intrinsic duty to figure out and then point to the greatest or clearest ways to access truth, to see it, to know it. We best point to it by being it. We best know it through glimpsing it, and then steadily, knowingly, resting in it. To be it is to know it, and to really know it is to be it. And we must remember - despite all our suffering, despite the (many) dark nights of the soul - that access to truth is never barred. We are never occluded from it. Ignorance is only an illusion.

I hear a giggle over my shoulder, gleeful and effervescent. Mystery Girl is smiling at me, nodding, as if in both agreement and approval of this last thought. Magically, psychically, as if she were right there with me riding the same train of thought, as if she too witnessed and processed these thoughts, she smiles and giggles, giggles and smiles, bats her eyes and nods her head gently, softly, sweetly in concordance. But something in her eyes glinting hazel brown, hinting of knowledge beyond her years as mine too have been described, shows more than just agreement. Beyond equality, she is elder. She holds a hitherto unseen understanding. Just beyond the waiting, knowing gaze, the enchanting smile, lips, eyes, and brow - she knows, always knows, the next conclusion, the next insight, has come to the next understanding already, ever beyond what I have gleaned, always a step or two (but no more than that) ahead.

And that's strike three; "To the principal's office!" yells Mrs Tumms. I get up from my seat to several loud oooohs, classmates seeking to capitalize on my banishment and win some hilarity points for themselves. I notice as I walk out of the room casually, not really caring about the trouble I'm in, that no one seeks to engage this girl. The class splinters into two's, three's, four's of kids grinning and commenting on the commotion. They are an undulating sea around her - the one, the one apart.

She waves at me for but a moment. I catch the gesture and wave back. Three kids who saw this exchange shoot me weird looks. My god, I think: they don't see her, Mystery Girl. Not even Mrs. Tumms appears to. No one does. I start walking to the principal's office, that dread-filled path, my mind and heart racing. I'm not afraid of getting in trouble at school, and my mother doesn't mind much either. She and I both know that what punishment I incur is more because I'm not a perfectly obedient little lamb. By the same token, I am by no means a dangerous wolf either. I walk past Mr. Germander's room and notice the little yellow flowers on the wall just outside, displaying all his students' names. I realize that outside every teacher's room, there is this: some are stars, some are plants, some are animals, seashells, the shape an action sound like 'Blaam!' is written in old comic books...

I backtrack to the Tumms' version of this: 26 of the 50 states, with my classmates' names each occupying one. I'm in Louisiana. I scan this stretch of wall over and over again, looking for a name I don't recognize. Matthew, Suzie, Lynn, Gavin, Joseph, Albert, Darnell...then I stop. My heart and mind stop. I see a state - a state whose shape I do not recognize - and whothehellcares because there's a freaking question mark in it! That's all. A state-shape I don't recognize, occupied not by a kid's name, but by a single, unassuming **?**

I file myself complacently to the principal's office. I'm done. I've had enough for the day, for the week. As I walk, her face flashes in my mind: the dark
hair, the playful, even bangs. The enigmatic smile and even more surreal, gentle laugh, soundless yet deeply meaningful like a key moment of one's dream. A steady flicker, in and out, there and not, as if my brain didn't or couldn't quite process her features like it does the rest of the real, tangible world. Either she's not real, or I'm losing my grip on what is. Huh.

Just in front of the office of offense and retribution, I decide not to go in. I have a theory to test out, outside. I walk towards the big double steel doors leading to the recess area, our shrinking field of sanctioned play. With almost all my boyish strength and arms outstretched to reach the bar that presses in to let you out, I do just that, and step into the fresh air of another overcast spring day.

The air - it's cold against my face and hands. I left my gloves in the classroom, but nevermind they're not essential for now. I've come to test the grounds of mind against the warp and woof of externality and see if there's even a difference, or if I can put this dubious dichotomy to bed. Haven't you had a sense of it, had a feeling all your life that 'inner' and 'outer' are false distinctions? That they're arbitrary, spoken - initially at least - only for ease of communication? But we lose our vigilance in time, fall into believing in and giving a hard reality to the words we use as symbols to represent and convey our experience. So easily, so carelessly do we forsake and displace our sacred truth: the prime, inarguable validity of experience.

Darkening swill, I turn my eyes from brown floor

to grey sky, and back, and back again.

Darkening still, I see her shadow and her outline;

her will, a deceptive thing. Or does the

deception lie with me? Evidence and

answer clear: from binary

thinking I'll do well to steer,

and instead, set the sails of focus near.

Reside with Me, live out of time, out

of mind, in the thoughtless sunshine

of a grey spring day, forever.

I see her, Mystery Girl, against the fence over there, and start running in that direction. I want to touch her and affirm her physicality. I want to know she's real. For naught, too hasty too hasty - she disappears. For a brief moment I turn back to the school and there she is, her back to the door that leads within, a smile and a wave. But now I know better. Go easy, for she vanishes with anything less than masterfully serene subtlety. I look out, past the fence I'm still hurtling towards, and there she is in the distance, out in the trim green field. Her back is to me; she's looking out into the distance. Where she looks, I want to be. Where she is is almost too rarified to glance at, to see. Perhaps that's why I seem to be the only one - Me - who has the eyes for this, this nakami. Not Kevin, not Mrs. Tumms, not Principal Lokin, not mom. Me.

With deftness I climb the fence and plop lightly onto the other side, stepping on moist, slightly spongy grass. Every step towards Her, a squish. Like tip-toeing on quail eggshells, I slowly and intently make my way in Her direction. If and when my mind flutters in doubt, distraction or fantasy, She begins to fade. Must hold my focus to see Her, to reach Her. Continue to engage that muscle, that subtle 'inner' muscle of focus. Sinking down, through, into and beyond the layers of mind, > of thought, > of thinking. Being; don't lose sight of being. Don't miss the mark. To know Mystery Girl, to reach *nakami* is to be sinless. Sinlessness to the moment, nothing precludes. Nearing Her presence, desirous of gnosis, I humble myself before her. One must die in order to know the face of God, the Jewish sages said, and so I quiet my mind before Her visage. The sun rises along with my surety, mine and its illuminatory quality one in the sacredness of mind-squelching focus, thinking at rest. Mind sunk into heart, I no longer stand behind Her, but beside. She looks to me, smiling gently. Glad I have understood how to reach Her, She extends Her hand and, wordlessly, takes mine. In these few moments I have been looking at Her, silence reigns and my heart is pounding. But once She takes my hand I relax and turn and look out into the sun as she does, the sun that has finally broken through the grey of the day. I cease to notice any objective features about her, cease thinking about anything at all and instead, simply stand with Her. Thinking stops. There aren't two people, anymore.

I. I sense. I sense sound, a sound, a sound in the distance. Thinking picks up - it's coming from the school, it's the end-of-school bell, buses will start up soon, I better...

Thinking stops, of its own accord. There is no one who starts or stops it, but there is an energy that perpetuates it, spirals it, spurs on the distractible dog allowed off-leash. Where does that take you? To what end? What result? What net gain? That same energy - the energy of intent or focus - can be channeled into knowing-being, which is to say, 'back' (it never left) to its source.

What happens next? Will the buses stall in search of me? Will my parent flip out, call the school, the police, and begin a search for me? Search for Me. Follow me into the luminosity of the sun. For that is where She and I are and will be. She. Me. Nakami.

One by one, then several at a time, the students of Mrs. Tumms' class and eventually she too looks out into the school's far field and behold a spectacle. Spontaneously, Principal Lokin looks out that way too, seemingly for no reason at all. For a quiet, breathtaking few magicseconds, all the people in all the rooms of the school with windows facing out to the field look, see, and stare, completely and utterly transfixed. They see a young boy and a young girl (who is she? they wonder) holding hands and walking slowly away from the building, away from the dull contiguous sheet of clouds covering ninety-five percent of the sky, and into the direction of the sun. Faintly, they notice a glowing orb breaking through in the distance. When they look back to the children, they're gone. School-wide, the audience to this vision notices two faint beams of light rising from where he and she were last seen, rising, co-mingling, uniting on their way to the sun.

Grandpa Seraphic

I remember when they led me, them with blue eyes,
those majestic beings, so masterful and serene.
I traveled west and then I traveled east,
found them (finding me) deep in a mountain valley.
They led with calm, their stares a care, bouts of silence
or conversation were one. They were unaffected.
I remember first seeing them in quiet awe, meeting them
each. Ancient masters embodied now, living stones
of human persuasion, care and patience pervading
their every action. So natural each movement, so complete
each gesture, each interaction they deigned worth taking.
You had nothing but faith in them;
it was vouchsafed by every act,
every deed you saw them do.
With tools and heavy packs they led me and friend August
by boat up the finger lake, docking on a side.
Yellowed switchbacks were our scenery
for the first two hours perhaps. Up into the valley,
verdantly green.
Green foliage, birdsong, and the steady babble of water from nearby
streams. The trail was worn in parts, but deeper into the valley did we
proceed. I found myself exhausted rather quickly with such a heavy pack,
but was able to continue, a source of inexhaustible strength nearby, quietly
emanating.

In the dusk of the wood we made camp, cooked dinner,
talked a bit, and slept - I, uncomfortably on uneven ground.
The following week passed thus: wake up, a cool dawn grey and blue;
work a good stretch of the day, fixing the trail and moving fallen trees,

quit work in time for an ample, restful evening, sometimes playing cards, sometimes not. Separately but at the same time together, we would sit in silence in the evenings, and imbibe the spirit of the forest in what ways we knew.

The quiet majesty,
the wordless understandings,
the steadiness of our work,
the utter dependency on each other,
the sheer replenishment the forest afforded us,
gifted us,
loved us with.
One evening, one of them said to me,
"There is a lot of light coming to the Earth right now.
A lot of beings are coming to help
us…coming to help the planet."
We sat by our own trees, either before or after that line,
separately but near each other.
When our work with them was done, August and I left,
hiked out the forest and down the valley to the shore of the lake,
stayed the night and got picked up the next morning by a postal service boat.

But also, I stayed with them, and they me led onwards, deeper into the valley, through seldom traveled passages, up, around mysterious bends, across scattered stepping stones set in streams,
by deer trails that followed the inscrutable curvature of Cervidaen logic
to new sights and perspectives that gave us a larger look,
a zoomed out view of the valley and its place in the mountain range,
through more forest thick,
yes through the heart of the plant kingdom's domain,
up and, eventually, to a clearing, to the edge of a meadow;

where they left me and I then turned from them and looked beyond
at what lay in front, what lay ahead.

What lay beyond, what lay in front was this: an immense and sunny field,
grass half- green, half-yellowed (it was nearly September), bounded,
encased on all sides by the reaches of the Cascadian forest. In the
distance, the mountains picked up again in their characteristic impressively
sharp crags, white-capped with snow year-round, like a badge mountains
wear at a certain point of size, at a certain level of majesty. My immediate
surroundings though were a small valley hidden among these American
Alps; a micro- climate, pristine, unseen, unknown, untouched except by
the workings of a divine Gaian intelligence - an escape from and an
improvement on logic itself. Yes, I could almost call it untouched, almost, if
not for the cabin I saw at the far end of the meadow, hugging the forest
edge, basking in the southern arc of the sun.

My solemn blue-eyed guides were nowhere to be found; they had slipped
silently (as expected) back into the forest behind. Darkening to the
impenetrable, foreboding in the extreme, I knew not, felt not to turn back.
This valley, this meadow, this scene was my destiny. That much was clear.
A gentle wind picked up as I stepped forward, out from the soft brown
ground of the wood and onto the yellow field-green. It was the time of
high-summer; the zenith of the season of growth had been reached, and
now all around the landscape showed that glorious, fleeting plateau of
life-cycle before the days got shorter and the rain picked back up, before
the plants died down and energy went back to root, the season of rest,
retreat and recharge. In other words, it was the global breath's pause
between exhalation and inhalation. The long grass swayed yieldingly with
the breeze, small birds chirped and danced in front of me while larger ones
circled overhead. In the distance I saw deer walking leisurely from a
resting spot in the soft warm field back into the forest, dense with

nourishment. There was sound, yes, but there was also a silence deeper than any I'd known before.

The cabin ahead of me, a distance slowly closing with my unrushed mosey through the field, was small and tidy. All its contents and resources were nearby, as though its tenant sought not to impose or sprawl onto the land. The logs that made up the cabin were thick, tan, and strong-looking, like they had been there for a while, and would be there for a while longer. In front, covered by the slight expanse of the roof out from the frame of the house, was a neat, trim stack of firewood, some fir, I'd venture. There was also a work bench in the trimmed grass in front of the house, and as I got closer, saw tools, circular garden beds, and some fenced-in chickens. The trimmed 'lawn' in front of the cabin was an unusual shape: triangular (the tip pointing down-field) and maybe a third of an acre total in size. I could also see there was some cleared land behind the cabin as well. The chickens clucked contentedly, and as I approached, their rooster made himself known. I admired some of the woodwork I saw: freshly made utensils (their sawdust nearby), hewn planks for seats, beams and poles that looked suitable for fruit and vegetable trellising. In fact, there were a few apple and pear trees espaliered at the center of some of the circle beds. To the sides of the cabin were various stone fruit trees, beautifully maintained and bursting with fruit. A few plums half-digested by detritivores or small furry mammals lined the trees' bases. I could've stayed here enjoying the gardens, animals, and orchardry for a while longer, but the breeze picked up again, ushering me along to the cabin's back, where I sensed there was much more to see.

At a low wooden table, in the augustness of an auspicious year, my grandfather, my father's father sat drinking tea. He sat with his feet to one side, the posture of a Theravadin monk, a big shiny kettle resting on a wool square on the table in front of him, sipping his steaming tea contentedly. Nearby, there were more fruit trees, nut trees, an outhouse and a sauna, and a large fenced circular pasture with a small flock of sheep. Irving Berkowitz, in his previous incarnation a Jewish-American and a smoking, thick-skinned, hustler-by-necessity-type New Yorker through and through, now sat in a way I wouldn't of thought possible for him, amid a backdrop I never in my imagination associated him with - a luscious Cascadian meadow valley. He looked more at peace than I ever remember him being; it was disarming yet also strangely reminiscent of some familiar state or expression, something at once ancient and near, rarified and common. His face, the whole demeanor of his being radiated a peace and a contentment more 'papa' than papa ever was when I knew him alive. His smile showed something he knew, something we all know before our idiosyncrasies grow out and entangle into knots of personality like unchecked plant growth after a month of alternating rain and sun, seemingly obscuring the clarity that is our natural state and birthright. Trim cleared grass inviting, subsumed in partial-shade that undulated with the sun's passing overhead, and with another stretch of forest flanking and beyond, stretching, it seemed, all the way to those snow-capped peaks, this end of the timeless and idyllic meadow in which I found myself now took on a husky orange hue, the dark orange of dusk. This warm dark orange glow to my entire field of vision pulsed and throbbed; these synesthetic waves I felt go right through me, incredibly in rhythm with my mood. A deep, restorative, supremely confidence-inspiring bliss washed over me, like I had stepped into a painting of the scene, and became a part of it. Smiling, and with his eyes most of the way closed, my grandfather beckoned to me with the calm excitement of wakefulness, using both his hands.

Startled as I was, overwhelmed with emotion as I became, I felt impelled towards him, as if in dream. "Hey Steven!" said a voice I hadn't heard since my youth: the raspiness of a lifelong smoker combined with the directness of a New Yorker. At once choked with tears, he saw this and continued, "Aw come on, it's okay. Have a seat." His voice was softer than

I remember it being. Of course, I thought, his suffering had left him, his burdens long gone. Speechless, I sat down at the wooden table directly across from him. With a smirk and a smile, he patted the ground next to him. I moved over quickly to his side. Who, after all, can deny their grandparent? He put his hand on my shoulder. "So whatcha been up to?" he asked, though I sensed, by virtue of his apparent sublimity, that he already knew.

 "Well Papa," I finally managed to say, "I'm finishing college now." "Recreation, right? I coulda guessed by how playful a kid you were that that's what you'd wind up studying: the field of fun!" he said with a laugh. "Hmm..." he remarked, becoming a bit more serious and looking away for a few seconds, "You saved up all summer to come out here, didn't you? To the Pacific Northwest, where the forests are finally big enough for you to play around in and not get bored!" His gaze returned to mine. What a countenance he held. What a loving intensity about him. I found that I simply couldn't lock eyes with him for longer than a moment, such a burning, sublime intensity there was about them. With a soft, sympathetic smile he said, "You'll find the one for you sooner than later, don't you worry kid." My god, he was reading my mind; he could see my thoughts and feel my feelings just as he could hear my words. It was very clear to me then just how transparent I was to him. He saw right through me, through everything.

For a while - just how long I can't say - we merely sat in each others' presence, sometimes looking at each other, sometimes looking away at something transpiring on his perfect mountain homestead. We listened to the sound of the birds or the sheep biting and chewing clover and grass. We heard some bees buzzing somewhere, faintly. The wind picked up, died down, and picked up again.

"Don't let your tea get cold." he said out of the blue. I hadn't even realized he poured me a cup. "I grew those herbs, in case you're wondering." Of course I was. He pointed at a small herb garden next to the cabin, complete with groundcover, shrubs, and vining herbs sprawling up the backside of his abode and onto the roof a little too. "I don't smoke anymore; I drink my herbs now," he said, again with his grin familiar. This made me happy to hear. Squelched his old habit, he had. Lovely.

"Well Steven," he began, "I think it's safe to say we can skip the small talk, and move right on to the big talk." What observant and gracious conversational mercy. "I like the direction you're headed. You've got some healthy habits and some important preoccupations. Truth? Life's thriving on planet Earth? Face time over screen time?" Here he knew and smiled at the pun he had made, "Not just anybody is committed to those things like you. I mean plenty of people are interested, sure. They'll weigh in casually and comfortably on some of the implications of technology, issues the world is facing. You let these concerns shape your life's direction. Plenty of people give into their impulses, for their phone first thing in the morning, for coffee, for sugar. You know the respite and freedom of awareness. Self-justification is the gemini of self-defeat. You know this, and actively work towards freedom." He looked around. So did I. A brief silence once again. "Someday, you'll be here. You'll have this, this home, this lifestyle you long for, inexplicably but undeniably long for. In fact, you already do. Like the statue already in the marble block, you only need to chisel away the excess and realize you've been here for all of time, looking your youth - energy plus doubt - in the face, telling him to wake up and get a move on." He smirked knowingly, and after a pause pregnant with understanding, winked. Hearing this, seeing him, I welled up with tears once more.

"You'll get there. I believe in you kid. And I love you *so* much!"
I was finally able to do it, to look into his eyes for longer than a millisecond. I doubled down and sustained my gaze. He beamed at me. My body

started to shake. Tears streamed down my face, releasing long-time sorrows and also expressing new heights of joy. A few tears trickled down his cheeks too. The longer I looked, the lighter I felt. Suddenly, I felt panicked and afraid; I felt like I was going to disappear. He made a micro-movement of his face, an expression saying 'have no fear'. I let go of fear, of all my apprehension, and in an instant saw him as me, me as him. There was no difference between us, no separation. The seeming time between youth and old age was nil. The portrait was complete, for even the viewer was gone.

The young have the seed of eldership within them. The elder help the young to remember this. In this way, 'young' and 'elder' have nothing to do with time, but denote wakefulness. There is only the wakeful, and those still nodding off.

"Go find your friends, Steven. Go and find the ones you'll inhabit this place with. You know they're out there." He stood up. So did I. I didn't want to leave. Though I knew beyond knowing that I'd be back, that residence here with kindred spirits was my destiny, I didn't want to leave him, Papa Smokey, my loving grandfather lost from me in my boyhood. I never forgot how we used to greet each other: I, running at him with eagerness and energy - him, arms wide open, seizing me with a hug and hoisting me up into the air, all laughter and smile.

"I never left you," he said, "my guile is yours, my photographer's eye. Hard to predict, we're wild cards and black sheep, both. But more importantly..." he stopped speaking and simply looked at me. And I knew. The seraphic spirit I felt destined to meet, felt destined to become, already am. Each step of the way towards completion of the work, completion already is.

With an arm around my shoulder we walked into the woods beyond the meadow, away from his cabin and into the forest eternal, the way that leads to the snow-capped peaks. Together and as one, smiling selfsame smiles we walked: two, one, none.

The Taste of Rosemary

Even as late as the night before my flight, I felt it was truly a toss-up as to whether or not I would make it, whether I should or shouldn't take it. My gut health was in a sorry state, some sort of infection had I, picked up from a naive combination of unfiltered ('pristine', I thought at the time romantically and foolishly) creek water and an unchecked consumption of sweets. This foolish, disastrous combo was from my first trip out to Washington state a few months prior, when I remediated hiking trails in the Cascade Mountain Range with the Forest Service and then visited Seattle and Portland for the first time. In the forest I drank the water, and in the cities I ate the sweets, you see. By the time I was supposed to fly back to Jersey where my family lived and where I was attending school, in the process of earning my B.A., my poops had become fast and loose. I remember telling my parents to try and not be alarmed. Fat chance of that, given my historically iffy digestive system. At that point, I'd already had years of bowel disease and one bowel surgery under my belt.

My symptoms began worsening into stomach aches and pronounced abdominal tenderness. I remember visiting my Chinese Medicine practitioner and explaining to her what had happened, the sequence of events while in WA that led to my seeing her sick now, when I had been the picture of health a mere month ago. "Maybe," I remember her saying, "your system could have handled the creek water but not with the sweets afterwards, or maybe the sweets without the creek water just before." In the mounting avalanche of my worsening GI symptoms, whatever investigation into causation there might have been was quickly swept to the wayside in favor of fast-acting symptom relief. The investigation, and ensuing cleanse of whatever I had picked up would come, but first, to stop the avalanche, to extract myself from that. Order of operations, you see.

Despite missing a lot of class that semester, I made it through, and, silver lining to my dismal state, got my internship, the last step in earning my bachelor's degree, approved. I was all set to intern on a small family farm on an island in the corner of Washington state, the northwest of the northwest. Though my degree was in recreation administration, my focus was community recreation, preparing me quite specifically to work in a federal, state or local municipal parks and rec office, or a community center like a YMCA or JCC. After Hurricane Sandy a few years before, I had a burgeoning interest in becoming more self-sufficient and not relying on large, indifferent and precarious systems for my food and utilities. So I put a 'growing food for the community' spin on the direction of my major, and sought an internship to pursue those skills. For the previous three semesters I had been first volunteering and then was paid to work for my school's organic demonstration row-crop farm. The Chair of the Recreation department at my university, the one who approved my internship, was a very kind, funny, and easy-going woman, and so when she okayed my somewhat off-base choice of internship for my major, I appreciated her flexibility very much. She knew of my lengthy, circuitous route to earning my degree, and she just wanted me to get the damn degree and get on with my life, bless her heart. Bless all her organs, in fact.

So there I was, several months after I had picked up and fed whatever pernicious pest I had picked up in the northwest, on the eve, the precipice of heading back and still on shaky ground health-wise. The night before my flight to Seattle I was staying with a friend who lived close to the airport I was flying out of, JFK International. She, a trained massage therapist, gave me a colonic massage (external, on my abdomen), which gave me some relief. "Life presents us with chance opportunities like this," she said. "I support your call to make your flight tomorrow and go for it, and I love you and am here for you if you decide tomorrow morning that you don't want to go, or if you decide you want to come back." So she said with compassion and wisdom. In the following day's nascent hours, she drove me to a nearby train station, hugged me goodbye and wished me well once more. I caught a train that took me right to the airport. Seven hours later I was on the other side of the country, breathing in Seattle's cool, moist air.

Before heading up to Orcas Island for my internship as a farmhand, I had arranged to spend some time with someone I had met the previous summer while doing trailwork. His name was Justin 'Dusty' Reynolds, and he and his wife Liz lived about an hour north of the Seattle-Tacoma International Airport, in a town by the name of Everett. "Hhhowzit goin' buddy?" Dusty asked in his trademark Mathew McConaughey meets Half-Baked stoner-surfer inflection as I hugged him hello at the airport, putting my tightly packed suitcase in the hatchback of his Subaru. "It's going," I replied, "I've been better but I've been worse too." I tried not to unload the full brunt and bore of my health woes on him all at once. "Something's been up with my digestion."

"Oh man I've been there. Some bad chicken, some dud fish and I'm down for the count. Happened to me a few weeks ago actually, and I was out of commission for maybe two and half days, three days. Yeah, I had a meal finally the night of the third day and was good."

"Yeah well, I think this is from the Cascade creek water I felt so good-n-groovy 'bout drinking when we were up in the mountains last summer. May not have been the best thing for me. My digestion's been off since then."

"Yep that'll do ya bud. If you didn't grow up drinking it your little internal microbial colony probably can't tolerate it. Like I've heard that people who grew up around the Ganges in India can drink that water. But it would put out you or me."

"Yeah that's right, people who live by that river do all sorts of things in it. They bathe in it. Dead bodies are sent floating down it in burning pyres."

"Yeah that's right…shit man that's crazy." Dusty laughed, continuing, "Yeah they can tolerate it but if ol' Dave from the auto-body shop in town were to go swimming around there you can be sure as shit he'd come back home with a busted gut."

"Sure as shit," I repeated.

We were cruising down Broadway, one of the town's major roads, aiming for a Trader Joe's to get some groceries for the week. "Figured we'd make a quick stop here on the way. Feel free to help yourself to anything in the fridge while you're here, whatever you can eat - you know better than I - and if there's anything you want in particular for yourself go ahead and get it. I'll usually do some eggs in the morning, bake some bacon, maybe cook up some fish if I can get my hands on a good filet. I got a couple of fishermen buddies so some good salmon usually makes its way into my freezer every season."

"Eggs and fish sound good to me. Do you happen to have any bones in your freezer?"

"Like for making broth? Yeah I think I do."

"Ah great well if you'd like I could make us a big batch of broth this week. I've been thinking of doing a bone broth reset to try and help get my gut in order. I gotta get well enough to be able to work on this farm."

"We'll do our best man, we will do our best."

We had made our run at TJ's and were back in the car, headed to his place, sipping on coconut water and munching on plantain chips. Dusty had also gotten a few bags of mixed nuts and dried fruit, favorite snacks of his I'd learn, as well as a few packs of bacon, a couple cans of beans, and an assortment of vegetables. We parked along the fence on the north side of his home, grabbed the groceries and headed inside. Once we unloaded, Dusty showed me where I'd be staying - the upstairs suite. "My daughter stays here when she's in town. It's yours for now." Though it was proving to be a cold and dreary March, the upstairs, the attic, amassed heat during the day, and, lucky for me, was the least cold part of what I soon found to be a drafty and not well heated home. I wasn't sure if that's how Dusty preferred it, or if he sought to save on his energy bills, or if the house was just built in such a way that made it hard to keep warm, poorly insulated maybe. Whatever it was, it was a cool time at the Reynolds house, in more ways than one.

After I hefted my suitcase up the steep staircase to what would be my room for the week, I walked back down to the kitchen and got to work on a big pot of bone broth. "Got some onions if you wanna toss one in," Dusty said. "Also gotta buncha herbs in the garden. Might be a good addition." Him and Liz did have a pretty great garden, maybe a quarter acre's mix of small veggie rows, dwarf fruit trees, berry bushes, and perennial herbs. Glistening, almost sparkling wet green against the blanket grey sky and the dank dark soil of the garden black from moisture and vermiculture compost castings, a rosemary bush, trim, contained, and standing prominent by itself, caught my eye. I walked towards it without trying, without thinking, a magnetic waltz. All else seemed to fade away in a vague multi-colored blur around the clear image of the plant locking and dominating my vision. The rosemary bush was beautiful, understated and perfect. As an east coaster I was impressed to see this common kitchen herb growing so effortlessly just outside the kitchen where it may very well get used. "She's been here for a while," Dusty said suddenly, momentarily waking me from my revelry, making me realize he was behind me, making me realize I was still on planet Earth and in Washington state, USA. "As long as we've had the place, that rosemary bush has been here. I'll use some of it for seasoning on occasion. It's potent. Hey you should try putting some in your broth." My eyes turned from Dusty back to the rosemary bush. "Yeah," I said, wrapt, "I think I will."

The day was turning to evening. The overcast sky parted to reveal the kind of truly glorious sunset western Washington often has. The Port of Everett, north of Seattle along the Puget Sound, looks west, along the same latitude roughly as the Strait of Juan de Fuca, the narrow channel that lets the waters of the Pacific in to fill the glacier excavated bath tub that is the Sound, an inland sea, similar to how the Strait of Gibraltar lets in the Atlantic Ocean to create the Mediterranean sea. In looking west that night - and all the nights Dusty and I would take our sunset walks - we saw some of the many distinctive features of the landscape visible and blessedly extant in the compact, moist terrarium that this part of the state is: from nearby islands (of which Washington has many, second in number only to mighty Alaska to the north), to the Olympic Mountains. South of us, Mt. Rainier, or Tahoma as it's traditionally named, was visible now that the clouds had mostly cleared away. East of us, the Cascade Mountains, where we'd met a few months prior, while to the north loomed Mt. Baker, Koma Kulshan. Furthest west, visible now from the vantage point of the hill we'd walked up and by the clarity of the clearing clouds was the Pacific Ocean - vaster than vast, seemingly endless, a great blue and multi-hued shimmering, dreamy infinity. All in all, I was growing more smitten with Washington by the minute, so packed full of amazing sights it is.

Where infinity refers to space, eternity refers to time, and time it was that occurred to me strongly and frightfully that first night with Dusty. Would I really be ready for farmwork in a week's time? The possibility, in the state that I was in, seemed like an ocean away. When we got back from our walk that night, hilly, breezy and beautiful, Dusty gave me some garden shears to clip the rosemary bush with. I did so solemnly, added the herb to my pot simmering thickly, bubbling like a true cauldron, and headed upstairs to rest. Stretching before bed, I was disappointed and frightened by my lack of mobility in some postures. I'm normally a pretty bendy guy; I've always been a regular stretcher, and can normally do full forward bends, wide-legged butterfly's and full wheel poses no problem. But now, I was concerned. I could feel the tenderness of my abdomen, particularly my lower left side, as I attempted to fold in half for a seated forward bend. And when I attempted the wheel pose - done by starting on your back, planting your feet in front of you and your hands just beyond your shoulders, palms face down, and then pressing up to lift your body into the air - I was very dismayed to discover that I couldn't get up very far. My tender tummy was tight at the skin, strained and pained with the inflammation of the infection I was facing as I attempted to press myself up. That's it, I thought, I've gotta pull out all the stops to get well, for me firstly and also to be able to do this farm internship. No matter what it takes. And so I resolved that night to fast and drink nothing but bone broth and water during my time with Dusty, so as to catalyze my body into autophagy and heal my gut. And maybe the rosemary, I thought prayerfully, would have some contributing effect, kill off some of the bad bugs plaguing me. Common kitchen herbs (think that of the classic Scarborough Faire) were reputed to have anti-microbial properties, hence their adoption into our cuisine, after all.

I woke up the next morning to the pitter-patter of rain raining down on the roof. I could hear Dusty up and about below me, likely in the kitchen. In conversation yesterday I learned that Dusty was essentially following a paleo diet. His morning routine usually consisted of meditation followed by baked bacon and bulletproof coffee. As long as it's not too noisy or chaotic, I actually like hearing people up and doing things in the morning while I lay in bed. I like hearing industriousness, hearing and knowing that people are awake and getting going with their day, being productive. To me there is something comforting about it, stemming from memories of hearing my parents up and about as I lay in bed as I child, I reckon, knowing that they were doing what needed to be done and that all was right with the world. As Dusty was starting to get his day going, as the March rain continued to come down, I turned over for another round of sleep. Why not? I thought briefly, happily, and apathetically. Why not? All there is for me to do this week is feel better, while away time.

When I'd woken up again an hour and a half later, sauntering down into the kitchen, I could confirm: Dusty had indeed cooked bacon that morning. The smell, unmistakable, still lingered in the air. "How's it goin' man? Hey your broth is looking pretty good. I popped the lid and took a look." I walked over to the lightly steaming, puttering pot and lifted the lid. "Whaddaya think? Think it's done?" The liquid in the pot looked rich and viscous with oil, and the smell of rosemary overwhelmed my nostrils. This was an agreeable overwhelm; to take command of my nostrils, to become olfactory first chair amid the symphony of smells present, the rosemary had my consent. I stepped back from the pot, and for a few moments, reeling in its potency and unable to answer Dusty straightaway, I considered the herb rosemary. A common culinary herb known to most all, so household a name as to be overlooked. It is a shame, I thought to myself, Dusty standing by for my answer, that we put exotic ingredients up on pedestals, and then by implication down-grade in our minds the power and value of that which isn't being hyped up as the superfood of the month. "Yeah," I finally replied, "She's done. Good and done. Dank! Rich!" I turned to my right, jubilant at seeing a successfully stewed broth, its potency quite apparent, and saw Dusty grinning. He, a practitioner of the Dharma and of metta (to consciously apply the mind towards thinking of others kindly and lovingly), was in joy at my joy. That's a cool thing some meditators figure out how to do: to be able to share in, not leech off of but share in and amplify the joy of others, the more functional, virtuous flipside of getting off on the suffering of others. "Other people's suffering tastes like honey," goes a cheeky Japanese saying I heard once.

I strained the broth, its rich, oily, rosemary goodness catching on the strainer I was using, flowing over the sides and running down the outside of the glass mason jars I was transferring it into. Still too hot to put into the fridge let alone drink, I set the three tall screw top jars I'd filled to the side on Dusty's kitchen countertop to allow for cooling, noticing the thick lightly green and yellow layer of oil that'd floated to the top, a full two inches thick each jar. As I waited, I drank some herbal tea, something with licorice, a long time favorite and true friend of my digestion. I heard Dusty's McConaughey-esque voice start up again at my side, "Hey man so I've got work at Stevens Pass tomorrow, and my mother-in-law's coming up from Portland tonight to stay for the next few days. I think she's gonna come and visit the ski resort at the tail end of my work day tomorrow. You can come up with her if you want, or you can hunker down here and just stay put and chill out, check out town here, whatever. It's up to you." Stevens Pass is the name of a ski resort about an hour east of Everett in the Cascade Mountains. Here the elevation and correspondingly lower temperature are such that what comes down as rain in Seattle and Everett comes down as snow. Not the dry 'champagne powder' of the inland Rocky Mountains, but the wetter, denser, coastal sort of snow known locally as 'Snohomish Sludge'. They take what they can get out here and enjoy winter sports nonetheless.

Later that day, just before dinner, Liz's mom/Dusty's mother-in-law Peggy arrived as prophesized. We greeted her in the garden-backyard area that also was their main way into and out of the house. I noticed that they didn't really use their front door much aside from receiving packages there. The back entrance, via the garden, led to the kitchen, and this was generally where most of the action in that home took place. Liz was away doing geological surveys in Alaska, so it was all up to Dusty to play the gracious host, a duty he executed well and with his characteristic unhurried charm.

Peggy was in her sixties, a fairly reserved and quiet person, which stood in stark contrast to talkative Dusty. She got a room at the Hotel Reynolds on the ground floor. Well and good, I thought, elders deserve ease, less steps, and bathroom proximity. Before going to sleep that night I tested my tummy tenderness by stretching again. Still tight, still tender, still painful. Well, I thought to myself, I'll fast on bone broth all week if I have to. Reset the fuck out of my digestion, whatever it takes. I was anxious to get well, to be ready to be part of a small community of hard-working, like-minded people sharing in the desire to live a life closer to the land, be more self-sufficient. I was dreaming of finding a sweet heart as a fellow intern on the farm or somewhere within the small island community. Some cute hippie chick who was down to spend all day with her knees in the dirt, who would cart wheelbarrow after joyous wheelbarrow of woodchips or manure with a smile on her face and a song in her heart. Who was intelligent and silly and cheerful. What a match we would be for each other; to find my better half, my chimeric twin to completion. Fantasizing thus, I drifted off to sleep.

By the time I got up the next morning, Dusty was gone. He left early on his days working up in the repair shop at Stevens Pass; drove to a certain point on the highway east where a company shuttle took employees coming from the Seattle area forth and back, a task that Peggy's Subaru Forester was well-suited for. I heated up some broth, said hello to the rosemary bush again, filled up a thermos and was ready to go. We stopped at the co-op in town first, and there I took the opportunity to load up on a few drinks in an effort to keep my self-imposed liquid diet interesting. On the drive into the mountains we talked about what you'd expect: where I was from, how I met Dusty, what I was up to in WA now, and of course why I was doing this fast, the digestive pickle I was in. By the time we reached the parking lot at the ski resort I was mighty hungry, sipping on cold brew trying to stave off my cravings. I was already feeling a bit better: the pressure from my abdomen had lessened, and that was all the encouragement I needed to keep my fast going. And with that rich, nourishing herbal bone broth by my side, I was feeling more confident that I could do this. At least I was resolute enough to try.

We really didn't do much at the ski lodge other than see where Dusty worked. That must have ticked off a box for the visiting in-law. We didn't spend enough time there to see the whole place, just the repair shop where he spent his days. Outside the shop he pointed around and told us what was where. The March day was already dimming, and it was time to drive back home, time for the eaters to cook up their dinner.

Some twenty-seven years prior, Dusty was setting speed records for incline skiing and schussing. There was a newspaper clipping on his fridge that I noticed and read, riveted. He's quoted in the article saying, "When you reach around a hundred (miles per hour), you're not touching the ground anymore. Your ski's hover just above it as you're skiing, but you're completely off the ground. You're essentially flying." That night, after their dinner, we went to use the sauna at his local YMCA, and I asked him about it. He said that back then in the early 90's he was in the process of qualifying for the Olympics. "Yeah, I was invited out to Europe," he told me, "but at that point I saw that skiing, as a sport, was getting less about having fun and pushing limits in an organic sorta way and more about technicality, endless drilling and precision. And so I decided to stop and pursue something else I was interested in: filmmaking. I moved down to Portland and started going to school for that." Dusty, like I would over the years, had taken the scenic route, a beautiful though sometimes trying path, to get to the stability of where he was now. As we sweat and stretched in the sauna he told me, easefully, joyfully, as was his nature, how he wound up not finishing film school and instead got into carpentry and construction, becoming a general contractor to support himself and his young family. All in all I saw why Dusty had gotten that far with skiing only to call it quits, and then return to it in a tamer, less high stakes way decades later. Whether it was physical feats like skiing, psychedelic trips or deep meditative states, Dusty Reynolds was very much interested in reaching and getting familiar with 'the edge'. He was all about having one foot just over the limit while one foot remained securely planted in the known. That way he could stick around, stay on earth to relay those boundary-bursting experiences to interested persons like myself. A Buddha, of sorts. To stick around and point out the way for those with little dust in their eyes. Sauna that night took the place of what was becoming our customary evening walk. I went to bed that night relaxed from the sweat-sesh and hungry from a full day of fasting, but feeling better symptoms-wise and more confident because of it. My flexibility in stretching had improved. I was on the right track.

The next morning I woke up to Dusty doing stuff in the kitchen, and feeling great myself. I felt like my tank was empty and my body was becoming able to do some autophagy, self-consume waste or infection (or both) and heal. I had enough bone broth for the day, but would have to get another batch going to have for tomorrow and the next day. As Dusty ate his bacon and sunny-side up egg on toast while sipping on his bulletproof coffee and casually looking at his computer - either looking at maps of the Puget Sound or finding old rare Grateful Dead live recordings or more likely flipping between both - I stepped outside. Spring morning in that Cascadian garden was fresh and moist, as one would expect. My friend the rosemary bush glinted at me a deep and knowing green, its small almost cylindrical leaves bursting perfumed and verdant. There was no wind in the air and yet it seemed to wave at me, saying, hello dear, how are you today? Do you need more medicine from me? Please take, please. As you need, my dear human friend, as you need. With a growing reverence for my floral friend, I clipped myself another potently scented sprig and held it close to my nose. I was falling in love with that scent. It was good medicine.

I took a moment to savor where I was, felt the morning mist sprinkling down on my head and wafting into my face, closed my eyes, heard the birds and the cars passing by, and took a deep fulfilling breath. With my eyes closed, rosemary sprig in hand and light precipitation still misting me not unpleasantly, I stayed standing there for a few more breaths, and a few more after that, savoring, focusing, happy, grateful for Dusty and for rosemary. After a bit, I walked back inside.

"Coffee?" he asked me. Dusty was and remains one of the most thoughtful, kind, and unconditionally giving people I know. When he wasn't jaws deep into some rambling pontification on the nature of reality accessible through psychedelics, meditation, or by riding the wave of a Grateful Dead jam, he was often offering someone something. "Sure," I said, "Can I try what you have? With butter and coconut oil?"

"Absolutely bud, coming right up."

As he got to work brewing and blending, I went back up to my room and put on another layer of clothing. I could've sworn it was chillier inside than outside at Dusty's place. Heading back downstairs, I found a seat at the round kitchen table, opened my own laptop and started to look up more about Orcas island, where I was due to land in a few days time. I happily and cozily settled into one of my favorite internet activities: exploring Google maps. I did this for hours at a time the year prior, familiarizing myself with the Northwest (as much as I could virtually) as I set my sights on moving there. Now, here I was. You could say that I 'manifested' it; you could also say that I set a goal and took practical steps to achieve it. Either way, I was on the other side of the country now, and on the precipice of spending some time in the nation's other armpit, or maybe one of its shoulders - San Juan County.

A steaming mug appeared in front of me. "Here ya go. Bon appetit," Dusty said, holding up his cup and cheersing me mid-air. "You still staying away from solid food today? This should hold you over for a bit." I thought about it. At the rate I was improving, I could probably afford to try a meal today. A nice, clean, home-cooked meal. If I were to have one, not three, not two, but one, then I would still benefit from an extended intermittent fast if I were to choose to do the same tomorrow. I would see how I was feeling, and I could always go full liquid again if the meal did more bad than good. "Yeah I think I will have some solid food for lunch today. I'm already feeling much better."

"I'm happy to hear that, man. I was starting to get a little worried. I don't think the 'no food' diet would fly on the farm."

"No, I don't think so either."

"You're gonna have to be able to replace the calories you're using up farming. Tilling the soil, digging, not to mention just being outdoors all day; that takes its toll too."

"Yeah and I don't want to be perceived as some holier than thou weird ass. I know from personal experience the social importance of partaking in communal meals. When you sit it out, you miss out on an important bonding ritual, and quickly become estranged from the group. I'd like to fit in with my fellow farmers."

"Yeah I reckon that'd be pretty important living in a small community on the edge of nowhere."

We passed the rest of the morning sitting in his kitchen, cloudy outside but a real social fire going inside between the two of us, such that I forgot about the chill, which, in all likelihood, was at least as much from my not eating as it was from his drafty house. We sipped coffee, and then tea, hot water with lemon too for actual hydration. Dusty and I shared a lot of the same health habits and rituals, such as valuing a cup of hot water with lemon and sometimes some salt. Mornings with Dusty, all but tweaking out on caffeine and talking about life and making all kinds of deep, sweeping connections and conclusions about the true and trippy nature of reality, holding in a torrent of pee to finish hearing what sermon he had for me, those were friendly and restorative days. True camaraderie and well-intentioned brotherhood. Eventually, despite the rain picking up, we decided to stretch our legs and go for a walk. In the Northwest, rain does not prevent this; it just calls for proper attire.

We walked a rectangular route: a few blocks south, an even fewer blocks east, and then another long side of the rectangle up north. On that side of the walk we passed an incredibly muddy park. It was at the base of a hill on three sides, and thus topographically destined for swampiness during the rainy season. Still, we saw some boot prints in the mud. Someone, some people were still using the park. Perhaps they were attracted to it all the more for its seasonal swampiness and general inaccessibility. Perhaps, I thought as we were passing it by, the park becoming peripheral as we moved along, perhaps people doing illegal things use the park more throughout the winter and spring, protected by a moat of mud.

When we got back to Dusty's house I offered to make us lunch. I cut slim coins of the carrots he had and started pan-frying them in coconut oil. As the carrots sizzled away I chopped up some kale and threw rough bunches of it in the large stainless steel pan. I added salt, a squeeze of lemon, and shook everything around, as one does in cooking. Then I cracked in four eggs - two for me and two for Dusty - added a splash of the batch of broth simmering away, put a lid on and let it steam finish. After about two minutes, I called it good. Off came the lid and presto, a steamy, delicious meal, dark green, vibrant seared orange, topped with a white and yellow square from the eggs that had run in together. And what a meal it was! The consumption of food is almost common enough, and the presence and availability of food is certainly ubiquitous enough for us to forget its vital importance. Almost. When hungry and having to wait another ninety minutes for a lunch break, or even when we arrive at a restaurant famished and are told there's a half hour wait, we are reminded by the inconvenience of food's quintessential importance to us. And when that meal finally comes…Imagine eating nothing for an entire day or two; one's appreciation and gratitude for food multiples exponentially. Dusty was plenty appreciative, and he'd had his breakfast that day.

Dusty hypothesized that there was something about Everett's latitude being on the same line as the Juan de Fuca Strait - a clear line out to the Pacific, as opposed to Seattle's being south of that line or Bellingham's being north of it, for instance - that affected Everett's weather, made it such that wind both swept in gales and swept out the cloud-cover quickly. Within a few hours spent in his kitchen, we could experience all microcosms of the four seasons and all types of weather conditions. After lunch Dusty took a nap. I did the dishes and cleaned up the kitchen generally, trying my best to express my gratitude for his taking me in in my week of need. Then I read a bit and decided to sit for a longish meditation. My first thought was to meditate up in my room, but then the thought jumped out at me, or maybe out *of* me: sit with rosemary. Inside, my rosemary-heavy bone broth was puttering away; outside, I sat with my herbal friend, my plant teacher, growing object and relation of increasing reverence and profundity.

His caramel smooth, trademark, "Hey bud," woke me gently from my state of absorption. I wasn't sure how much time had passed; when one forgets about time, intentionally or incidentally puts time out of mind, what feels like ten minutes could actually be an hour. By the time I opened my eyes to smile at Dusty in greeting smiling at me, the sun was beginning to set for the day, the grey-blues of the Cascadian sky putting on a few yellows and oranges, as if someone in a higher dimension, a higher order of life had just started a fire. Maybe that's what weather truly is after all: some beings to which we are ants going about their lives in such ways that affect us minute three-dimensionally grounded beings as profoundly as weather, the turning of day into night and night into day. Atlas tires, and shifts his burden to his other shoulder. Zeus gets irate, and a storm occurs, affecting millions. I'm not convinced the ancient Greeks were wrong.

We take our usual late afternoon sunset walk, and as we reach the ritzy part of the neighborhood that overlooks Everett's naval base, Dusty explains to me how the edge of this hill the neighborhood is positioned on is eroding, which, looking down from where we were standing, was plain to see. The town, he tells me, led by a team of military civil engineers, is about to start a project to shore it up, secure the hill (and its inhabitants therefore) and prevent further landslides. It's just the sort of work that his wife Liz does, he tells me: surveys an area deemed important for environmental and energy reasons and determines what must be done to ensure the geological integrity of the place is maintained, and specifically in her line of work, so that whatever energy project that's been proposed is determined to be of negligible impact on the land. Fault lines, water tables, mountains and stuff. Big 'destiny of an ecosystem' kind of stuff. "Speaking of Liz," he says, "she'll be back tomorrow. Getting into SeaTac late in the morning from Anchorage. So I'll be shooting down there after breakfast to pick her up."

  "Great," I say. I'm happy to meet her, partner to my kind and interesting host I resonate with so much. To see his other half, she that balances he. Sounds great.

When we get back Dusty makes dinner. I skip it. One meal is a good start. I don't wanna push it. I'm grateful that I seem to have digested lunch well, no deleterious effects noticed thus far. I sit with him and sip my batch of broth. Another potent, flavorful concoction. I am satisfied. We're both happy. We talk a bit and decide to make an early night of it. Dusty heads to his room for another 'sit', another meditation session, and I head upstairs. Performing my nightly stretches and abdominal tenderness check, I was very pleased to find that I could stretch (particularly noticeable in wheel pose) deeper and more easily, and that my abdomen and especially the part in question, my lower left side, wasn't as tight. My self-administered healing regimen was producing noticeable results. This was a good thing, I thought, smiling as I lowered myself into bed. I was finding success. Keeping this up, cautiously, slow and steady, I felt I would be farm-ready in a few days.

That night I had a dream. Sometimes with dreams there is a knowing sense, a sense of knowledge or relation that is, that feels implied, feels like a given, even if there aren't any direct happenings or action in the dream to evidence the implication, the given, the thing that is known. Like if in your dream there was a person that didn't look anything like your brother or your ex, some brain-generated rando, and yet you *know* somehow, even without it being made explicit why, you just *know* that person *is* your brother, *is* your ex. Or if everyone in your dream was purple and had a third arm and you knew, as a given, that that was well and fine and normal: the acceptance of an unexplained abstraction as natural and not needing explanation. If Siegmund Freud left a lasting impression on the western world, it was undoubtedly our inclination to psychoanalyze our dreams, supposing them to be entirely reflections of our mental subconscious. While I do think this is true for the most part and amply proven anecdotally (if anecdotes be proof), I don't think that's all there is to the phenomenon of sleep and dream. I think that in dreams we can also be contacted by or communicate with others.I think there is also plenty of anecdotal evidence to support that. It is uncommon, psychotic even, to suppose that all the waking world is a figment of one's own mind. Why then do we accept solipsism as truth for our dreams?

On this night of nights, my third at Dusty's, there visited me in my dream a powerful, loving woman, whose name I knew, just knew to be Rosemary. We met in a dimly lit enclosed space. It felt like a tavern or a cave, dare I say a womb. The dream meeting wasn't long and there wasn't that much to it besides her cheerful face, her joyful smile, the warm, welcoming way she stood and held her arms open outward to her sides, her palms up, inviting. And while she didn't physically touch me in the dream, I felt engulfed in and supported by her embrace. Rosemary had my back. Rosemary was looking after me, devoted to helping me regain my wellness.

Though I'd begun to allow for a midday meal, the observation of a long intermittent fast was still something I was intent on. I realized that one strategy for success with fasting was simply being awake less. And so, once again, with nothing on the agenda but feeling better, I turned over for another round of sweet healing slumber. When I woke up again Dusty was gone. Peggy evidently had gone with him. It was nine-thirty in the morning, which meant that he was on his way down to the airport to pick up Liz. I texted him, asking if he'd like me to have lunch ready for all of us by the time they got back. I heated up some water to have hot with lemon as I waited for his reply. I drank it down and stepped outside into the garden, sitting down next to Rosemary, admiring her shape, her unique perfumey scent. I closed my eyes and settled into meditation.

Some twenty minutes later I stood up, taking in the surprisingly clear, not rainy morning. Inside I checked my phone and saw that Dusty had replied: "just got her. thanks but we're gonna grab something in the city." That meant Seattle. Liz was probably well-ready for some cosmopolitan faire after spending the last several weeks close to the Arctic Circle. Fair enough, I thought to myself. Reckon I'll head on down to the co-op and get some grub there.

The sun decided to disappear, or maybe it was the clouds that decided to come out the moment I set out to walk into town. With flannel and rain-proof shell layer on, and as it occurred to me last minute, a grocery bag in case I decided to bring anything back, I began the short walk downhill into town. Everett's downtown is a nice manageable size, a few blocks wide by several more blocks long, east of which ran soulless chain-store ridden Broadway. But downtown had some soul. I walked past a yummy looking Venezuelan restaurant, several pubs and tattoo shops, a crossfit studio, and finally, a popular bakery and cafe, one that evidently prided itself on using local ingredients and supporting the community. Next block down was the Sno-isle food co-op, Sno for Snohomish county, and isle for…? That part I didn't understand or care enough to ask about. At the hot bar I got butter chicken with long grain basmati rice (the kind that almost curls at its tips), a sauteed vegetable medley, and my I must have been feeling confident in myself and my digestion because I got a slice of gluten-free marionberry pie for dessert. I still had an insurmountable sweet-tooth then, and still registered gluten-free as 'harmless'. I ate the meal with relish (the enthusiasm, not the condiment) and picked up a few grocery items: more eggs, more bones, more vegetables, and some grass-fed ground beef from the freezer. I couldn't help myself and also bought an interesting seeming flavor of kombucha (the bottle said, "champagne oolong") and a chocolate coconut-milk smoothie drink, complete with various price-tag justifying superfoods. From there it was about a fifteen minute walk back to Dusty's, going uphill this way.

After I put my groceries away, I went up to my room and read for a while. This whole time I'd been corresponding here and there with one of the farmers about my arrival time. When I landed in Washington three days prior I told him, "within the week." Feeling better as I was but wanting to give myself a bit more time to be sure, I gave the farmer (Sam was his name) a call and told him I'd be over Friday. It was Wednesday. I reckoned I'd be feeling even better tomorrow, and all but normal and ready for work in forty-eight to seventy-two hours. With the end of my stay here now in sight (Dusty of course had initially offered me to "stay for as long as I wanted or needed to") I began to calculate: how much food we had left and how many meals I'd be eating here in my remaining time, how many more jars of broth I'd need, for it was still those that were carrying me through the day. After a touch of pragmatic thinking, my mind, tiring of that, is prone to reorient itself to abstraction and philosophizing. I considered the problem I'd come here with: a busted gut, tight, hard and painful, along with the sorts of other dysfunctional bowel symptoms you might expect to go along with that. Was it the fast or the broth that was really moving the needle on my getting better? Was it the change of scenery? Moving from New Jersey to Washington, place of my fantasies for going on a year now, was a big change. Sometimes it is exactly change like this that's needed to get past stuck points, to counteract stagnancy, which is what I was experiencing in a very literal biological sense for months back east leading up to this week. We try and pick things apart, isolate the variables, determine the controls, all in an attempt to single out what object does what; that is the aim and method of the Hellenistic scientific tradition that so strongly informed the deductive processes of the western world, and as of the last century practically all the world. But there is another way of thinking and of viewing things: looking for the effects of objects in relation. Just as I could never know if it was the creek water or the sugar that led to my gastric affliction, instead concluding that it was very likely a combination of both, so too can I only surmise now that it was exactly and irreducibly *everything* I'd been doing at Dusty's plus the overarching life change that was the move itself that was leading to my getting better.

"Nice to meet you, Dusty's told me a lot about you," Liz said to me, a very kind, authentic smile drawn across her face. She looked happy, a little weary, and was probably glad to be home. "Uh oh," I said back, "not entirely sure what that means."

"All good things," Dusty chimed in, "all good things." At this, we all laughed. "So Steve here's been doing this bone broth fast to fix his gut, and it's been working yeah?"

"I would say so. In fact I was just on the phone with one of the farmers and I told him that I'd be arriving on Friday."

"Okay great, we can make that happen. I don't work that day so I can take you up there, you just let me know." I wasn't expecting that, door to door service from Dusty, from airport to farm and room and board in between. What a guy. I was also wondering just exactly what his work schedule was. It didn't seem very regular or predictable to me at least. "That would be mighty kind of you Dusty, thank you. You've got quite the charmer in your life Liz. Quite the gentleman."

"That he is," she said, smiling again, running a hand along his shoulder.

"We've had a fun week here with your mom around and Steve getting back on his feet. Just taking it easy, watching the rain come down. Yeah, spring's not so bad over here. You'll have a good time on the farm. It'll likely be a mixed bag of rain, sun, and more rain. But it'll be nice to be outside all the time, growing your own vegetables. They got animals over there?"

In the garden we four sat, Dusty, Liz, Peggy and I. I told them more about the farm where I'd be interning, what little I knew of Orcas island and the San Juan Archipelago. The three northwesterners chimed in here and there with their experiences of those islands, what short trips they'd made over the years. I was very excited for what was in store for me. All around us the plant life glinted as the sun shone down on the nearly ever-present moisture and dew. Small birds chirped around us, and on the power lines sat the crows, watching, waiting, being. Just behind me was that plant ally I would be remiss to forget, lovely Rosemary, herbaceous and hardy through persistent rain and summer drought. And with strength enough to pass some on to me.

Less than forty-eight hours later, Dusty and I were up early to begin the drive north. It was about an hour to get to the town of Anacortes, and from there another hour's ferry ride to Orcas. I wound up leaving some bone broth in Dusty and Liz's freezer for them, for which they were thankful. By the end of my time with them I'd really perfected the recipe, and my final batch was the tastiest I'd made. Making a few passes back and forth between house and car to load up all my stuff, I saw my friend standing there, alone where she was planted in the garden but content seeming nonetheless. She waved at me one last time, and one last time I walked over to her, knelt down to her base, took in her strong scent, and said my thanks. I was well. Ready for my next adventure. After this week I would never forget the kindness Dusty showed me, and I would never forget the look, the smell, or the taste of rosemary.

From inside the warmth, the coze, the hearthheat of my second-story apartment, you wouldn't be able to tell there was an ice-wet chill to the air outside, save for guessing provided the context gleaned from the wintry optics: leafless maples, naked alders and cherry trees, the telltale permaglisten of the season that adorns all exposed exteriors outside. Inside, humidifier and heater run and ceiling lights illuminate the space kindly on in the time ample past the early sunset. A shockingly early sunset, year after year.

On my desk atop three thin cardboard coasters rests my evening brew. Steaming oily glistening, dark and hot. My sunset drink, to help propel me on through the season's elongated dark hours. Before lighting and electricity, did people living north spend that much more time asleep? Candles, of wax, of tallow, whale or bear fat, must've been integral. But also likely was more rest, more time spent asleep. To rest, invest in oneself and for months of the year recoup from all the demands, energetic and social, all the repeated bandwidth max-outs of summer, and then, as the calendar renews and the new year is celebrated, to begin to bank energy, eventually letting it pent up for summer at long last. The mature hawthorn tree in its glorious spring bloom, the lengthening days having awakened it's exuberant mane of white, pink, or red flowers after months of photosynthetic hibernation, is as good a symbol and substantive example of this annual, seasonal energetic parabola as can been seen. The tree's excitement can be felt with ease so long as one hasn't reasoned oneself out of the sense of biophilia, an important connective empathy we are born with and so many tend to lose, yet another senseless circumcision rite much of society engenders.

Before the sun is up, I am. Usually I rise with the sun. But today I've got much to do. Though I'm getting on in my years, my needs, though now less and simplified, remain much the same. Food, water, shelter, clothing, medicine, satisfaction. I have an inkling that these needs will remain until I am no longer. Until the elements that conspired together in confluence to form and animate give up the ghost and disperse, scatter back from whence they came, disunited. Until I the sandcastle return to the beach. Until I the snowman return to the ground. Until I the tributary return to the ocean.

I am up early today to get in a good, long meditation before I go 'on the hunt'. Today I seek to replenish my store of a certain fungal friend and longtime ally, the black gold of the forest - chaga. Inonotus Obliquus, as it goes by in Latin, *obscured ear*. I brewed up my last cup yesterday, dark and earthy, almost caramel in flavor, and today I must find more. But first, in the darkness that heralds the coming day like amniotic fluid, I will sit in still absorption and observe the primacy of consciousness, the presence of Shiva that is my blessed opportunity to remember each day.

After a long and lip-smacking draught, I place my mug back down on the three thin coasters just left of the center-front of my desk. I imagine that my mug, which I so highly revere, bought from its artisanal maker a few year ago, likes resting on that coaster pillow when not in my hand. I'll take a moment to acknowledge that hyperbole: a pillow would make a terrible coaster. Even so, I'll stand by the animism I've just ascribed. Objects may 'like' things because no 'thing' is an object solely. The term, so common as to be trampled over in thought, merely denotes the relation of a perceiving subject. And who is to say that some objects categorically cannot be subjects also? Who are we to intimate the potential consciousness of another? Who are we to declare, knowingly or by implication, its definitive absence? I the subject adore both the object of my mug - a clay tankard/stein in the medieval style - as well as the liquid object it contains, my daily brew. It being late afternoon, I opt for half-caff coffee as its liquid base. Otherwise, the recipe is the same as my morning brew: into the dark equatorial bean-tea I add some powders of some herbs of repute: he shou wu and chaga. Sometimes I add cacao powder and sometimes even less often but still sometimes when adding cacao I'll add a sprinkle of cayenne. Just a sprinkle. Before all of this though, first in the mug softening at room temp and awaiting the hot coffee is approximately two tablespoons of salted butter or ghee. Grass-fed, lest I gain some acne. All of these things I procured earlier today just a few blocks away at the shopping center I live by.

Through the east-facing double-paned glass windows of my cabin, the first rays of the rising sun alight gently on my forehead, and I know it's time. My cabin is a hexagon with windows on all its sides but north, so that the sun, in its southern arc across the sky, illuminates my home throughout the day. Magnified by the glass windows and the solidity of the cabin, that distant sun provides me with some warmth each day too, even as far north as I reside. I grab what I need for the day: a satchel for collecting the mushroom, a small axe to extract it from the tree, and a rifle for protection. This is Alaska, after all. I turn the kettle on to warm some water for the day out there and put on some more clothes, thick pants over the long johns I'm already wearing, a sweater, a second pair of socks, thick wool ones over the cotton ones I've already got on my feet. Into my tall green thermos goes the hot water, and as I set it down on the kitchen counter my dogs perk up. They know this sound, know well what it means. They come up to me, wagging and snuffling, the first animal noises I've heard today. We say hello by pets and licks, and I reach down to remove a wooden plank from the floor in order to access one of my in-house coolers, pulling out some ground venison and filling their bowls. AM chow-time, a ritual most revered by my canine companions. I put my coat on, gather up my things, and grab two small bits of bone-marrow from the cooler. Leo, my husky, has finished his chow and is waiting excitedly by the door. I place one bit of bone marrow in little Fyodor's bowl. He's a cavapoo, a smaller breed and not as voracious an eater. As he finishes, I greet Leo with his piece of marrow, which he eats with precision right out of my hand. I need my boys strong and well-fueled for today's cold, outdoor adventure. Fyodor waits patiently at his bowl as I retrieve his wool socks that have been drying over the wood-stove from yesterday's outing. I slip them on his feet. He allows this, seems to appreciate them in fact. It's cold out there, and the snow is deep. My boys, valiantly struggling to stifle their yelps of excitement, shuffle in place by the door, all but ready to burst out of the cabin. They sit for me once more as I approach, scratch them each behind the ears, and out we go, into the small clearing immediately surrounding our home, around which the Tongass, the great rainforest of the north, envelops us endlessly.

I went for a good hour's walk as the sun began to set at 3:30 in the afternoon today, listening first to the last two songs of the Baroness album I'd been working my way through, followed by a talk and Q and A by one of my favorite Buddhist teachers, the monk Ajahn Punnadhammo. The walk culminated by design with me reaching the post office located conveniently in my nearby shopping center to grab some items my email told me had arrived. Had arrived yesterday, actually; they take an afternoon to sort and place incoming mail, so it's always the next day that I go to retrieve. Though I make an occasional foraging foray into the woods (the Olympics are a lovely place to do so), and though I grow some winter squash each year in a bed in my local community garden, the vast majority of what resources I need I acquire in a fashion like this: I go to a place where they've been sent to or have them sent to me from somewhere else. I appreciate these things - food, medicine, gadgets - though I note with a touch of sadness how disconnected I can feel from them when I remember I know not the conditions by which they were grown or manufactured, the care or lack of care with which they've been produced, assembled and sent to me. It is a big unseen economy by which so many of us live, like a machine self-aware and yet so large that no part, no one cog can see all others, can see the machine entire. It is disjointed in the experience of it, though it works. It supports so much life.

Leo and Fyodor and I work in wordless, command-free sync and synergy. By subtle cues I didn't even know I was giving, by my timing and emphasis this morning my dogs know, somehow, that we're not out to hunt and we're not out for just a walk. Somehow, they know it's the third thing we do outside: forage. They know intuitively in this endeavor to stay quiet and not announce our presence to the quiet abundance of winter life that surrounds us. Stealth mode: it's in their genes. As I take step by cautious step, Leo bounds sleek and almost noiselessly both on our well-worn trails about our home as well as off into the untrodden snow, clearing fresh canine trails and revisiting ones he's already started. Little Fyodor stays in trails already cleared; he knows better than to collide into snow more than twice his height. Sometimes Leo has a good lead and his spontaneous trails lead me to something useful. Most of the time it's excitement, following the scent of something past.

It's amazing to really take it in, that his sense of smell is the strongest sense operating among us. However, what we're after, the chaga mushroom, doesn't have much of a smell, not even to a dog. So it's my eyesight that's actually the sensory MVP today, and already I'm scanning the trees, though it's unlikely any so close to home will have the hallowed black tumor-like growth that is the medicinal, harvestable part of the chaga. That's what we're after, something a human would be mortified to find on themselves but plenty lucky to find on a deciduous tree. I'm looking for such hardwoods, this time of year stoic and leafless. Famously it's on living birch trees that chaga grows, though I've seen them on alder trees this far north too. The cold, moist air feels good on my face, an inversion of the climate I grew up in. On the Atlantic coast, winters are dry and summers are humid, whereas on the Pacific coast it's the opposite. And that is how I prefer it. One must be on watch for mold, yes, but I find that to be an acceptable trade-off for not being blasted with an oppressively muggy summer. I haven't felt that sort of gross heat, stifling and buggy, for many years…

Today was my day off, and on such a day I may wake up (having decided the night before) with a vigor and a resolve to get done what needs doing: to run the errands that need to be ran, to make some solid progress on my school work or make some power moves in my garden bed. Or I may decide the night before it's appropriate to sleep in, to rest, wake up when I do and allow the day to play out more organically. This often means giving in to impulse and enjoying the mental relaxation that comes with not saying no to myself. Within reason. This might look like heading to a cafe shortly after waking up, getting an overpriced coffee drink and penning out a few pages whilst I sip. I may meet a friend at a cafe, and do less writing and more talking. Or, more in line with the reticence of the wintry season, and as I have decided to do on this day, stay home, put on some instrumental music like jazz or classical or something ambient, and drink down coffee after buttery coffee, all but tweaking out as I explore the virtual world in a fast-forward manner, again letting impulse fly, reading and then opening a tab on my laptop to look up the region just mentioned in my book, writing and then opening another tab or two to pursue some flight of fancy I entertain about moving up north and living in a smaller, more remote town where it's even more cloudy and rainy and I'm indoors writing or concocting herbal medicine most of the time or outdoors connecting nourishingly in the deep, deep green forest, hunting moose or finding mushrooms or just sitting contendly on a plush mound of moss, fully attuning my sense to all the frequencies of the forest, labeling or differentiating nothing. Another moment or two and the reverie bursts, and I get back to what I was doing, writing, studying. Now, I am at the tail end of this session for today. I grow antsy in my seat and it's time to get up, time to move and get some fresh air before the sun sets and the dark hours lay in.

Leo chases off a snowshoe hare. Slowed down by breaking fresh snow, he'll never catch it. He is playing out his instincts, taking unquestioning direction from his genetics. This gets us into trouble sometimes, we humans with our laws and upward strivings. Most of the time, though depending on the person certainly, we resist our more base instincts, much like someone who fights to swim against the current in order to reach a better place upstream. I see the autonomic glee animating Leo, his wolf-like face alert and engaged, see his hardwired neurochemistry alight the handsome, sharp lines of his powerful canine maws as he holds out in hunt-mode for a moment longer before returning to my side. He impresses me.

We trod on, still walking a path of mine through the snow and into the woods, our main path from which arterial ones spring out. It is highly likely that we'll create a new outshoot, a new branching path today in our conk-driven quest, our mushroom hunt. I note with a relieving sigh as forward the dogs and I go, our eyes, ears, and their noses on sensory fire from the endless input of the forest pristine and sparkling reflective from the ubiquitous snow, how it is well and good sometimes as a human to relax, relent, and allow for impulsive behavior at times. Nothing malicious or destructive, but how blessedly relaxing it can be at times to forgo one's agenda, one's upkeep and strivings, and float for a little along the river of the way the day goes. So much of my life, or more specifically my internal experience, could be summed up attitudinally as swimming against the current of deep-seated habit, with bits of reprieve here and there, relax and drift before resuming the belabored kicking of my mental legs, the striving swim. With the habits I value now second-nature to me, there is no swimming, no striving anymore. I have reached the river's far side upstream, and it is here I dwell for good. For now, for the remainder of this life.

Sip after buttery sip I make progress on the present, and fantasize, dream, and delight about what's to come. Where I'd like to visit or end up, what sorts of things I might like to do. Places. Possible careers. What fulfillment might look like in the decades to come. Presupposing I'll live that long. Presupposing fulfillment *isn't* already, that something is missing or needed. I would do well to remember that this is all speculation. This mental activity is one part plan-orienting and five parts play. Years from now when that supposed fulfillment is reached, is ripe, will it still look like what I envisioned decades prior? Ought I to hold doggedly to a vision and not deviate no matter what comes or develops over the course of life's co-creative unfoldment? Or should I be fluid, open to my own changes and how the world around me changes in time? I might imagine now, for instance, that I'd like to be an English professor, that I'd find real fulfillment doing that. But what if by the time I'm teaching or shortly after starting, AI does my job for me or makes it unnecessary? I am happy now, happy with where I am and what I'm doing. And though it seems to me there are pieces missing - a partner, land or a building to call my own - I know, if I really stop and feel into my being that I am full and happy and complete at all points and stages.

We've been out for a few hours now, getting warm internally from near constant movement and externally from the low risen sun moving slowly across its short winter arc. It won't be out for long today, but at least it's out, which is bright and glorious. Never taken for granted. We are out of the radius surrounding the cabin that I am intimately familiar with and fairly certain is bereft of chaga. For this season at least. Now, we are cutting new trail. Fyodor falls in line behind me, and me behind (for the most part) Leo as I make sure to displace more snow than I have to with each step so as to make a path for the little guy. "What's that?" I say out loud, getting Leo's head to spin. "What's that?" I say again, and this time point to a tree maybe fifty feet away that appears to have the tell-tale black and tan lump.

A parasitic fungus, inonotus obliquus spores enter their host tree through poorly healed wounds, spreading to the tree's inner heartwood. The fungus will feed on the living tree for any number of decades depending on its health and size. At some point, seemingly when the chaga 'infection' has gained the upper hand, a sterile, harvestable mycelial mass is produced. What I know and love and am looking for today. This medicinal part of the organism so sought after is technically not a mushroom but a different fungal organ called a sclerotia, a compacted mass of tightly branching filaments that works as a defensive control center for its parasitic endeavors as it continues to slowly nom on its host tree. Despite being referred to as a mushroom, it's not. Mushrooms are the spore-spreading sex organs of certain fungus species. Most, perhaps. But not chaga, not inonotus obliquus. It is important to harvest this forageable part, this dense block of medicinal fungal armor, while the tree is still alive. Harvesting the sclerotial mass off a dead tree would likely result in acquiring a no-good, mold-ridden hunk.

Leo is at the tree sniffing around, astute and determined olfactory detective he is. I'm walking towards him, with Fyodor at my heels behind me, dodging sticky snow clumps. As we get close I see, veritably, what I suspected: chaga, inonotus obliquus, a solid hunk about eight inches tall and between two and three inches thick, healthy looking and ready to be axed out. Doing this won't kill the tree or the fungus, for its spores are already set confidently in, of which this dark sclerotial mass hangs as evidence. The black gold of the northern woods, here at my fingertips.

Mm mm mm, I smack my lips and savor the last buttery sip of this morning's cuppa. Cup two, and I'm out. Out of butter, out of chaga. On top of my shit as I usually am, I know that I have a shipment of the stuff waiting for me at the post office. Knowing my chaga stash was nearing its end, I'd put in an order with my supplier, Birch Boys, last week. After lunch I'll go on a good walk, forty-five minutes to an hour long, grab more butter and swing by my PO box to re-up. Ingredients I ritually ingest that fuel my potential, actualizing daily.

The pot on the woodstove sputters and steams. In it a fraction of the chaga-treasure we found decocts. Now, it's busted up into many smaller pieces and dust from a few hammer blows while wrapped in cloth, a trick I learned long ago from a hunter in the Adirondacks. Another move in his honor - we're having bear stew tonight for dinner: local bear (of course) and carrots and potatoes I grew myself. Gotta give the bear meat a long cook to kill off any potential trichinosis.

Fyodor sits by the woodstove warming up. Leo sits and stands, walks and wags alternately by the front door, already ready for our next outing. He may be ready, but like Fyodor I'm done for the day. Not because I'm absolutely wiped, but because at this point in my life I know well the value of conserving my strength. So I can venture out again for hours more tomorrow. So I can run (for a bit) with my furry companions in the dune-like snow. So I can say hello with a quiet and conscious smile to the amazing ecosystem in which I live, this gloomy though joyful bastion of life that is northern Cascadia. I love it all and want to savor my time remaining with it, within it, sometimes a happy spectator and other times a eager dance partner.

The sun is up and so am I! Though it remains under its grey cloud blanket for now, I have thrown my blankets off and begin my day with vigor. Inner fire, inner sunshine is what it takes to get through Cascadia's winter and enjoy doing it. Zip, zap, zoom! I'm moving around my kitchen like a scientist, heating this, brewing that, taking that out of the fridge and putting this back in, blending myself a satisfying smoothie to start my day. I'm playing a playlist of bebop jazz from the tv mounted on the wall, and even before my first sip of the wonderfully frothy buttery brew I've made for myself, I feel energetically in line with the tempo and general vibe of the music. One more *vrrrr* to blend the butter in my brew and the instant chaga powder too, and then to sip. I purse my lips to the lid of my clay-fired steiner and ahhh, perfection.

The sun's been down for hours now. My dogs are each in their respective beds dozing. By the light of a whale-fat candle given to me by a nearby Tlingit family, I write about the day's adventure. It took me the longest time to start writing regularly in a diary. Maybe that's because there were always so many other things to do, so many things competing for my attention. But now and for some twenty years prior, my life's been simple. Blessedly simple and free, beholden only to nature and her rhythms, predictable enough to the extent that we don't muck them up. I do not in the slightest mind being beholden to the rhythms of the earth and the heavens because, beholden as I am *to* the elements terrestrial and celestial, I am held *by* them, our original and primary parents.

For a good while now my chaga tea has been puttering away soothingly on the stove top. I reckon it's time. Walking over, I lift the lid and steam pours forth, giving me a light facial I was looking forward to. Oh yeah, it's ready. My chaga tea, dark black with a crackling, almost iridescent dark orange caramel accent. Yes. Time for a cup. I'll pour some when cooled a bit into my dog's bowls too. We will sip this glory brew. And by it, so empowered, greet tomorrow smiling, renewed.

Chornii Oolitsa - an excerpt

1: Collapse

Ilyana was born into turbulent times. For some, turbulence meant hardship and trauma, while for others it meant profitability and the securing and amassing of power. Peculiarity of the human species, that: chaos could cut both ways, devastation for some, opportunity for others. Practically everyone Ilyana knew or even saw growing up then, the first twelve years of her life, belonged to the former camp - camp hardship, camp hunger, camp regularity-of-sorrow. Despite its prevalence, no one would choose to stay at that camp if they didn't have to. Advertising to get others to willingly join such a camp would be difficult at best.

Beyond the three dimensions of space necessary for creating a human city, or put another way, complicit in the perception of such a thing as a city, is time, a fourth dimension: the subjective measurement of the length of existence within the aforementioned three dimensional space we occupy. Those first three dimensions are nigh inarguable, mathematically foundational in fact, and taught in school the world over. Number four, time, gets trickier to comment on objectively, though certainly, undeniably, inescapably, it orders our lives, lining up and syncing our movements in space. Now, what lies beyond that? What's next? Things become even trickier and less agreed-upon from there on out, though, it bears remembering, that that which is, *is*, regardless of whether we can cogently express what *it* is.

Time is pregnant with possibility, and therein lies the key to the next, the fifth dimension. Just as movement in space implies time, our potential movements across time suggest another dimension to be considered. In one 'time line', an individual loses their job and their home as the USSR plummets; in another, they somehow capitalize on the chaos and amass more wealth and influence than they ever had before…if this job was taken instead of that one, if more initiative was shown on a particular day when the boss happened to be looking, if a train on a particular day was or wasn't taken, if a scholarship was or wasn't awarded, and on and on the forking path of life that at each step of the way almost never seems as consequential as it actually is. And yet also, differences across time needn't always be profound. They can also be as mundane and meaningless as having had a mole or not, receiving a green shirt on your birthday instead of that blue one, differences with no damning or lucky repercussions.

Ilyana was born in 1988, in Moscow, Russia. Crumbling Moscow, depressed Moscow, everyone-in-it-for-themselves Moscow. Quite possibly the worst time ever to have been born in Moscow. The 'collapse' of the Soviet Union is a very appropriate term to describe what happened, and what life for some time subsequently was like. No one knew this better than the citizens of Russia, of Ukraine, of Belarus, of Georgia and all the other satellite states of the former USSR that, bitterly sweet, now had more independence than they'd had for the better part of the last century, but realized that while standing abandoned in the rubble of their economy, their nation, their way of life, a way of life that somehow, despite it all, kept going like a river dried down to a thin creek still weakly flowing. Camaraderie, in both political philosophy and practically in everyday sentiment, had bottomed out. Mistrust and destitution: this was what collapse looked like socially.

Moscow is a city of concentric circles. For hundreds of years that is how it expanded, with its wealth and power concentrated in its bull's eye center, or else hidden in Lenin-knows-where, somewhere outside the city, in a place remote and unexpected, easy enough to pull off in the largest country in the world. Secrets and exceptions to the rule aside - of which there are probably many - the further out from the center of the circle, the poorer the people and the more run-down the infrastructure. The center of Moscow would be the very first place in all the former USSR to bounce back; the historic parts of the city most readily benefited from international tourism, and with the Iron Curtain down that's exactly where foreign money went at first. But on the outskirts of the Kremlin and Red Square, beyond the intrigue of swirling onion-domed buildings were seas of dismal poverty: rows and rows of apartment buildings, deteriorating and grim-looking, uncared for and uncaring, that housed millions of people in need, all getting by as best they could, which for many meant inundating themselves numb with alcohol, that ever-flowing, destructive reprieve. There was no more mother state to give them the essentials (not that it always did the best job), and for the first time in several generations people truly, not even de facto, but really and truly had to fend for themselves. Suspicion and paranoia, seeds densely planted and regularly watered during the last seventy years, were now full-grown weeds, rampant, invasive, and cruel. No one was easily inclined to help unless they had a reason to, transactionary or by bond. Familial bonds didn't guarantee help in life. But friendships often did. Ilyana had two childhood friends, friendships so strong and natural it was as if they had come into this life together on a vow to help each other make it through the circumstances they were born into. Their names were Natalia and Yevgeny.

2: Black Street

Ilyana, Natalia, and Yevgeny lived forty minutes by subway from Moscow's bullseye, an hour or so by car depending on the state of the roads, and several hours walk. They did not go to the center of the city that often, a few times here and there with family or for school, as a matter of national pride. They mostly stuck to their district, venturing sometimes into neighboring ones as they grew older. Their apartment building, tall and painted a brown fading into tan (or maybe it was tan fading into brown, or maybe it was originally yellow) sprouted up strainingly from the drab grey streets. Money for the improvement of local roads hadn't come down the great Red pipeline in many years. Sidewalks were crumbling, or partially or wholly overtaken by grass; potholes in the roads were at the frequency of several to a block; minor depressions or dips in the ground due to lack of maintenance on top of hasty construction to begin with led to a preponderance of what were small skating rinks for most of the year and puddles to splash in in the springtime. Sources of amusement for children, the ubiquity of potholes and generally deteriorating roads was a source of frustration for vehicle-driving adults and teens. For those without a vehicle, the many potholes, extant and in formation, were less of an issue. However, it was unavoidable for those living in this city, in this country, in this part of the world, that rundown roadways, crumbling sidewalks, and shabby, unmaintained, uncared-for buildings and public spaces were a constant backdrop for their lives.

Growing up in the same apartment as Ilyana - Chorni Oolitsa, it was called, which meant Black Street in Russian - Natalia and Yevgeny each had two parents, man and wife, that sometimes fought and sometimes seemed to ignore each other and sometimes cooed in reconciliatory love. Ilyana's one parent, her mother, followed similar patterns within herself. "Where is your papa?" Natalia asked Ilyana innocently at a large tenant get-together, a big cookout one summer early on in the trio's friendship, the second or third time they'd met, as four-year-olds. To which Ilyana blankly and matter-of-factly replied with the same stock answer she'd been given, the one Ilyana's mother Sophia told people casually, people she knew she wouldn't get to know very well: that he had been in the military. Sometimes adults got the hint - more from Sophia's tone than her actual words - and wouldn't ask any more and the subject would quickly change. Sometimes though - and especially in Ilyana's case where she was talking to other kids, stubbornly curious, socially unaware kids - sometimes someone would ask more: what position, what rank, or in what conflict. To which Sophia would reply, returning the tactlessly inquisitive volley with a definitively game-set-and-match tightening of her mouth and annoyed glare of her eyes, either that it was "an accident in training" or "which one do you think?", referencing the failed Afghan conflict that was the straw that broke the camel's back for the Soviet Union. She then might say, "why don't we talk about something happier, huh? How is your job going?" The person she was talking to might very well not have a job, and the conversation would become, somewhat awkwardly though intentionally, about them and their gripes. "My papa was a hero. He was much stronger than your papa - the strongest and bravest in the world! He wasn't afraid of the dark, or the cold, or even cockroaches," Ilyana would state triumphantly. "He could do anything."

Natalia's parents, both academic by trade and aptitude, had lost their jobs as professors at a college for the humanities in a different, more well-to-do part of Moscow, but being resourceful, determined, and lucky, found work at a supermarket and relocated, drastically downgrading and downsizing to their Chorni Oolitsa apartment. Natalia's mother became a cashier, while her father donned the long, heavy grey jacket of someone who spent their time in walk-in refrigerators and freezers all day, working in the meat and dairy sections of the store. Their good fortune at finding steady work quicker than most meant, among other things, that Natalia's clothing often looked nicer than Ilyana's or Yevgeny's. Ivan and Lyooba ran a tight ship in terms of household economics, often scrounging on food quality, taking home stale goods from the store when they could, and waiting on repairing things in need of repair so that Natalia could look her best, which they rightly reasoned translated into her feeling her best. Lyooba, as a psychologist, was keenly aware of this. As such, Natalia was often the jolliest and most confident of the trio of friends, but a bit less adventurous, not wanting to do anything that would dirty or damage her clothes. She was aware - at first on an unconscious level that informed her perception and self-concept, but more and more consciously as she grew older - of her family's relative stability and good fortune, all signified by her cleaner, newer looking clothes, and the consistency of food on the table. One year while celebrating Natalia's birthday, she and the other children of Chorni Oolitsa gathered around the small off-white square table in her family's cramped but tidy kitchen, eating the red and pink frosted cake her parents had made, wooing and fawning over her birthday presents, immaculately knit by her mother and grandmother in bright, luscious colors: a beautiful, long carmine red scarf and snow-white mittens embedded with glitter, so she wouldn't lose them in the snow. While the other kids were content forking cake into their eager little mouths, blissed out at this infrequent and inordinate amount of sugar, cleaning their plates of any morsel of remaining frosting, Natalia took Yevgeny and Ilyana discretely over to her room (the room she shared with her parents), and gave Yevgeny her old yellow scarf and Ilyana her old red mittens, both in practically new condition. She shushed them as they thanked her, nodding in return with a little smile drawn across her face and telling them to hide the gifts in their pockets so the other kids present wouldn't see. They all knew there and then that they had formed a special inner circle amongst themselves, the *d'yeti* of Black Street.

If the three had drawn lots just before their birth, it was Yevgeny who'd drawn the shortest. Even before his birth and before the collapse of the nation, Yevgeny's parents, Demetria and Steppan, did not have a healthy relationship nor much financial stability. For the entirety of his adult life and for some of his teenage years too, Steppan had been involved in black market trade, a sizable shadow industry in a country that had either closed itself off or been closed off from the markets of most of the world. Like a bear in its den for a long winter, with its waking and coming out an inevitability, uncomfortable (to say the least) for those in the den to witness it, Steppan had spent his life on his tip-toes to one day realize that the skill he had - the niche he had supported himself by for so long - was of rapidly evaporating relevance. Technology from outside the Iron Curtain, music recordings, clothing material formerly inaccessible to and so highly sought after by the corrupt and wealthy elite, and of course, his mainstay, his saving grace - drugs - now all poured in and could be gotten by anyone with a little money. It was all accessible now, and so he found himself an unnecessary and unwanted middleman.

Yevgeny's mother Demetria saw something in Steppan one day, something more than his slicked back hair and unusual and somewhat mystifying green eyes. The one day-turned-weekend that he had chanced to stop in the small town of Abakan near Krasnoyarsk, where he had been spending time then getting rich off the illicit desires of the wealthy in that out-of-the-way city, Demetria and he were fated to meet. What was supposed to be a quick run of premium European merino wool ("from the pastoral foothills of Greece. So soft you'll swear you're on Mt. Olympus") turned into, when they saw each other from across the street and attracted like magnets, a prolonged stay, the act of conception in her cold, creaking wooden artist's loft, a shacking up of sorts that despite its quickness felt right, impassioned and true. This was followed of course by pregnancy and eventually, on Yevgeny's first birthday, marriage. That too, new economic realities aside, slowed him down, made his trade and lifestyle less plausible. Eventually, through many mishaps and frustrations chasing false leads, decreasing interests and hollow opportunities, and the child, always the child needing something, they found Chorni Oolitsa and slithered in, Steppan's first promise to Demetria of "not wanting for anything" by that time a sore cut that had scabbed over and been reopened many times. Now finally settled down in Moscow, Steppan and Demetria sought to let it heal, to let themselves heal and live up to the happiness they felt so strongly together earlier on in their relationship, but it was a near-constant challenge.

3: Play and Seasons

Ilyana, Natalia, and Yevgeny grew up in a very free, hands-off kind of way, as if their parents were so preoccupied bailing their family-ships of water to keep them from sinking that they often didn't have the time or the energy to enjoy the ride with their children.

They went to school when they were supposed to, most of the time. And most of the time, the teacher showed up to teach. Outside of school, which was the one relatively stable institution in their young lives, they had their run of the place, for better or for worse. In summer, when all around them life had completely thawed and there was so much green and all things could happen uninhibited, when people were naturally more inclined to joy and to saying yes, affirmative as the many rays of the sun shone over its long days, they would start each day practically exploding out from their respective apartments into the vibrant outside world, maybe having a bite to eat first (if their parents could catch them and had something at the ready) or more likely given a snack to take with them for when they got hungry. They would meet each other on the stairs heading down to the ground-floor, sometimes colliding with each other in their enthusiasm, sometimes bumping into an older tenant, too drunk on summer or alcohol to care.

In school they learned their language, numbers and colors, simple object words that they'd be encountering often enough anyway, like bird, fish, snowflake, and apple, and their corresponding image, which was easy enough. Then they went on to compound them: the red bird, the blue fish, the white snowflake, the green apple, and so on. They learned how to write their names, and started learning basic arithmetic. Thankfully, they were fed lunch from a big pot of soup, a piece of bread for each child to go with it. They would fight over the thick, crusty butt end of the loaf - the prized *gorbushka* - which, unless their teacher intervened, usually fell to

Anton, who asserted himself the most aggressively. When on his good side, when he had been given proper deference to, Anton might share the *gorbushka*, in his regal magnanimity, with Yevgeny or one of the other boys, or playing the gentlemen, give part to one of the girls, a Casanova smile smug across his face.

Natalia lived on the fifth floor, Yevgeny on the third and Ilyana on the second. They would usually find each other rather quickly by listening for each others' voices or laughter - a kind of sonar unique to them - and then out into the long day they would go, down the stairwell and out to the always dirty ground level entryway (what in finer establishments was called a lobby), past the hardy scarfed *babushkas* gardening their cherished large square of a garden plot, and then anywhere, anywhere the day would take them: to the park, to the other park, to the supermarket where they might be given some food: fruit, stale bread or the mother of all hauls - a piece of candy, a *confectka*, shiny-wrapped and sweet beyond belief. If their parents had given them a few *kopecks* as they were headed out the door, they would have money when it was time for food or hydration. Rye *kvass* and sometimes sweeter sodas soothed their parched throats on those sun-soaked summer days.

Sometimes they would hop the fence and play in their school's playground, a very different experience in the summertime than during the school year. A small creek ran seasonally nearby, drying up by late summer. When it was running and when it wasn't didn't matter, there they would play taking turns standing at the top of the creek's edge, yelling something heroic or something silly before jumping or sliding down into the voluminously big-leafed plants growing in the creek below, child-sized landslides of dry dirt and rubble cascading down with them. Each year they experienced with the same wonder how the plants growing in the rich soil of the creek's bank would sprout, and then, in concert with the lengthening days, grow prolifically, quickly reaching their heights and surpassing them with ease.

Fall meant the air was getting crisper, the days were getting shorter, their parents were forcing more layers on them and the trend was to spend, to their dismay, more time inside. School was in session again, which meant for them that the day would be more structured by adults than themselves. There would be more adult voices, more yelling, more commands, more rule-following. They learned to accept this as par for the course, as they accepted that the leaves begin to fall off the trees this time of year too, their crunch on the ground outside becoming synonymous with this time of tightening after the unbounded freedom of summer. They were now forced to mingle with other children, some they liked and some they didn't, as well as some kids only one or two of the trio liked, like how Yevgeny liked Anton (or rather, sought to please Anton) while Ilyana and Natalia decidedly did not.

In the garden, the old ladies and old men were harvesting big squash and pumpkins, a contest implicit each year as to who could grow the biggest or whose were the most oddly shaped. They took down their trellises, stakes, rope, and bean-poles, the fruits long gone in advance of the first frosts of October, sometimes September, or else found withered, rotten and mushy on their dark brown stalks or dry on their lifeless tan vines, though this was infrequent; the old gardeners of Chorni Oolitsa were masterfully thrifty, resourceful and attentive in optimizing their harvest. 'Waste not, want not' was hard-wired into their very genes by a lifetime of attending to survival.

Winter was an intensification of this general trend, the nadir, the darkest and coldest period of the year, with a few events that spiced things up and helped the people make it through: the holidays, Christmas and the New Year were always looked forward to. For a brief period of time there was an agreed upon reprieve from the cold (in terms of both temperature and attitude), as something resembling the joy, light, and openness of summer shone forth, albeit in a pale, somber aspect. Adults were more relaxed and giving. Doubtless, the children of Chorni Oolitsa and indeed children

Moscow-wide appreciated the brief change, the relent in adults' otherwise crummy and stressed behavior even more than the gifts. Though this is something the young ones would probably not readily admit.

Then, also, there were the drunks. Swollen in numbers since the collapse, though undoubtedly a class of folk that had always been, the drunkards of Moscow are an indelible part of the city, an unpredictable, sometimes violent and almost always sorrow-drenched ambience. There are of course countless casual drinkers on the spectrum of social drinkers to closet alcoholics quietly or noisily ruining their and their families' lives, a slow biochemical as well as moral corrosion. But the drunks as such were the ones out on the street and so flagrant in their disorder that their dysfunctional relationship to the substance and its chaotic effect on their lives was on full display. They were no longer in control of themselves, and the object of their desire, the state of consciousness they sought and the substance necessary to get there, was in control of them. There were those who drank and roamed the streets by day, by night, and then those wretched souls who drank day and night, whenever possible, as if seeking oxygen. Children on their way back from school or out with their families celebrating the holiday season would see them blundering around, burping, hiccuping, breaking things, cursing people, talking to themselves, or eerily quiet though still clearly drunk. And always they were alone. For however many of them there were, that was their hallmark: they just couldn't connect to anyone or anything except the liquor, and so they drank for and by themselves. Holiday season, despite the cold, brought on a surge of drunks and drunkenness, whose red noses looked much like the amanita mushrooms that popped up in the fall.

In Moscow, spring comes late and doesn't last long. The first signs of vegetal life, green sprouts poking through the ground where the snow has melted and uplifting vernal birdsong, usually come in May, and by then the rapidly lengthening days mean summer is already well on its way:

snow-watered grass greening and growing, earth-worms wiggling through and aerating the soil, leaves filling back up the terrestrial canvas, shooting out and towards the sun in a desperation and jubilation every Muscovite understands. The children of Chorni Oolitsa were much the same way, though school and other human aberrations on nature's calendar served to thwart their instincts. In the spring of 1995, when Ilyana, Natalia, and Yevgeny first started to have their own adventures together, they scurried out from their apartment building so excitedly one day that they hadn't realized there was still at least a foot of snow on the ground, and since it was still freezing nightly, quite a bit of ice. As they ran outside, faces red mostly from excitement but also temperature differential, Yevgeny slipped, first on his untied boots, then on an ice slick right in front of the main doors of the apartment complex. He waved his arms around and, grasping reflexively, managed to take Ilyana and Natalia down with him. Some people were outside already shoveling snow, or obsessively buttoning, zipping or lacing up their children into their puffy layers. No one turned an eye to the reckless trio, parentless, without supervision. Landing in the snow through its crunchy top layer and into its soft, fluffy core, the three friends quickly looked up from the wet cold and laughed peals of laughter, experiencing the hilarity of a slap-stick-like accident in good, blameless stride. Their day of free-range play was off to an exciting start. For them at least, spring had sprung.

4: Babs and D'yeds

With their own parents as busy as they were trying to keep their familial ships afloat, the youthful trio found adult attention elsewhere. Fortunately for them, these influences were mostly positive, from wise older folk who had lived through a hell of a time. Elderly people of Chorni Oolitsa who had the good fortune of not having to work for money, who had their family to support them as they had done for them during Soviet times, had at this point in their lives the time and good sense of time to be doing various life-enriching activities just outside the apartment, as the weather permitted. Gardening, for instance, once essential, was now supplemental for most families, though still important and oh so appreciated, both for fresh food and putting away preserves. When times were tough, when the supermarket supply slowed to a trickle, when the freeze of winter made fresh food a memory and a longing, gardening was appreciated. Much of the apartment grounds over the years that followed collapse were converted, season by season, year by year, square plot of land by square plot of land, into gardening space by these industrious old folks, the *babushkas* and *d'yedushkas* of Chorni Oolitsa. The landlords of the apartment complex - there were several - were seldom seen and didn't seem to care. The *babs* and *d'yeds* always kept things neat and beautiful anyway, so who could complain when you were greeted by an assortment of eye-catching flowers everyday when you stepped outside; huge, beautiful pumpkins vibrantly yellow, orange, red, even blue growing into the fall; hardy cabbages started in spring and summer in an intelligently planned succession whose basal leaves grew wide in a fervent effort to catch as much sunlight as they could when it was out and whose heads grew large and sweet in the winter.

And they were always willing to share. More than willing, they often demanded. Morning after morning as the children passed by, the *babs* would try to give them a vegetable to take for the day, one they could snack on like a carrot or cucumber. As the children returned home in the afternoon, a day of adventure under their belts, sloshing around in some creek bed or playing 'don't touch the ground' in some park, the *d'yeds* would hawk another vegetable at them. "Here, take this, take this potato home to your mother for soup. No it's good, we have too many here, you must." There was no refusing them.

Not all the gardeners of Chorni Oolitsa were old or profusely giving. Sergei was a short, muscular man, clearly younger than the *babs* and the *d'yeds*. He worked silently and ceaselessly, always the first one in the garden and the last one out, and could be seen working from their windows even as the snowflakes fluttered down thickly and mercilessly in winter. What was he doing then? Fixing the fencing, polishing tools, laying straw down on the beds - winter work. The children did not know it yet, but Sergei was ex-military. He fought in the Soviet conflict in Afghanistan, referred to and remembered by many as Russia's Vietnam. He always wore a headband around his head in memory of his unit. Most people did not know this much about him, though the *d'yeds* and the *babs* did. They spoke with him, to the extent he was willing. They knew why he didn't smile anymore. Gardening, it was clear, brought him some peace.

There was one *bab* who interacted frequently with the trio. Her name, as she instructed them to call her, was Babushka Tatyana, *babushka* being the Russian word for grandma, also often used as an insult to someone who isn't. The next time Yevgeny slipped on the ice outside (which was the afternoon of that same day, after snowball fights and snowpeople building) she saw and walked over, calmly and carefully but with the speed of adult concern. "*Ostarozhen d'yeti*! You must be careful around the ice. Use your eyes please and watch out for each other." With one strong arm she picked up Yevgeny and, before he knew what was happening, dusted him off and patted him kindly on the back. "There you are strong boy, all better." Yevgeny and Natalia laughed and began to go back inside, hungry and tuckered out. Babushka Tatyana then turned decidedly to Ilyana, catching her attention just as she was about to head off to join her friends, and with a twinkle in her eye handed the young girl a small jar of apple butter. "This is for you and your mother. Show her first please before you go opening it up." She smiled knowingly and returned to the garden. The young friends didn't notice it, and even if they did they wouldn't have understood why, but Babushka Tatyana had a soft spot for Ilyana. Maybe she in particular reminded her of herself as a little girl, or someone else. Suffice to say, she saw the seed of something special in her. They didn't know, and at that age, didn't know they didn't know.

5: Sophia Frolova

With a cold glass jar of tightly packed apple mush in hand, Ilyana knocked on her apartment door with her free hand and called, "Mama, *ya doma!*" Her mother always kept the door locked, a must in those hard times, but was always quick to come and let her in when Ilyana called, back from the day's adventure. *Latch. Snap. Snkt.* The door swung open and Ilyana collided with her mother in embrace, hugging her legs as children sometimes do. Sophia Frolova bent down and wrapped her arms around her daughter, closing her eyes and smiling a sighing smile. Ilyana would have been happy to stay like this, melting into her tall enshrouding mother forever, but Sophia, being more mindful of time and place, drew her daughter back into the warmth and safety of their home, closing the door behind them. *Snap. Snkt. Latch.*

Ilyana's mother Sophia stood five foot eight inches tall and had wavy brown hair down to her shoulders. She had piercing, near startlingly sky blue eyes. To look into them for too long, many people felt though few would say, was unnerving, unmasking, as if she - and not by her own choice but by some either supernatural, delphinic or primal, animal process - laid bare your consciousness, and whether you wanted to show her or she wanted to see or not, she saw the true intentions of everyone her eyes spied. This may or may not have actually been the case, but it was how the object of her gaze almost invariably felt.

She was beautiful,but not a demure, docile beauty, rather an untamable sort. As a girl growing up in Vladimir, a few hours east of Moscow, she was, at first, regarded as cute and angelic, and people were frequently moved to give her chocolate or other small gifts, pats on the head or shoulders. As she grew up however, people stopped viewing her as merely a cute, harmless thing. She became like a doll come to life. There was an unnameable action in her eyes at most times, a searching. Through no fault or act of her own, boys who pursued her would start to feel lost, self-conscious and doubtful, as if in a maze, as if in a state of woods-panic navigating the seemingly inscrutable forest of Sophia. What did not help was that she was not talkative at all, and so rarely diffused the enigma of her gaze, so seldom clarified her mystifying countenance. And so, relating to her, attempting to gain intimacy with her was like walking through a fog-ridden forest. Invariably her would-be suitors would give up and partner off with another more approachable girl, or having realized something about themselves in the curious, soul-barring experience of courting young Sophia, another male. Throughout her teenage years, the 70's, she became increasingly aware of herself and the effect she had on people. Without any explanation for it, without any guidance from a wise, caring female role model to ease her into understanding herself, to help become comfortable with herself, Sophia's own confidence was shaken. By her late teens, she couldn't help the suspicious edge that tinted her powdery blue eyes. What girlfriends she had from before puberty faded away from her like overshadowed trees. As she walked around her high school, every look of hers was a gorgon-stare, no matter how innocent or nebulous her intent, every glance down the hall, at the teacher to ask a question or merely looking on at the instruction provided was like a flash flood her peers wanted to avoid getting swept up in.

Once, in organic chemistry, their teacher so lost her train of thought after getting lost in Sophia's eyes that she proceeded to give the class the wrong instruction and ruin the experiment and the lesson for the day.

Similarly, despite her own innate dance ability, it was a skill for her that could never take flight, as her dance partners would either be avoiding eye contact with her or get lost in her gaze and trip them up. She developed a reputation in high school for waltzing herself and her partner into dinner tables at socials. It became a challenge among the boys, a running bet: who could dance with Sophia the longest before messing up, not riding a bucking bronco so much as a disaster swan.

Though undeniably beautiful in a regal and alluring kind of way, she was like a circus oddity to most people, and by the end of her high school years was essentially friendless and inwardly quite sensitive and paranoid. She couldn't explain it, no one could - her parents were no help either - and so she internalized a sense of "somehow this is my fault." She knew by that age - the late 70's, early 80's - that she had a power she didn't understand, and though it felt more like a curse, it was one that if turned around, when finally understood and gained mastery over, would be a great asset, a superpower. This she knew.

"Momma, look," said Ilyana, "Look what Babushka Tatyana gave us!"
 "That's very nice of her. This will be great on our toast tomorrow morning, don't you think?"
"Or tonight for dinner! Momma, can we have *hleb e yablikee* for dinner tonight?!"
 "That does sound tasty..."
"*Vkoosni, vkoosni!*" Ilyana parroted back.
 "But what about the potato salad we made yesterday? It's tastier when it's fresh. If we don't have it tonight it won't be as good tomorrow, and especially tomorrow tomorrow."
 "Okay momma, but what about these apples? Will they be bad tomorrow, and really really bad tomorrow tomorrow?"
 "No my dear, they will stay tasty because Babushka Tatyana preserved them. They are safe in this jar like you in your bed wrapped up in your

blankets at night. That's why you are such a tasty girl! *Vkoosni, vkoosni!*" Sophia said playfully as she pinched Ilyana like a hungry crab. "Momma don't eat me!" Ilyana cried in reply, laughing and trying to escape her mother's little nips and pinches. In the trust and love of the parent-child relationship, their eyes met - Sophia's sky blue and Ilyana's forest green. Sky nurtures forest, forest nurtures sky. With her crab pincers extended, Sophia ran after the fleeing Ilyana, shrieking with delight. Someone who is not afraid to look at me, and someone I want to look at. It *has* all been worth it, thought Sophia as she gave chase.

6: Sprung

The days were getting warmer and longer. Everywhere snow and ice were melting, making for an ample drink to nourish plant growth as well as an irresistible slippery muddy wonderland for children, for children who liked mud, that is. This time of the year Chorni Oolitsa was more like Korichnevy Oolitsa - 'brown' street more so than black.

Ilyana and Natalia were anxious to get outside and play on this gorgeous weekend morning but Yevgeny had not yet turned up. "Let's go knock on his door," said Ilyana. They were already on the third floor, their usual meeting spot, and walked over to the door they'd seen Yevgeny come from and go back to, apartment #314. As they approached the door they heard yelling, first a man's voice, then a woman's. Then they heard a loud crash. Then the door popped open, surprising the girls and causing them to stagger back, as out Yevgeny briskly came, quickly closing the door behind him.

"What's happening in there?" asked Natalia.

"My p-p-parents are fffighting," said Yevgeny, who had a stutter. "Let's go. They d-d-do this sometimes," he continued as they descended the stairs. "I d-d-don't know if they lllike each other anymore," he said matter of factly.

"They still like you though, right?" asked Natalia, skirting a few broken beer bottles on the incoming step.

"Yeah I th-th-think so."

Stepping outside into the springtime morning air, still fresh from rain that had gone all the night before, trickling slowly to a stop only an hour ago, Natalia enthusiastically suggested that they go to a new place today, a new park (new to them) that her parents had recently taken her to for the first time. It was larger and further away than they were used to trekking to. "I remember the way," Natalia declared with a confidence that was all the other two needed to hear, a confidence Ilyana and Yevgeny were beginning to associate with the sense of 'this is not a conversation anymore; this is the way it's going to be'. Besides, they each felt looking at each other, who could say no to the promise of adventure? This much, becoming their credo more with every outing, they said to each other without saying, as if telepathically.

They walked out of their apartment complex, past the *babs* and *d'yeds* who were gardening away like human worker bees, and turned left when they reached the street. There was a large crack in the sidewalk, seismic-looking and splintering, and at least three potholes in the road within view, each completely filled with water. Ordinarily the trio wouldn't pass up splashing in them, playing a game to see how high they could jump, imagining themselves and their knee-high boots ascending up into the stratosphere as their heroic little legs rocketed them, each jump higher (or so they imagined) than the last. *Whoosh! Splash!* And a tumult of laughter, awe and approval if the splash and its impact were extra big. But not today. Today they were on a mission, a journey to a new and far off land. They were intrepid adventurers braving an expedition from their homeland to a far less familiar, mythic place. To weather the journey from the known to unknown is an essential excitement, a rite of passage for children whose imaginations haven't dried up yet, who haven't been scared, intimidated, or otherwise convinced - by themselves or something else - into non-creative status-quo complacency, dull, drab, and grey, into consensus of the primacy of what adults tend to call the 'hard, physical world' or the 'real world', 'concrete reality'. What they are referring to, and consciously or not, taking on faith as their de facto religion, is merely the most common and boring denominator, the most overlapped segment of reality on the spectrum or continuum of perception, so shared as to be very nearly inarguable, but also so common, so basic as to beg improvement, building up, adornment, expansion. It invites imagination, which is not creating something from nothing. Transformation, of the dull into the whimsical. It is as if some adults, bullies really, insist loudly and oppressively that we all worship and work with the sandbox, the mere fact and frame of the sandbox, without being so bold as to play with the sand. Lack of play, isn't it, that dries up the well of imagination. And then they call that normal and you crazy, or immature, or some other specific and convincingly contrived diagnosis, for deviating. Natalia, Yevgeny, and Ilyana deviated from the norm that day, bless their still curious hearts, while around them ten millions others were content or coerced into their usual grooves, nothing more from the raven's eye than ant-like perambulations, predictable geometrics, regular quadrangular orbits: the calling card of the human mind in its purely functional, uninspired state.

A right at the yew tree, Natalia remembered, her parents taking the opportunity to teach her an uncommon tree species. Glorious sun now shone through the parting clouds, bringing out a greater depth of color in Natalia's red, Ilyana's blue, but not Yevgeny's grey spring jackets. Natalia's and Ilyana's were rubber, and would keep them from getting wet if it started raining again. Yevgeny's jacket was warm but not waterproof, an oversized wool jacket he grabbed on his way out the door as he dodged hurled furniture and hurtful words that flew above his head. The jacket, in fact, was his mother's. He just wanted to grab something and get out the door.

Another puddle passed. Ilyana had to put the passing up of all these splash opportunities from her mind. A greater prize lay ahead. She told herself, gauging from the enthusiasm with which Natalia was shepherding them along. Meanwhile they were each keeping track of cars they saw that were the colors they were wearing. "One more for me!" Yevgeny said triumphantly whenever he saw a grey car. By the time they made the turn onto Pushkin street, lined with white birch trees on both sides all in their first week of leafing out, Natalia was up to five, Ilyana four, and Yevgeny eight. Every time they saw a car of a different color, one not represented by them, like black or green, Ilyana would say jokingly, "One more for Dima!" Natalia, giggling, joined in. "Look!" she said, seeing a yellow taxi cab, "One more for Dima!" the two girls laughing more and more every time Yevgeny asked - with increasing mock outrage, consciously helping to create the joke with his response - "Who is Dima?"
  "Red," said Natalia, "One more for me."
"Look everyone, there's one more for Dima!"
  "Who is Dima?!"

They laughed and laughed, a breeze blowing through the birch tunnel they'd been walking through, their new leaves fluttering sequentially in the wind like dominoes falling, a photosynthetic wave soaring free and joyful above the trio's carefree antics as they echoed out into the street. They were completely unaware that, not far away, danger lurked, fitful and nauseous.

The trio soon reached a small stone bridge as the road and sidewalk they were walking along crossed a stream. As they approached, their laughter still ringing out openly, a man stumbled out from under the bridge. His clothes were dirty and tattered, his face was flushed, his eyes yellowish and his nose red. The overcoat he wore was large, positively cavernous to the children's eyes, and sadly full of holes. He was also, unfortunately, missing a shoe. Clearly drunk, he was even holding the bottle to prove it. As he continued to stumble towards them he yelled, slurring his words, "You're bbbeing too louddh!" Ilyana, Natalia, and Yevgeny now came to a halt, and quickly understood, young Moscovites they were, just what they were looking at, who, what sort of person had entered the scene. As they saw the tell-tale giveaways marking the presence of a drunkard - and an ornery one at that - they felt his chaotic presence, an adult in pain and unable to help himself. It was a non-intellectual assessment their limbic systems performed automatically. Something, several things likely were awry with this man, and they knew this before knowing him, before speaking to him, which, due to their training from home and from school on how to handle this sort of encounter, they did little of. Without needing to confer with each other, they quickly fled the scene, nimbler than he, rushing across the bridge as he continued to stagger up the slight hill from the creek. "You hear me?! I'm talking to you!" he yelled as the trio scurried past him. "You're m-m-missing a shoe!" Yevgeny yelled back. The destitute man threw his bottle at them. It shattered on the side of the bridge and rained back down in shards on where he just was, his hangout, his drinking spot under the bridge. "Ungh!" he yelled, the children's feet clacking on the cobblestone bridge as they scampered overhead. He did not pursue.

The children were a bit rattled, and breathing hard when they stopped running. Natalia was the first to say something. "We're almost there!" They had walked almost two miles now, many steps for their little legs. But their journey, even with its close call, had paid off. They were rewarded with a beautiful park to play in, one worth traveling to indeed. A large open field dotted with beautiful spring flowers, a miraculous break from the monotony of snow, loomed expansively ahead, forever it seemed to them. On one side of the field was an intimidating bramble hedge, thickly impenetrable rose and berry bushes, flowering white, white-pink, pink and red flowers. On the other side of the field were many tall trees. They shaded out all but lucky patches of wildflowers as the trim grass, lawn-like, continued on into the woods. Strangely, eye-catchingly, it was a forest without an understory. Their run away from the bridge drunk had slowed to a reverent saunter, slow and wide-eyed. Wordlessly, they walked through the field and into the woods, enrapt. No snow, not even living on in the cool shade of large trees, no leaves, trim grass - the park was uncharacteristically well-maintained for this side of Moscow. It had a manicured look one usually only seen in the affluent innermost neighborhoods of the city.

Now under tree cover, in the cool, damp shade of an early spring morning, They played one of their favorite games: Fairies in the Woods, in which Ilyana and Natalia were both beautiful and innocent fairies, frolicking through their enchanted glade of a home - as is the chief activity of fairies, frolicking daintily and unseen in places verdant and rarified - whereupon Yevgeny would jump out and chase them, playing the mean, angry troll. "Unngh!" he would yell, stumbling after them ogreishly, arms flailing, step by heavy step changing directions as Ilyana and Natalia, the frightened fairies, flitted about swiftly and fearfully. The game had several variations. Sometimes Yevgeny was a charming prince, and interacted amicably with the fairies as they bestowed fey blessings upon him: fairy wands and fairy potions, fairy stones and fairy flowers, sometimes eating them (flowers are fairy food, after all). Sometimes Ilyana would play as a shy deer or a keen, stalwart hunter. Natalia however always wanted to be a fairy princess.

Today the two girls were fairy sisters, and Yevgeny a handsome prince lost in the woods. He had run away from his family's castle, not wanting to become king. He wanted to stay young forever, shirk the duties of the human world and live in the forest, with its trees and creatures, with its drama-less peace. As they walked around the park, a new adventure for the trio, its beauty and newness - novelty, in a word - led them to an experience of awe and a certain sense of magic, something utterly unlike the order, rigidity, and predictability adults imposed upon their scheduled days. Their game today, so far removed from their usual world of Chorni Oolitsa, sparkled with an aliveness that absorbed them, commanded their full attention, made the 'game' feel realer than real. Large trees - oak, maple, and cedar, who knows how old? - loomed overhead and all around, encasing and enwrapping them in the world of the game, the micro-world of the park, the adventure of the day, all so far away from the sometimes stressful and disappointing 'normal' world. Birch and poplar trees, thinner and with a white, sometimes silvery bark, shimmered in the rainfall they'd collected last night. The occasional spruce, with thick, mighty bark and needles so tough you couldn't grab without feeling pain, was an impressive site for the children to behold, so much bigger than them and so much older and immovably established. In the sun of the day, warming the moist and mycologically active forest, toadstools popped up as if right before their eyes, bulbous russolas and boletes, agaricus species, shaggy manes, as well as the classic looking amanita muscaria, perfectly fairy-like with its bright red cap bespeckled with white polka dots. Here and there small purple orchids bloomed, fairy slippers as they're sometimes called, and fawn lilies, milky white. There were no bushes in this part of the park to obstruct their play, no ditches to avoid or broken-glass to sidestep, unlike the city streets.

Natalia pranced around primly. Ilyana, in imitation of something she didn't yet understand but nonetheless had seen, bated her eyes at Yevgeny, fluttering them and then turning her head, feigning seduction and tease.

Yevgeny, prince of the moon he called himself, regally walked toward the fairies and, with the manners and solemnity of a prince truly noble at heart, called to them, earnestly seeking their counsel.

"Oh fairy sisters of the magic woods,
hear my cry and do me good!
The kingdom that will be mine
I do not wish to rule.
My father, the world, fate,
all so cruel!
Instead I wish to be in your realm,
fast, with four legs, and horns at
my helm.
If you'll make my heart's wish come true,
I swear that forever I will protect you!"

To which the fairy sisters chimed in unison:
"Dear prince, dear prince,
do not be afraid!
We fey of the forest come to your aid.
The human world is cruel and short;
We will make you our woodland consort.
Grazing upon flowers and mushrooms you'll
spend your days, on four legs you'll soon
learn our caring ways.
We tend to the forest.
We keep it safe and neat, and live in places
untrammeled by human feet.
Deer prince, deer prince,
spin around three times each way.
We bid you welcome to the land of the fey!"

In the immediate span of forest around them, several butterflies floated. The sun shone down in thick yellow-gold streaks alighting variously around them, beaming down in unbroken diagonals from the vernal firmament and onto a fallen branch, a patch of woodland grass, the body of a cedar tree. Unseen by the children, several deer were grazing nearby, their young buck of four points stoic in duty, keeping watch over his harem.

Ilyana, Natalia, and Yevgeny played on through the day, without a care, moving, sounding, and acting like the creatures they played as, their laughter resounding into the woods with no one around to hear it. With no detracting adult presence to take away from the focus of their imaginative play, they were able to lose themselves in their game. It took on a magical quality, inspiring shortcuts to unnameable feelings and emotions in concert with the adult lives they imitated, if also mythical. Eventually they felt, internally, magnetically, the sense to return home, calculating on some subconscious level their distance from home against where the sun was in the sky. On the walk home they spoke and joked around less than earlier, feeling the quiet of being satisfied with their adventure, their day of play and potent make-believe. Instead they each mostly thought their own thoughts and didn't necessarily feel compelled to share them. A bit unusual for eight year olds perhaps, but the children of 90's Moscow were an unusual generation: more independent, self-motivated, self-starting, and also, typically, prone to introspection.

Natalia felt proud that she had led such a successful adventure, and was excited to tell her parents about it. Yevgeny was hoping that his parents had cooled down by now. There was a good chance they had and that they would be in one of their more loving, reconciliatory moods. Those were his favorite. As they passed back over the bridge and saw that the man from before was no longer there, they each looked at each other and sighed relief; the walk home would be smooth and uneventful this time. Despite his absence, Ilyana continued to think of the man they encountered earlier. Natalia and Yevgeny were already planning their next adventure, their excitement, they couldn't help it, brimming over into thoughts of the long summer ahead. But Ilyana stared straight ahead, unblinking. Her legs moved as if carrying her on auto-pilot, her arms stock-still at her sides, her head and neck straight. She was in something of a meditative absorption, a trance, as she reimagined the man they saw earlier - drunk, possibly homeless, stumbling oafishly, throwing his bottle in confused anger, no doubt inwardly tormented - as a nice man, well-dressed and smiling. Instead of a wrinkled, pock-marked face with furrowed brows knit by the habits of suspicion and conflict, she imagined a handsome man in a suit, as she'd seen men wear on tv or when she visited Moscow's center district.

She imagined him smiling and instead of throwing a bottle, offering them each a balloon and a piece of candy. He became a happy man, giving because he had enough in life and wanted to share his joy with others, simple of motive and pure of heart. She wished this not just for themselves or for other children, so they wouldn't get a scare like they did when crossing the bridge earlier to get to the park, but for him. As they walked the long walk home, she thought intensely about the details of that man having a different life, a happier life, in broad emotional strokes as well as minute details: how he would have grown up differently to make him so happy, how he would have looked differently, felt differently and so would make or at least contribute to others feeling differently when they saw him, greeting them with a smile and treat, not a snarl and a hurled glass bottle. She not only played through this visually in her mind as she took step after automatic step alongside her friends on their way home, responding to them when they engaged her, dodging traffic and generally navigating well as any pedestrian; she also *felt* how he would feel given these happier, more joyful circumstances, this changed and blessed life. This happiness, this joy burned through her body as if she was experiencing the happy life she was wishing for him, her brain neurochemically stimulated all the same as she imagined and wished, desired and willed this all intensely and repeatedly.

Ilyana came to and realized where they were - that they were back home at Chorni Oolitsa - when she saw Babushka Tatyana, simultaneously smelling her comforting *babushka* scent and picking up on her kindly *babushka* vibes. The sound of her friends reached her ears. Natalia and Yevgeny were in the middle of telling her about their day. "Wow, I am glad that man didn't hurt any of you. Please be careful *d'yeti*. What a lovely sounding game you played in the park! That forest sounds beautiful. I think I know the one. I think I went to that park when I was young, too. I am glad you all had such a good day. Spring has sprung, *d'yeti*! Here, each of you take a cabbage. Sergei worked hard to grow them over the winter. They are a gift from him." The trio looked over at Sergei beyond the wooden fence. He paused his wheel-barrowing, looked at them and nodded in recognition, the smallest hint of a smile visible at the corners of his mouth.

At the Ghost Spa

One fine day on Edmount Island, a jingling of keys preceded the opening of a large, creaking wooden door. This metallic jingling and wooden creaking, an auditory break from or addition to the almost constant birdsong, happened every day on Edmount Island. Morgana Feyestres Ballantine, known to most as Fey, was opening her Ghost Spa set on a small island on Lake Ballinger just north of Seattle.

It was May. The sky that day, a bright and cloudless blue, shone a nearly full moon faintly hanging, high and distant, while the effulgent sun blasted a long beam of yellow-gold sunlight through the open doorway, trailing into the vestibule of the building. Bathed in solar warmth, the smell of the cedar from which the facility had been built was pleasantly pungent. The spa was a large two-story affair made from reclaimed building supplies and some pieces, boards, etc. not originally purposed for building by a team of talented DIY hippie builders, carpenters and all around good-natured weirdos she knew from over the years and had invited out to Edmount Island when she was first awarded the incredible and serendipitous opportunity to 'hold a space for the spirit world' from Washington State's ever-progressive government, ever-expanding the lists and boundaries of marginalized organisms they deemed worthy of respect and support. When famously (and to the mocking laughter of other more traditional, anthropocentric states) Oregon and Washington decreed first elementals (rivers, mountains, grasslands) and then the spirits of the deceased as persons in the eyes of the law worthy of rights, respect, and financial aid, the opportunity to build and oversee a spa-sanctuary for spirits quickly unfolded for Fey, the sort of sparkling mix of intention and serendipity that is the signature of a cooperative universe. Over the course of her tragically interesting life, she had ample experience both with the spa and service industry and with spirits, ghosts, demons, and other entities. She had worked the front desk for naturopathic clinics, and thanks to plenty of her own interest-driven research had an encyclopedic knowledge of pharmaceutical medications and herbal remedies, as well as magick. All her life she had felt an intense connection to that which most could not see but were impacted and influenced by nonetheless. She had had her own circuitous, rambling journey over the years, pacifying various pernicious energies in her life and the lives of those close to her, and when as a young woman she'd more or less gotten a handle on her innate and atypical talents, she cultivated her own rich relationship with spirit guides and other entities from the astral realm, a domain and dimension of life perilously under-represented. And so you could say that Fey, with her unique set of proclivities, interests, and professional experience, was born for this, to manage and run a spa for ghosts.

Growing up in the suburban outskirts of Seattle as well as the city proper, Fey had passed by Lake Ballinger for many years, for the nascent decades of her life into the demands of adulthood. She had on more than one occasion foraged around the perimeter of the lake: willow bark and shoots, stinging nettle, oyster mushrooms, salmonberries, ocean-spray blossoms and pearly ever-lasting flowers, just some of the bounty of the pacific northwest. After years abroad from Cascadia - down in the Sierra Nevada range of California and a momentous, full circle sojourn to the desert in Arizona where she was born - Fey Ballantine had returned to her family home in Snohomish county, the next county up from the Seattle area's King county. Re-establishing herself in the Puget Sound, full of skills, knowledge, and calm confidence, Fey was gracefully entering her august years. She was content with her home life, where she grew herbs and extracted their medicine, made art and clothing. She produced a surplus of these things and sold them at the local farmer's market as well as online, and thus she was able to pay for her groceries, utilities, and other bills. Occasionally she would offer a class on any number of the different skills she'd grown proficient in over the years: make-up, fly-fishing, how to do your taxes. Herbalism of course. Her schedule was varied and completely her own. She was her own boss, and a boss in general. And she was happy. She was at peace.

She remained connected to 'the world' and news happenings, but in a distanced way, no longer emotionally invested in or affected by national or international politics. It had been a long journey, but she had finally found a 'home' within herself, and felt centered. All her life she would say she was never quite comfortable in her human body, but now, at this age and stage, she was okay with it. Those around her, whether casually passing her on the street or those who actually knew her could feel this centeredness of her's, could almost see it alter the air immediately around her, like the unhurried center of a storm. One day while having coffee with her good friend Mars Morrigan, they told her about an amazing opportunity that the state government was offering to the most qualified applicant.

"Oh my god, Fey, you won't frickin' believe this: Washington State is offering a grant to build, to create, a sanctuary for spirits."
  "Wooooow," she replied, "really?"
"Yup. 1.6 million dollars to purchase land and curate a space for our state's "restless deceased". Those without a proper home, lost, meandering and unsatisfied with their situation on the astral plane.'"
  "Holy…wow. Duuuuuude…"
"That's what the call for applicants on the state government's website literally says."
  "That is just…incredible."
They continued sipping their coffee and chatting, making each other laugh as they were wont to do. Around Fey's patio where they sat, the birds chirped and the squirrels and the chipmunks made their strange kind-of intense little noises as the late morning sun grew higher and bolder in the sky, heralding another gloriously sunny and temperate day of Western Washington's spring season. Together the two friends chomped on pickles

and tasty gluten-free sandwiches, whiling time away and enjoying each other's company.

For the rest of the day and into the next, Fey sat with that opportunity, the call from her state's government that she wouldn't have thought in a thousand years would've been a possibility. The day after her brunch and conversation with Mars, she was driving past Balinger Park at the top of the lake, and couldn't believe her eyes: a plot of land for sale on the small island in the middle of the lake. And wouldn't you know it: it was within the budget of the grant the government was offering. In her mind, an idea was forming. Something was coming together, like planets aligning. And opportunities like this, she knew, ought not to be ignored.

Two years later and her spa for ghosts had been up and running for several months, and had had a very lucrative first quarter, in fact. Lucrative how, exactly? Appreciative spirits spontaneously left her all sorts of things, including sometimes stacks of hundred dollar bills. From whence? This Fey did not ask, a selective non-investigation. She merely smiled to herself each morning when she stepped towards the offering circle in the spa's entranceway and saw what had appeared overnight.

While she still had her family home not far away, she lived on the island most of the time. Mars, who lived a touch northeast of Seattle, usually stayed over four nights a week, Thursday through Sunday, the busiest days at the spa. They would be away Monday through Wednesday, returning to the island Wednesday evening or Thursday morning with supplies and provisions from the mainland as well as special requests members of the spa asked for. The wants of the wandering dead were numerous; it was in their very nature, usually, to be sticking around for something - an object returned to them, a broken relationship mended - and this Mars executed with vigor. This was a role they had adopted with enthusiasm and a sense of honor on their days away from the spa: to be something of a detective and track things or people down for their deceased clientele. They kept track of their hours and were paid all the same.

The spa gradually came to life, so to speak, as Fey walked through it. It was during this, the first walkthrough of the day, that she began to set things up that had been turned down the night before. The spa's hours, catering towards spirits, were from 8pm to 4:30am. Sometimes Fey stayed awake through the night for the whole shift, other times she retired to her hut an hour or three before closing. She slept for as long or as little as she liked, and then simply enjoyed the space and the island during the day, sometimes with friends who'd come for a visit and perhaps work-trade to help out a bit, sometimes with students from the mainland she'd taken on who would visit her here and there for a lesson in magick or herbalism, but most of the time by herself, savoring her solitude. Islands, like towers, mountains, and caves, are special places to inhabit; they are natural focal points, places at which power and intention naturally concentrate. It isn't hard to go mad on an island by oneself, and it is easier, also, in such a place, to grow in both personal power and in one's understanding of the nature of things, what with the hustle and bustle and typically labyrinthine confusion of life and the proliferation of conflicting desires seemingly natural in an urban setting no longer an obscuring influence. What with the smokescreen of *maya* gone or minimized, or at least easier to spot. And so Fey, after waking up whenever she damn well pleased, would usually walk from her hut at the island's edge to the spa at its center, roughly a tenth of a mile. Among the first things she would notice would be the deep dark blue of the lake against the cerulean powder sky, with Cascadia's many shades of green set in between the two. This time of year she would drink in the bloom of the wildflowers growing amongst the lengthening grass, her narrow path, trodden daily, kept down and inviting of passage. The birdsong, becoming veritably symphonic in May, would drive out any irritating or anxious thoughts she might have woken up with. She would smile at the trees, leafing out pridefully or lengthening their evergreen tips, the new growth of which, light, green and eager, she might collect for medicine, for tea, snap off and gnaw on on the spot (pleasantly citrusy and bright), or simply admire and let be and not harvest *because* of how potent and beautiful they were.

After the jangling, creaking entry into the spa, after seeing with pride and a cold warmth in her heart the many offerings left by the previous night's pale patrons (sometimes straightforward and appreciated, like money, sometimes charmingly random like old dolls, candy, or single earrings), she would snap her fingers crisply and clap twice loudly to summon her imp helpers. They, small, dark, and many, tidy the place up, typically from 4:30-7am everyday. After a few hours break, they are called back to help set up, which they do eagerly for Fey, first collecting and putting away the offerings, and then turning on the soaking pools and ecto-sauna. The prize of the show, the spa's ecto-sauna was specially designed by Fey and other occultists for use by the incorporeal, utilizing negentropic energy produced by harnessing the 'cold energy' generated by employing Planck's isothermal-isobaric process in a vacuum in everdark. It was a complex, multi-disciplinary process that not many understood. But Fey did. And when a government official came up from Olympia to check out and report back on what the grant winner was doing (make sure it was following all the OSHA standards for spirits), they were confused, in awe, and somewhat frightened by what they found at the spa on Edmount Island. But Fey, confident, articulate, and charismatic, made sure the state official heard what they needed to hear, saw what they needed to see, and had all their boxes ticked to sign off on a positive report about the grant-funded spa-sanctuary and make Governor Robo-Inslee the 4th and his constituents happy.

Fey's imps moved around like small high-speed shadows. The crew was efficient and exactingly trained, though it was interesting (and for Fey, quite the relief) to realize that not very much sanitization was needed in a spa for ghosts. Humans, messy with their biology and so large as to be host organisms of the microscopic realm, demanded hard, anti-microbial sanitization, and especially in Western Washington, needed active mold prevention strategies for their buildings. Spirits, on the other hand, aren't affected by pathogenic bacteria, viruses or mold; they in fact enjoy cob-webs and dark, dank environments. And so all Fey usually had to do in the afternoon before the spa opened to its ghastly public was walk around with either sage or palo santo, with the windows open of course, to energetically sanitize the space. She preferred to think of this not as 'sanitizing' but as clearing any residual energy and restoring the spa to a more blank, neutral status before its guests arrived. The ecto-sauna was always on; its psychethermal, dark intelligence picked up on whether there were visitors inside of it, incorporeal or otherwise. It was time now, in the course of opening the spa, to check in with Sam in the mechanical room that was essential for the pools to work.

Fey walked to the back of the building where this room was to be found. Runed phasmophobic hydrostone, a material both inflammable and one ghosts could not pass through, outlined a space ten feet high, twenty feet long, and twelve feet wide. In this room lived another one of Fey's good friends who'd committed to helping her run the spa. In her previous life as a human with a body, Samantha Tehota was a successful facilities director and all-around pool systems and hydrotherapy wizard for a much-loved human spa in Seattle. After decades at that job, with its many ups and downs, frustrations and triumphs, Sam was glad to hear what her friend Fey was doing. When Sam made a blood oath with the mechanical room of her spa years ago, it proved very powerful and lasting, but it wasn't infallible. Things still happened on a fairly regular basis that baffled her, and over the years she had grown tired of this disconnect, this incomplete relationship with the mechanics of the facility she was charged with overseeing. A blood oath got her close, but not quite close enough to seamless communication and understanding with the pools and their filters and boilers, motors and pipes. When she approached Fey with the idea of merging with the plumbing and mechanics of her ghost spa, Fey did agree that would be a good idea, a best case scenario for an overseer of a hydrotherapy system, but wanted to make sure her friend felt this way for certain, was fully aware of what she was getting herself into and the lasting implications of this decision. She was about to commit herself to being soul-bound to a room and all that lay within it, to be master of this ten by twenty by twelve foot realm for as long as its foundation would stand. "Girl I know what I'm doing; I got this," said Sam, no slouch in the ways of magick herself. And so just before the spa was about to open, when everything was set up and ready to be tested out, Fey, Sam, and Mars performed the exacting and exhausting ritual required to bind Sam's soul to the mechanical room of the ghost spa. Sam's human body fell limply to the floor as a gust of energy pervaded the room like a small cyclone. Their hair and clothing fluttered, and loose objects around them like the candles and stones used to perform the ritual were blown out or knocked over. "OH YEAH!" said Sam, feeling a surge of indescribable power in her new, non-human form. "This is what I'm talking about! Woooow! I can see so much! It's all so clear! There's a problematic air bubble in this pipe over here," the pipe rattled and glowed, and Mars quickly went to work disassembling it and remedying the issue. "There's some sort of blockage in this pipe here," again, a tell-tale rattle and a green glow, obvious enough to her friends. "Oh it's the sealant. You guys applied too much and it dried in a clump that's partially blocking the flow of the pipe." Fey began to open that pipe, saw what Sam was talking about and started scraping away the surplus sealant glue. "This is uh-mazing," Sam said, a voice now coming from nowhere in particular but audible to all in the room. "I can see all the problems so clearly, because, it's like, I can FEEL them. Man. I'm glad I lived a life with a human body but this…this is something else. I should've done this years ago."

"If you had done this years ago at the spa in the city, you would've been bound there, and it would've been very, very hard to get you transferred over here," said Fey.

"Yeah…yeah, you're right. Okay other stuff: the sauna seems to be working fine."

"Thank the goddess, that was such a bitch to set up," Mars exclaimed.
"I think it's the first of its kind in like, the entire world," said Fey.

"Yeah, that's something. Would ya look at that?" answered Mars. At this, the two human friends laughed and laughed, and their friend who was now in essence a functional poltergeist laughed as well, a pleasant sourceless echo that filled the room.

And so on this day, as everyday, Fey checked in with Sam, who knew the workings of the spa amenities like the back of her hand, quite literally. It was easy, a perfect arrangement, because Sam always knew, intimately and down to the last detail, what was going on with the mechanics of the spa, exactly what and where something was wrong if there was anything wrong. "Good morning Fey, welcome to work," said Sam cheerfully, sounding from nowhere and still loving talking to her friends in her non-physical form. "Welcome to work Sam. It's four in the afternoon."

"Okay, okay. You know I have no sense of time anymore."
"I know, I know. How is everything today?"

"Not bad. There was an owl perched on top of me for three hours recently! I guess that was early this morning."

"Cool. How are the facilities?"
"Oh, yes…ummmmm doin' great! Pools are all good, boilers are good, it's so nice we don't have to worry about chlorine levels anymore."

"Yeah, ghosts don't give a fuck about chlorine."
"Not a single fuck."

"Very good, very good. Thank you Sam." Fey turned around and started to walk out the door.

"Hey Fey,"

"Yes Sam?"

"Would you uhhh come hang out with me later? It's not like I can go anywhere or do anything not related to this spa anymore."

"Of course. I'll be back to see you before we open tonight."

"And you'll come see me while we're open too, right?

"Of course. I appreciate you Sam."

Though the sun was still beaming in the sky when the spa opened that night, its patrons were used to it. Ghosts and other creatures of the night, crepuscular deer for instance, are well aware of the highly diurnal, sharply oscillating times of light and darkness in the north. The days grow long so quickly in May in Washington, it's like a fire of inspiration, after months of short, grey days, that can consume. Newcomers to the region may be overwhelmed by the sudden bursts of energy they start to feel, the wherewithal seemingly from nowhere to wake up with the birds and get out and do stuff, and as the lengthening days of spring grow into the towering days of summer, spread themselves thin socially, overpromise and overextend themselves, social backpay for so many days spent inside with only one other person or alone. At this point in her life, living on a small island on a small lake, Fey did not mind the time of year. Centered in herself, she did not allow herself to be influenced so much by the cosmos, or rather she did but on her own terms. She was the gatekeeper of herself: the gatekeeper, the gate, and the palatial city of cells beyond.

She assumed her place at the front desk, with all the quiet grace of someone who's doing something they've been doing for decades. To her left, her shadow imps scurried over, climbed on top of one another and formed into one, one large shadow-shape roughly hominid, without a face and with large black arms pointed at their ends, its dark featureless head pointed too. Formerly when working front desk jobs, Fey would walk over to the front door of the establishment, unlock it, open it, greet the guests who'd been standing outside oh so ready, roll out a carpet for them. Now, Fey did this all with a wave of her hand, with telepathy. In walked, or rather, floated, some usuals. "How are you today Fey?" asked the ghost of a man named Thomas Shipley.

"I'm well, Thom, how are you?"

"Good, good. Can't complain. Except for uh, y'know, fucking dying last year. Motherfucker not looking where he was going merging onto I-5. I was just minding my own business, heading down to banya for a schvitz, and what do I get? Collided with at high fucking speed. Fuck."

Fey, used to Thom's tirade and the disposition of the disgruntled dead in general, wasn't actively listening. She acknowledged his name on the check-in sheet for the day, which prompted Imp to gesture to the guest, in this case Thom, to enter the spa. But Thom, as usual, prattled on. "I mean, look, I don't *really* mind being a ghost, I think it's kind of fun actually, there's a lot I don't have to worry about any more, like rent or being politically correct, but the one thing I'm worried about is, who's taking care of my dog?"

"Your sister is."

"...really? You're sure of that?"

"Mhm, she updates me on occasion. The other day she let me know that she's doing well. At her checkup the other day she got a shot, took it like a trooper, and the vet noted that she'd gained…what was it…1.25 pounds. Enjoy your soak." Fey finishes by saying as Imp steps forward and reaches out a dark shadowy tentacle towards Thom.

"Thanks, I appreciate it," says Thom as he moves from the lobby to the spa floor, half of his own volition and half through intimidation on the part of the hulking black creature increasingly interested in him. Fey has had this same interaction with him every day Thom has come in. He'll get it eventually, she thinks. Ghosts can be stubborn. They sort of are by definition.

The smoldering sun lowered towards the horizon, yellow into orange into burning red, with all manners of blue and purple dancing around and opposite, the spectrum of color perceivable to the human eye splayed out across the canvas of the sky. What the spirits entering and leaving the ghost spa saw, we may very well not know until we join them. Occasionally Fey took a break from checking in her ghost patrons and would walk around the spa, making sure everything was running smoothly. And indeed on this night, like practically every night since the spa had been in operation, things were. She stepped inside the mechanical room, saying "very good" to Sam and spending a few minutes with her. She walked over to the tea lounge and topped up the mugwort tea. The butter platter was always in need of replenishing, even though all spirits entering the spa signed forms explicitly banning "activities pertaining to or resembling insatiable hunger and/or unquenchable thirst." Fey didn't want to exclude ''hungry ghosts' from the spa-sanctuary, but she did want to put a clamp down on unsustainable appetites like that, for no one can, by definition, afford to feed or ever satisfy a hungry ghost. The faire in the tea lounge changed on a rotating basis to accommodate spirit snack preferences from around the world. Sometimes, scone-like currant soul cakes were put out. Sometimes beer and pretzels. Sometimes it was desserts with ube or smyrna figs or persian mulberries. Pumpkin and turnip jack-o-lanterns adorned the spa during Samhain, and some ghost patrons just loved hiding in those, attempting to spook whatever humans might be working in or visiting the spa. Once a month Mars would bring blood sausage and bone broth back from Seattle, and the ghosts would have a field day.

Just as she finished sprucing up the tea lounge, Fey heard a commotion coming from the lobby. She walked down the stairs and back over there quickly and purposefully, and saw Imp with five tentacles out attempting to contain several ghosts in conflict, yelling, hissing, shrieking and howling at each other. Imp turned its featureless black head three hundred and sixty degrees to face whoever had just entered into the lobby from the spa, and then, seeing it was Fey, cocked its head to the side, uncertain of how to proceed with this tense situation and imploring Fey to help. Before she said or did anything, she sized up the situation: she saw three human ghosts, a water spirit in the form of a bipedal dragon standing eight feet tall, and a large rat-like-looking ghoul. The three human ghosts were yelling at them in English with fisticuffs raised, saying things like, "Why don't you two go back to the sewer you came from?!" and "No vermin allowed!", while the dragon hissed loudly and the rat ghoul shrieked with anger, bearing claws and fangs, clearly ready to fight.

"What's going on here?" Fey asked aloud, drawing all attention to herself. The flailing of arms, murid legs and pads, and the hissing of forked tongues stopped in an instant, and seven more sets of eyes were on Fey, taken aback by the powerful living entity that had just announced itself. In addition to the five spirits in conflict there were two others hanging out in the lobby waiting to be checked in. At this, Fey felt slightly embarrassed. "Actually, hold on a sec. Let me check these two in. Thank you for waiting so patiently; my apologies for the disturbance."

"Just another day in paradise, eh Fey?" asked Roger, one of the non-aggressor human ghosts, jokingly. "I think this might be the purgatorio," said Dave, the other one waiting to be admitted. Smiling knowingly, they walked into the spa together. "If not the inferno," Fey heard Roger say faintly as the two disappeared into the spa.

One of the three human ghosts spoke first: "They tried to cut us in line. We'd been waiting patiently and then they just show up and…"

"You lie, foolisssshhh human," said the water spirit, "we did not even come in together. I know not this sssssspirit, but now it ssssseeemsss we are bound, by fate and inssssult."

The rat-spirit, who did not speak English, hissed and shrieked furiously with spittle flying everywhere in its attempts to explain its take on the matter. The rat-spirit was not dumb, however, and in its attempt to express itself it pointed to the human ghosts and then to the dragon and then itself. The water spirit, a naga, took up the task. "Thesssse ones were checking in alright, and when they ssssaw me walk in, and then our friend here, they ssssstarted to laugh amongssst themssselves, and were even ssso bold asss to call usss out. They thought we were a pair fresssh from the sssewer and made fun of usss."

"Not true!"

"We did no such thing!"

"Imp?" asked Fey, "What did you hear? What did you see?" At this, Imp dutifully extended yet another tentacle over to Fey, gently wrapping around her wrist and ending with a soft tip in the palm of her hand. Fey closed her eyes and saw the scene play out as Imp had seen it just a minute or two ago: the three human ghosts had come in first, all together. They began checking in with Imp. None of them had been here before; they were all newcomers. Then in walked the naga, the dragon-like water spirit, standing behind the ghosts, towering above them. Then in walked the rat-ghoul, scraping its left leg along the floor as it walked, an old injury, Fey noticed.

First, one of the ghosts looked back, then a second one and soon after him, the third. Just as the naga said, they snickered amongst themselves, eyes bulging, failing to suppress their laughter. Finally one of them said, "Look mates, they must be redoing the sewer lines today and these two musta got flushed out!" The three ghosts laughed and laughed, the naga looked appalled for a moment and then looked angry, while the rat-ghoul, sensing it was being laughed at, flew into a rage right away and dove at the human ghosts. Imp caught it in mid-air with an outstretched tentacle, and the sense-memory playback stopped. Fey opened her eyes and looked at all involved once again, the offenders and the offended. First she spoke to the three ghosts: "I'm sorry but due to your actions I'm going to have to ask you three to leave the spa. You've verbally assaulted other patrons here and made them feel unsafe. This place is a sanctuary, where the deceased come to find rest and peace, and as such harassment of any kind is not tolerated."

"This is ridiculous," one ghost said.
"We didn't do anything! They started harassing us!" said another.

"Patently untrue," said Fey. "We have it on record that you three were the instigators of the conflict. Look, I know the afterlife can be rough. I may be among the living, but that's not to say I'm unfamiliar with your particular plane of existence. There are places to rage and places to terrorize, in which such behavior would be totally valid. This, however, is not one of those places."

"We're sorry," one of them finally admitted. "Can we come back again some other time?"

"That's to be determined. I will reach out for further correspondence and a final decision on the matter. But for now, please leave." The ghosts looked at each other, looked at the dark shadowy creature she had referred to as 'Imp', and then finally at her, the living human woman, as if sizing her up and seeing if they could take her, defy her and do as they pleased, run amok throughout the spa perhaps. They saw a fire in her, first glowing in her eyes, and then, as the seconds passed, an actual green flame growing out of her hands. Fey looked calm, intensely so. It was clear to all around that she had full control of the room, and that she could probably take all the spa patrons on at once if she had to. The ghost trio in error had seen enough. With a mix of waving, bowing, and other supplicatory gestures, they backed out of the spa. The fire in her hands and in her eyes died down. She looked over at the naga and the rat-spirit and said, "My sincerest apologies. We strive for our spa to be restful and joyful, and those guys were jerks. Your entries today will be comped, so please don't worry about leaving an offering on your way out. You two have been through enough. Please, enjoy your time here.

"Thankssss," said the water-spirit naga. "Shshkagwhash!" said the rat-spirit, nodding its unsightly head in a show of appreciation. Once the spa doors had closed behind them, Fey asked Imp, "Wanna take a break?" Imp paused for a few seconds, conflicted, perhaps thinking…and then vigorously nodded its head 'yes'.

As the evening wore on, more and more satisfied ghost guests left the spa, and the offering pile had started to grow, though this wasn't something Fey really paid attention to the sight of. As it was in a specially devised chalk-lined circle, there was no risk of supernatural theft. Moreover, most beings that passed through the spa doors understood and respected its sanctity, the offering circle's being a way of saying 'thanks' to the human realm that had made their spa experience possible. And though the spa industry - whether for the living or the dead, it did not matter - had its share of unsavory interactions as par for the course, this line of work also had plenty of lovely, inspiring interactions that made it all worthwhile. A couple of old ghost grannies were laughing and smiling together as they were leaving the spa that night. They looked refreshed and sublimely happy, as happy as a ghost could look really. "Thank you dearie," one of them said to Fey with a smile as they waltzed joyfully past the front desk. Another one paused, looked Fey in the eyes and said with gravity, "Thank you, truly. This night has been so great. We all feel so happy and light and young again. The spa has really lifted our spirits, hehehe!" she laughed witchfully.

"That makes me happy to hear," Fey replied, "Come back anytime. Have a good night ladies!"

"Eehhehehehehheeee!!" their laughter, continuing on as they left the building, could be heard prominently from outside.

In the wee hours of the morning, the witching hour to be more exact, Fey left the front desk for her break. She walked through the spa, spying patrons, regulars and newcomers alike, having a riotously good time. Just like a spa for folks alive, there were moments, minutes of loud congenial conversation and camaraderie shared across the spa, in the pools and in the sauna, new friendships forged and existing bonds strengthened, as well as times of quiet, of deep relaxation and a silent, shared sentiment and trust in the healing powers of quietude. As Imp held down the front desk ably for the next half hour, Fey glided past the utterly unique healing environment she had brought into manifestation. She was not a particularly prideful person, but in this moment she did feel a welling-up of joy and satisfaction from it all. She and some regulars exchanged smiles and nods as she walked about. She checked the tea room one more time and put out more butter. Then she headed into the mechanical room. "It's that time of the night, isn't it?" asked Sam. "You know it," Fey responded.
 "I've already got her nice and warmed up for you."
"Sam, you're the best."
 "I know. Another day, another slay! Get in there, enjoy."

Fey opened a small square door on the floor. She took the ladder down, down, down, step by careful step, until she found her footing on the earthen floor she liked so very much. A few more steps and a thick slab stone door in front of her opened inward. As soon as Fey walked in, the door swung shut behind her. A steamy, cavernous, earthy dream, the subterranean steam room was Fey's own personal spa amenity. A sweet floral scent pervaded the air; she changed what herbs she had in the steam room as she pleased. For the duration of her break, Fey would forget about time, would forget about everything. Sam would gently let her know if the front desk needed her. Whatever concerns she had left in her storied life would melt away. She would not become anything more than she already, remembering her unity with Gaia, with Earth, with Mother. Another night passeth at the ghost spa, and the moon grew full.

An Enigmatic Loop

Mark Perdue wakes up bleary-eyed and under a cloudy sky, blinking, gasping, and for a few stunned moments, choking on his own saliva. Coming to dumbly, it was as if his eyes had forgotten how to shutter and perceive, as if his throat had amnesia and his epiglottis had Alzheimers.

He stands up and feels stiff in just about every part of his body - his neck and lower back especially - and looks around. He is in an alleyway, classic-like with the concrete not flat but softly angled so rain amassing from all the buildings and dropping down does not collect and flood but empties into the storm drains that appear throughout the alley's middle, like bones in a filet of salmon or rockfish. Working through the strain in his neck (in fact, marveling at it a bit as he does) he looks around, takes stock of where he is, for he has woken up not knowing where he is and wonders how he got there and why his body has racked up this surprising and unusual tab of pain. He has come to on a pile of cardboard. A makeshift bed it seems. There is an overstuffed dumpster to his right, and an oval puddle to his left. The smell of the dumpster sinks in now, stinging his nostrils and surpassing his bodily pain as the most jarring thing in his sensory experience. The air is cool and moist - that's humidity in late Autumn for you - and the glistening, wet concrete of the alleyway tells him (along with the puddle) that it had rained recently, last night most likely. Yet he is completely dry, save for a little blood he tastes in his mouth. Wonder: what is the effective recycling rate of us drinking back in our own blood? How much heme iron and plasma do we get back versus what we lost when it trickled or spurt out from our sensitive flesh?

The scent of the garbage and the sensation of the fresh, moist air are waking him up, something like a combo of smelling salts and cold water...something like that, and he starts to move, a bit unsteadily at first, past the puddle now providing a bath to a few pigeons. Curiously, he walks right by them, rather close, and they don't seem to care; they don't fly away, nervy, precautious calling-card of most birds. It is as if they do not notice him, as if he isn't there. In his raw and blunted state, he isn't impressed much by this, barely notices it, in fact. But consider it for yourself, can you imagine approaching a group of small, flighty birds, getting closer and closer, and them *not* flying away? As if egging you on boldly, "Come on biped, come on. Get a little closer whydontcha?"

It hurts to move, to walk. It hurts to think, like his brain's running on spent oil. The mystery of how he got to where he is right now - dots unconnected - doesn't bother him as much as the pain in his body and the dullness of his brain, something like a hangover, dehydration, head trauma and withdrawal from some heavily adulterated black-market smack. Mark has experienced each of these rude awakenings in his time, but never all at once like this. The pain is potent, and there's a slight ringing in his ears that he begins to notice comes and goes.

As he stumbles down the alley he creates a mental checklist, very simple and direct, that he must complete to undo his stupor, to dissipate the fog he's woken up into: he needs hydration (a pint of mineral water with a good half a lime), he needs coffee (today, a quad shot, at least, maybe spring for a Turkish), a hot shower (he can take that back at his apartment...hopefully he's woken up in the same city), and something relaxing like a sauna, a massage, or an acupuncture session. Hell, on a day like today, maybe all three. Unusual times call for unusually restorative measures. And then, he figures, body, mind and spirit restored, then he can work on figuring out what the hell happened to have him waking up here, like this.

Nearing the end of the alleyway, he runs his hands along his legs, for the first time since waking up feeling for his pockets. Nothing. His stomach rumbles and he can't help but laugh to himself. He is really, truly empty.

Seattle's overcast skies give way to a gentle rain. Par for the course. It's the rain you see before you feel, so slight, so limp is this sort of drizzle. Seattle doesn't get too many hard rains a year, and thunderstorms remain a distinct rarity, but this sort of precipitation, weak and persistently intermittent, is common. During this time of year in the northwest, the days are short, the skies are grey, the roads, sidewalks, fences, telephone and streetlight poles glisten slightly with perma-wetness, the ground remains soggy, and everything mechanical outside slowly corrodes, while everything structural slowly, if unattended to, grows moss. The denizens of these places - Seattle, Portland, Vancouver - must make their own sunshine, or else flounder into a vitamin D-less depression.

Hands in empty pockets, Mark walks up to the intersection and gets his bearings. 37th and Olive. Okay, he thinks to himself, I'm twenty-five minutes from home by foot. Without his phone or wallet he can't get a ride, no taxi, no Uber, no app-activated electric scooter or bike. No friend he can call to pick him up. Even though knows how much he has in the bank, it's useless without an intermediary device to retrieve it. Even though he knows several people that would stop whatever they were doing to come and pick him up, it's useless without his electronic rolodex, his practically necessary pocket companion. How's that for technology improving convenience, increasing ease: we are all now effectively boarded off from our own hard-earned capital if we lack the paradoxically high-tech and ubiquitous hand-held device to withdraw it, to permit us access to what's ours. A powerful technological middle-man, one that has become essential to all but life's most basic functions, a utility that someone else has made, that a company owns and loans to you, dictating ominously nebulous terms of service so dense as to be dissuasive from fully evaluating, so expansive and uninteresting as to buck our trained short-leash attention spans from even beginning to investigate the extent of what we're agreeing to by their usage. This becomes today's societal show of faith en masse: implicit trust in the benevolent or at least neutral, transparent intention of others, not individuals but companies, faceless and detached, commodifying our attention spans faster than smallpox swept through the New World.

How helpless we are without our things, he thinks, walking past crushed energy drink cans, a half-eaten package of supermarket sushi now being picked apart and finished by crows, and a grey-green tent with a blue tarp over it. Not an uncommon sight in this town: someone outpriced and down on their luck, making their home on the sidewalk. Squatting publicly is almost legal here, until the city decides it's not, until your encampment is found to be on or near the site of a new apartment complex. Hearing some movement, some rumbling coming from within the tent as he walks by, he feels lucky to have the meager space he does, small studio apartment it is, and the job he does, however boring and menial it is. Come to think of it, he's not even sure what day of the week it is; he very well could be missing work right now. Oh heavens, he thinks sarcastically, laughing to himself a bit, levity much appreciated on a day like today, whatever will the meat department of his Safeway do without him? Sling cheap chicken and overpriced beef and lamb all the same.

As he reaches his apartment on the intersection of Martin Luther King Way and Columbia Street, he begins to anticipate the conversation he's about to have with his landlord. She lives on the first floor of the old building, and is, lucky for him, generally pretty chill. A relaxed landlord, another blessing he can count. By now he has grown used to the bodily pain he woke up with today, and is craving coffee and calories. Relishing in the familiar movement his hand makes as he punches in his passcode to get into the building, 7138, he is comforted by its familiarities: the weight and heft of the entryway door, the smell of the first floor - a combination of mold and some perfume, plug-in misters to cover it up, something the average person or new tenant might raise an eye at, but to him, used to it, comforting. Especially today.

The colors of the carpeted floor, red, tan, brown, with little green accents, a 'Persian rug' of a hallway carpet, along with the striped tan walls, let him know he is home. He sees Janice ('Jan') Rhyner at the front desk, his landlord. Very convenient, he thinks; she's right here, no borrowing phones and attempts to track her down needed. As usual, she doesn't notice or greet the individual who just walked into her building (not a great trait for a property owner, perhaps). When she's seated at her desk like this she's usually either reading or looking at something on her computer. Today, it's a book, he notices as he approaches her, trying to actually make a little noise so as not to startle her. He puts his weight down pronouncedly to sound the wooden floor. It looks like she's reading something called 'Antecedents of Dwemer Law'. Strange.

"Jan. Hiya. I'm locked out. Need your help."
"Mmokay Mark, be right with you." She hasn't looked up from her book yet; no doubt she is finding a break in the page to stop, the next page, the next paragraph, wherever makes sense. Jan's not one to gush customer-service. Mark inhales a full, deep breath, looks at the hallway to the left of the desk, his left, her right, and looks back at her. Exhales. She inserts the bookmark and sets the book down.

"Mark, what happened to you? Were you mugged?" she asks semi-seriously. Understandable. Mark knows he doesn't look like the picture of health right now, can feel it even though he hasn't seen his reflection today. Or has he? Didn't he spy his quaking reflection in the undulating puddle he walked past as he left the alley this morning? He screws his eyes up to the upper-left, thinking. Vague memories of a liquid mirror, something like the bad guy from Terminator 2. But he can't place it for sure.

"Uh hello, earth to Mark...you wanna get back into your apartment and sleep it off or what?" Jan takes the lead, walking out from her desk. The jingling key ring she's holding wakes Mark from his reverie. Jeez, he thinks to himself, I really need something...a cold shower and a strong brew. Sounds good. Coming right up. He follows her somnambulantly down the hall and up the stairs to the second floor. 218. Mark's home sweet home.

"Thanks Jan," he says "I'll make sure to rest up good today, screw my head back on,"

"You do that Mark," she says, with a little more concern in her voice this time. "And let me know if you find your key or not. I'll have to take something from your deposit if you've lost 'em. I don't know what it'll be...just let me know and I'll get a quote on copying a new key for you if need be. Shouldn't be much, ten, twenty bucks at the most."

"Thanks Jan. They've got to be around here..."

"I hope they are. Otherwise someone out there's got access to your place...oof that might mean we'll hafta change the lock...oof."

"I'll let you know. I have a feeling they're in here."

"You really don't remember? What were you up to last night? Did someone slip you something?"

"Ha," he hadn't considered that. "Nah," he says, trying to smile, trying to laugh slightly in order to diffuse this interaction. But truth be told, he doesn't know for sure. He thanks her again, walks in and closes the door on her, a concerned look stuck on her face.

I'll be alright, he thinks, I'm home now, I can reset and get back in control. But as he advances into the kitchen, somewhere between passing the sink and seeing an unwashed wine glass and tea mug in it and placing his hand on the refrigerator door, he's struck with a strange, discomforting sense of deja vu. He hears a loud and shocking sound, like glass breaking, and tastes metal in his mouth. Then he hears a ringing in his ears - shrill, loud, softer now, gone. I'll be alright, he tries to think loudly, pushing all the other thoughts out of his mind, crowding them out for mental space. I'll just have to fake it till I make it, he thinks. I've been here before.

Next to the glass and ceramic mug in the sink, sits his phone, wallet, keys and pocket knife in a tidy stack. Something he would do, arrange them like that, only not there by the sink. Strange. Whatever. He opens his fridge and takes out some carbonated mineral water. It came all the way from a spring in the Italian Alps, across an inland sea, an ocean, and a continent to him. For his lips, for his gullet. He should feel special, count that among his blessings. He grabs a lime from the basket on top of his refrigerator, slices it and squeezes a segment into his water. Nice, he thinks as he notices his small tub of raspberry flavored electrolyte powder, forgot about this. He dashes a spoonful into his glass, hears the sizzle as it meets the carbonation, swirls it and knocks it back. The bite of the seltzer, the sweetness of stevia and the acidic edge from the lime: hydration perfected. He sets up his moka pot, turning the stovetop burner on low, and heads into the shower. The hot water is revitalizing, bringing him to the next level of wakefulness that only submersion or being doused in water can, that daily ablution holy without us calling it so. But then it hits him again, briefly this time: he hears glass shatter, tastes metal and sees stars, buzzing, ringing, feels a sense of deja vu. How strange: recurrent deja vu. Must mean something. Something he doesn't quite have the desire or the courage to investigate right now. Then he feels the sting of shampoo in his eyes, remembers he's got coffee on the burl, finishes up and steps out. He dries himself off with the royal blue towel he's had for at least a decade, still holding up, and runs a brush through his hair. Half-decent now, he thinks, catching his reflection for a moment before going over to his dresser to put on a fresh pair of clothes. He's not sure if a single wash cycle will purify the clothes he came in with, woke up wearing, slept in and did whatever he did last night in. He doesn't know whether to hang onto them for a few rinses, bury them or burn them. It wouldn't be right to give them away, feeling about them as he does. That would be like passing on bad juju. And no one likes bad juju.

He reaches his kitchen just in time to catch his moka pot beginning to hiss. Into his favorite mug, one that says "South Dakota" near the top and has a pretty wildlife scene set around it of ducks and pheasants flying out from the brush of a creek. Pretty as the scene is, it's kind of like it's seen from the perspective of you, the hunter, the way those birds have made a splash and a rustle as they flap their wings intensely to fly away. He watches the crema of his coffee swirl as the steam flies away. Rich and dark. Gusto crema.

Memory is a funny thing. It's not straightforward or necessarily truthful even - it's a take. When you remember something, you're only recalling your perspective of it. We don't see things from a bird's eye view; even if we did, that would just be from the perspective of another animal, one that we think tends to see things from *above*, as if that were somehow closer to omniscience. But then that only tells you more about our perception, doesn't it? What we, as animals ourselves, following a certain logic that originates from the strengths and weaknesses of our senses and in line with the patterns we tend to notice, see, or fabricate; the way we make sense of the gaps in what we see, the way we connect the dots. Which is nurture *and* nature, nurture being nature in long form, played out over eons of evolution, thousands of successive generations learning from and adapting to the conditions present in the petri dish Earth. Scientists are implicitly faithful in the security of their variables and controls, unquestioning of certain long established axioms, handed down to them from on high, religiously devout to the beings whose shoulders they stand on. Listen to a hundred human beings talk about the concert they went to last night: do you learn more about the concert, or about the similarities and differences of those hundred human souls?

It's this sort of thinking that coffee stimulates in Mark. If he's not channeling his caffeinated brain into a task, it channels itself into philosophical musings. Imagine if the Greeks, the Romans, the Han Dynasty had access to coffee. How might the artwork of the Tlingit be different if they did? Would it've made the Blackfeet or the Lakota Sioux even fiercer? Maybe Custer's Last Stand would've been somewhere else. What if the Mayans had been drinking coffee? They likely had their own stimulants. Did Beethoven have coffee? Did Bach? Creativity unleashed. Creativity unhinged.

Well, Mark realizes about himself, I am certainly more awake now. Certainly more alive. Brain's online. Time's as good as any to grab a few essentials and hit the road. Get going on this quest to recuperate and figure out how last night brought him to this morning. It's Friday; he doesn't have work today, fortunately. He checks his fridge: eggs, ground beef, miscellaneous fermented vegetable matter...he doesn't feel like hanging around and cooking a meal, he wants to keep up the forward momentum. He grabs a small triangular wedge of goat cheese (it's raw dairy, paprika rubbed into and permeating its rind), and begins to eat it as he walks out the door. Quick pocket check: phone, keys, wallet, pocketknife, and he is complete. Time for a massage, and he knows just the place.

The rain has not lifted. The gloom continues to blanket the sky greyly, and all underneath it continue to be exposed to the subtle misting of the terrarium Cascadia. Flying into or out of the pacific northwest this time of year, it is clear: this is a climatologically distinct zone; the ocean gales and hydraulic outlooks trapped into a certain area flanked by mountains makes it so. The mountains - the Cascades and Coastal ranges - are because long ago different tectonic plates started to collide, decided they wanted to inhabit the same space, and their friction gave rise to mountains, bulbous and beneficent planetary acne. And thus, Seattle, Vancouver, and Portland are the way they are. Further up the coast, cities like Prince Rupert, Ketchikan, and Juneau sit right up against these tall coastal mountains, catching the precipitation of the Pacific's hydrological cycle year-round. In places like this, someone who's lived there for a while is appropriately referred to as a 'mossback'.

Mark, now equipped with the essentials of functional personhood in the 21st century, drives himself to his favorite place to get a massage: New You in the Columbia City neighborhood. After spending a classic six minutes orbiting the spa to find a parking spot, he parallel parks himself into a cramped space and walks a block back to get to New You. It's the smiles of the people you happen across that kindle the fire, the warmth, the sun inside this time of year. The lack of exterior sun, of vitamin D (which apparently is more an exogenous hormone than a true vitamin) has us withdrawn, pruning our social interactions into brief and tender head-nods, quick, curt yes's, thanks', sure's and you got its', preservations of energy as we wait for the riotously (by comparison) outgoing eruption of sociality and extroversion inextricably tied to summer's long, sunny days. And if during the winter someone is caught being less than enthusiastic, if a store's employee's face says I'd rather be home right now and I'm here today simply putting in the hours until I can be, we Cascadians understand. We get it. We are not unlike plants, preserving our energy inwardly for a good chunk of the year. If some joy can be brought out from within and your torch can help keep someone else's going, whether by smile or compliment or silently cheerful presence, that is a victory of sorts. You've proven yourself a successful crucible in sublimating the unique energetic landscape and seasonal rhythm of a temperate coastal maritime climate closer to the north pole than the equator.

That is exactly what Mark gets as he walks in the door. Sheila always greets him and all her customers with a smile. No one besides her close friends and family knows this, but it's because she's grateful to be here, grateful to be alive let alone running a business. Her parents narrowly escaped the Khmer Rouge, fleeing Cambodia in the 70's to land in Seattle. By the skin of their teeth, by the squeak of their dumpling did they make it out alive, bringing their little girl (soon to be dubbed with an English name) with them. Thousands of customers have passed in and out the doors of her family's business not knowing their story, not knowing the reason deep down for her indefatigable smile. Not them, not Mark either. However, he appreciates it as he settles into the first room on the left and is greeted by his massage therapist Cindy. She knows exactly where to spend the forty-five minutes he's bought, exactly the pressure to apply. Today though, he asks for more pressure than usual when she gets to his lower back, and again on his neck and shoulders. She wonders why (he does feel tighter than usual) but her sense of professionalism and even more so her imperfect English keep her from asking any questions. She is clean, confidential efficiency at work. A speed bump here, a knot undone there, the muscle fibers and fascia relent and lengthen. Growing deeply relaxed, Mark almost falls asleep. Cindy and the light spa music playing in the background have put his brain into a theta state. He is calm, and his physical pain has all but faded away.

Suddenly he realizes the massage is over. A quick, quiet, "all done, thank you," and Cindy's left the room. He sits up after a moment, relaxation-dazed, stretching, slight grunt of satisfaction. It is only when he stands up, his vertebrae stacking, that he remembers his back pain. Still there, though less so. And then it hits him: he hears a loud and shocking sound, like glass breaking, and tastes metal in his mouth. Then he hears a ringing in his ears - shrill, loud, loud, LOUD...softer now, softer still, gone...

In spite of this, he keeps on. Must keep the momentum going, he thinks yet again. It's becoming a mantra for him he knows he must follow, 'just keep going', don't think, don't feel, just move, just do, lest he slide down into an emotional darkness he knows he's capable of descending into, a familiar place, a blend of aimlessness, incompetence, and helplessness. Without saying another word, he pays for his massage, tips Cindy, and walks out. In walks another customer, and Sheila smiles once again.

Mark is hungry. But before satisfying that need, he decides to do what's better done on an empty stomach than a recently-made-full one: banya. Not just a session in a sauna, but the full on hot, cold, hot, cold experience that is banya, the Russian word for that high heat sauna and cold water combo of an experience. There is one he goes to on occasion, right in the middle of town, not far from the Space Needle. Now that he has his phone, he calls them to check their availability...and they can take him in the very next hour block, which is in fifteen minutes. Perfect he thinks, and even says on the phone with the banya employee. And he's in. Simple as that. Looks like he's got time to get some spring water from a store somewhere on the way. This is what he loves about the city: ease of access and amenities; the ability to rapidly formulate plans and get a bunch of different things done in a day; so much going on at once in an urban setting, so many options and potential outings clamoring for your attention and your dollar.

He starts his 2003 Toyota Celica and drives the eight minutes it takes to get from New You to Belka e Strelka, the Russian-style sauna house. With red lights and a little midday congestion - people on their lunch break - it takes him twelve. He parks in their cramped, diagonal, nose-in-only lot in the alley behind the building and walks briskly inside. Didn't have time for the spring water, he remembers suddenly. Oh well, they have water here. They have lots of water here. At the front desk is someone he hasn't seen before. A new hire, he concludes. The new staff member does take an extra minute to check him in, and his rote vocalization of the rules and recommendations of the facility comes off scripted and somewhat less smooth than some of the more seasoned staff that have checked him in before. He'll get it down soon enough, Mark thinks to himself. Mark even smiles as he thanks the one who checked him in, handed him his locker key, sandals and towels. He did not ask his name. Mark changes quickly in the locker room and enjoys the warm downpour of the shower as it hits him. Our affinity for warm water, he muses, gotta be from the womb. On some level we all miss that womb-time, that warm wombic embrace where everything was provided for us and there was nothing for us to do except be nourished and grow; we just had to *be* to realize our potential then, and nothing more. No posturing, no competition. Nothing to figure out, no problems to solve. Those were the days.

Out on the spa floor and in his bathing suit (he usually keeps one in his car for trips here or to the beach), towel in hand, Mark grabs a cup with his free hand and fills it with filtered water the spa provides. The cup looks like clear plastic, but it is made of compostable material, of course. This is Seattle, after all. He drains an entire cup and fills it up again. Gotta stay on top of hydration when there's sauna involved. As he walks into the high-heat sauna, he begins to hear the ringing in his ears again. No, no, he thinks. Go away. Sitting on the highest and hottest bench, he closes his eyes, less-than-consciously tightens nearly all his features and attempts to ride it out, or rather drive it out, whatever's wrong with him, whatever's been following him around today. He hears other people coming into the sauna, talking, leaving, back and forth carefree and unaware of the quiet, close-eyed man sitting up top by himself grimacing at what he's going through.

It doesn't get any worse. Miraculously, the ringing stops this time short of the shell-shock, grenade-detonation-esque fever pitch it's gotten to throughout the day today. Thank goodness, Mark thinks. Thank me for taking care of myself like a goddamn adult. I'm getting over this, getting through this. Hallelujah.

A few more increasingly sweaty minutes and Mark steps out of the sauna, its comely wooden door swinging softly shut behind him, a comforting and familiar thing. Interesting how we tend to either adore or despise that which doesn't change, he thinks to himself briefly. Thought stops as he steps into the cold plunge, sinks, fans his hands to keep himself submerged for a few seconds more. Just as the brainfreeze starts, he relents and rises head first out of the forty-six degree water like a bear out of a freezing mountain stream. Extreme temperatures bring out our animal nature. Extremes in general do this. He shakes his head and wipes his face with his almost numb hands, steps over to the edge of the pool and climbs out. He downs his cup of water, can't help but "ahhh" in satisfaction and dispenses himself another. Then he goes back into the sauna. For the next hour he follows this circuit: sauna, cold plunge, big sip of water. The holy trinity of hydrotherapy. And it works its magic on him, or its science as we say nowadays. The science works on him, refreshing his circulatory system, promoting detoxification, calming inflammation. Not magic, science.

By the time Mark's checking out of the sauna house, there's someone else at the front desk. Either the newbie's shift is over or he's taking a break. "Thank you," says Mark. "Have a good rest of your day," says the person working the front desk. "You as well," says Mark as he walks out the front door, not bothering to look back. You as well.

When he gets back into his car he checks his phone reflexively and sees a text from his friend. "Pho?" asks his friend Haydn. "Pho" Marks texts back. "Pho sure". The puns that delightful and nourishing Vietnamese soup lends itself towards are many, and people and businesses don't hold back. "See you at Pho King in 15," comes Haydn's reply. Mark knows the place, of course. They go here fairly regularly - 'they' plural and 'they' singular; Haydn identifies as non-binary and often wears a "They/Them" pin to let others know.

It is good to sup the soup: in general, after sauna, after a noxious night out. Soup meticulously simmered, with bones, herbs, meat and tendons, is a veritable panacea. Chicken soup, the old Jewish penicillin, Mark remembers as he pulls into a parking space in front of the dingy restaurant. When you arrive at a place to consume pho and see that the decor and general aesthetic is dingy and worn with time, you know you're at the right kind of place for good, authentic pho made without cutting corners. The old way, the right way. Without cups of sugar to mask a lack of depth. For Mark and Haydn (who's walked in a minute after he did), there is no need to look over the menu, and the server who knows them knows this too. Still, not assuming every last detail, she waits for them to say:
"Beef special please," - Mark
"Chicken and tofu please," - Haydn
  "Okay, one beef special and one chicken and tofu, double protein," - the server, so that Haydn's aware they'll be charged extra for the second protein.
  "Thank you," Mark and Haydn chime together. Haydn's aware. Haydn's been aware for twenty something visits to this place. The server walks away and Mark says with a smile, "Double protein eh? You trying to get swole Haydn?"
  "Veg protein and animal protein, just covering all my bases."
"Good, good."

A few long seconds pass. In that time the two friends hear the tv mounted on the wall playing the local news and the bell of the door opening, announcing someone's coming or going.

"What've you been up to, Mark? It's a day off for you, right?"
  "It is a day off, and an off-day too."
"Oh yeah? Safeway been working you hard?"
  "It's not that so much as…" Mark trails off, looks away from Haydn, away from their table for a moment as he begins to hear that damned ringing in his ears, low but consistent. Trying to fend off upset at its return, he struggles to pick up where he left off, finish a damn sentence with intelligence for once today.
  "It's not that so much as I just woke up today in pain."
"Oh?" Haydn puts in, attempting to keep up the momentum of the now troubling conversation. "Physical pain? Emotional pain? What's up?" Haydn can now tell that something is up, truly up. Though he didn't look it at first, they can tell by how Mark's conversing that something is amiss.

"I just sorta woke up out-of-sorts today, generally and all-around out-of-sorts. Physical pain yes, though the massage I got earlier helped. Banya helped."
  "Good, good," Haydn likes and visits the sauna-house too.
"Uhh…" Mark rallies, not wanting to get Haydn too concerned. He certainly won't be telling them about where and how he woke up this morning. But he realizes he can't withhold everything. That would be unrealistic and concerning in itself. "I've had this ringing and buzzing in my ears today, kind of throughout the day, coming and going intermittently. Again, the massage and the sauna helped, but…I don't know man. Heh," he chuckles as their pho arrives. "Maybe this soup will help." Haydn's face squirms slightly with concern for their friend, which Mark, busy adding in the toppings - beansprouts, cilantro, jalapeno slices - does not see. The sweet-n-savory aromatic steam from their bowls rising up into the air

between them obscures Mark's face from Haydn and Haydn's face from Mark. But Mark isn't looking at his friend anymore. He's just relieved the meal is here so he can have a break from trying to explain himself, a nourishing excuse to pause the uncomfortable conversation. Haydn tries for a few seconds more to peer through the twin torrents of steam and glean what they can of Mark's confused countenance. Then they give up and begin adding in the toppings they like: the beansprouts and a few jalapeno slices, but not the cilantro. Haydn is one of those people who detest cilantro, can't even begin to understand how anyone could enjoy it. Genetics, they say.

Between burnt tongues and slurping rich slightly sweet pho broth, the two lose themselves in the meal. Haydn begins to talk a bit about a show they've been watching with their partner, a podcast they think Mark would like, and finally, how their cat is doing. "She's on death's door."

 "Sorry to hear that," Mark replies. That one was easy. An automated answer, a readymade reply, a social expectation - something that would appear as a suggestion at the bottom of an email whose subject matter is something morose, from what the email's intelligence engine can gather about it. Usually snarky about things like that, readymade replies suggested to him from the rapidly learning AI of his device, this time Mark is appreciative. The soup is nourishing, tasty, satisfying the hunger he's had for hours now…but still, it feels like work. Work to gather the noodles and the meat with his fork, work to lift it towards his mouth, to bite down, to chew. And it will be work for his digestive system to process the meal, turn it into nutrients and calories for him. At least it's hydrating. At least it's soup. Soup is an old thing, an ancient method of preparing food for consumption. If barbecue is the father of culinary history, soup is the mother. Between thoughts like this, the sound of blowing on the food and slurping it up, the audible crunch of beansprouts, Mark and Haydn make their way through their big bowls of pho. Lunch, the ritual, gets taken care of: the food, the social engagement, thanks for the meal here in the form of payment and ritual words, and ah's and grunts and belly pats of approval as they walk out the door, bell chiming at their backs, announcing their going.

"Alright well, it's good to see you Mark," Haydn says, a touch of sorrow and finality in their voice, some resignation that Mark just barely picks up on. Something is off with my friend, I'm not sure exactly what it is nor what, if anything, I can do to help. C'est la vie. Gotta get on with mine - to summarize Haydn's thoughts just then. "Gotta get back home, feed my cat, plug away at these blog posts I'm supposed to write," they say as if they don't actually know what they're doing or don't agree with what they're doing, a slightly resentful, slightly comical shrugging gesture. We've all got bills to pay, life's implicit toll by toil. "Yeah, yeah, we've all got bills to pay," says Mark. Haydn's gaze lingers, and Mark meets their eyes. Their face returns to a state of concern, concern better expressed non-verbally, after all. "Take care of yourself, alright? Put on a meditation app, get a good night's sleep, okay?"
  "Alright buddy,"
"Promise?"
  "Uh-huh," Mark intones, going in for a quick hug. The hug can say more than he can with his mouth. They hug, they part ways. Mark's car starts with a gasoline roar while Haydn's Leaf comes to life noiselessly.

Looking down to tap on and check his phone, as is now habit, Mark sees a text from another friend of his, Allain. Pronounced 'Allen', he refuses to go by 'Al'. Allain is a professional, classical concert pianist, composes scores for films and documentaries, and has a touring season every year where he travels the world and puts on piano performances, usually solo but sometimes with cello or violin accompaniment. He lives in the Seattle area most of the time and puts on invite-only house concerts on occasion.

Having friends in high places with spacious homes and grand pianos makes this possible. Mark always gets an invite from Allain, about one every other month or so when he's in town, and usually chooses to attend. Mark's friend is something of a savant; having memorized piano sonatas of Chopin, Schubert muzurkas and Mozart's nocturnes, he plays without sheet music, entirely from memory and with much emotion and panache. Tonight, Mark sees from the text, Allain is playing at a home in the Madrona neighborhood, not far from where he lives. That'll be nice, Mark thinks, I can park at home, walk there and walk back and have an easy, early night. Wake up tomorrow right as rain, like nothing out of the ordinary even happened to me. The desire to overwrite and move on from how his day began so very strangely is superceding his desire to investigate it.

Classical performances, unlike rock concerts, tend not to go on late into the night. There's usually an afterparty with plenty of hor d'oeuvres and wine and pomp and social posturing, but Mark usually skips out on those, leaves after the performance after saying good job and thank you to Allain. He enjoys his pianist friend's playing quite a bit, but those environments of haughty old urban wealth nauseate him. Oh well, he thinks, I can stomach it. For Allain, for the enjoyment of some fine piano playing, I can stomach it. Mark drives home, feeling the best he's felt all day.

Car parked, body relaxed, stomach satiated, Mark begins the walk over to the recital. He hasn't heard or felt that ringing, shattering deja vu-addled noise-sensation for a while now, not since lunch. A good sign, a very good sign. When improvements in one's health are noticed, when symptoms lessen or go away seemingly of the body's own autonomic accord, it is a thing of joy. Anyone with chronic health conditions, a scarily increasing percentage the reality and real number of which we are perhaps shielded from, knows this. I remember when I was young, Mark thinks to himself as he walks, kicking a can down the block, disease seemed so far away, rare, something that your grandmother's chain smoking cousin was afflicted with, something you heard news stories about, people suffering from strange and rare ailments in towns you'd never heard of in parts of the country you hadn't been to. Now, it's practically everyone. Now, it's only a matter of time until Pestilence, on a pale horse, rides past you with a sickly wave of his bony hand.

Mark rounds the corner from Pine onto 37th avenue. The day, now in late afternoon, is different from how it began. It's mostly sunny now, with just a few clouds in the sky. Oftentimes that proves to be the case in the northwest: the sun powers and peeks through the clouds at some point in the day, either overtaking them till sunset or for precious, fleeting snatches of time. Oh to drop everything you're doing and run outside to snag 5 IU of vitamin D. We Cascadians have all been there.

Mark feels the temperature of the air dropping. Inside, all over the city, across this latitude of the earth people are turning on their heat. Outside, all surfaces man-made and plant-made are still darkly damp with the day's intermittent rain. The quickening cold and the persistent damp make being indoors all the cozier. The house in which the concert's taking place tonight is actually a condo, turns out, one that's part of an attached block-long row of them. As he approaches the door, Mark reflects on something he often thinks on walks and drives: how despite what the exterior of the home or building looks like, you really don't know what's inside, to the extent there aren't glass walls or large windows displaying the interior for you. And even more intriguing, you really don't know how it *feels* inside, the mood that day, the vibe generally, the particular arrangement of things and furniture that contribute to making the place feel just so. Whether how the homeowner-designer has arranged things is in accord with feng shui principles or flagrantly violating them, whether they know that or not, are trying to live up to some varnished ideal or following their own intuitive or idiosyncratic feel, so many interior spaces remain locked away, like so many possible and hidden realities, perhaps accessible, perhaps not, pending our boldness or awaiting the invitation of another. This home Mark has just entered, hanging his raincoat and sliding off his shoes at the entranceway, seems harmonious. Harmonious and yet…distant.

Like most of the homes Allain plays in, it's the home of someone obviously wealthy. Things looked too ornate for Mark's tastes and so sterile as to appear unbelievable and out-of-touch. It's interesting to think, strange is probably a better word, how for the many drug-addicted or mentally ill houseless folk living nearby, that just beyond the walls of this building is a life and a lifestyle beyond their dreams. Heck, even for your common housed people, splitting a house five ways or rocking a dingy studio like Mark, living pretty much paycheck to paycheck. The disparity of wealth and circumstance…ah, but what's to be done? Enjoy the music. Be appreciative that your talented friend thinks to reach out to you and go get yourself a cup of tea or wine or both and sit down and alternate at closing your eyes and watching him play and just enjoy the music. Just enjoy. And this Mark does. As per usual, Mark introduces himself to his hosts, in this case two men probably in their fifties somewhere, one rather flamboyantly gay and the other the muted, masculine sort of gay. And then Mark avoids lingering around the kitchen where drinks and snacks sit out for self-service, avoids striking up or being stricken up for conversation with anyone else, finds his seat in the corner of a ridiculously comfortable couch across from the piano where Allain will play, and sits. And sips. And as the greying, well-dressed Seattle elite converse in pairs, trios, or quartets, he hears the sorts of things, snatches of phrase, that one would expect to hear from caricatures of wealth, from Thurston Howell the third or the anti-heroine of a Jane Austen novel, things like, "Well I never," and "simply to die for," and "the darling," and "be a dear," and "I simply couldn't bear it." Mark, his gaze trained on the carpet floor as he sips his wine, actually hears someone say, "Well, you *must* come to our new summer home on Crane Island this year." Hearing all of this, some morbid sense of wanting to disturb them all arises in him. Jar them. Do something really outlandish and unexpected like let the wine dribble out of the front of his mouth and fall down on the carpet and fake a seizure, raise everyone's blood pressure for a bit, make sure they still all know that life is mostly a messy thing out of our hands.

But that is only a thought for Mark, a morbid, normal thought, because Allain has stood up, everyone in the room has quieted down, and he begins to talk about what he'll be playing tonight. A round of applause and he begins with Eine Kleine Nachtmusik - Serenade No. 13, by Mozart. A recognizable and appropriate little start, a cute parlor trick. A short tune, Mark's tea is now at a sippable heat. He sips. Next Allain breaks into Schubert's Fantasia in F Minor. Minutes of intense concentration, both on the part of the performer as well as the audience, and no sound at all but for piano and the occasional clearing of a throat. A flourishing finish, a lingering moment maintained with eyes closed, such focus, such intensity sustained you could almost see the still air crackle around him the performer. Applause again, this time louder. Allain stands up and announces, "And now, for the next twenty minutes or so, I would like to play for you some of my own music." Mark shifts in his seat, finishes his glass of wine.

Allain's own compositions are wonderful, sometimes powerful and dramatic, sometimes understated, but always deeply moving. Mark enjoys Allain's originals the most; that's right, even more so than the works of the classical masters. He imagines how he might say that to someone here if they were to ask him, catch him say at the end of the recital as he was headed for the door. "With respect to the classics, I do adore Allain's pieces the most out of what he plays." Versus how he would say it to a family member or a coworker who asked him what he did on his day off: "Went to a friend's piano performance. Had a pretty great time. My friend does famous classical stuff as well as his own. I like his stuff better." As Allain launches into his piece, entitled, Lamas 18, Mark looks around the room: black tiled floor in the kitchen and dining room, cream carpet elsewhere, white walls leading up to a high ceiling, a spiral staircase to the second floor. That's cool but it's a bit much, Mark thinks. What a way to declare your wealth, that you have the means to spiralize the walk up to the next part of your home. A large granite island in the kitchen area and the same granite all around it for the countertops, hard, dark, and speckled with a few lighter accents here and there. And of course, such a home would not be complete without a glass chandelier above the dining room table, its chairs having been taken from their usual spots to serve as seats for the show. The music carries on: next Allain plays a piece he created as an ode to Beethoven, entitled 'Slowly Growing Deaf'. Refilling his tea (rooibos with ginger and jasmine), Mark enjoys the stark, bouncing emotion of it; it's like you can sense the frustration in the piece that the master must've felt as he suffered through that tragic and astoundingly ironic affliction.

Mark makes his way back to his seat, still rumpled looking, but as Allain begins his final segment of the concert, Chopin, Mark just can't get comfortable. With his new steaming hot cup of tea and glass-o-wine number two, Mark feels squirrely, though he can't quite place why. Looking around, he feels a strong sense of being out of place, what with all the richie riches around him decked out in clothing that would probably cost Mark a month's wages a piece. And now there is something about the sound of the piano, the way it's resounding in the large, high-ceilinged room, the acoustics he formerly thought quite good he now finds menacing. He feels his heart begin to race. No matter, he says to himself as he tries to return to calm, tries to talk himself down. We've already turned the day around quite a bit, we can take this on too. No matter, no matter, courage, courage. Encouraging phrases and words flash through his mind in a barely bidden procession, a cruise-control of his own 'how-to-deal-with-panic playbook' he's amassed through the years. You get to a certain age, or maybe not a certain numerical age but a certain level of maturity and you no longer need or necessarily have to have anyone to talk you down. It's gotta be you, at a certain point. You that stops the buck, you that rides and subdues the bucking bull. You that rescues you from the avalanche of you.

The rapid cascade of keystrokes that is Chopin's Piano Sonata No.2 in B-Flat Minor, Op. 35: I. Grave Doppio movimento has begun, accelerating Mark's mind and feeling as the piano melody propels forward without relent. The second movement, Scherzo, keeps these feelings, this mood of Mark going for a bit before slowing down. Mark however, does not slow down; his mind is still racing: what am I doing here? Why aren't I on a homestead in Alaska forgetting about the world and its problems? Why aren't I living easy in a quiet, small town on the west coast of Tasmania, eating mangos and working three or four hours a day for room and board? What am I doing in this offensively expensive town working my ass off to merely tread water with the semi-regular slip of salt-water in my mouth?

Mark gets up. He has to move. Unsettled, frantic chi within him, bounding around his poor meridians, and he has to move. He's still in a room full of people, but he feels invisible. Somewhat comforting. All eyes on his friend Allain, so very talented and deserving of eyes. And ears. Movement three: Marche funèbre lento, the funeral march, that slow, steady, measured and tragic procession of notes, grave, solemn, and resigned much like a group of people carrying a coffin. It's his coffin, Mark thinks to himself in his mounting paranoia, pawing at his peace like an inconsolable child. Mark realizes he's been standing, still and undecided, hearing the music yes but entirely in his head and overwhelmed with discomfort for the last several minutes. But once again, Allain has saved him the group recognition of this odd posture he's taken up unconsciously, this social faux pas, by playing so dramatically and excellently. He has cast a spell over his audience, their attention transfixed on him and him alone. Not the weirdo standing with a cup of tea in one hand and a too-full glass of wine in the other. Mark takes a sip, drains it down to a manageable, not embarrassing amount, one he can walk around with and not risk spilling all over this nauseatingly ritzy home. Some part of him wants to. Make a mess quietly and leave. Leave it to them to figure out, clean, repair or replace. They could absolutely foot the bill. Maybe turn it into a tax write-off somehow for charity for a Seattlite in need of help, in need of some cathartic action.

Movement four: the finale, a natural end to the funereal procession that precedes. It's short compared to the three movements of the sonata before. Mark is standing in the kitchen again. He takes one more big sip of wine and one more big sip of tea. As if they are his last. Mark knows the concert is reaching its climax, and he feels so unhinged that his emotional state feels detached from his own self-center and instead dependent on and reflective of the music being played. He's known this mood once before: once on a most-of-the-day-long solo hike he took in the Olympics two years ago. The day started sunny and so did he. When it became cloudy, so did he. When a thunderstorm broke out he felt exhilarated and terrified at the same time, like the force of nature was in command of not only the physical reality around him but his inner experience too. And now, similarly, Allain is playing his very own emotions with each note, each keystroke of the piano. He stands up, announces his last piece for the night, Chopin's famous Ballade No.1 in G minor, and sits down to the keenly awaiting hush of the crowd. Even Mark's mind stops for a moment, like briefly coming up for air before plunging back down with the music. The piece begins with such a strong, single note, it sends a shiver up Mark's spine. As if jolted awake, as if given smelling salts and coming to sharply, he sets his beverages down and, wanting to feel completely unencumbered, takes everything he has out of his pockets and places them neatly next to his drinks. No one in this crowd steals, he thinks to himself. Well, at least not gross physical objects. Small potatoes for these folk. He takes several laps around the granite kitchen island. Once again, no one sees, all eyes on the pianist par excellence. For three minutes the ballade builds, through a flourish of beautiful and dextrous complexity. The tinged, repeating five note refrain, *dun dun dun dun dun*, repeats several times and is abandoned as the music gets faster and faster, more and more passionate, a harder attack on the keys each time. Just as Allain slows down and begins the passage for which the piece is known, that enchanting sequence of notes that inspires a certain je ne se quais, Mark's head begins to spin. He hears that shrill ringing-shattering in his ears, the one he's been running from and attempting to soothe away all day. The issue he thought was over…is back. And the sense of deja vu (how else to put it into words?) that he's experienced this before. Spurned on by the music? By his own anxiety? By some inner, hidden ailment impossible to figure out that will be the death of him? Is it cancer? he wonders finally and irresponsibly, giving up and giving in to his greatest and most paranoid fears. He needs space. He needs to move away from these people, from the music, beautiful as it is, and its suddenly skull-pinging volume. Without anyone seeing him, he walks up the spiral staircase - he's been interested in it this whole time and let's be honest, so has everyone at the concert without a spiral staircase of their own - and reaches the second floor of the condo. The second floor of this bad dream, this panic fugue. Mark gets the spins. This isn't going away this time but intensifying, and bits of silver show up in the corners of his vision and he feels unsteady. As Allain launches into the speedy part of the second round of the melody of renown, Mark moves blindly towards some light, some relief: light pouring in through the long oval window he semi-sees as he turns around. He paws forward almost blindly to the light that blinds and brings relief simultaneously. He might as well be crawling on all fours. He considers it. That melody sounds for the fourth and final time, and then another quick passage, the last in the nine minute piece of music. Mark, in pain, ears ringing, vision blurry, mental state oh so confused and uncomfortable, stumbles forward toward the light suffusing through the glass window, faint source of warmth and paltry comfort in this dismality. Senseless, the sensation of the sun redoubled by the glass window is akin to the graceful mercy of God. Allain races flourishing down the piano, high to low, as Mark, encouraged by the warmth he feels, his one solace in this moment, in this house, on this day, in this city and in this life, is bidden him forward to be engulfed more completely in its embrace. A moment of silence as the performer slows down to play the final notes, closing the ballade as it began with powerful, somber single notes, and Mark, increasingly desirous of the sun and its comforting warmth, walks through the oval window, shattering it easily. After the shattering, after the crashing of the glass, a millisecond of rushing air dilated into timelessness passes him and he hears the final notes of the piano ringing triumphantly as he crashes down onto a stack of cardboard in the alleyway behind the condominium, blacking out.

Molding, Glowing

I began my career in education as a para, as in paraeducator, as in 'side educator'. The term is apt, for we, the less qualified though undeniably stout of heart 'marines' of the grade-school world, often sat, crouched, or stood to the side of the student we were working with. My job as a para commenced with employment at Lucienda Memorial Middle school, LMMS, halfway through the school year. My girlfriend and I had moved to town the previous fall, and spent a few months sorta looking for jobs but mostly enjoying settling in, going on hikes together in nearby mountain trail systems or taking long ambling walks around town, attending an event at a yoga studio or sampling the town's holiday markets. People in this town were friendly, we found, and so we were quick to begin a few friendships, with business owners, with people our age and of our general ethos that we saw repeatedly at the apothecary or the food co-op.

As the early winter snow accumulated and hardened each night in temps increasingly below freezing, the heating bills rose. Two mouths to feed, and not cheaply but to feed well, began to eat away at our savings. We thrifted for most of our furniture, got a great deal on a slightly broken washing machine (easily repaired), and yet still, the need for income was real, and was beginning to be felt. With that looming financial reality came a lowering of the bar, a willingness to apply for and accept jobs we wouldn't normally be interested in. I won't demean those jobs or the people who work them by listing them specifically, for its different strokes for different folks and hey, people at various points in their lives have differing bandwidths to be able to slog through a job to make end's meet, but let's just say I didn't move halfway across the country to work retail. Not my thing.

The town's school district, I heard and saw amply online and by signs around town, was hiring in several departments, and with a moderate sense of desperation, it seemed. They were, for instance, in dire need of substitute teachers. I, however, was in dire need of regular employment. So I looked into, applied for, interviewed for, and at long last got the job of paraeducator. In this role, I would often be assigned to work with a specific student in need of extra support, either in class or separately off to the side, in a different room, during a study hall period, or after school even. I might be with the same student all day, several students, or sometimes as generalist assigned to a class (and no one in particular) waiting for raised hands like a game of whack-a-mole.

Perhaps it was my multifarious experience working with tweens and teens that I demonstrated in my job interview, or perhaps it would've been the case any way: I was thrown right into the frying pan of middle school life - after one full, tedious day of online training, that is, shlumped into a chair that was too comfortable to be productive in in the corner of the school's library.

"Mr. Berkowitz," I was called and would rapidly have to get used to responding to, "here is your schedule for today," one of my new colleagues, Mr. Albis says, handing me a freshly printed out piece of paper with a descending list of how my day would unfold, names, times, class locations and numbers in a tidy spreadsheet taking up half the page. It looked like for that day at least, I was mostly assigned to a student named Chuck, Chuck Bogsworth, his full name read, while also providing general support to a few classes to break things up.

Mr. Albis and I walk over to room 129, Ms. Demetriou's math class, where, as we stood in the doorway, he discretely points out Chuck to me. In the second row of the class he sat, first desk from the left side of the room (from the student perspective, aimed at the teacher, digital screen and whiteboard up front), a blank paper and his head on the desk. With both of us seeing quite clearly the issue, the reason for my supporting Chuck as a paraeducator, Mr. Albis bid me adieu and good luck. Ms. Demetriou was busy helping other students one by one all around the classroom as they took their quiz on algebraic expressions. Sure it was within her capabilities, her job description even to nudge awake the occasional sleepy student, but the student who was falling asleep in her class most days? Not turning in assignments and proving himself a negative asset in partnered and group work? It's this situation precisely that calls for a para. I walk through the doorway that separates hall from classroom. It was not my but Chuck's time to shine.

"Hey there," I say softly and in a friendly, non-accusatory tone, touching him gently on the shoulder as I squat next to the napping seventh-grader seated in semi-consciousness at his chrome and tan desk. "My name's Mr. Berkowitz." Chuck was waking slowly, eyes just beginning to peep open, his face taking on a perturbed and confused expression. "I'm here to help you out. Looks like you guys are working on a quiz today huh?" I end with a question on purpose so as to begin to engage him, to contribute to wakefulness. "Huh, oh, okay," he grumbles, I think, and his head goes back on his arm-acting-as-pillow. "Come on dude, we gotta take this quiz," I say, working in another get-on-their-side tactic: referring to what *he* has to do as what *we* have to do, a helpful deception in language for the greater good. No answer from him, no more stirring awake, instead a decided turn back to sleep, sleep, as I'll soon learn, this boy so desperately needs, so stupidly and tragically is not encouraged to get at home. "Chuck," I say again, my touch a touch more forceful this time, "come on man." "Ungh," he moans in protest, dismissive, reluctant. "Come on Chuck. It isn't time for sleep, it's time for math. Sleep you gotta do at home." This time he doesn't make a sound, but instead shakes his head 'no' with it still buried in arms. Though I admit to myself that a child is warranted some childishness, this sort of unreasonable, immovable stubbornness ought to be behind a seventh grader. This is exactly why I'm here, I think to myself. I knew this was going to be difficult, akin to prodding awake a sleeping bear.

The teacher is already moving on, onto the main lesson now, and it seems as though all Chuck has accomplished is saturating the corner of his still blank quiz with a small circle of drool. The quiz was only supposed to take up the first fifteen minutes of class, a review, a knowledge check of what they've been working on. Even if he was fully awake and alert, applying one hundred percent of his malnourished brain cells, he still would not be able to complete the quiz. With the help of a para like me, it may take Chuck the entire class period to get through this short quiz. Or, as I'll soon come to learn is Chuck's habitual speed and style, it will take most of the period for him to begin the quiz. He'll start it, and if we're lucky he'll get through the first page. Then it will take him another study hall period - an open class period for students to catch up on work, at the expense of one less elective period - to finally get it done. For me, for all adults present, it's practically unbearable. For him too, only he hasn't worked this out for himself yet, tumult of garbled, unprocessed emotions and trauma that has on his plate, that he comes to school with everyday.

At least, I learn about him the following week - more wakeful and, blessedly, more smiley and social - at least he knows how to split and stack firewood, how to keep his family's fireplace going, an absolute necessity during Wyoming's long and challenging winter season. Maybe he can even start a fire. For Chuck, I learn, is a physic - a category of human that best makes sense of the world through and is generally best suited towards physical work. Stuff with his hands, imminently real and right in front of him, free of abstractions and heady concepts. That much would be clear to anyone within ten minutes spent with him, that he is best suited to build, repair, fix, or cook. He ought to, and perhaps in another country would be fast-tracked to an apprenticeship in the trades. But not in our education system. No, we don't like to specialize youngsters, even though specialization is the reality of the job market. We want obedient, well-rounded little enlightenment thinkers, with the bulk of their antiquated, idealistic courseload bordering on useless, and with only so much instructional time, taught at the expense of more pertinent and practical skills, like how to create and a balance a personal budget. We set our youth to the ridiculous task of being or at least proving to us that they can sound as though they're one part Montaigne, one part Marie Curie and two parts Isaac Newton. We want our youngsters growing up today to know to kowtow to The Science, and look at all else, all other ways of thinking and interpreting information or life itself as novel or primitive, always the disparagement of 'civility' implicit. Always. Never take those glasses, those viewing lenses off, child. Forget as quickly and completely as you can that you're even wearing them. There you go. Good. Here's a small, irresistibly sweet little reward to drive that lesson in and feed your pathogenic gut bacteria so you develop an autoimmune disease before the age of thirty and are all the more dependent on the system that taught you how to think and guided you to pick up a hundred socially-sanctioned dysfunctional lifestyle habits. And now, as an adult, you'll contend with limiting and sub-par health issues for years, for decades on end. From that, you could work to change yourself, improve yourself, but you'll have to successfully wade through the thicket of information and perspectives aimed at convincing you that this is normal, this is okay, this is right. This is just what growing older is…right? And it was clear enough to me that Chuck was already on the path to dysbiosis, for his breath often smelled like my grandfather's did, which is to say, of mold.

My days spent mostly with Chuck in this manner piled on. It was almost always an uphill battle to get his assignments done. He would have a good couple of days, maybe a good week even, but then seeing him again the following monday, it was always a roll of the dice as to whether last week's momentum was still there, or if something happened over the weekend to derail him, anger him, confuse him, scar him. It was clear with pretty much all of the kids we worked with that they didn't have the best lives at home, not the most supportive or functional families. From the smattering of information about themselves and their lives - shared innocently enough when students were asked on a monday how their weekend was, or on a friday what they had planned for their weekend, around holiday breaks in the school year - we educators and support staff were able to paste together a partial, often curious and sometimes unsettling collage of information from which we could make inferences outlining broken homes, violent and/or drug-addled parents, absent or short-tempered 'guardians' in their lives. Weekends spent with family in towns two or three hours away and for unclear reasons. Sleep deprivation, the hallmark of their age and of our screen-filled times, whether more or less forced from poor parenting or self-imposed through staying up into the night to play video games - again, poor parenting. In this way it was often two steps forward one week, and one, two, or four steps back the next. This was the unavoidable nature of the job. We got those kids for seven hours a day. Seven hours to learn, to get required work done. Seven hours to make good impressions, to be a positive influence in their lives, to help them grow in their abilities and feel the satisfaction and smile the sort of smile that only comes from growth in proficiency and competence. And everyday, there was another seventeen hours for which we had no say, another seventeen hours to run counter our influence or perchance in concordance. Often times in our cohort - the ROC or Rise Over Challenges program - kids would get sent home or worse: sent out to social services, to the town's youth crisis center, to the psyche ward at the town's hospital. It was truly always a toss-up where our ROC students would go ('the rock' as we and they referred to our little group), what direction their moods would take them: up the hill of progress and positivity, skill-growth, competence and confidence, or to slide back down, stumble, falter, or avalanche into disruption and outrage. Volatility, and being able to work with whoever showed up that day and however they showed up was the name of the game.

A few months into the job I am assigned another student to shadow and support regularly. Trent Baker is in the 7th grade like Chuck, but distinct from him in several key ways. Like Chuck, he is on the lethargic/apathetic/defiant side of the student behavioral spectrum, as opposed to the hyper-active, seemingly interested but trouble-focusing side. But there appeared to be more to Trent, a depth, something in his eyes, further evidenced by the sorts of things that would occasionally come out of his mouth, that belied an old soul. A degree of wisdom incommensurate with his woeful circumstances and bitter anger at being stuffed back into a body riddled with hurt for another sixty to a hundred trips around the sun. Despite his being categorically in the lethargic camp of students, Trent was a bright kid, that much was noticeable upon my first conversation with him. I also noticed an interesting pattern that began to repeat for the two of them: while I would often, not always but often, be working with Chuck to fight off sleep and in dimly lit rooms, I would always, even in the hallways, encounter Trent in a bright, fully illuminated setting. I wasn't sure what that meant or that it meant anything really, but I have a tendency to notice things like that, aggregate pattern data without analyzing or searching for the 'why' of it, just noticing, just taking in.

Trent seemed terribly disinterested in school. But most of the time he was a calm sort of defiant, often sitting cross-legged on the floor at the back of the room in a near perpetual state of protest. When presented with work that didn't appeal to him, which was most things, he would state with calm and immovable certainty (as stubborn as Chuck, though awake, alert, intelligent and discerning), "I don't wanna do that." To a teacher or para he perceived as old or out of touch, he might react more stand-offishly. With me, he was relaxed. I didn't know the whole story with him, his upbringing, his life at home, but hearing that he went to a Montessori school for his elementary school years, I figured his parents were alright, that they must have been decent and somewhat progressively-minded people, at least as regards the education of their child, where and how he would spend his seven-ish obligatory hours of education a day. By his own review however, he did not enjoy his time there, which said a lot about him, that even in the freedom and self-direction of the Montessori system, he still found the compulsivity of education repugnant.

My schedule shifted eventually from being a generalist in an aeroscience elective class (which I have no knowledge of and was absolutely no help in) during period two of the day to joining Chuck and Trent in their period two computer science class. This was also not my area of expertise, but I was determined (and excited, actually) to rise to the challenge and instruct myself in the course material, catch up on where they were at in the class as fast as I could, and help those boys to make it out of Mr. McCullough's comp sci class with a passing grade. I could see right away that I was more interested in the subject matter than they were, and though I asked about switching them out and just getting them into another study hall period, I was told by guidance counselors that it was too late into the semester for that, and that even if they didn't do well in this class that it wasn't the end of the world as it was only an elective, not a core class like Math, English, Science, or History. The core four, as they were called, and were the most important targets for these middle schoolers to be developing their knowledge of and fluency with. And so with the pressure off of them (and me), I focused on getting them through the class and trying to have some fun along the way. Because, I learned as I got into it myself, what we were learning about and doing in that class *was* fun. From our little territory at the back of the room (stemming from Trent's insistence on staying back there, his refusal to join Chuck and I at a table station like everybody else) we took in Mr. McCullough's presentations on coding. Middle schoolers learning to code, I thought to myself on the second or third day helping them out in that class, now I'm really in the 21st century. A brave new world, and then some. Well why not. We must keep up with the times, mustn't we?

The issue with the class, for them, was how fast-paced it was. We would learn about, practice and build on mathematical concepts pretty quickly, and so these lethargic, apathetic boys were getting left behind. The average computer science class went like this: everyone sat at their seats with their school-distributed Chromebook at the ready and followed along with the new concept Mr. McCullough presented, which always built on something we'd learned previously. We practiced the new thing, and then maybe every other week had a project that would demonstrate what we'd been learning. We used short USB cables that connected the laptops to little green motherboards, from which we could make all sorts of things happen. On the laptops we'd log into a Microsoft code-learning software and input commands to do anything from attempt to create our own mini alarm system, light differently colored LED lights, make small mechanical levers move when a certain button was pressed. One kid, a real prodigy in the class, assembled his own remote controlled robot, BattleBots style. The project weeks were usually a check-in at the beginning and then open class periods to work on whatever the programming mission was, last week's lesson now to be exemplified in a physical, tangible display of comprehension and as a group effort. So we, Chuck and Trent and I, were a squad. Though I tried to get them excited about the objectively cool assignments we were given, it was always like herding bulls, or stubborn young bison rather. Chuck was enjoying the novel and usually not allowed experience of sitting on the floor in the back of the room, as well as the comradery of having me and Trent at his side, on his team. Chuck and

Trent got along, and I got along with them. We joked about things, people, talked about how our weekends went, whether we saw a movie that had just come out and what our review of it was. And though the concepts and steps to executing each project were often out of their league - no offense to them, just not their proclivity - they thought the project design and the end results were cool. Like when we thought of making an alarm system for Batman so that when the Joker or some other villain were to enter the Bat-cave, Batman would be alerted and the intruder would be punished with a big spring-loaded boxing glove fist. That project never quite made it from dream to manifestation, but the gathering and garnering of their interest was a win itself. That motivated them, sorta, for what we decided we would go with for our final project of the year: making a 'musical instrument' out of an orange and a banana.

We all thought this would be both a funny and entertaining project to complete for the final. Pretty much as soon as we decided on it, both boys, Chuck and Trent, lit up like Christmas trees. Gone for the moment, for the rest of the class actually, was their usual lethargy and resistance. For once, they were both excited about their school work. But I realized instantly that what they were excited about was the *idea*, the idea of what the end result would be. Would I be able to keep their interest throughout the work to get there? That would be the challenge. Throughout the rest of school that day, when we saw each other in the hallway, during their lunch period, when I popped into their gym class, those boys greeted me with a smile and a fist to pound, remembering our aspiration of musical fruit. I matched their enthusiasm, even as I felt a sinking feeling that their interest might not translate into productivity, and that I would be carrying the project once again. We would do this (realistically, I would do this) by linking small pressure-sensing probes to the motherboard/computer console connection. On the coding software accessed via Chromebook, our task would be to input commands to make the computer play a certain note if the banana or the orange were squeezed separately or together, for a total of three different possible notes.

As this was the class's final project, it was late May, and so in this high altitude mountain town, solidly Spring. There was still snow up in the mountains, still plenty of frozen alpine lakes, but finally and blessedly temperatures were consistently higher in town and nearby woods. Plant life was in bloom and pollinators were clearly busy and happy after their long, frigid wait in 'suspended animation' as it's called for insects. There was one morning late that month my girlfriend and I were completely floored to wake up to see still perky, cheery-looking flowers outside our front door, freshly bloomed in just the week past, that morning gripped by thick icicles after the night's snap freeze. 'False Springs' happen everywhere. This is especially true when you're living more than a mile high.

It's not just plant life that was responding to the increasing temps, lengthening days and fertile rain of Spring. We heard more birdsong of course, and saw a marked increase in the presence or visibility of frolicking bunnies running around the lawns and alleys of our neighborhood. We saw more deer out and about. The bison in the plains just outside town seemed happier and were covering more ground, likely not feeling the need to be as conservative in their caloric expenditures. And the town's stalwart non-migrating crows that hung in there so bravely all winter long, clinging tenaciously to the leafless trees (now abundant with leaves again) that swung helter-skelter in the frigid wind, they were getting rewarded with a seasonal reprieve.

And so it was of course with humans too. There were some intrepid locals who rode their bikes around town year-round, wearing large oven mitt-looking gloves to grip their bike handles throughout the winter. Now, they put their bulbous bike gloves in storage for the season. Now they were free. Hardy exercise enthusiasts aside, there were definitely more people out and about in general. For the first time since moving here I saw people having barbecues, heard music being played by speakers as people hung out in their front or backyards. I even started seeing the year's first influx of tourists. It was spoken by locals with a mix of humor and honest, pining reverence, their eyes distant and full of hope, about how for two months a year this high mountain town set in a geologically flanked, earthen wind tunnel turned into paradise. At this point in the year, I was starting to see what they had been talking about.

"Alright boys," I said the following day, sitting in between the other two members of the 'back of the room crew' and logging into our Chromebook. "I know we think this is a really cool idea, but now we have to bring it into reality. How are we gonna do that?"

"Ummm I don't know," Chuck replied reflexively, in the sort of cartoonishly quick voice that he would employ when feeling silly and energized.

"We gotta, like, connect the cables to the thing, oh um to the computer and to the microchip and from there to the fruit, and set up the right codes and then squeeze them and make music. Right? Yeah, yeah, that's right. Right Chuck?" Trent reached out his open hand and Chuck dapped him up.

"Yeah! Connect the wires to the thing and the fruit and…yeah!" Chuck replied, keeping up the nonsensical responses.

"Okay, okay. That's it, in essence, but we gotta figure out the specifics: the right cables going into the fruits and the processor chip and the computer, and from the computer, the right codes. The codes will be the commands that will allow for the whole thing to work. Otherwise, we're just squeezing fruit."

"Haha, 'just squeezing fruit!'" Chuck parroted back. I could see where this was going. I would attempt to string them along, to guide their energy this morning, the second day of the project, into actionable steps. Could this energy of theirs - right now being displayed in energized silliness - be translated into doing the work? It was my job to work with them, believe in them and their innate potential. But once again that sinking feeling, born of witnessing seemingly implacable behavioral realities day in and day out, welled up inside me. Or perhaps it wasn't inside me but in the air, in the atmosphere, something they were feeling-effecting too. Only they weren't aware of how to harness their inner power and focus and knock out some work they didn't want to do. A chief difference between middle-schoolers and adults. Some adults, that is.

"Let's have one person do the coding and the other do the wiring, and you guys can switch in ten minutes. Sound good?"

"Okay!" replied Chuck with the same exaggerated enthusiasm. "I'll do the wiring," Trent said, slyly staking his claim to the far less complicated of the two jobs.

"Alright here you go Trent," I replied, handing him the small green processor-chip, the USB cables and the fruit. "And here you go Chuck." I set the Chromebook on his lap. "Don't worry, I'll help you out. I am here to help," I said caringly, emphasizing the last three words.

Not a second after I gave Chuck the laptop, I started to smell an off-putting smell, something like mold. Chuck had very quickly gone from all fun and games to serious, quiet, and nervous-looking. Perhaps this was a stress response via body odor? That happens sometimes, right? Especially, perhaps, to 7th graders, high-grade hormone factories their bodies are. "What's that smell?" asked Trent. I looked over at him and without answering saw that he was jamming the cables into each other and the processor and the fruit repeatedly and excitedly. There was no rhyme or reason to what he was doing; he was still excited, and this was how it was manifesting itself. His skin color, I noticed, now seemed lighter than usual. Or was it the light around him that seemed to have begun to intensify, as if someone had turned up the light dial but for just the area immediately around him? I had no time to ponder or investigate. "Hey please don't break those."

"I'm not breaking them."

"Please don't jam them together repeatedly. You could damage them and that's not what we're supposed to be doing anyway. Let's go about this in a calm, scientific manner, like an engineer would."

"Someone better engineer some deodorant for my boy Chuck over here cuz he be stinkin'!"

"Shut up Trent!"

"Guys let's keep it civil, come on. We're a team and we've got work to do."

No longer playful or excited or positive at all, Chuck was now scowling and hunched, pretty clearly, to my semi-trained eye, in a psychologically defensive posture. The mold smell that seemed to be emanating from him was intensifying, and it appeared as though the pallor of his skin was changing too. He was looking paler and…greener? Is that right? Is he sick? Am I seeing things? I wondered. "Chuck are feeling alright? Do you wanna step out and go see the nurse maybe?"

"I'm fine," he said definitively and pouting, literally crossing his arms in front of himself in a show of almost unbelievably stereotypical obstinance. When people do things like this, commit behavioral tropes like running out of the room and slamming the door to end an emotional conversation prematurely, it makes me realize that life does sometimes imitate art more than art imitates actual life. And it shows me that that person has been watching too many family sitcoms, too many cartoons, or modernly speaking, too much TikTok. I attempt to keep the project moving forward. "How we doin' with the commands for our fruit keyboard Chuck?" He sits there for a while, arms remaining crossed while he looks away from the both of us, not answering: one of the few forms of control a kid can exercise in an uncomfortable situation. "That's alright," I say, "let's get a refresher from Mr. McCullough." I could use another adult in the mix at this point, I finally admit to myself. I lock eyes with the teacher standing at the head of the room and wave him over. He walks over to us right away, immediately squatting down next to Chuck with the laptop, which frees me up to attend to Trent who's sensed he's hit a nerve and is doing something he shouldn't with the cables and sensor-wires that are meant to go into the fruit. And so, a natural contrarian, he doubles down, ramming the things into each other and clipping the sensor clamps to parts of the USB cables, just generally wreaking havoc. "Trent please don't do that. You know that's not how those are to be used," says Mr. McCullough straight away. He then begins a valiant struggle to help Chuck while not showing that he's rapidly become overwhelmed by the student's apparent BO.

"So we need to string together a series of commands as inputs for the sensor cables," he indicates the wires and clamps Trent's been fucking around with, "so that when they're in contact with the two pieces of fruit you've got here, the computer will play music in response to the pressure of your touch when we squeeze them. Do you remember how to create input commands on our coding software?" There's a pause, Chuck saying nothing while he either attempts to remember or sits in his embarrassment at being so utterly out of his element. The embarrassed silence is palpable, and not unlike someone sitting in their pants they just wet. At this point, as I attempt to productively redirect Trent, the teacher and the student are out of my sight, out of my periphery even as I fully physically turn and reorient myself towards Trent, who's now singing manically, "The cable goes here and the clamp goes there, the clamp goes here and the cable goes there!"
  "Uhhhh," I hear Chuck say, guttural and searching like the human equivalent of a loading screen.

Mr. McCullough, continuing to brave Chuck's undeniable odor, went from kneeling to sitting cross-legged next to the lad. "If you're unsure how to write a line of code," he said, "take a look back at the powerpoint from Unit 2, which you can access through our online syllabus." That much, Chuck could do. We all, Trent now included, watched mutely as Chuck clicked clumsily through the bulleted list of links to lessons in the way of videos, webpages, and .ppt files. "There it is," Mr. McCullough said, "No not Unit 2 overview, lesson 2.1. There ya go. Alright, take a look at that; that lesson goes into detail on how to write lines of code with our Microsoft application. I've got to go help other students. You got this. Good luck you guys." This was exactly where the standard teacher's job ended and the paraeducator's began. This was exactly why I was here.

"Uh Mr. Berkowitz?" Chuck says, his inflection belying the beginning of a question I think I already know the answer to. I play dumb in my response, at first. "Yes?" Even though I know what he wants. He wants to be handed his fish, not catch it himself or even try. "I don't know how to do this." I don't give it to him right away. Instead, I choose to engage his teammate. "Trent, how do we do this? How do we code?"

"I have no clue," he replies emphatically. "And I don't care. This is dumb."

That's right: the study of computer science is 'dumb' according to this disenfranchised seventh grader. This pronouncement, obviously wrong on its face, is in actuality a statement of how he feels, an emotional explanation of his disinterest.

"I guarantee you I'm never going to use this. Like, not once in my life." As Trent speaks, as I focus my attention on the boy sitting not a foot away from me, he grows more animated and…brighter. Again, I notice that strange phenomenon I'd seen before in Trent, and now would have to ask other school staff, other paras about in order to corroborate whether it was true or whether I was hallucinating that he and the area immediately around him was growing brighter. Unlike Chuck's scent, no one else seems to notice this, though I was on the verge of asking Chuck, strange as it was. "I wanna go outside man," Trent continues, his tone of voice growing faster, higher in pitch and more frenzied, "Mr. Berkowitz, can we go outside?"

"Not during Computer Science class. We got a project to do."

"School sucks," Trent says with emphasis, "this is some b.s." Like a lightbulb getting screwed in with its corresponding switch already turned on, Trent's skin and features glowed brighter and brighter. I wonder if he was hot to the touch. "Trent, are you warm right now?"

"Nah,"

"Well you look like you might have a fever. You look warm." It wasn't even exactly that; I just didn't know how else to describe what I was seeing and wanted to engage him to figure it out with me.

"I'm just done with this shit," he says, "I got this Aztec screaming whistle yesterday, check it out." I catch him just in time as he pulls a small whistle that looks like a skull from his pocket and puts it to his lips.

"During recess, or gym, if you get your teacher's permission."

A few more minutes of fielding distractions and their (successful) attempts to put off the work this project demands, and the bell rings. Another five class periods for them, another five hours of what they consider imprisonment, and then they're free. Until tomorrow.

Students and overworked faculty alike are now counting down the days, the tomorrows left till summer's undeniable and resplendent freedom. Spring had had its quick run in our quiet mountain town. Now, as school's end loomed near, it was feeling like and everyone was acting more like it was summer. Socially, summer is expanded as much as it reasonably can be in this place, where after months of intense cold and interminable wind our yearly angle towards the sun, so cosmologically slight and yet so terrestrially profound, finally makes life on the high steppe of Wyoming temperate. Even the mountain lakes sitting upwards of 10,000 feet begin to thaw. The increasingly erratic energy at LMMS continued, while we adult personnel did our level best to keep the ship of integrous academia sailing.

At this point in the year, we were settling for staying afloat, let alone smooth sailing.

The next day, and despite my wanting to give them the benefit of the doubt, it turned out that Chuck and Trent still did not want to work. From the start of class that day, now in the second to last week of school, something was clearly amiss with each of them in their own way, not only carrying over the seemingly stress-influenced peculiarities they'd exhibited the day before, but intensifying in them. One pleasant surprise awaited me as I entered the room: they were already seated neatly and somewhat obedient-looking in our spot, our territory at the back of the room. That much was good; no cat (bison) wrangling to waste the first six to eight minutes of class. But before I even sat down next to them I could see how oddly bright Trent was looking and how glum and sickly pale-green Chuck appeared. Their physical postures were in accord: Chuck was hunched over, sitting with his legs crossed, his elbows on his knees and his hands propping up his face, while Trent, also sitting with his legs crossed except with his back straight upright, was looking around the room wildly and rocking back and forth, shuckling as if in prayer.

I retrieve our Chromebook from the class charging station and sit down between the two, as I usually do, trying, at first, to act like everything's normal, like everything's alright. I continue to wonder, even more strongly and incredulously today, does no one else see what's up with these two? What's off with these two?

"Alright guys let's get to work," I utter one of the many 'ushering on' phrases that winds up coming out of the paraeducator's mouth about a hundred times each day.

No response.

"Hey guys, we got a project to do." I look to my left, and without even consciously deciding to I bring my left hand to pinch my nose as I take in the fetid sight and smell of Chuck. "Uuuhhuhhuhhh," is the sound he's emitting, something low and droning, groaning, sounding like a continual stream of uncertainty and like he'd been socked in the gut. "What's going on dude?" I ask him. From his hunched posture, with his pale-green skin, he turns his head still propped on his hands and looks at me. His dark beady eyes lack pupils, and out of its corners something green-white is leaking, softly oozing out from behind his eyes and onto the area of his face just around them. I puzzle for a moment over what I'm seeing. Mold. It's mold, like what might grow on food left in the fridge for too long or on compost left unturned. And then I see some growing on his jet black hair. As I'm taking this all in, now not just baffled but with growing alarm, Chuck lets out another low, pained-sounding moldy-breath moan, "Uuuuhhhhhh." Despite holding my nose, his smell hits me, breaks in like an enemy army breaking through a castle's defenses. Autonomically I blink a few times to ward off the sting my eyes begin to feel. I shake my head in disbelief, and turn towards Trent. While seated, his upper body is moving with the franticness of somebody desperately needing to pee. He's looking around the room, right, center, then left, left, center, then right, over and over again. He appears to be on drugs, like an amphetamine based drug, yet I know from his file that he's on downers, SSRI's. And again, his skin is bright, so luminous it looks like a small star is about to burst out from within him. "Trent how about you? How are you doin'?"

 "I'm doin' great Mr. Berkowitz," Trent says in a high pitch and at a low volume, sounding like he's dehydrated. He continues shaking his head from side to side as he continues to answer me, "Just great." I catch his eyes on his next pass to the left, as I am what is to his immediate left. His eyes are bulging out of their sockets, and coming from behind them, suffusing out the sides is light, white yellow light bursting out from behind his eyes, as if he's just seen the Ark of the Covenant and he's about to pop.

I am in disbelief. The student's flanking me are way out of line. How could they possibly finish their project like this? How could they work? It's not right to come to school like this. It's irresponsible to send your child to school like this. I can no longer contain myself. I don't know what else to do. Seeing this middle-school computer science class going on operating like everything's fine and dandy, I stand up and shout, "Does anyone else see what's going on?! I've got one kid molding and one kid glowing over here!" The entire class turns their heads in sync and looks at us, as if of one mind, as if executing a mass coordinated movement like the murmuration of a flock of birds in a sky of tumultuous weather. They all look at us at the back of the room as if they don't understand, as if we, or they, were aliens. I hold my arms up into the air, entreating, and shout once more, "Help us! Why won't someone help these boys!?"

The Butcher of New Norfolk

"I won't ever forget that cunt, " said Steve to the squirming discomfort of his American company. Seeing this, and in fact before the word had even left his mouth, he knew he had to explain. "You see, in much of Australia and the UK, the c-word is used very casually, even affectionately. When you're close enough with someone to joke around, it could be and often is swapped in place of 'mate', 'man', or 'bro'.

"Is it used as an insult?" asked a curious friend.

"When the 'c' and the 't' are pronounced sharply," said Steve, "Then you know you are witnessing true wrath. There was only one time I heard him say it that way. The situation absolutely called for it, and still, it made my hair stand on end. You see..."

The crowd gathered around the fire casually noshed and sipped on pot-luck faire as Steve told his tale, a recounting of one of his adventures in Australia. The smell of wood-smoke was in the air, and if you were standing close enough to the food table, a garlic-y vegan curry.

"I knew coming into Hobart that I wanted something different, I was over working vague hours with ill-defined expectations and boundaries, issues that can plague work-trade arrangements."

"With the exception of my first week in Brisbane, spent with American friends also visiting, my two and half months in Australia up till then had been passed in work-trades, arrangements and connections for the most part made through an online directory, matching prospective hosts with work-willing travelers, and vice-versa. All in all, these experiences helped show me what we're often told in platitudes and unconvincing philosophical stances: that people are by nature good, and that everyone has in common the desire for happiness and fulfillment. I also learned very quickly doing these sorts of things that what sets us apart - sometimes magically, sometimes in ways that are hard to smooth over, and often in ways that just flat-out make you laugh - are our quirks and eccentricities: the way we just have to have something done or presented, cooked or arranged. *The towels are folded and hung this way in my house*, or *oh no don't bother, those can just air dry overnight*. But also the charm of a person, the inspiring and attractive way they carry themselves, how they speak, how they punctuate their expressions with facial features and other body language, or how they don't. I'm talking about the characteristic raising of an eyebrow at a certain kind of moment, the gleam in one's eyes, half conscious and half not, toward a phrase's end that puts a charming sparkle on what was said. There are a lot of people doing awesome things in a unique way in this world, in a given country, in a single city, in small rural towns and out of the way places you'd likely never visit if not connected by an online directory listing people with projects putting themselves out there. Fascinating people, sometimes amazingly wise and enlightened-seeming and sometimes type-a and often irritable and impatient with help that comes their way. It is an untold number; we will have to be content with not knowing about all the cool shit that's happening. All the crazy creative natural-style buildings being built; all the small-scale farms growing colorful, delectable heirloom vegetable varieties; solutions to the problems of waste-management and plastics composting from inspired 'lightning in a bottle' types of genius inventors that we don't hear about because their solutions solve problems in ways that aren't easily monetizable; couples with a love so bold and a combined skill set so broad as to be an Ark of two. Everyone is doing their life's work with unique perspectives and also with many weird quirks and eccentricities that only make sense to them or their family because of how they live in, find comfort in and are inspired by where they are."

"By the time I arrived in Hobart, fresh off a month of work-trading split between the yang-like owner of a small-scale orchard and gin distillery and the yin-like owner and operator of a hippy hostel on Tasmania's wild, undeveloped west coast, I wanted more autonomy and a more defined schedule. I wanted to find a job and work six to eight hours a day for pay, select my living space, purchase and cook my own groceries, and maybe save up a little on the side, if I could get into a groove and exercise some thrift. After months in remote (and also, it must be said, beautiful) locations, without tempting but actually mediocre restaurants or sleek superfood-laden snacks (it had been far too long since my last raw cacao goji berry spirulina maca dusted acai reishi ball), I was excited to take in Tasmania's big city. I did look for jobs...while mostly eating my face off on the hydra-like mission of sampling the endless food offerings of an urban environment. About that saving up thing..."

"Fairly quickly, I found part-time work at a butcher shop. And lo and behold, it must have been meant to be, it was a whole-body butchering shop, sourcing their animals from nearby Tasmanian farms they'd checked out themselves and approved the ethics and operations of. I walked in one sunny day shortly after the new year and met Bert, the head butcher, and Deb, the owner, operator and rancher supplying highland angus to the store. I could tell right away that we saw eye-to-eye regarding the righteous resurrection of proper animal husbandry, processing and consumption. And while they couldn't offer me a forty hour work week, Deb promised to keep me in the loop about learning opportunities with Bert and part-time work each week."

"Now Bert is the cunt I really wanna tell you about. He was a refreshingly different voice to hear three months into living in Australia. With a British accent, and more specifically, London Cockney, he brought with him to Australia, like me, another totally unrelated life from the other side of the world. I came in for work two days that week and three days the next week, during which we connected, quickly establishing a chummy rapport with the ease and jocularity of a couple of middle-school age boys, the plethora of obscenities included. It wasn't long at all before 'handling meat' jokes became a regular part of our discourse."

"As far as work went, in all honesty I'll bet that I was, at first, more of a hindrance than a help, bumbling around as I was in a post 'welcome back to civilization, allure of the sights sounds and smells of the city, grain-brain addled glucose fog' by which I mean: it had been a long time since I'd stuffed so much carbs and sugar down my gullet, and it was slowing me down. For my first three weeks in Hobart, I think my body's chief occupation was staying on top of adequate insulin production. As nice as it was to enjoy the tastes of Hobart, I was also relieved to be moving out of the hostel right across from what was high in the running for being the island's best bakery, and up to my new friend Cameron's place for the week. There, I did more of my own cooking, and felt my brain-fog quickly lift. I began to move faster, more intelligently and efficiently at work, retaining information better and just generally being less of a putz. "Stop being such a cunt; take a day off for once in your life," Bert would say in his gritty but somehow charming Cockney, mostly joking, though with some truth to his request likely, his words belying a slowly eroding patience. My suspicions about the true extent of his patience aside, it initially did take me some time to get used to how he expressed his friendship: through comical though unsparing jocularity and good-natured ribbing, with the invitation implicit (and eventually on my part, acted on) for it to be mutual. "Taking the piss out of each other", as he called the nature of our banter. Always sounded gross to me, but it was a uniquely English turn of phrase, I learned."

"Here we were: two different native English speakers in yet another English speaking country on the other side of the world, both very far from our homelands and both (didn't we know it) in search of friends. Bert had sixteen years on me, the last eight of which had been spent in Tasmania. At this point, he was a lifer; it's where he wanted to be, far as he could see. I on the other hand was only taking a short detour, skipping winter that year, and would definitely be heading back stateside a few months later."

Here Steve took a meaningful pause in the telling of his tale, savoring his affinity for home, how nice it was to be back and among dear friends, a pause long enough to enjoy a raven's *kaaaw* and a gust of wind, rattle of leaves in the forest that encircled the gathering. "What does he look like?" someone asked.

"I would say he stood just shy of six feet tall. He was a big guy, in a stocky sort of way. Formerly, before a shoulder injury, he had done regular weight training, and that aside, his profession as a butcher called for spurts of heavy lifting on a daily basis. In his own words, a gorilla of a man, and from the way I saw him, at forty-five, carry a fore-quarter of beef, I'd call him a silverback at that. He kept his head shaved, wore sneakers, and glasses with small rectangular frames. At the butcher shop he wore a long university labcoat over a checkered button-up shirt, freshly ironed every morning as the second to last thing he'd do before heading out the door to drive to work. At work, we wore thin denim aprons draped around our torsos and up to our necks. I thought they were pretty slick."

"Good morning Steve," he'd say to me as I arrived to work, a slight uplift, a hint of cheer in his voice. "(Good) morning," I would reply dutifully, my Yankee accent standing out next to his, and both of our accents standing out, probably, to the typical Aussie customer. My next moves were to apron up, mop the shop floor with a disinfectant solution, and then check in about what was the next most pressing thing to do, probably help put meat out on display and ticket them with labels and prices, or make mince meat if we needed; veal, pork, beef, then lamb was the order if we were doing them all or several successively, for each meat can take residual amounts of the previous without losing its own distinctive flavor. If you were to mince goat (which we did once, at my request), that animal would go last."

"Despite his Paul Bunyan-esque appearance, Bert truly was a kind, sensitive, and funny guy. He was conscious of his people invading this land, and in his sensitivity, tapped into and assumed collective ethnic guilt, deserving of it or not. "If an Aboriginal were to come into the store," I heard him say once, "I'd turn on an Aussie accent, because I'd rather sound like them than stand out like the bloody Pom I am." Brits in Australia, you see, are sometimes and especially amongst each other referred to as "Poms", short for pomegranate - the shade their skin was after their voyage at sea to reach the land down under."

"Bert could have me burst into diaphragm-shaking laughter at a moment's notice. Once, while cleaning and closing up the shop in the last hour of the work day, he looked at me seriously and began to ask, checking in with me about our closing procedures, "Have you done this...have you done that...have you…have you… have you ever seen a man as fat as me, as fat as me, as fat as me?" bending and standing, swinging his arms in song, "Have you ever seen a man as fat as me, as fat as me, as fat as me?"

"Deb had just hired another butcher a week before I came into the picture. The store also had a high school age girl working as their retail hand most days. So, when she came up with a regular schedule, Deb had me working just one day a week - Tuesdays. I tried to find more work at other places, hotels and other butcher shops, to no avail. With my week at Cameron's winding down, and not having secured enough work to afford to stay at one of the hostels in town again, I had to contemplate options outside of Hobart like harvest work with fruit farms or more work trades for room and board."

"Bert, in his perceptiveness, picked up very quickly one morning that something was off with me, that I was wearing a heavy heart, which was surprising as not fifteen minutes in our morning together at the shop had gone by. "Are you alright?" he asked me, a question, I've learned, serious as it may sound to the American ear, can be more casual in British English, a sort of "how are you?" I replied in earnest that no not everything was alright, and that I'd have to leave Hobart soon if I didn't find more work. Without missing a beat he said, "Well you could come stay at my place. Wouldn't cost you anything. I have some landscaping work that needs doing, if you'd be interested."

"Really?"

"Yeah I just have to check in with Jess but I'm sure it'll be alright." He checked with his partner Jess, and when I asked him again at the end of the day, he reaffirmed; yes I could come and stay with them for as long as I needed. It was settled. Next week I would depart from Cameron's and move in with Bert and Jess in New Norfolk."

"On the way over, Bert and I talked naturally for much of the forty minute drive, and for the first time outside of a work environment, no longer 'on the clock'. While I'd already heard about much of his past life in London, the conversation turned at one point to past lives after he asked me if I was a religious person. I probably told him that I believe in plants, which was my standard response to questions like that at the time. "I'm not religious at all," he said, "never cared a bit for it. I grew up on the streets of London where defending yourself and your own was priority. I wouldn't even really call myself a spiritual person," he continued "though I do believe in certain energies, people have energies, vibes you know. And I believe there are things that exist that we can't see."

"But can sense," I clarified, "if we are sensitive or perceptive enough."
"Right," he said.

"It's all there," I went on, "that which is does not require belief to be, like how gravity does not require anyone's belief in order for its effect to be felt. It's very much there regardless."

"Thas'it," he said, a favorite reply of his. "There's a woman I see sometimes in town, in New Norfolk. She's an energy worker, a psychic type. First time I saw her she was a bit taken aback. She must have seen my aura and felt it was heavy, that there was bad spirits following me or hanging onto me. As she began our first session she said, "You're going to feel so much better after this." And I did. I felt much lighter afterwards. Somehow she'd seen into my past lives and said that I used to be a fierce Mongolian warrior. Fancy that! I mean, look at me; I reckon I was!" We both laughed."

"As we pulled off the riverside highway and into town, switching subjects, that remark stayed with me. Both consciously and not, I made a mental note of that: Bert, butcher in this life and Far Eastern Warrior of time past; for something about it seemed significant and true. For a man who worked in a trade that most would consider harsh, crude, of dense physical realities and blunt bloody truths, Bert was very perceptive and could pick up fast on the felt but unsaid dimension of life. Before that conversation and as long as I knew him afterwards, he appeared to me psychically and energetically aware, despite - as he would so often say in his own words - his oafish, butcherly appearance."

"New Norfolk reminded me of towns I'd encountered in the Catskill Mountains of New York State, which is to say: not a big town, not a nothing town, surrounded by mountains on all sides, and by the looks of it - from its worn buildings with their fading facades to its junkyard-looking homes and the many yappy anxious barking dogs in its residential streets - has seen better days. Whether towns like this, towns that once were and could again be a place of interest survive to see some new invigoration is up to the current and coming generations, whether they'll deem it broken enough to be hip, faking it till they've made it so, or leave it to flounder, fail and fade away."

"Approaching Bert's home we passed a most interesting property. Surrounded on all four sides by streets, it stood alone, two acres or so non-contiguous with any neighboring properties. "This used to be the old neighborhood schoolhouse. Now someone lives there. We almost bought it ourselves. Wished we did," said Bert as we drove by. For the little I saw of the place, it made an impression on me. Firstly, I was struck by its garden potential: it had a golden half acre at least of a yard behind its main house that appeared to get great sun exposure throughout the day. The property was fenced in sturdily, which would keep out the local crepuscular fruit and vegetable thieves, and was garlanded by a couple of large, majestic looking oak trees. It was one of those places that very soon after looking at it I had to hold myself back from fantasizing about turning it into a five to ten year homesteading project. "Those lions are interesting," I said to Bert.

Soon as they passed into my vision, they were gone. If I'd blinked, I would have missed them. But I didn't, and now, pulling up to Bert's street, I couldn't get them out of my mind. "Yeah, they are," said Bert, "I notice them too, every time I pass by." They were the Chinese sort of stone entryway guardian lions. In Europe, their grotesque analogs perch atop cathedrals. Similarly in China they were (and still are I suppose, though now to evoke the past) positioned in front of temples and palaces, on guard for the sake of precious persons or contents therein. The car came to a stop and the engine turned off. A silent moment before either of us said anything or made a move to exit the car. As if reading my still-fixated mind, Bert remarked, "There's something about them, isn't there?" "

"The question lingered in the air, drifting and unanswered for only a moment longer before our reverie was definitively brought to an end by the sudden barking onslaught of Bert's dogs. As I would soon learn was the case with practically all of New Norfolk's canine familiars, Bert's three dogs suffered from a pretty bad case of fence-anxiety. If you were on the other side of the gate, the window, or the door, his dogs would bark at you thunderously and unceasingly, acting out the role hard-wired into their genes by thousands of years of being the organic village alarm system, faithful friends they are. On the far side of the screen door, beyond the window walking by innocently in the street is the Enemy: the scout of the rival tribe, the wolf stalking the farm. But as we crossed the threshold of the yard and then the front door, the alarm system seamlessly transitioned into a celebration, a great rejoice for pack members safely returned from hostile lands. Sooky, Frodo, and Missy were sweet and loving dogs. Once inside their home, all they'd want to do was either play (Frodo), sit on your lap (Sooky), be given food (Missy), or lick you (all of them). Within ten minutes of our arrival, after I had set down my stuff in Bert and Jess's guest room, I quickly and intimately got to experience all they were about, and was reminded yet again that as hand is to human, tongue is to dog."

"Jess proved to be a gracious hostess, showing me around and helping to make me feel at home, which I did rather quickly. Once or twice a week she would make some extravagant dessert. Their refrigerator generally was bursting with food. They had a big screen tv, a comfy couch, and a lawn that needed some work. I was set. In the mornings I would wake up anywhere from six to eight-thirty depending on the day, whether or not we had to get to the shop early or pick up supplies like paper bags or butcher's paper on the way in."

"I learned right away that Bert was an extremely light sleeper. A creaking step, the latch of a door being fully closed, any noise in the night was enough to potentially wake him up. "I live in constant fear," joked Jess. He couldn't explain it himself, even after clinical testing with electrodes hooked up to his head, he once told me. I saw it as a residual trait of his old warrior nature: always on alert, always ready for combat, ready to protect and to destroy, even and especially someone or something his alarm dogs missed. I looked at him - smiling as we all shared a laugh later in the day the morning of which I had accidently woken him up - and imagined he slept with meat cleavers under his bed, always kept sharp, along with a full suit of armor like that of a terracotta warrior. After he related an episode in which he once fought off a steadily increasing number of people in a bar in London - people who, after the fourth or so person to join the fray, didn't know him, didn't have anything against him but were drunk and amazed at the ox of a man out back taking on all comers and holding his own - it was an image I had no trouble imagining."

At this point in the evening, the sky had darkened considerably and there was a chill in the air. Night falls fast for half the year north of the 45 (degrees latitude). A few people such as those with children to put to bed had left. Brooke and her boys took their bacci set and said their goodbyes. With the number of savory offerings at the potluck table dwindling, Steve's friend Sean quietly and dutifully started making batch after batch of dessert waffles with a cast-iron waffle mold over the fire. His friend Trinity, absorbed in the story and intent on hearing more, held her guitar lovingly as she listened. Rosa, a founding member of the local chapter of the 'Strong Independent Woman Overachievers Club' was staying up past her bedtime and decided that that was okay. She loved being with her friends. Steve continued.

"On my first day in New Norfolk I went for a long walk for most of the day, getting the lay of the land as I always like to do in a new place. Doing so, plus time, plus routine, changes the way a place feels to me. Or rather not 'change' but render out more fully, like turning a sketch or an impression into a full-fledged painting. A place in the world, a time in your life, the music you were listening to, your interests then and your outlook at the time on the spectrum from depression to exuberance: all colors on our artist's palette in the fine art of living (the finest art there is), in cultivating the felt experiences of our lives as well as our memories of them. In this sense, there is the act of painting and the completed portrait, the latter meaning that time has passed, you have left that place and are engaged in the act of authoring new works of life-art, and of past works are left with memory, with reckoning, a very different and retrospective paintbrush with which we repeatedly paint over the portraits in our collection every time we remember them, whether we want to or not. In sharing this story with you, am I showing you a portrait or am I guiding you to feel what painting it was like? I submit that for your silent contemplation, for there is still more of my New Norfolk painting to see, even as we now paint together on this very night the sight, the sound, the story of our time together here and now."

"New Norfolk is bisected by Tasmania's second longest river, the River Derwent, which begins at Lake St. Clair to the north, flows south past Hobart and terminates in Storm Bay, part of the Tasman Sea between Australia and New Zealand. There's a vital bridge in town crossing it and connecting the more residential north side (where Bert and Jess live) to the more small business-oriented, town-hall-having south. It is a town of 5000 something people, and as I said before, many anxious barking dogs. Getting my lay of the land on that hot summer day under a mighty blue sky, listening to the band Oh Sees, I stopped in at the first cafe I saw and rather impulsively had a scoop of gelato. What everybody truly needs on a hot day is H2O and electrolytes; what everyone wants on a hot day is ice cream. Therefore as long as there are hot days and as long as there is want, the selling of ice cream and other cool treats will be a viable business. I walked past other cafes, a pharmacy, an alternative medicine clinic, even a small pet food store, all to the fuzzy, distortion-driven tones of the Oh Sees' album Face Stabber. At the supermarket I got coconut water (another hot day cash crop) and a few snacks that I decided would be my lunch. I sat in the shade outside the store and switched over to a podcast (because no one should eat to garage rock) as I snacked and sipped away. It had become windy and cloud cover had blown in over the small formerly baking Derwent River Valley. Indirectly, taking my time, I walked back to Bert and Jess's place."

"A week came up when the two other regular employees had both taken off, and so I picked up the slack at the shop, working more days than usual. It turned out to be a stressful week: a customer was playing phone tag with Deb complaining that a cut of meat wasn't as tender as promised, we had to triage and throw away a bunch of mince meat and stew bones for freezer space, the guy from the chicken farm didn't know how to vacuum seal the chickens he was dropping off and had to be walked through it as we were working, and to top it all off, Bert's latest batch of black pudding burst out of its casing while being boiled! Bugger! as the Aussies would say. I checked my moon-phase app and sure enough, it was the week leading up to the full moon, in which there is great potential, likelihood I'd say, for high intensity times. I think Mercury may also have been retrograde; I don't remember exactly but it sure felt like it. Fateful timing, it was also my last week staying with Bert and Jess. Deb had some work for me at her ranch as well as a place for me to stay. As much as we enjoyed each other's companionship (at home, on the commute into Hobart, while working), and made each other laugh (usually at meat jokes), I knew that Bert and Jess, those lovebirds, wanted their space to themselves again.

They'd been talking a lot about wanting to have kids together soon. It didn't occur to me then but maybe they were hinting at something…"

"On Saturday afternoon, the last day of the work week and this particular week the night of the full moon of February, Bert popped the top off a beer, took a sip, "ahh", sighed with thirst quenching relief. "Man, I am knackered. This week really wrung me out." I shook my head empathetically and probably said something in an attempt to verbally pat him on the back. As head butcher he took his job very seriously. The cuts of meat we put out, the decision to start making old-world specialties like black pudding and haggis, these were his calls, quarterback of the cutting room he was. I shared in the joy of his successes - compliments from customers, the perfecting of a recipe - and also to a smaller extent his woes, like losing several gallons of premium pig's blood because the sausage casing was frozen before use (that's what black pudding is by the way, in case you were wondering). I also think he was disheartened because just as I was becoming useful, becoming teachable beyond simple shop tasks, I was leaving. He wanted, he needed and deserved a full time apprentice, someone in it for the long haul, someone he could mold from a blank slate to learn to do things his way, as he would put it. It could've been me. I looked down the well of a potential life in Hobart, Australia, and I saw water. I liked the city a lot. A fair, temperate climate with good hills to hike and cold water to swim in. I'd made a few friends outside of work, and had even gone on a brunch date with a really sweet girl with whom there was absolutely relationship potential. In another life, in a parallel universe, it could've been me. But I knew I had something very special waiting for me across an ocean and up ninety degrees of latitude. Sorry mate, I said to him as well as thought to myself at times; it just wasn't meant to be."

"We were halfway through an episode of some show Jess and Bert liked on netflix and I was most of the way through a portion of our spicy chicken stir-fry dinner when we heard them. Distant yet still remarkably loud, dogs in what sounded like the next neighborhood over began barking, first one, then several, shrill and incessant. Like a row of canine dominoes, more dogs joined in with each passing second. What the hell? we all wondered aloud in our own words, beginning to conjecture as to what may have been happening. The dogs closer to home began barking, their volume of course even louder, their collective panic increasing. By now they'd formed a veritable lunatic symphony: some dogs barked the deep bass parts, while others, little dogs surely, yapped away in their grating brand of soprano, pizzicato yips. A minute had transpired since the first bark we'd heard, and in that time our own dogs had gone from ears-perked-up attentive to nervous pacing to now, yes, joining the discordant choir themselves. As dog owners will do, Jess and Bert began to try and yell their dogs down. There was however, no calming them, no placating their frenzy. It was when Frodo began foaming at the mouth and jumping doing 360's that I began to feel viscerally unsafe and made to leave the room. The cacophony of barking berated us from all sides; even behind closed doors there was no escape from the intense ear-splitting barrage. I came back, standing in the doorway with earplugs and saw Bert attempting but failing to assuage his dogs. Jess was on the phone. She could have been calling the vet or the police; the latter seemed just as appropriate by that point. Then, in an instant, as if receiving directions from a doggy hive-mind, they went for us: Sooky running to bite Jess, Missy attacking Bert, and Frodo, eyes all white and mouth frothing, went for me. Darting out the front door, I slammed it shut on the possessed pooch mid-leap. Running outside, I saw that our neighbors had fled their homes and were coming out onto the black-top of the street as well, converging in their curiosity-wrought-with-panic. Dogs were already out roaming the block, biting the tires of every car they saw. By now, police sirens had added to the oppressive atmosphere of noise, though they were not yet on our street. I felt a hand on my shoulder; it was Jess. "Where's Bert?" I asked her straight away.

"He's still inside trying to calm the dogs," she said, tears streaming down her face. "What? How?!"

"I don't know but he doesn't want us to get hurt and he doesn't want anyone to hurt the dogs. He said to head to the other side of town. We should get away from where most of the dogs are. And the other side of town connects to the highway, just in case..."

"In case we need to leave," I finished for her. I understood what we had to do.

"Okay let's go."

We mobilized. Jess, myself, and many of our similarly besieged neighbors began walking hurriedly down the street towards the river, towards the bridge. Some people had makeshift weapons in their hands - brooms, hard rakes, shovels - while others had actual ones: axes and kitchen knives. On our way to the bridge, an eight block walk, we were attacked several times by crazed singular berserkers as well as cooperative packs. When we saw people under attack - in their yard confused and horrified at having to fight off their formerly loyal companion - we helped them fend off the four-legged assailant, and cleaned and bandaged any wounds they might've had (someone had the wherewithal to bring a first-aid kit as they fled their home). Most of those we encountered joined us after saving them. A few insisted on staying put and waiting for the police while others simply didn't see the sense in leaving their castle. Lone wolves and wolf packs much the same, us humans."

Those sitting by the fire hearing Steve's story listened on with either dropped jaws or jaws full of ice cream and waffle, expressing shock with their eyes while taking care not to choke on their food.

"When we reached the bridge many others had gathered there too, evidently following a similar train of thought. At our backs was a horde of frenzied, lunatic dogs; ahead of us, more human infrastructure and a greater chance of safety. Jess and I looked at each other, unsure of whether to continue without Bert. That decision was soon made for us as two mammoth, malicious looking stone lions stepped into view. Amid the throng of dogs-gone-mad, the twin stone lion guardians from the property I envied, come-to-life and hulked out to at least five times their original size, crushed lawn and pavement alike with every booming step they took. Their glowing red eyes, terrifying to look at, seemed to be the source and seed of their evil animation. Though wordless and monstrous, they seemed to know what we were up to, our intentions of escape, and seemed intent themselves on thwarting our plan and feasting on our lives."

"The dogs and now the lions were rapidly closing in on us, and it seemed now that even crossing the bridge would not ensure our safety, as they were so close that they would surely follow us over, or more likely, reach us while on the bridge and slaughter us in a helpless bottleneck, with nowhere to turn save for the suicidal option of plunging into the dark and flowing river beneath us. We, the doomed denizens of New Norfolk, shared together a helpless eternity of a few minutes dwelling in this realization, inching backwards towards the bridge in despair. Then, suddenly, a new figure appeared; yet another variable was entering the already nightmarish mix. When the figure was still fuzzy and indiscernible in the distance but nevertheless clearly hurtling towards us, I thought to myself, wonderful, delightful, how much worse can this get? Bring it on."

"When we could tell the thing was bipedal we sighed with relief. When we saw who it was and what he was doing, we stood there now not paralyzed by fear so much as awe and surprise. Running towards us clad from head to toe in leather-hide armor and brandishing two massive knives was Bert.

He did indeed look like an ancient Mongolian warrior gone Anglo. He stopped in front of the crowd, placing himself between us and the lions, which by now had stopped their march to assess this new target in their path. The horde of mad dogs had stopped also, forming a semi-circle around the lions."

"Bert spoke to us, "All of you, cross the bridge. I'll hold them off here. They won't get past me." Several people, including Jess, rushing closer to him, protested his command. "I won't hear a thing about it," he said with the utmost surety, "I know who I am, what I've done, and what I'm capable of. I know what my strengths are, and what my destiny is. When I'm through over here I'll see you on the other side. Now go, off with you." In hindsight the ambiguity of his phrasing stands out to me. In the heat of the moment we all understood it naturally as meaning 'the other side of the bridge,' but the linguist in me savors his choice of words, for he could've also and perhaps did truly mean the other side of death. Perhaps, a thousand years ago, he saved us all once before on the plains of northern China or on the bare Mongolian steppe. Perhaps *every* thousand years there is a lifetime in which he remembers who he is, recalls his warrior dharma and, like a dormant volcano merely biding its time, erupts, and he saves and slaughters with the resolution and mastery of an untapped eon."

" "Right you lot," he said aloud, turning to face his foes and wiping his weapons - two massive golden meat cleavers - against his armor. "These here are my friends and family you're after." One of the lions let out a bomb of a roar, its red eyes gleaming as sharp as its teeth. Bert, holding his cleavers out to his sides, began rushing at them as he roared, "In Londontown they called me the Ripper; long ago I was known the world over as Attila. No creature on earth has bested me, and there's nothing my blades won't cut through." One by one and then several at a time the dogs began to whimper and back away. I could see a smile on his face, heroic yet sinister, as he yelled to his enemies, the lions, now bounding towards him too, "Do you know who you're up against?" He raised his cleavers over-head and with a leap he yelled even louder, "I'm the butcher of New Norfolk you cunts! Tonight you meet your doom!" "

"From the other side of the river, I only saw that first blow: his cleavers broke stone as they connected with one lion's face and the other's shoulder, while one of their massive column-like paws swiped him hard across the torso. It looked like the thick leather armor he wore took the brunt of the blow and he might've made it out okay, though I couldn't be sure. I had gotten swept up in the commotion this side of the river. Several towns' worth of police-force along with EMS and firefighters had arrived on the scene, tending to people's wounds and strategizing about how to deal with a few hundred mad dogs and what seemed like town-wide property damage. I spent the night along with many others in one of several churches that had opened its doors to those of us who didn't want to or couldn't go back home just yet. The emergency personnel pulled an all-nighter that night in New Norfolk, scouring the town and hopefully getting paid overtime. Needless to say, no one slept well, exhausted as we all were."

"The next day Deb picked me up from the doorstep to Bert and Jess's now vacant home. I'd walked back there to get all my belongings, passing two thoroughly busted up stone lion statues whose rubble now lay for all to see, commemorating the stand-off at the bridge, the time the human population of New Norfolk was brought to its knees. Jess had gone to stay with her parents. Bert hadn't been seen yet. Through the quiet beauty of Deb's hillside ranch, further still out from Hobart, I was able to process over the next few days what had happened, and more or less satisfactorily soothe my adrenals, lovingly coax my fight-or-flight response off. But maybe now you'll forgive the seeming vulgarity of the term, in this case an endearment. Maybe now you'll understand me when I say that I'll never forget that cunt, Bert, the butcher of New Norfolk."

When my brother told us all for the first time that Papa had visited him in a dream, it had only been a few weeks since he'd died. "He called me on the phone," my brother said, "and told me about where he was - a waiting room. He said that he was okay, no longer in pain, just waiting."

This is right in line with the traditional Jewish concept of the afterlife that my eldest son described to me once. He said he heard it from a History Channel special on the Old Testament. Apparently for Jews there is no hell, and until the messiah comes no ultimate heaven either, but instead something like a sleepy waiting space akin to a train station at dawn or dusk, where the deceased hang out faintly, not doing much but not suffering either. Despite my father's wishes, despite how he was raised and the life he lived, we, his children and grandchildren, never were great Jews. We didn't have even close to the same pride as he did in where we came from, our ancient culture that narrowly escaped extinction recently and many times over before the 20th century. Oh well, dad. So it was and so it is. We loved each other fully nonetheless.

When I heard that my brother dreamt of our father again, and then a third time, and that one of my sons did too, I was not just amazed but also began to feel jealous. I am his daughter after all. I am the first-born of Edward Faerber, son of Jack Faerber, who took that simple monosyllabic first name when he emigrated from Hungary to the U.S. with his family in the late 1930's to escape religious and ethnic persecution, where, as my father would always remind us with such disgusted passion, they were killing Jews in the street. It was one of the only topics of conversation that had him lose his cool, each and every time he spoke about it.

Naturally I started to wonder: why wasn't I dreaming of him? Why wasn't he visiting me in my dreams? The first question is much easier to answer than the second.

Maybe I wasn't dreaming of him because I don't really dream anymore, period. I do experience the sort of strange half-dream thoughts one has sometimes when drifting off to sleep and the short one-scene dreams one has sometimes just before waking up, the kind that occur as the brain gently shifts from the waking, logical state to the relaxed, restful non-executive processing state that is sleep, and back again. But beyond those liminal thoughts, faint and tantalizing as they are, there is nothing for me once I conk out. Just a black-out. Just the oblivion of unconsciousness. It's been this way for decades. If I'm being honest with myself I know why. It's because I regularly use cannabis to fall asleep, which is known to disrupt REM sleep, which is when we dream. It is, as I said, a multi-decade habit without which I simply wouldn't be able to fall asleep. It is also a habit my father never approved of, and one I mostly kept him in the dark about. As someone who works six and a half days a week, not falling asleep isn't an option. We all know the hell that is a sleepless night. I'll pass on that as often as I can.

Why else don't people dream? Could there be other reasons? I'd much rather chalk it up to something physiological than lack of worth as to why I haven't dreamt of my recently deceased dad. And so upon hearing of more and more family members dreaming of him, I set out to explore the potential reasons for myself.

Since he passed away at the very end of 2020 at the age of 82 (of diverticulitis, not COVID, it must be said given the time-frame), my and my brother's families took stock of my father's home, the home my brother and I grew up in, and beyond that, the home of our parents for over 50 years. We cleaned it up, organized it. There were family treasures, personal effects, kitschy junk and troves of expired food. I learned through this process that my parents had been inadvertent preppers for decades. Nowadays we semi-seriously call people holding onto sets of canned or boxed non-perishable goods 'preppers', and people holding onto miscellaneous junk for no logical reason so much so that it begins to crowd their house and violate fire safety laws, hoarders. But to my parents who grew up in the wake of the Great Depression and WWII, they were just being sensible. My father, the second son of Jewish immigrants who were blessed to make it out alive, was raised to be thankful for what he had. To always clean his plate, to never throw away food unless it was visibly and undeniably spoiled, an attitude that did not mesh well with his diverticulitis diagnosis later in life. Contributed to it, most likely.

The horrifying full extent of my mother's Alzheimer's was revealed to us now without dad to take care of her, shield her, shield us from her degeneration. She would not be able to live on her own without him, that much became clear very quickly. No one of the family was going to live with her nor take her in and devote ourselves to caring for her, though we did hire a live-in caretaker for the first month after his death, which proved itself to be an unsustainable arrangement. Instead we found an assisted living facility not far from the apartment my husband and I were renting. That had been talked about before, had been in the cards as a distinct possibility for some time as my parents grew older and their health issues presented themselves, and with unusual foresight my father had arranged with his health insurance that in the event of his death his wife would be well taken care of in this way. Towards the end of his life he would often sign off phone calls with the refrain "take care of yourself." Well, he took care of mom, that was for sure, saint of a man he was.

After months of effort, experiencing nostalgia and breathing in more than our fair share of mold spores, we were able to sell my childhood home. There was so much to take out, distribute to family near and far and to just plain get rid of. That house was packed. There was expired food dating all the way back to the 70's, spice mixes so old they may as well have been dust. Just below the surface of the house's clean-looking, aesthetically acceptable appearances, beyond that thin veneer of sanity, civility, and homeliness, hundreds of boxes, pouches, and cans of expired food lived on defiantly just beyond the cupboard door. In some places mice had discovered this, got into the food stores and thrived on the cache they found. There were so many unnecessary items and redundancies - packages of batteries, cheap emergency ponchos, boxes of the same bowtie pasta all lined up like the grocery store they were bought from - we realized that my parents must have had a standing grocery list and just got the same things every week or biweekly or monthly, regardless of their trends of actual use. Whether they were entirely self-aware of this hoarding of theirs and their Great Depression-informed, 'clean your plate' psyches, relishing in the surplus and safety of knowing they had way more at any one time than they'd ever need, or whether they weren't so self-aware and were rather more simply and dutifully getting what was on the shopping list each week like unquestioning broken records, we'll never know. Without my father to ask or my mother in her right mind, that'll be their secret.

And then, there was the library.

It was no secret that my father was an avid reader. Often reading five or six books at a time, it was one of his main interests in life. He influenced me and two out of my three children to always be reading a book. When my firstborn wrote his first book, a collection of short stories, he dedicated it to him, "to Edward Faerber, for inspiring a lifelong love of literature". My father, who was alive to see this, shed tears of joy when he was given a copy of that book and saw the dedication. Every night of his adult life, and probably similarly in his youth, he would head up to his room at around 8pm or so, sometimes earlier, and lay in bed and read till only God knows when. He had an impressive collection of books in his own room, one he didn't share with my mother on account of his sleep apnea, ranging from Jewish scripture to the poetry of Borges, from Ancient Greek civilization to modern psychology. There were books here and there throughout the house, as one might expect, more as decorations and social offerings. Then there was the garage, which housed his motorcycle, their garbage and recycling, some yard tools, and stacks and stacks of books forming a row twelve to fifteen feet long and chest height high at least. Against the far wall of the garage was a long set of storage shelves a library or a warehouse might have, completely stuffed with books. It didn't end there. In the basement, where the mold smell was strong enough to sting our eyes, were even more books, all sorts of old board games lost to time, and in one corner what appeared to be a collection of rare books: books with unique silvery covers, a couple of first editions, several books entirely in French (which the man, to our knowledge, did not speak), and one very important and sacred looking copy of the Torah. When we were finally convinced that we'd taken full stock of the sum total of the books in that house, we lovingly referred to his collection as the Edward Faerber Memorial Library.

Another personal effect to deal with was his motorcycle. Yes, my father, the straight-laced bifocal wearing, book-worm baby boomer he was, owned a motorcycle. He rode one along with his brother from his teens up until just a few years before he passed. Though in the last decade or two of his life he didn't ride it out of the tame suburban neighborhood in which he lived. When I saw his motorcycle in the garage, on its kickstand tilted like he had just come home from a ride, I felt fond memories wash over me of him taking me for rides when I was growing up. And then on my wedding day, before the ceremony, when he took me for a celebratory ride to the Hudson river. He always looked after me with such care, such tenderness and unconditional love.

As my brother and I finished saying goodbye to our childhood home, I was struck so vividly by the memories it held, in particular the ones that were daily occurrences. We took them for granted then, just another part of the golden days of youth that never end until major life events like marriage, children, or the death of loved ones tell you you've aged. As we stood in the cream-colored carpeted front hallway, I remembered how everyday when we heard his car pulling into the driveway in the late afternoon, my brother and I would yell, "Daddy's home!" and stop whatever it was we were doing and run to the spot where I was standing now, waiting gleefully as he unlocked the front door and said dutifully, each time, "let me wash my hands before I give you a hug."

As the weeks turned into months, the first months of 2021, and the house went up for sale, my desire to understand one secret, one mystery, only grew stronger. At first I thought it was just the men and that was that; that Papa was only visiting male family members in their dreams (my brother, my two sons, my husband) like things would be in a traditional sexually separated orthodox synagogue. I thought maybe, being a pious Jew, he observed this rite in death. But then one day he appeared in my daughter's dream, and out went that tidy little theory. It was at that point that I had to admit to myself that something about my lifestyle, maybe my cannabis use, maybe undealt with stress, was messing with my ability to dream. My other son, my middle-child, mentioned noticing this too in his own experience: that whenever he took a break from smoking he would experience a rush of intense dreams, pent-up REM releasing or taking place at last. Now knowing this, if I was being real with myself I had to at least entertain the possibility that my nightly habit was preventing possible communication with my father from beyond the grave. Thinking this felt mystical, but I had to admit, possible too. Suggesting this aloud to others - my husband, my coworkers, my cousins - felt surprisingly more validating than I'd expected. Holding back from voicing my thoughts because they might seem silly or even obnoxious to others is something I've alway done, even, if I'm being honest, to the effect of withholding the expression of love when love was my only intention. I think my parents did that too. That's not to say that I didn't feel loved by them. But as I grew up and saw more families and more walks of life, I saw more passion, more expression of emotions both joyful and angry. Like meeting my husband's family way back when, for instance; I was struck by how their yelling at each other seemed to be a normal aspect of their communication. My parents subscribed to a post WWII middle to upper-middle class baby-boomer set of virtues and manners. In a nutshell, it was this: let all your actions be done as if always in full view by the rest of society; act like your every deed was done in public. If you were home and it was just family, you could relax a little, let your hair down, be silly, make faces, be a character. But in any other setting it was suck it in, hold it back, sit up straight and proceed with caution.

This mentality seemed right and proper, second nature to me, modeled by my parents who only deeply wanted to be successful as success was defined by their parents. And not necessarily have this defined, specific-looking success seen by their parents. They didn't need them to say 'good job' or pat them on the back. I think it's that they internalized a specific vision of what success and living well and living right looked like. And as first generation Americans, they internalized those ideas of success and decorum strongly mixed or confused with the desperate sense of survival that their parents came to this country with. As stuck in my ways as I'll admit to being, my parents were *really* stuck in their ways. I don't think they were capable of breaking their molds, no, not even bending them.

—------------------

In order to see my father again, in order to dream, I realized I would have to bend or break my mold. Posing the question to Dr. Google led to many (too many) possible causes of poor sleep and lack of dream: stress, cortisol level, anxiety, light pollution, circadian rhythm being out of whack, vitamin D level, blood sugar and glucose metabolism, hormones and menopause…I exist at the center of the storm of all of this, and smoke pot in the evenings to escape it all, to relax, to unwind what has been wound up inside me over the course of an average day, to laugh, to decompress, and finally, after a little book reading, to fall asleep. To be able to fall asleep I do something that keeps me from dreaming. Thinking about this consciously for the first time, I became aware of this profound paradox of my everyday life. That year after his passing, thinking about my father and my family life as I grew up had become a habit for me, a reasonable obsession you might say. As I drifted off to sleep one night a month or so after my parent's home had sold, I remembered sweetly our summer vacations in the bungalow in the Catskills they rented out for two weekends a year, Memorial and Labor Day weekends, the gateways to and from the idyllic freedom of summer. I took pride in how playful my father was compared to the other dads lounging about or cooking up food. My father, Edward or Eddy as he was known, would act like a wild gorilla and chase us little kids around, puffing out his cheeks and bounding around on all fours. If only I could visit those summer days again in my dreams…

But the dreams don't come. Only the reprieve from thought and activity, the 'turning off of the tv screen' that is deep sleep. Restful for the body but not much for the mind, or so I've learned, is the difference between deep and REM sleep. There were many things I could do, it turned out, to retrain myself to start dreaming again. I asked my eldest, something of a self-taught encyclopedia on herbs and supplements, and did a little internet investigation of my own. I wrote down everything I found out and picked out just two to start with so as not to get overwhelmed.

- Quit cannabis
- Take something called GABA
- Take magnesium
- Meditate before going to bed
- Be done with screens an hour before bed
- Exercise over the course of the day
- Have some hot water with honey and apple cider vinegar an hour before bed
- Drink herbal tea with (I found a number of herbs) hops, mugwort, chamomile, passionflower, valerian, or skullcap

Exercise I had down. As an exercise instructor I was already doing this for hours each day. The other ones were mostly helpful, from what I could tell, for falling asleep, not necessarily for inducing dreaming. So I decided that in addition to stopping smoking I would try the honey and apple cider vinegar combo, and see where that got me. That day I felt a certain amount of dread and anxiety at the thought of not partaking in my nightly ritual, something I did with my husband every night like sharing an evening glass of wine. But every time the dread at the thought of it crept up, I remembered why I was going to try this. And I was just trying it, after all; no lifetime vows or resolutions. Just trying different things here and there and seeing what happened. Seeing if anything, any one habit or herb or lack of an herb, ahem, would lead to my desired results: to see my father again in my dreams.

"So you're really not going to come and hit this joint with me?" my husband Roy asked in disbelief. Expecting my usual post-dinner request to go take a walk and smoke a fat joint, he already had one rolled. "I've got to give this a try," I told him. "Alright," he replied, "I respect that. It'll be here if you do wind up wanting it. I'll just go hit the one-hitter a few times." He walked down the steep steps of our apartment to our garage. In our living-room, feeling a little strange and a little anxious at passing up our evening doobie, I began doodling with markers on a large blank sheet of paper. First tracing out many shapes and loops of similar sizes but totally random in their orientation, I filled the page with black-lined curves. Then, I took out my large colored marker set and began to color them in. Usually I choose a theme or suite of colors that make sense together, but tonight, inspired by how unhinged I felt, I picked colors completely at random; it was like a stream of consciousness coloring session. I always find this to be a relaxing, mentally soothing activity, and it's become something I do now almost everyday.

I heard Roy's footsteps coming up the stairs, followed by his voice, "So what's on the menu for entertainment tonight, m'lady?" he said with a smile. I couldn't help but smile back as I suggested we try finding a nature documentary to watch. When my husband Roy is in a happy, playful mood, it's one of the best things in the world. It's contagious. We made our cups of ice cream topped with granola and settled onto our large L-shaped couch. Just as I expected, it felt strange to be doing this in a sober frame of mind, but I remained resolute. In the name of relaxation and trying to make it an easeful night, I resisted the urge to check my phone for work texts or emails. Over the years I, the group fitness manager of the gym I worked for, have established the unfortunate precedent of being reachable outside of my work hours. Now I was trying to undo this, make people forget or no longer think to reach out to me past five or six in the evening. Though it was trying and anxiety-producing in its own way to not check my phone this late in the day (and for the sake, ultimately, of reducing my anxiety, ironically), eventually I was able to relax into the moment as my husband and I ooo'd and ahh'd and laughed at the scenes of nature from around the globe that unfolded before us on our tv screen. Still a screen, but I guess one was enough tonight. A reasonable reduction, something to be proud of.

One of the treasures we found buried in my parents' basement was a vhs of our wedding! We thought this was long gone, that no one had a video recording of this momentous day in our lives. But it was there, and for once I was grateful that my parents held on to almost everything. We no longer had a vhs player however. But my husband Roy did not accept defeat; he found someone who was able to convert the vhs into a dvd.

Reliving this incredibly special day was an emotional experience beyond belief. Years before our children were born, before grandparents had become 'grand' and when older friends and relatives were still around and kicking, the video was truly a window looking back into another time, an era of our lives both familiar and distant at the same time. My friends were there, thinner and without their husbands, Roy's friends were there and still had full heads of hair. Still a novel experience back then in the early 80's, friends and family took turns in front of a tripod mounted video camera and recorded us well-wishes, some nervous and awkward, some with coke-jawed enthusiasm, but all loving and sincere. These clips were interspersed with the footage of the party following our exchange of vows.

Our parents, not yet old and feeble, left us messages this way too. Roy's father, his hair done up in a jheri-curl and with his characteristically quirky sense of humor, wished us well but said (perhaps joking but then again maybe not) that the party was great but that the fruit cups could have been better. When my parents stepped in front of the camera, they were beaming with love and pride that their daughter had found her life partner. I still remember how loving and sincere my dad's voice was when he wished us good health and all the happiness in the world together. He wished that in our marriage we would have the strength to take care of each other. I would say that this has indeed been the case, and I'm happy that both sets of our parents lived to see this ring true. Needless to say, we were both in tears at this point in the video. With my father's death came an unexpected reminder of the day my married life began, a gift from him even though he was gone.

As usual, I followed our nightly time together in front of the tv with some solo reading time. I was always in bed before Roy; it had been this way for quite some time. As I read my book, not stoned, I felt tense, not as comfortable and relaxed and ready to drift off as I normally was. I consciously tried to relax myself, each muscle in my body and then finally my mind. I concentrated on watching my thoughts, slowing them down. As new trains of thought arose I gave them no more energy, instead imagining I was playing whack-a-mole as I hammered down each new thought as it arose. Whack-a-thought. Eventually I put my book away, closed my eyes and lay there, as physically comfortable as I could manage to get.

I laid and laid there, not drifting off to sleep.

Eventually Roy entered the room, quiet as he could, turned off the lights and climbed into bed with me. Maintaining my somewhat meditative state, focusing on observing and nothing more, I felt the bed shift and heard it creak as he lay beside me. Shit, I remembered, Roy snores like a bear. If I don't fall asleep before him…too late. The man was fast asleep in a matter of minutes. As the rabbi said at our wedding ceremony, in sickness and in health…in snores and in sleeplessness.

I laid there still, not drifting off to sleep.

I opened my eyes and looked around the room, mostly dark with a few small bright lights from things plugged into the outlets that surrounded us, our wifi modem on top of the dresser in the corner. I heard the steady drone of our air purifier provide background noise like a sitar drone for my husband's bear-like snoring heaves.

Still, I laid and laid there, not drifting off to sleep.

My patience, my attempt at zen was losing out. I began to experience the stressful mental parade that sleeplessness brings: the anxiety, the squirminess, and of course, worst of all and known to everyone who's ever struggled to fall asleep, the self-questioning and the self-blame. Thoughts of 'what's wrong with me?' and 'the person next to me fell asleep so easily, why can't I?' And then thoughts of tomorrow, of the day that will be so thrown off by the sleepless night at hand. I couldn't take it any longer, not when what I knew would put me right to sleep was so close by. I got up from bed somewhat angrily, grabbed my one-hitter out of the drawer in our bathroom we keep it in and headed down to the garage to take a few puffs.

—------------------

I wake up the next morning a bit pissed off and not feeling as rested as I normally do after a night's sleep. Oh well, I think to myself reassuringly, I'm trying new things. There will always be growing pains in attempting to break out of one's routine. It's like swimming or kayaking against the current; it will be difficult, but there's a reason I'm doing it. Attempting it. I do some pushups as I wait for the shower to get warm, and step in. I can hear music faintly, coming from the kitchen. It's Roy of course. He's up and at 'em, as he is every morning. He's usually up before me, has his cup of coffee and packs me lunch for the day. He's semi-retired and has taken it upon himself, in his loving, dutiful way, to run the house, so to speak: cook, clean, fix or repair what needs it. I still do the painting if we ever decide to repaint the walls, that's my thing. But he's on top of just about everything else. He's always been very proactive and exceptionally good at that, keeping the ship running smoothly, whatever it takes. He smiles at me as I walk into the kitchen and sit down at the dining room table, and I can't help but smile back, replying 'good morning' both verbally and not. "Have you ever had a lucid dream?" he asks me all of a sudden.

"Mmm," I start to think, "No, I don't think so."
"Maybe that's something you can try. Apparently it's a skill one can develop."

"Can one?" I reply cheekily.
"One can," he says back, humorously sagelike. "You can. You can be that one."

So while I'm at work that day, when I have a free moment here and there, I look into it. Articles and webpages claim that lucid dreaming doesn't have to be something that happens magically or randomly. It is something you can practice at and eventually reliably train yourself to be able to do, they say. I poll my coworkers on lucid dreaming, and the results are mixed: a little less than half of them tell me they've never had a lucid dream, a little more than half say that they have once or twice in their lives, and one guy, Kevin, our administrative assistant, says he taught himself how to lucid dream about a decade ago. "You have to practice having a 'reality check-in' throughout the day," he tells me.

"What the heck is that?" I ask.
"Something like looking at the clock regularly, looking at your palms regularly throughout the day. And every time you do, you pair that with asking yourself, 'am I awake or dreaming?' That part is very important. Time after time during the day, you know what the answer will be. But it's important that that question, that reality check is part of it."

"Umm okay…how often do I need to do this?"
"I don't mean obsessively, to the point that you're not doing anything else and you just look like a crazy person checking your hands all the time. But the idea is to have this check-in regularly enough that your brain will dream

of you doing it, and in that moment you ask yourself, like you did a hundred or so times over the course of the day, am I awake or am I dreaming? The formula is ingrained."

"And what happens when I finally do it in my dream?"

"The reality check then should make you conscious and aware, since you've been practicing throughout the day being conscious and aware. And once you realize you're dreaming, you can kinda do whatever you want. The normal laws of physics don't apply."

"Can I create whatever I want? Make objects or people appear in my dream who weren't there before?"

"Ehh, well I've never done that. It was always me and only me I became fully in control of when I would lucid dream. Like, I would realize I was dreaming, and then I would fly around like Superman."

"Do you still do this?"

"Nah,"

"Why not? It sounds amazing."

"Well, maybe I'm not the most creative person, but I just got tired of it. So what if I could fly around or move really fast? Your dream is going to do what it's going to do, going to be what's going to be. It's like a pre-loaded script created by your brain. And it was never long before whatever I might've chosen to do in the dream, even if it was a conscious choice, perhaps in spite of it being a conscious choice, would end the dream, would wake me up. Like flying too far away from the scene of the dream, or messing too much with what the main characters in the dream were doing. It's like your brain knows and wants to do or express whatever it has queued up to do or express, and time and time again I would 'break the dream', end it and wake up. I never got anything meaningful out of lucid dreaming. But! That's not to say you shouldn't try it. I don't want to dissuade you. It is cool, for sure. You should totally try it."

And so, I spent a moment every half hour for the rest of the day (I set a reminder on my watch) looking down at my hands, noticing my engagement ring and my wedding ring, the lines that ran through my palms, and asking myself, am I awake or am I dreaming? A few times when driving on the way home, when stopped behind another car, at red lights, I checked my palms, am I awake or am I dreaming? Once during our dinner that night I took a moment to 'check-in', and of course Roy asked me what I was doing. "Lucid dreaming practice," I explained. I thought it was interesting that even though the answer to the question I was posing to myself was always the same, it helped me to notice just how often I'm basically on auto-pilot throughout the day. This continued into the following couple of days, as my lucid dreaming practice, my reality check-in helped to insert moments of awareness and clarity into life's repetitive mundanities: taking the same roads to work each day, doing the same things at work each day, seeing the same clients and coworkers there each day, driving home, eating dinner, doodling, going for a walk and then relaxing in front of the tv each night before bed. I had rejoined Roy each night in splitting a joint together; that night without it and the thought of how many more nights like that I'd have to face before I was finally able to fall asleep without it (and that was a big 'if', really) was just too much. I decided to take it easy on myself and just keep it at one thing to support dreaming at a time.

I didn't expect to be lucid dreaming after one day of doing this, or even two or three, but after day three I did start to wonder. On day four I asked Kevin shortly after getting to work. "I started becoming lucid after…" he paused to think, literally scratching his head as he did so. "Um, I think it was somewhere in week two."

"Great. Flippin' fantastic," was my reply.

"Keep at it. It's going to be worth the effort."

I kept at it alright. Noticing my irritation at what was really such a small thing, a small investment of my time and energy but one, apparently, that took its time to pay out, I reflected on my sense of want and reward and how it's changed over the course of my life. Changed so fast and without very much reflection on my part. Where once I was more than content to save up my allowance for the better part of a year in order to buy myself a bike, now I was pissed if my Amazon delivery took longer than 48 hours. I suppose when near instant gratification becomes the norm, even a costless habit that takes time to see the results of can be annoying. The virtue of delayed gratification, something my generation and my father's especially grew up with, is pretty much lost to us now. 'Don't care how, I want it now!' sang Veruca Salt. She could probably run for president and get elected now on that campaign slogan alone.

To quiet down my impatience as I kept up my lucid dreaming practice, I remembered how life used to be. Now slow-seeming by comparison, growing up in the 70's it was all we knew. Taking your time, saving up your pennies, clipping coupons. And slow, steady, daily diligent practice. That was something my father embodied strongly and effortlessly. I remembered how on the weekdays if I woke up early enough in the morning I would catch him in the kitchen with the day's newspaper on the table, his breakfast eaten and his lunch (usually a sandwich) already packed, doing his morning exercises: push-ups, sit-ups, and chin-ups holding onto the wooden door frame that separated the kitchen from the front hallway. Mom wouldn't be up yet, and so we shared this quiet time in the early hours of the day, now sacred in my memory, in which we wouldn't say much at all to each other but just slowly and diligently each start our day on the right foot. In this way, my father impressed upon me discipline, an early to bed-early to rise mentality, and a lifelong commitment to the importance of exercise and taking care of yourself. Coming up on two decades in the fitness industry, he must've made a bigger impression than I'd previously considered.

Eventually, on the night of my sixth day of practicing, I had a dream. I was on a street in the town I grew up in. As dreams go, there was no clear evidence of this, I just *knew* that to be the case. My grandparents, my mother's parents, passed me by in their Cadillac convertible. It was a picturesque sunny day in suburban New Jersey. I was sitting on a street corner, their car top was down, and they turned to look at me as they drove in front of me. As they passed me by they did so in slow motion. I waved at them. My hands! I suddenly remembered my hands, remembered to ask myself the question, and realized I was not awake but dreaming. Before I thought about what I could do with that information, I looked back up at my grandparents. They smiled, somewhat eerily, but did not wave back. Then, when their car had passed me, they resumed their normal speed, the normal speed of a car sauntering down a residential street, fifteen to twenty miles an hour probably. When they'd fully left my sight the dream ended, and I woke up. My first feeling was one of the excitement of success; I had had a dream, fully formed and more vivid than I'd had since…I don't even know when. And it was semi-lucid, I'd say. I became aware but didn't act on my awareness. It didn't feel like I had time to. Strangest of all though was the fact that this was an almost exact repeat of a dream I had when I was a girl. My grandparents, those grandparents specifically, had gotten into a car accident when I was eleven years old. My grandmother, Nana we called her, was killed on impact. My grandfather Sam lived out his remaining few years with us. Back then, in the early 70's shortly after they'd had that accident, I had this dream. The only difference was then I wasn't in the habit of looking at my palms and questioning reality. That was the only difference; otherwise it was an exact repeat of that meaningful dream I had all those years ago, waving them goodbye after their car accident, only now I'd become aware in the dream that I was dreaming.

I told Roy about it that morning, my children and my brother too that day. I didn't know what to make of it. It did feel like progress; I did have a dream about deceased family, and it was nice to see them again, fleeting and surreal as it was. But still no Papa, still no dear ol' dad. In the time I'd made it my mission to dream of him, my two sons had dreamt of him again twice. I decided it was time to try another potential dream-inducer. My eldest son had good things to say about the herb mugwort. He was always willing to help out with advice on what herbs or mushrooms to take for this issue or that, and as soon as I said the word he mailed me what he promised was a potent 'mugwort elixir' made in the San Juan islands where he lived. Knowing the passionate quest to dream I was undertaking, he shelled out and sent it by express post. "How should I take it?" I asked him by text. "Start with one dropper full an hour or so before bed in some warm water. Try that for a few days and increase to two droppers if you're not getting any results. The further away from dinner you take it, the more effective it'll be."

When the small package arrived, I took it home and opened it up in the kitchen. I felt an unusual sort of reverence as I held the small dark green glass tincture bottle in the air. Remembering my son's instructions on proper storage, I resisted my impulse to look at it in the sunlight that was streaming into the room. "Keep it in a cool dark place, out of direct sunlight." I placed it in my night table drawer next to my side of the bed, and again felt a peculiar almost mystical sense of reverence as I closed the drawer. I felt the stillness in my room for a moment, heard the wind rustle through trees outside, saw the dust or skin particles wafting carefree through the air in the room, and then walked back into the kitchen. I heard the garage door. Roy was home.

"How did you shoot today?" I asked him knowing he'd just returned from the gun range he visits once a week or so.
 "Not bad, not bad. I shot fifty rounds with each gun, and I had a nice group grouping at the center of the target by the end of it."

"Nice. Well when the zombie apocalypse hits I know who to stick around with."

"Ha, I do it for no other reason than the enjoyment of it, and I hope you'd be sticking around me when the zombie apocalypse hits for other reasons first."

"Yeah, yeah. But the marksmanship helps…"

I had to head back to work for another two pilates clients that night at the gym and was finally done with work for the day at 8:30pm. I ate dinner on the drive home, something the cafe at my gym makes called a San Remo wrap, my favorite. By the time I pulled into our garage, parked and headed up the stairs, Roy and I were SO ready for our evening joint. That whole process, the walk out of our apartment complex, the smoking and then the walk back takes about twelve to fifteen minutes. When we stepped back into the house from that, I remembered my dream elixir I was supposed to take. I squeezed the small black rubber bulb of the tincture dropper into some water I'd heated up on our stovetop kettle. It tasted sweet, slightly alcoholic, and…herby. I don't really know how else to describe it. Herbaceous, that's what they say on Chopped and other food shows. Herbaceous. Then, more of the usual rituals of our evening: ice cream, shows, book, bed. Anyone married or with a steady job can relate to the groundhog's day that life can be. Especially if you've got both going on. Shoot, I thought to myself as I put away my book and got ready to fall asleep, Steven said to take the elixir on an empty stomach. Oh well.

That night I didn't dream, big surprise. The next day was much the same, except I didn't return home for a few hours' break early in the afternoon and didn't have any evening clients. I worked straight through till six and then headed home. I had dinner at home that night, it was ready when I got there, chef Roy be praised. I skipped on dessert that night so that my mugwort potion could be more effective. Still had some pot though, of course. As I lay down to sleep that night, I did notice a difference. It was hard to put into words, but I felt calmer and sort of dreamy even before I had fallen asleep, if that makes any sense. I couldn't tell if I was just expecting something to happen or what, but I felt like something was going to happen, an excited but chilled-out feeling of anticipation. In hindsight I'm still not sure if this was a placebo effect or the elixir starting to work its magic, this pre-sleep feeling. But once I had fallen asleep that night, something had definitely taken effect, because I dreamt. Vividly.

I had a dream that night it was my bat-mitzvah, the Jewish coming-of-age ceremony that takes place around age thirteen. Near-perpetual persecution must have led to an expediting into adulthood for us Jews. I was back in time but with my adult mind and full knowledge of everything that had happened since then, as dreams go sometimes. Back then in 1976 my bat-mitzvah was one of the first to be had in the temple since the completion of the renovations it had been undergoing for most of the year prior, so there was a certain sense of newness and awe on my day. In the dream I felt these feelings again as if for the first time: how immaculately clean the new carpeted floor looked, the (for the time) avant-garde large aerial sculpture-chandelier thing held aloft by wires on all sides about fifty feet into the front hallway that twinkled metallic gold, the fresh coat of paint on the walls that led all the way up to the high ceiling of the main temple room where daily services were held and where my bat mitzvah ceremony took place. I was in a small room connected to the main temple area where people about to go up and lead the congregation waited, normally rabbi's or other times guest speakers, and whenever there was a coming-of-age ceremony like mine today, where the bar or bat mitzvot (boy or girl about to be 'adulted') waited. I sat there at the small brown wooden table with a folder with all my prepared materials in it: the programme for the ceremony, people I was supposed to remember to thank and honor at different times throughout, a small speech I would make at the beginning introducing myself and my family line and a larger speech I would give towards the end that was my 'lecture' on the Torah portion I was assigned to speak about, one that coincided with and was traditionally read that time of the year, the beginning of June. I felt all over again the nervousness I felt then at this highly important coming-of-age event. It was a monumental day and to my father, a religious man, especially important. There was as I sat waiting, however, a certain awareness. I knew who was there - friends, immediate family and more distant relatives - even though I hadn't seen them, again, another dream peculiarity. There was also an awareness with my adult mind present of 'oh I've been here before, doing this again eh?' that I certainly didn't have on that day all those years ago. That's what helped it kick in: I'm dreaming, I realized suddenly and starkly. I'm dreaming and I'm in a place where I know my dad is too. I can find him. I've got to try and find him. I stood up and started to walk out of the room when the rabbi stopped me. "It's not time to go out yet Zelma," (my Hebrew name), "the cantor has to sing the opening recitation and announce you." I looked up at the rabbi and he was just as I remember him being on that day, old and sage-like with kindly eyes and grey hair going white, a beard too. With frustration I realized what was going on and how strange it was: my dream, my own subconscious mind, was stopping me from rushing the dream along prematurely, and also in a way that made sense for the occasion, just as the rabbi would've done if I tried to do this back on the actual day of my bat mitzvah. I did not attempt this back then, by the way. These layers of awareness, this meta-cognition while dreaming was a pretty damn trippy experience, I must say. Afterwards I realized it would've fit right into the plot of a Christopher Nolan movie.

"I need to see my dad," I said to the rabbi. "Why? What's wrong?" he asked, just as he would've if this were playing out in real-time wakefulness. "There's something I need to tell him, I just remembered." I struggled to find a good enough reason, struggled to come up with something meaningful or convincing enough to let him (my dream, aka me) let me go to my father, who I knew was just beyond the door to the temple hall, in the very front row not ten feet from the stage. "You'll see him in just a few minutes. You'll see everyone very soon. Are you nervous Zelma? Don't be. You've spent a lot of time preparing for this day. I've heard you chant your Torah portion. You did it beautifully at the rehearsal just the other day. You are ready, you know it in your bones!" He said all this smiling at me, trying to ease my worries and encourage me. Inspire me. He (me) was doing exactly what rabbi's are meant to do. Maybe I would've made a good rabbi, I thought then and there in the dream. Then I thought about that: that I was consciously self-assessing my rabbinical skills of consolement based on how a subconscious aspect of me was talking the conscious aspect of me down. Whoa…

I felt so frustrated, so close and yet so far. Feeling that the dream would end right before I went out to begin the service, or that the service might commence but I wouldn't get the one-on-one time I wanted with my father, I decided to make a break for it. I turned sharply from the rabbi whose hands were on my shoulders and ran for the door, my arms outstretched so I would open it on impact. Even if that meant bursting out onto the temple stage loudly and abruptly and shocking the entire congregation, I was willing to do it. I was willing to do anything to see him again, to be able to look into his eyes, kinder than anyone else's on the planet. To be able to hug him again, feel the strength of his arms wrap around me. "Zelma!" yelled the rabbi. I burst out through the door to the temple stage, a crashing rush, and ended the dream and woke up.

———————————

I woke up the next morning as one does from an intense dream: emotional and in a kind of awe. I'm not one to lay around in bed, so despite the strong feelings I was feeling, feelings I couldn't yet put a name to, I got up to begin the day. How real our dreams can feel, and despite that how quickly they fade away…I was remembering the inherently sad and unrequited nature of dreams most of the time, now that I'd had two recently. People do have happy dreams, but those seem to be exceptions to the rule. Most of the time - according to what I hear from family and from coworkers, and according to my own recent experiences - dreams are incomplete and unresolved, sleepy expressions of our frustrations or insecurities or unfulfilled desires.

Roy and I sat at the kitchen counter that morning eating toasted bagels and lox that he surprised me with. I told him about my dream. He listened attentively, lovingly. He didn't offer advice or suggest what I could've done differently, he just listened. I figured this dream I had last night was close enough to seeing my dad, so I told the rest of my family about it too. And my brother and sister-in-law. Nobody commented one way or the other, approved or disapproved of this dream of mine entering into the non-existent file of 'dreams about Papa'. They all just listened to me, and said more with their eyes and smiles than with words. Their looks were the same we all have worn at various times since his passing, in talking about him, in remembering him. Non-verbal, I think those looks and facial expressions mean something like, "we all loved him, he loved all of us, we were all blessed to have been the ones he loved in this life, and we are united and even closer now, if saddened, by his departure."

I had just one pilates client to instruct that day. I would head to the gym for that session, do a little admin work, and then come back home and spend the day with Roy. On the drive there, taking the roads I know better than the back (or front) of my hand, I reflected on what this months-long mission to see my father again had accomplished. It involved the changing of my habits, which was hard. It involved thinking of him daily, which I bet I would've been doing anyway, but perhaps in a less intense and methodical way. I reflected on the good times we had together and the life lessons he gave me, and as I pulled off the highway and into my gym's parking lot it hit me: I am his first-born child embodying his habits more so than anyone else. I am his greatest representative in existence currently, and now that he's gone, the most 'Edward Faerber' kind of person alive. I am diligent with my exercise and work schedule, love to read, and am silly with my children. For the ones I love, I love them quietly, but with the strength and sureness of a mountain. I take care of my kids, I take care of my husband, my exercise clients, and am getting better at taking care of myself, as my father would so often remind me. Part of taking care of myself now, I realized, would be giving up this obsession, giving up this desire to see him again so long as it eats away at my peace of mind. Stepping out of the car and walking towards the large double doors of my gym, I realized the recent victories I'd had were enough. I was dreaming again. It *was* possible for me. From that day on, I no longer actively tried to search for or induce my father into my dreams. But, as long as I was dreaming, I could remain hopeful. I would no longer devote so much time or energy to the task (for there was no 'task' anymore, it felt to me), but rather just be relaxedly open towards it, open towards the possibility of him stopping by to say hello some time. Until then, and beyond then, I had a living, breathing, pulse-having family to take care of, starting with me.

Acknowledgements

Many people, places and things were directly and indirectly influential in the creation of these stories. Names have been changed in most cases for anonymity's sake. Here are the explicit mentions that really ought to be acknowledged:

'Birch Boys', mentioned in *Inonotus Obliquus,* are an excellent Adirondack-based, sustainable mushroom product company. I have no financial affiliation with them; I just love what they make.

In *An Enigmatic Loop*, I mention a book called 'Antecedents of Dwemer Law', which is an item in *The Elder Scrolls* video game series.

The ode to Beethoven in *An Enigmatic Loop*, 'Slowly Growing Deaf', is also the name of a song by the band Mr. Bungle.

The themes and style of the auteur, Christopher Nolan, were highly influential in the creation of *An Enigmatic Loop*. As well, Nolan is explicitly mentioned towards the end of *Learning to Dream.* For his wonderfully out-of-the-box, mind-bending thematic proclivities and pioneering techniques to achieve them, he forever has my thanks.

Thanks to the band Oh Sees for making the album 'Face Stabber', mentioned in *The Butcher of New Norfolk*. It was an excellent album to walk around a new town to.

This book is dedicated to my family and a few dear friends.

To my friend Aaron, for being the incredibly giving person that he is, for long talks and trips that go way out there just beyond the furthest limb of the tree of reality, for being there in my times of need.

To my friend Orest, for being such a hilarious and joyful warrior-doctor of truth. May we continue to find and uplift each other life after life. Thank you for your friendship, your humor, and your tireless commitment to the Sanatana Dharma.

To my marvelous partner Morgan, for not giving up, for a loving partnership and for helping me make this book as good as it could be. Your willing and attentive editorship has been truly invaluable.

To my friend Lili, for being such a strong and ever-present friend in my life, for camaraderie and laughs on laughs on laughs, for pushing each other to do better and stay longer in the cold plunge, for being consistent in a world of social fickleness.

To my family, starting with my dad,

What can I say? It's understood. You have been the sun in my life, the all-provider, Vishnu incarnate. For being an indefatigable source of inspiration and oomph to get things done, get well and move onward, ever onward to embodying the biggest bravest hero I know I can be. For our shared love of music, the deep in my bones appreciation of which has been such an incredible gift. For being the shoulders on which our family has grown and launched off of to crowd-surf the concert of life. With you it's been god mode, all-weapons since the start. Life's challenges never stood a chance.

To my mom,

So much of my inner self, habits and sense of discipline have grown from your effortless example. The way you carry yourself and steadily go about both what you have to do and what you love to do each day has been a model for me to follow and live my life by. Your appreciation of nature, and dogs and plants in particular has shaped the trajectory of my own life and interests in ways you might not even realize. The way you are so comfortable by yourself has had even more profound impacts on me, and your tireless work ethic is a continual inspiration!

To my brother,

To one of the friendliest, most loyal and compassionate people I know, who also happens to be my brother! There are few things I love more than when we get together and talk and laugh and comment on life. You are so humorous, so joyfully-inclined, so optimistic and thoughtful. You have such a good head on your shoulders, and I have the utmost confidence that you will continue to do well and live well into your adulthood. You are such a strong and stable presence in the lives of those you love; you probably don't even realize how much of a blessica you are to us. May you live long and live well!

To my sister,

Whenever I hear about what you're up to with your job, your hikes and exercise habits, how you're taking such sweet care of your little furry baby dog, I am filled with love and admiration. Whenever I tell people about you or show them the picture of you doing a headstand on a paddleboard on a lake surrounded by mountains, I am filled with such pride. You have so many amazing qualities: you are kind and loving, you are thrifty and good with money, you are disciplined and clearly have an incredible work ethic, you are silly and hilarious. I may be five years your elder, but I look up to you quite a bit!